the devil knows you're dead

"TERRIFIC!"

San Diego Union-Tribune

"THE BEST . . .
It takes the steady hand of a cool pro
like Lawrence Block to monitor the erratic pulsebeat
of New York City without faking it . . .
Block has the offhand grace to make it look easy."

The New York Times Book Review

"COMPELLING . . .
Loyalists will hang on every word
as Scudder makes his facinatingly uncertain way
through an increasingly uncertain world."

Kirkus Reviews

"FASCINATING . . .
A superior storyteller . . . Block has an awareness
of the pain and pleasure of living.
It is a gift that not all authors have."
San Antonio Express-News

D0012020

"BLOCK EXCELS!"
Chicago Tribune

"REMARKABLE . . .
Scudder's first-person tales are as much about the
fears and pleasures of life in today's New York City
as they are about solving mysteries."
The Wall Street Journal

"DARK, SEAMY . . .
Succeeds not only as an intriguing mystery,
but also as a meditation on the mysterious processes,
coincidences, and accidents that make up
human existence."
Mystery Scene

"RECOMMENDED . . .
A complex and compelling work"
Montgomery Advertiser

"EXCEPTIONALLY VIVID . . .
An excellent book from a writer
whose norm has come to be no less"
The Armchair Detective

"EMINENTLY READABLE . . .
A moody page-turner"
Chicago Sun-Times

"A MASTER . . .
The Matthew Scudder novels are among the
finest detective novels penned in this century."
Jonathan Kellerman, author of *Bad Love*

"SIMPLY THE BEST WRITER
working at his trade today . . .
I can't think of a nicer Christmas present
for any reader of PI mysteries than this book."
Mystery News

"RESONATES WITH DRAMA AND PATHOS . . .
Crackling, quotable dialogue . . .
Block has Fun City's folkways down cold"
Rock Hill Herald

"ONE OF OUR BEST
and most popular mystery writers.
I recommend his work."
Nashville Tennessean

Other Avon Books by
Lawrence Block

A DANCE AT THE SLAUGHTERHOUSE
EIGHT MILLION WAYS TO DIE
IN THE MIDST OF DEATH
OUT ON THE CUTTING EDGE
THE SINS OF THE FATHERS
SOMETIMES THEY BITE
A STAB IN THE DARK
A TICKET TO THE BONEYARD
TIME TO MURDER AND CREATE
A WALK AMONG THE TOMBSTONES

Avon Books are available at special quantity discounts for bulk purchases for sales promotions, premiums, fundraising or educational use. Special books, or book excerpts, can also be created to fit specific needs.

For details write or telephone the office of the Director of Special Markets, Avon Books, Dept. FP, 1350 Avenue of the Americas, New York, New York 10019, 1-800-238-0658.

LAWRENCE BLOCK

the devil knows you're dead

AVON BOOKS NEW YORK

If you purchased this book without a cover, you should be aware that
this book is stolen property. It was reported as "unsold and destroyed"
to the publisher, and neither the author nor the publisher has received
any payment for this "stripped book."

AVON BOOKS
A division of
The Hearst Corporation
1350 Avenue of the Americas
New York, New York 10019

Copyright © 1993 by Lawrence Block
Published by arrangement with the author
Library of Congress Catalog Card Number: 93-411
ISBN: 0-380-72023-X

All rights reserved, which includes the right to reproduce this book or
portions thereof in any form whatsoever except as provided by the U.S.
Copyright Law.

Published in hardcover by William Morrow and Company, Inc.; for information address Permissions Department, William Morrow and Company, Inc., 1350 Avenue of the Americas, New York, New York 10019.

First Avon Books Printing: October 1994

AVON TRADEMARK REG. U.S. PAT. OFF. AND IN OTHER COUNTRIES, MARCA
REGISTRADA, HECHO EN U.S.A.

Printed in the U.S.A.

RA 10 9 8 7 6 5 4 3 2 1

In Memory of Sandra Kolb

Acknowledgments

I am pleased to acknowledge the substantial contributions of the Writers Room in Greenwich Village, where the preliminary work on this book was done, and of Marta Curro, at whose house in Chelsea it was written.

May the road rise to meet you.
May the wind be always at your back.
May you be in heaven an hour before
The Devil knows you're dead.

AN IRISH BLESSING

On the last Thursday in September, Lisa Holtzmann went shopping on Ninth Avenue. She got back to her apartment between three-thirty and four and made coffee. While it dripped through she replaced a burnt-out light bulb with one she'd just bought, put away her groceries, and read the recipe on the back of a box of Goya lentils. She was sitting at the window with a cup of coffee when the phone rang.

It was Glenn, her husband, calling to tell her he wouldn't be home until around six-thirty. It was not unusual for him to work late, and he was very good about letting her know when she could expect him. He'd always been thoughtful in this regard, and his solicitousness had increased in the months since she'd lost the baby.

It was almost seven when he walked in the door, seven-thirty when they sat down to dinner. She'd made a lentil stew, enlivening the recipe on the box with garlic, fresh coriander, and a generous dose of Yucateca hot sauce, and she served it over rice, with a green salad. As they ate they watched the sun go down, watched the sky darken.

Their apartment was in a new high-rise on the southeast corner of Fifty-seventh Street and Tenth Avenue, diagonally across the street from Jimmy Armstrong's saloon. They lived on the twenty-eighth floor with windows looking south and west, and the views were spectacular. You could see the whole West Side from the George Washington Bridge to the Battery, and on across the Hudson and halfway across New Jersey.

They were a handsome couple. He was tall and slender. His dark brown hair was combed back from a well-defined widow's peak, with just the slightest touch of gray at the temples. Dark eyes, dark complexion. Strong features, softened the least bit by a slight weakness at the chin. Good even teeth, a confident smile.

He wore what he always wore to the office, a well-tailored dark suit and a striped tie. Had he taken off the suit jacket before sitting down to dinner? He might have hung it over the back of a chair, or on a doorknob. Or he might have used a hanger; he was careful with his things. I picture him sitting at the table in his shirtsleeves—a blue pinpoint Oxford shirt, a buttondown collar—and tossing his tie over one shoulder, to protect it from food stains. I'd seen him do that once, at a coffee shop called the Morning Star.

She was five-two and slender, with straight dark hair cut modishly short, skin like porcelain, and startling blue eyes. She was thirty-two but looked younger, even as her husband appeared a little older than his thirty-eight years.

I don't know what she was wearing. Jeans, perhaps, turned up at the cuffs, showing a little wear at the knees and in the seat. A sweater, a yellow cotton crewneck, the sleeves pushed up to bare her arms to the elbow. Brown suede slippers on her feet.

But that's just a guess, an exercise of the imagination. I don't know what she was wearing.

Sometime between eight-thirty and nine he said he

had to go out. If he had removed his suit jacket earlier, he put it on again now, and added a topcoat. He told her he'd be back within the hour. It was nothing important, he told her. Just something he needed to take care of.

I suppose she did the dishes. Poured another cup of coffee, turned on the television set.

At ten o'clock she started to worry. She told herself not to be silly and spent the next half hour at the window, looking out at their million-dollar view.

Around ten-thirty the doorman called upstairs to tell her that there was a police officer on his way up. She was waiting in the hall when he got off the elevator. He was a tall cleanshaven Irish kid in a blue uniform, and she remembered thinking that he looked just the way cops were supposed to look.

"Please," she said. "What's the matter? What happened?"

He wouldn't say anything until they were inside the apartment, but by then she already knew. The look on his face said it all.

Her husband had been at the corner of Eleventh Avenue and West Fifty-fifth Street. He had evidently been in the process of making a telephone call from a coin-operated public phone at that corner, when someone, presumably attempting to rob him, had fired four bullets at close range, thereby causing his death.

There was more, but that was as much as she could take in. Glenn was dead. She didn't have to hear any more.

2

I met Glenn Holtzmann for the first time on a Tuesday evening in April, which is supposed to be the cruelest month. T. S. Eliot said so, in "The Waste Land," and maybe he knew what he was talking about. I don't know, though. They all seem pretty nasty to me.

We met at the Sandor Kellstine Gallery, one of a dozen housed in a five-story building on Fifty-seventh between Fifth and Sixth. It was the opening of their spring group show of contemporary photography, and the work of seven photographers was on display in a large room on the third floor. The friends and relatives of all seven had turned out for the occasion, along with people like Lisa Holtzmann and Elaine Mardell, who were taking a course Thursday evenings at Hunter College called "Photography as Abstract Art."

There was a table set with stemmed plastic goblets of red and white wine, and cubes of cheese with colored toothpicks stuck in them. There was club soda, too, and I poured myself some and found Elaine, who introduced me to the Holtzmanns.

I took one look at him and decided I didn't like him.

I told myself that was ridiculous and shook his hand and returned his smile. An hour later the four of us were

4

eating Thai food on Eighth Avenue. We had something with noodles, and Holtzmann drank a bottle of beer with his meal. The rest of us had Thai iced coffee.

The conversation never quite got off the ground. We started off talking about the show we'd just seen, then made brief forays into other standard topics—local politics, sports, the weather. I already knew he was a lawyer, and learned he was employed at Waddell & Yount, a publisher of large-print editions of books originally brought out by other publishers.

"Pretty dull stuff," he said. "Mostly contracts, and then every once in a while I have to write a stern letter to somebody. Now there's a skill I can't wait to pass on. As soon as the kid's old enough I'll teach him how to write stern letters."

"Or her," Lisa said.

He or she was as yet unborn, due sometime in the fall. That was why Lisa was drinking iced coffee instead of a beer. Elaine was never much of a drinker, and doesn't drink at all these days. And, one day at a time, neither do I.

"Or her," Glenn agreed. "Male or female, the kid can plod along in Daddy's boring footsteps. Matt, your work must be exciting. Or am I only saying that because I've watched too much TV?"

"It has its moments," I said, "but a lot of what I do is a matter of routine. Like anything else."

"You were a policeman before you went on your own?"

"That's right."

"And now you're with an agency?"

"When they call me," I said. "I work per diem for an outfit called Reliable and take whatever free-lance work comes my way."

"I suppose you get a lot of industrial espionage. Disgruntled employees peddling company secrets."

"Some."

"But not much?"

"I'm unlicensed," I said, "so I don't tend to get corporate clients, not on my own. Reliable gets its share of corporate work, but most of the stuff they've used me on lately has involved trademark infringement."

"Trademark infringement?"

"Everything from fake Rolex watches to unauthorized logos on sweatshirts and baseball caps."

"It sounds interesting."

"It's not," I said. "It's the street equivalent of writing somebody a stern letter."

"You'd better have kids," he said. "That's a skill you'll want to pass on."

After dinner we walked to their apartment and did the requisite oohing and aahing over the view. Elaine's apartment has a partial view across the East River, and from my hotel room I can catch a glimpse of the World Trade Center, but the Holtzmanns' view had us badly outclassed. The apartment itself was on the small side—the second bedroom was about ten feet square—and it sported the low ceilings and construction shortcuts characteristic of most new housing. But that view made up for a lot.

Lisa made a pot of decaf and started talking about the personal ads, and how she knew perfectly respectable people who used them. "Because how are people supposed to meet nowadays?" she wondered. "Glenn and I were lucky, I was at Waddell & Yount showing my book to the art director and we happened to run into each other in the hallway."

"I saw her from the other side of the room," Glenn said, "and I made damn sure we happened to run into each other."

"But how often does that happen?" Lisa went on. "How did you two meet, if you don't mind my asking?"

"The personals," Elaine said.

"Seriously?"

"No. As a matter of fact we were sweethearts years ago. Then we broke up and lost track of each other. And then we happened to run into each other again, and—"

"And the same old magic was still there? That's a beautiful story."

Maybe so, but it was on the thin side. We'd met years ago, all right, at an after-hours joint, when Elaine was a sweet young call girl and I was a detective attached to the Sixth Precinct, and a little less firmly attached to a wife and two sons on Long Island. Years later a psychopath turned up out of our shared past, dead set on killing us both. That threw us together, and yes, Lisa, the same old magic was still there. We stuck, and the bond seemed to be holding.

I'd call it a beautiful story, but since most of it went untold you couldn't get much conversational mileage out of it. Lisa told about a friend of a friend, divorced, who responded to a personal ad in *New York* magazine, went to the designated meeting place at the appointed hour, and met her ex-husband. They took it as a sign and wound up getting back together again. Glenn said he didn't believe it, it didn't make sense, he'd heard half a dozen variations on the theme and didn't believe any of them.

"Urban folklore," he said. "There are dozens of stories like that. They always happened to a friend of a friend, never to somebody you actually know, and the truth of the matter is they never happened at all. Scholars collect these stories, there are books filled with them. Like the German shepherd in the suitcase."

We must have looked puzzled. "Oh, c'mon," he said. "You must know that one. Guy's dog dies, he's heartbroken, he doesn't know what to do, he packs it up in a big Pullman suitcase and he's on his way to a vet or a pet cemetery. And he sets the suitcase down to catch his breath when somebody grabs it and takes off with it. And ha-ha-ha, can't you just picture the look on the poor bastard's face when he opens the stolen suitcase and what does he find but a dead dog. I'll bet you've all heard at least one version of that story.''

"I heard it with a Doberman," Lisa said.

"Well, a Doberman, a shepherd. Any large dog."

"In the version I heard," Elaine said, "it happened to a woman."

"Right, sure, and a helpful young man offers her a hand with the suitcase."

"And inside the suitcase," she went on, "is her ex-husband."

So much for urban folklore. Lisa, indefatigable, shifted from personal ads to phone sex. She saw it as a perfect metaphor for the nineties, born of the health crisis, facilitated by credit cards and 900 numbers, and driven by a growing preference for fantasy over reality.

"And those girls make good money," she said, "and all they have to do is talk."

"Girls? Half of them are probably grandmothers."

"So? An older woman would have an advantage. You wouldn't need looks or youth, just an active imagination."

"You mean a dirty mind, don't you? You'd also need a sexy voice."

"Is my voice sexy enough?"

"I'd say so," he said, "but I'm prejudiced. Why? Don't tell me you're considering it."

"Well," she said, "I've thought about it."

"You're kidding, right?"

"Well, I don't know. When the baby's sleeping and I'm stuck here—"

"You'll pick up the phone and talk dirty to strangers?"

"Well—"

"Remember before we were married when you were getting the obscene phone calls?"

"That was different."

"You freaked out."

"Well, he was a pervert."

"Oh, really? Who do you figure your customers would be, Boy Scouts?"

"It would be different if I was getting paid for it," she said. "It wouldn't feel like a violation. At least I don't think it would. What do you think, Elaine?"

"I don't think I'd like it."

"Well, of course not," Glenn said. "You haven't got a dirty mind."

Back at Elaine's apartment I said, "As a mature woman you've got a definite advantage. But it's a shame your mind's not dirty enough for phone sex."

"Wasn't that a hoot? I almost said something."

"I thought you were going to."

"I almost did. But cooler heads prevailed."

"Well," I said, "sometimes they do."

When I first met Elaine she was a call girl, and she was still in the game when we got back together again. She went on turning tricks while we set about establishing a relationship, and I pretended that it didn't bother me, and she did the same. We didn't talk about it, and it became the thing we didn't talk about, the elephant in the parlor that we tiptoed around but never mentioned.

Then one morning we had a mutual moment of truth. I admitted that it bothered me, and she admitted that she had secretly gotten out of the business several months previously. There was a curious "Gift of the Magi" quality to the whole affair, and there were adjustments to be made, and new routes to be drawn on what was essentially uncharted terrain.

One of the things she had to figure out was what to do with herself. She didn't need to work. She had never been one to give her money to pimps or coke dealers, but had invested wisely and well, sinking the bulk of it into apartment houses in Queens. A management company handled everything and sent her a monthly check, and she netted more than enough to sustain her life-style. She liked to work out at the health club and go to concerts and take college courses, and she lived in comfort in the middle of a city where you could always find something to do.

But she had worked all her life, and retirement took some getting used to. Sometimes she read the want ads, frowning, and once she'd spent a week trying to put together a résumé, then sighed and tore up her notes. "It's hopeless," she announced. "I can't even fill in the blanks with interesting lies. I spent twenty years diddling for dollars. I could say I spent the time as a housewife, but so what? Either way I'm essentially unemployable."

One day she said, "Let me ask you a question. How do you feel about phone sex?"

"Well, maybe as a stopgap," I said, "if we couldn't be together for some reason. But I think I'd feel too self-conscious to get into the spirit of it."

"Idiot," she said affectionately. "Not for us. To make money. A woman I know claims it's very lucrative. You're in a room with ten or a dozen other girls. There are partitions for privacy, and you sit at a desk and talk on a telephone. No hassles about getting paid. No worries about AIDS or herpes. No physical danger, no physical contact even, you never see the clients and they never see you. They don't even know your name."

"What do they call you?"

"You make up a street name, except you wouldn't call it that because you'd never get anywhere near the street. A phone name, but I'll bet the French have a word for it." She found a dictionary, paged through it. "*Nom de téléphone*. I think I like it better in English."

"And who would you be? Trixie? Vanessa?"

"Maybe Audrey."

"You didn't have to stop and think, did you?"

"I talked to Pauline hours ago. How long does it take to think up a name?" She drew a breath. "She says she can get me on where she works. But how would you feel about it?"

"I don't know," I said. "It's hard to predict. Maybe you should try it and we'll both see how we feel. That's what you want to do, isn't it?"

"I think so."

"Well, what is it they used to say about masturbation? Do it until you need glasses."

"Or a hearing aid," she said.

She started the following Monday and lasted all of four hours of a six-hour shift. "Impossible," she said. "Out of the question. It turns out I'd rather fuck strangers than talk dirty to them. Do you want to explain that to me?"

"What happened?"

"I couldn't do it. I was hopeless at it. This one dimwit wanted to hear how big his cock was. 'Oh, it's huge,' I said. 'It's the biggest one I ever saw. God, I don't see how I can possibly get the whole thing inside me. Are you positive it's your dick? I'd swear it was your arm.' He got very upset. 'You're not doing it right,' he said. Nobody ever told me *that* before. 'You're exaggerating. You're making the whole thing ridiculous.' Well, I fucking lost it. I said, 'Ridiculous? You're sitting there with the phone in one hand and your dick in the other, paying a total stranger to tell you you're hung like Secretariat, and I'm the one's making it ridiculous?' And I told him he was an asshole and I hung up on him, which is the one absolute no-no because they reach you by calling a

900 number so the meter's running as long as they're on the line. The one thing you don't do is hang up before they do, but I didn't care.

"Another genius wanted me to tell him stories. 'Tell me about the time you did a threesome with a man and a woman.' Well, I've got real stories I could have told, but am I supposed to take something that actually happened and share it with this jerkoff? The hell with that. So I made something up, and of course all three people were hot and gorgeous and perfectly synchronized sexually, and everybody came like the Fourth of July. As opposed to real life where people have bad breath and skin blemishes, and the women are faking it and the man can't get a hard-on." She shook her head, disgusted. "Forget it," she said. "It's good I saved my money, because it turns out I'm unemployable. I can't even make it as a telephone whore."

"Well?" she said. "What did you think?"

"Of Glenn and Lisa? They're fine. I wish them well."

"And you don't care if we never see them again."

"That's a little harsh, but I'll admit I don't see us spending all our free time with them. There wasn't a whole lot of chemistry operating this evening."

"I wonder why. The age difference? We're not that much older."

"She's pretty young," I said, "but I don't think that's it. I think it's a lack of anything much in common. You go to class with her and I live a block from them, but aside from that—"

"I know," she said. "Not much common ground, and I probably could have predicted that going in. But I found her very likable, so I thought it was worth a try."

"Well, you were right," I said, "and I can see why you liked her. I liked her myself."

"But not him."

"Not especially, no."

"Any idea why?"

I thought about it. "No," I said. "Not really. I could point to things about him that I found irritating, but the fact of the matter is that I'd already made up my mind to dislike him. I took one look at him and knew he was somebody I wasn't going to like."

"He's not a bad-looking man."

"Hardly," I said. "He's handsome. Maybe that's it, maybe I sensed that you'd find him attractive and that's what put my back up."

"Oh, I didn't think he was attractive."

"You didn't?"

"I thought he was good-looking," she said, "the way male models are good-looking, except not as pouty as they all seem to be these days. But I'm not attracted to pretty boys. I like grumpy old bears."

"Thank God for that."

"Maybe you didn't like him because you were hot for her."

"I already knew I didn't like him before I even looked at her."

"Oh."

"And why would I be hot for her?"

"She's pretty."

"In a fragile, china-doll way. A fragile, pregnant, china-doll way."

"I thought men went crazy for pregnant women."

"Well, think again."

"What did you do when Anita was pregnant?"

"Worked a lot of overtime," I said. "Put a lot of bad guys in jail."

"Same as when she wasn't pregnant."

"Pretty much, yeah."

"Maybe it was cop instinct," she said. "Maybe that's why you didn't like him."

"You know," I said, "I think you just hit it. But it doesn't make sense."

"Why not?"

"Because he's a promising young attorney with a pregnant wife and an upscale condo. He's got a firm handshake and a winning smile. Why would I peg him as a wrong guy?"

"You tell me."

"I don't know. I sensed something, but I couldn't tell you what it was. Except that I had the sense he was listening awfully hard, as though he wanted to hear more than I wanted to tell him. The conversation dragged tonight, but it would have sailed along just fine if I'd told some detective stories."

"Why didn't you?"

"Maybe because he was so hot to hear them."

"Like phone sex," she suggested. "He had the phone in one hand and his dick in the other."

"Something like that."

"No wonder you wanted to hang up. God, do you remember what a disaster that turned out to be? For a week afterward I wouldn't say a word in bed."

"I know. You wouldn't even moan."

"Well, I *tried* not to," she said, "but sometimes I had no choice."

In a Nazi accent I said, "Ve haff vays of making you come."

"Is that a fact?"

"I suppose ze Fräulein demands proof."

"I suppose I do."

And a while later she said, "Well, I wouldn't call it the best evening we ever spent, but it certainly had a nice finish, didn't it? I think you're probably right, I think there's something sly about him, but so what? We'll never have to see them again."

*   *   *

But of course I did have to see them again.

A week or ten days after our first meeting I walked out of my hotel one evening and got halfway to Ninth Avenue when I heard my name called. I looked around and saw Glenn Holtzmann. He was wearing a suit and tie and carrying a briefcase.

"They kept me working late today," he said. "I called Lisa and told her to go ahead and eat without me. You had dinner yet? Want to grab a bite somewhere?" I had already eaten, and told him so. "Then do you want to have a cup of coffee and keep me company? I'm not up for anything fancy, just the Flame or the Morning Star. Have you got the time?"

"As a matter of fact," I said, "I don't." I pointed up Ninth Avenue. "I'm on my way to meet somebody," I said.

"Well, I'll walk a block with you. I'll be a good boy and have a Greek salad at the Flame." He patted his midsection. "Keep the weight down," he said, although he looked trim enough to me. We walked to Fifty-eighth and crossed the avenue together, and in front of the Flame he said, "Here's where I get off. Hope your meeting goes well. Interesting case?"

"At this stage," I said, "it's hard to tell."

It wasn't a case at all, of course. It was an AA meeting in the basement of St. Paul's. For an hour and a half I sat on a folding metal chair and drank coffee out of a Styrofoam cup. At ten o'clock we mumbled our way through the Lord's Prayer and stacked the chairs, and a few of us stopped in at the Flame to take nourishment and other people's inventories. I thought I might run into Holtzmann there, lingering over the dregs of his Greek salad, but by then he'd gone on home to his little cabin in the sky. I ordered some coffee and a toasted English and forgot about him.

Sometime in the next week or two I saw him waiting

for a Ninth Avenue bus, but he didn't see me. Another
time Elaine and I had a late bite at Armstrong's and left
just as the Holtzmanns were getting out of a cab in front
of their building across the intersection. And one afternoon I was at my own window when a man who might
have been Glenn Holtzmann emerged from the camera
shop across the street and walked west. I'm on a high
floor, so the person I saw might as easily have been
someone else, but something in his walk or stance
brought Holtzmann to mind.

It was the middle of June, though, before we spoke
again. It was a weekday night, and it was late. Past midnight, anyway. I'd been to a meeting and out for coffee.
Back in my room, I picked up a book and couldn't read
it, turned on the TV and couldn't watch it.

I get that way sometimes. I fought the restlessness for
a while, until around midnight I said the hell with it and
grabbed my jacket off a hook and went out. I walked
south and west, and when I got to Grogan's I took a
seat at the bar.

Grogan's Open House is at Fiftieth and Tenth, an old-
fashioned Irish ginmill of the sort that used to dot Hell's
Kitchen years ago. There are fewer of them these days,
although Grogan's has yet to earn a bronze plaque from
the Landmarks Commission, or a spot on the Endan-
gered Species List. There's a long bar on the left, booths
and tables on the right, a dart board on the back wall,
an old tile floor strewn with sawdust, an old stamped-
tin ceiling in need of repair.

They rarely get much of a crowd at Grogan's, and this
night was no exception. Burke was behind the bar,
watching an old movie on one of the cable channels. I
ordered a Coke and he brought it to me. I asked if Mick
had been in and he shook his head. "Later," he said.

This was a long speech for him. The bartenders at

Grogan's are a closemouthed lot. It's part of the job description.

I sipped my Coke and scanned the room. There were a few familiar faces but no one I knew well enough to say hello to, and that was fine with me. I watched the movie. I could have been watching the same picture at home but there I'd been unable to watch anything, or even sit still. Here, wrapped in the smell of tobacco smoke and spilled beer, I felt curiously at ease.

On the screen, Bette Davis sighed and tossed her head, looking younger than springtime.

I managed to get lost in the movie, and then I got lost in thought, caught up in some sort of reverie. I came out of it when I heard my name mentioned. I turned, and there was Glenn Holtzmann. He was wearing a tan windbreaker over a checked sport shirt. It was the first time I'd seen him in anything other than a business suit.

"Couldn't sleep," he said. "I went to Armstrong's but it was too crowded. So I came here. What's that you're drinking, Guinness? Wait a minute, you've got ice in your glass. Is that how they serve it here?"

"It's Coca-Cola," I said, "but they've got Guinness on draft, and I suppose they'll give it to you with ice if that's how you want it."

"I don't want it at all," he said, "with or without ice. What do I want?" Burke was right in front of us. He hadn't said a word, and didn't say anything now. "What kind of beer do you have? Never mind, I don't feel like a beer. How about Johnny Walker Red? Rocks, a little water."

Burke brought the drink with the water on the side in a small glass pitcher. Holtzmann added water to his glass, held the drink to the light, then took a sip. I got a rush of sense-memory. The last thing I wanted was a drink, but for a second there I could damn well taste it.

"I like this place," he said, "but I hardly ever come here. How about yourself?"

"I like it well enough."

"Do you get here often?"

"Not too often. I know the owner."

"You do? Isn't he the guy they call 'the Butcher'?"

"I don't know that anybody actually calls him that," I said. "I think some newspaperman came up with the name, possibly the same one who started calling the local hoodlums 'the Westies.' "

"They don't call themselves that?"

"They do now," I said. "They never used to. As far as Mick Ballou is concerned, I can tell you this much. Nobody calls him 'Butcher' in his own joint."

"If I spoke out of turn—"

"Don't worry about it."

"I've been in here, I don't know, a handful of times. I've yet to run into him. I think I'd recognize him from his pictures. He's a big man, isn't he?"

"Yes."

"How did you come to know him, if you don't mind my asking?"

"Oh, I've known him for years," I said. "Our paths crossed a long time ago."

He drank some of his scotch. "I bet you could tell some stories," he said.

"I'm not much of a storyteller."

"I wonder." He got a business card from his wallet, handed it to me. "Are you ever free for lunch, Matt? Give me a call one of these days. Will you do that?"

"One of these days."

"I hope you will," he said, "because I'd love to really kick back and have a real conversation, and who knows? It might lead to something."

"Oh?"

"Like a book, for instance. The experiences you've

had, the characters you've known, I wouldn't be surprised if there's a book there waiting to be written.''

"I'm no writer.''

"If the material's there it's no big deal to hook you
up with a writer. And I've got a feeling the material's
there. But we can talk about all that at lunch.''

He left a few minutes later, and I decided to pack it
in myself when the movie ended, but before that happened Mick showed up and we wound up making a
night of it. I had told Holtzmann I wasn't much of a
storyteller but I told my share that night, and Mick told
a few himself. He drank Irish whiskey and I drank coffee
and we didn't quit when Burke put the chairs up on the
tables and closed for the night.

The sky was light by the time we got out of there.
"And now we'll get something to eat,'' Mick said, "and
then 'twill be time for the butchers' mass at St. Bernard's.''

"Not for me it won't,'' I said. "I'm tired. I'm going
home.''

"Ah, ye're no fun at all,'' he said, and gave me a
ride home. "'Twas a good old night,'' he said when we
reached my hotel, "for all that it's ending too early.''

"The last thing I want to do,'' I told Elaine, "is write
a book about my fascinating experiences. But even if I
were open to the idea he's the person least likely to get
me to do it. All he has to do is ask me a question and
I automatically look for a way not to answer it.''

"I wonder why that is.''

"I don't know. Why would he want to talk to me
about writing a book? His company publishes large-print
editions. And he's not an editor, he's a lawyer.''

"He could know people at other houses,'' she suggested. "And couldn't he have a book-packaging operation going on the side?''

"He's got something going."

"What do you mean?"

"Just that he's got a hidden agenda. He wants something, and he doesn't let you know what it is. I'll tell you something, I don't believe he wants me to write a book. Because if that was what he really wanted he would have proposed something else."

"So what do you figure he wants?"

"I don't know."

"Be easy to find out," she said. "Have lunch with him."

"I could," I said. "I could also live without knowing."

I didn't see him again until the first week in August. It was the middle of the afternoon and I was at a window table at the Morning Star, eating a piece of pie and drinking a cup of coffee and reading a copy of *Newsday* that someone had left on an adjacent table. A shadow fell on the page and I looked up, and there was Holtzmann on the other side of the glass. He had his tie loosened and his collar open and his suit jacket over his arm. He smiled, pointed at himself and at the entrance. I figured this meant he was about to join me, and I was right.

He said, "Good to see you, Matt. Mind if I sit? Or were you expecting someone?"

I pointed to the chair opposite mine and he took it. The waitress came over with a menu and he waved it off and said he'd just have coffee. He told me he'd been hoping I'd call, that he'd looked forward to our getting together for lunch. "I guess you've been busy," he said.

"Pretty busy."

"I can imagine."

"And," I said, "I don't honestly think I'd be interested in doing a book. Even if I had one to write, I think I'd be happier leaving it unwritten."

"Say no more," he said. "I can respect that. Still,

who says you have to have a book in the works in order for us to have lunch? We could probably find other things to talk about.''

''Well, when my work schedule thins out a little—''

''Sure.'' The coffee came and he frowned at it and wiped his brow with his napkin. ''I don't know why I ordered coffee,'' he said. ''Iced tea would have made more sense in this heat. Still, it's cool enough in here, isn't it? Thank God for air-conditioning.''

''Amen to that.''

''Do you know that we keep our public places cooler in the summer than in the winter? If this place was the same temperature in January that it is right now we'd complain to the management. And people wonder why we've got an energy crisis.'' He grinned engagingly. ''See? We can find plenty of things to talk about. The weather. The energy crisis. Quirks in the American national character. Be a cinch for us to get through a lunch hour.''

''Unless we use up all our topics ahead of time.''

''Oh, I'm not worried about that. How's Elaine, by the way? Lisa hasn't seen her since school let out.''

''She's fine.''

''Is she taking any courses over the summer? Lisa wanted to, but she decided her pregnancy might get in the way.''

I said that Elaine would probably enroll for something or other in the fall, but that she'd decided to keep the summer open so that we could take long weekends.

''Lisa was talking about calling her,'' he said, ''but I don't think she got around to it.'' He stirred his coffee. Abruptly he said, ''She lost the baby. I guess you wouldn't have heard.''

''Jesus, no. I'm sorry, Glenn.''

''Thanks.''

''When did it—''

"I don't know, ten days ago, something like that. She was just into her seventh month. Bright side, it could have been worse. They told us the baby was malformed, it couldn't have lived, but suppose she carried it to term, even had a live delivery? Would have been twice the heartache, the way I figure it."

"I see what you mean."

"She was the one who wanted a kid," he said. "I got along this long without any, I more or less figured I could go the distance. But it was important to her, so I figured why not. The doctor says we can try again."

"And?"

"And I don't know if I want to. Not right away, anyhow. It's funny, I didn't mean to tell you all this. Shows what a good detective you are, you get people talking even without trying. I'll let you get back to your paper." He stood up, pushed two dollars across the table at me. "For the coffee," he said.

"That's too much."

"So leave a big tip," he said. "And call me when you get the chance. We'll have that lunch."

When I recounted the conversation to Elaine, her immediate response was to call Lisa. She made the call, got the answering machine, and rang off without leaving a message.

"It occurred to me," she explained, "that she can deal with her grief just fine without my help. All she and I ever had in common was the class, and it ended two months ago. I feel for her, I really do, but why do I have to get involved?"

"You don't."

"That's what I decided. Maybe I'm actually getting something out of Al-Anon. I'd probably get even more if I went more than once every three or four weeks."

"It's a shame you don't like the meetings."

"All that whining. They make me want to vomit. Other than that they're great. What about you? Do you like Glenn any better now that he shared his grief with you?"

"You'd have to," I said. "But I still don't want to have lunch with him."

"Oh, you won't have any choice," she said. "He'll keep grinding away at you until you wake up one day and realize he's your new best friend. You'll see."

But that's not what happened. Instead six or seven weeks passed during which I never caught a glimpse of Glenn Holtzmann, or gave him a passing thought. And then somebody with a gun changed everything, and from that point on Glenn was on my mind more than he'd ever been in life.

3

Within the hour, I knew as much as Lisa Holtzmann did.

Elaine and I had gone out to dinner after an early movie. We got back to her place in time for all but the first five minutes of *L.A. Law*. "I hate to say this," she said when it was over, "and I know it's not politically correct, but I've had it up to here with Benny. He's so relentlessly dim."

"What do you want from him?" I said. "He's retarded."

"You're not supposed to say that. You're supposed to say he has a learning disability."

"Okay."

"But I don't care," she said. "You could find a higher IQ growing in a petri dish. I wish he would smarten up or ship out. But then I feel that way about most of the people I meet. What do you want to do now? Is there a ball game on?"

"Let's watch the news."

And we did, half watching, half listening. I paid a little more attention when the perky anchorwoman began talking about a Midtown shooting, because I still respond to local crime news like an old Dalmatian to the ringing of the fire bell. When she mentioned the site of the shooting Elaine said, "That's your neighborhood." The next thing I knew she was reading the victim's name off the teleprompter. Glenn Holtzmann, thirty-eight, of West Fifty-seventh Street in Manhattan.

They went to a commercial and I triggered the remote and turned off the set. Elaine said, "I don't suppose there's more than one Glenn Holtzmann on West Fifty-seventh Street."

"No."

"That poor girl. The last time I saw her she had a husband and a baby on the way, and now what has she got? Should I call her? No, of course not. I didn't call her when she lost the baby and I shouldn't call her now. Or should I? Is there anything we can do?"

"We don't even know her."

"No, and she's probably surrounded by people right now. Cops, reporters, film crews. Don't you think?"

"Either that or she hasn't heard yet."

"How could that be? Don't they hold back the name of the victim pending notification of next of kin? You hear them say that all the time."

"They're supposed to," I said, "but sometimes somebody screws up. It's not supposed to happen that way, but lots of things happen that aren't supposed to."

"Isn't that the truth. He wasn't supposed to get shot."

"What do you mean?"

"Well, for God's sake," she said. "He was a bright young guy with a good job and a great apartment and a wife who was crazy about him, and he went out for a walk and—did they say he was making a phone call?"

"Something like that."

"Probably to find out if she needed anything from the corner deli. God, do you figure she heard the shots?"

"How do I know?"

She frowned. "I just find the whole thing very disturbing," she said. "It's different when you know the person, isn't it? But that's not all. It just seems wrong."

"Murder's always wrong."

"I don't mean morally wrong. I mean in the sense of a mistake, a cosmic error. He wasn't the kind of person who gets shot down on the street. Do you know what this means? It means we're all in trouble."

"How do you figure that?"

"If it could happen to him," she said, "it could happen to anybody."

The whole city saw it that way.

The morning papers were full of the story. The tabloids led with it, and even the *Times* stuck it on the front page. Local television stations gave it the full treatment; several of them had studios within a few blocks of the murder scene, which gave it a little added impact for their employees, if not for their viewers.

I didn't stay glued to the set myself, but even so I saw interviews with Lisa Holtzmann, with people from the neighborhood, and with various police officials, including a detective from Manhattan Homicide and the precinct commander at Midtown North. All the cops said the same thing—that this was a terrible crime, that such outrages could not be allowed to go unpunished, and that all available police personnel would be working the case in around-the-clock shifts until the killer was in custody.

It didn't take long. The official estimate of the time of death was 9:45 Thursday night, and within twenty-four hours they were able to announce an arrest. "Suspect charged in Hell's Kitchen homicide," the newsbreaks chirped. "Film at eleven."

And at eleven we watched the film. We saw the suspect with his hands cuffed behind him, his face pointed toward the camera, his eyes wide and staring.

"Jesus, will you look at him," Elaine said. "The

man's a walking nightmare. Honey, what's the matter? You can't possibly know him.''

"I don't know him," I said, "but I recognize him from the neighborhood. I think his name is George."

"Well, who is he?"

I couldn't answer that, but they could and did. His name was George Sadecki, and he was forty-four years old, unemployed, indigent, a Vietnam veteran, a fixture in the West Fifties. He had been charged with second-degree murder in the shooting death of Glenn Holtzmann.

4

Saturday morning I rented a car and we got out of the city and drove a hundred miles up the Hudson. We stayed three nights at a refurbished colonial inn in Columbia County, sleeping in a canopied four-poster bed in a room that had a dry sink and a porcelain chamber pot, but no television. We didn't look at TV or read a newspaper all the time we were there.

It was Tuesday afternoon by the time we got back to New York. I dropped Elaine and turned in the car, and when I got to my hotel there were two old guys in the lobby discussing the Holtzmann shooting. "I seen the killer around for years," one was saying. "Wiping windshields, hustling spare change. All along I said there was something wrong with the son of a bitch. You live in this town, you develop an instinct."

The Slaughter on Eleventh Avenue, as one of the tabloids felt compelled to call it, was still very much in the news, even in the absence of continuing developments in the case. Two elements combined to give it a hold on the public imagination: The victim was a young urban professional, the sort of person to whom such things were not supposed to happen, and the killer was a particularly unattractive soldier in the vast army of the homeless.

The homeless had been with us a little too long, and their numbers had grown too great. What charity fund-raisers call "compassion fatigue" had long since set in. Something within us made us long to hate the homeless, and now we had been given good reason. We had always sensed that they represented some sort of low-grade danger. They smelled bad, they had diseases, they were louse-ridden. Their presence gave rise to guilt, coupled with the disquieting intimation that the whole system was failing, that they were in our midst because our civilization was falling apart around them.

But who would have dreamed that they might be armed and dangerous, apt to come out shooting?

Round 'em up, for God's sake. Get them off the streets. Get rid of them.

The story stayed in the news all week, but lost some of its hold when the suicide of a prominent real estate developer took over the headlines. (He invited his attorney and two close friends to his penthouse apartment, served them a round of drinks, said, "I wanted you here as witnesses, so there won't be any of the usual horseshit about foul play." Then, before they'd had time to digest what he'd said, he walked out onto the terrace and vaulted the railing, plunging sixty-two stories in utter silence.)

Friday night Elaine and I wound up at her place. She made pasta and a salad and we ate in front of the television set. A woman on the late news tried to segue from one story to the other by contrasting the developer, who presumably had everything to live for but took his own life, and George Sadecki, who had nothing to live for yet took another man's life. I said I didn't quite see the connection, and Elaine said it was the only way to get both men into the same paragraph.

Then they ran a taped interview with a man identified only as Barry, a rawboned black man with white hair and hornrimmed glasses, whom they described as a friend of the alleged killer.

George, he said, was a mellow dude. Liked to sit on benches, go for walks. Didn't bother people and didn't care for people to bother him.

"What a revelation," Elaine said.

George didn't like panhandling, Barry went on. Didn't like to ask nobody for nothing. When he wanted money for beer he'd collect aluminum cans and bring them back for deposit. He always put the rest of the trash back neat so folks wouldn't get upset.

"An environmentalist," she said.

And he was always peaceable, Barry said. Had George ever said anything about owning a gun? Well, Barry thought he might have said something along those lines. But, see, George said a lot of stuff. George'd been in Vietnam, see, and sometimes he got confused about then and now. He might be saying he did something, and it sounds like he's talking about yesterday, and it's something he maybe did twenty years ago, if he even did it at all. Like what? Well, like burning up huts with a flamethrower. Like shooting people. When it came down to huts and flamethrowers you knew it was twenty years ago if it happened at all, because huts and flame-throwers didn't turn up much around West Fifty-seventh Street. But shooting people, well, that was something else.

"This is Amy Vassbinder in Hell's Kitchen," the reporter said, "where there are no huts and flamethrowers, but where shooting people is something else."

Elaine hit the Mute button. "I notice they're calling

it Hell's Kitchen again,'' she said. "What happened to Clinton?''

"When it's a story about rising property values,'' I said, "then the neighborhood is Clinton. That's when they're talking gentrification and tree planting. When it's gunshots and crack vials, then it's Hell's Kitchen. Glenn Holtzmann lived in a luxurious high-rise apartment in Clinton. He died a couple of blocks away in Hell's Kitchen.''

"I figured it was something like that.''

"I've seen Barry before,'' I said. "George's friend.''

"Around the neighborhood?''

"And at meetings.''

"He's in the program?''

"Well, he's been around it. Obviously he's not sober. You just saw him drinking a beer on camera. He may be one of those guys who stays sober between drunks or he may just come around now and then for the coffee and the companionship.''

"Do a lot of people do that?''

"Sure, and some of them wind up getting sober. Some aren't alcoholic at all, they're just looking to get in out of the cold. That's a problem for some AA groups, especially now that there are so many people living on the street. They've stopped serving coffee and cookies at certain meetings because the refreshments tend to draw too many people who don't belong. It's a tough one, because you don't want to exclude anybody, but you want to make sure there's a seat available for the alcoholic who wants help.''

"Is Barry an alcoholic?''

"Probably,'' I said. "You heard him tell the world how he spends his life on a park bench with a beer in his fist. On the other hand, the acid test is whether or not alcohol makes your life unmanageable, and only Barry could tell you that. He might say he's managing just fine, and maybe he is. Who am I to say?''

"What about George?''

I shrugged. "I don't think I ever saw him at a meeting. I guess we can call his life unmanageable. His dress and grooming might pass for eccentricities, but when you gun down strangers on the street it tends to suggest that something's not working. But was it the beer that did it? I have no idea. I suppose he could have scavenged enough empty cans to drink himself into a blackout, but he could just as easily have been cold sober and decided that Glenn Holtzmann was Ho Chi Minh's kid sister. The poor son of a bitch.''

"Barry said he was mellow.''

"He probably was," I said. "Until last week, when he got a little tense.''

I stayed the night and didn't get back to my hotel until sometime the following afternoon. I stopped at the desk for my mail and messages and went on up to my room. A Mr. Thomas had called twice, once the night before and again at ten-thirty that morning. He had left a number with a 718 exchange, which would put him in Brooklyn or Queens. I didn't recognize the number, nor did the name mean anything to me.

The other message, logged at eleven the previous evening, was from Jan Keane, and the number she had left was one I recognized. I spent a long moment looking at the eight letters of her name, the seven digits of her number. I hadn't dialed that number in quite a while, but if she hadn't left it I don't think I would have had to look it up.

I wondered what she wanted.

It could be anything at all, I told myself. It was probably AA-related. Maybe she was serving as program chairman at a meeting in SoHo or Tribeca and wanted to book me to speak. Maybe she'd run into a newcomer whose story was similar to mine and thought I might be able to help him.

Or maybe it was personal. Maybe she was getting married and wanted to let me know.

Maybe she'd ended a relationship, and for some reason wanted me to know that.

Easy enough to find out. I picked up the phone and dialed her number. Her machine kicked in on the fourth ring, and her recorded voice invited me to leave a message at the tone. I had just started to do so when her actual unrecorded voice cut in. I waited while she disengaged the machine and then she was back on the line, asking me how I was.

"Alive and sober," I said.

" 'Alive and sober.' Is that still your standard response?"

"Only to you."

"Well, I'm both those things myself, old friend. I celebrated another anniversary in May."

"May twenty-seventh, isn't it?"

"How did you remember that?"

"I remember stuff."

"Yours is in the fall, and I *don't* remember stuff. This month or next?"

"Next month. November fourteenth."

"Armistice Day. No, I'm wrong. That's the eleventh."

Neither of us had been sober when we first came into one another's lives. We'd met in the course of a case I was working. Years before, a woman in the Boerum Hill section of Brooklyn had been stabbed to death with an icepick, ostensibly by a serial murderer. After I'd left the force they finally pulled in the serial killer, and it turned out he couldn't have committed this one particular murder. The victim's father hired me to sift the cold ashes and try to find out who was responsible.

Jan Keane had been married to a man named Corwin at the time of the original homicide, and had been a neighbor of the dead woman in Brooklyn. She had long since divorced and moved to Manhattan, and my investigation eventually led me to her loft on Lispenard Street, where the first thing we did was crack a bottle and get drunk together. The second thing we did was go to bed.

It seemed to me that we were a pretty good match at both of those activities, but before we'd had a chance to practice much she announced that she couldn't see me anymore. She'd tried AA before, she said, and was determined to give it another chance, and the conventional wisdom held that it wasn't a good idea to hang out with a heavy drinker while you were trying to get sober yourself. I wished her the best of luck and left her to the world of church basements and sappy slogans.

Before I knew it I was finding my own way into that world, and not having an easy time of it. I hit a couple of emergency rooms and detoxes. I kept putting a few sober days together and then picking up a drink to celebrate.

One night I turned up on her doorstep, unable to think of any other way to get through the night sober. She gave me coffee and let me sleep on her couch. A couple of days later I went over there again, and this time I didn't have to sleep on the couch.

They advise against getting emotionally involved during early sobriety, and I have a feeling they're right. Somehow, though, we both stayed sober, and for a couple of years we kept each other company. We never lived together, but we did reach a point where I was spending more nights at her place than at my own. She cleared out a dresser drawer for me and made some room in the closet, and an increasing number of people came to know that they could try me at Jan's if they couldn't reach me at my hotel.

So it went on for a while, and it was good some of the time and not so good some of the time, and there came a time when it coughed and sputtered and died like a car running on empty. There were no big fights and not much in the way of drama. We didn't run up against any irreconcilable differences. We just ran out of gas.

"I have to talk to you," she said now.

"All right."

"I need a favor," she said, "and I don't want to get into it over the phone. Could you come down here?"

"Sure," I said. "Not tonight, though, because Elaine and I have plans."

"I met Elaine, didn't I?"

"That's right, you did." We'd spent a Saturday afternoon wandering through galleries in SoHo, and at one of them we'd run into Jan. "That must have been six months ago."

"Longer than that. I saw you at Rudi Scheel's show at the Paula Canning Gallery, and that was the end of February."

"Jesus, has it been that long? I don't know where the time goes."

"No," she said. "Neither do I."

The words hung in the air.

"Well," I said, "tonight's out. Jan, how urgent is this?"

"How urgent?"

"Because I could run down there right now if it's really important, or if tomorrow's time enough—"

"Tomorrow would be fine."

"Do you still go to that Sunday afternoon meeting on Forsyth Street? I could meet you there."

"God, I haven't been to Forsyth Street in ages. Anyway, I don't think I want to meet you at a meeting. I'd rather you come here, if that's all right with you.''

''It's fine with me. Pick a time.''

''You tell me. I'll be home all day.''

''Two o'clock?''

''Two is fine.''

After I'd hung up I sat on the edge of the bed wondering what sort of favor it would turn out to be and why she hadn't wanted to request it over the phone. I told myself I'd find out soon enough, and that I evidently didn't care all that much or I would have gone straight down there. I didn't have anything important to do before I saw Elaine later. There was a welterweight fight on *Wide World of Sports* that I was planning to see, but no one was billing it as the Fight of the Century. I wouldn't eat my heart out if I missed it.

I picked up the phone again and dialed the 718 number, and when a man answered I asked to speak to Mr. Thomas. He said, ''Uh, did you say 'Mr. Thomas'? Or did you want to talk to Tom?''

I checked the message slips. ''It says 'Mr. Thomas' here,'' I said, ''but my messages tend to be more or less accurate depending who takes them. My name's Matthew Scudder and somebody left two messages for me to call a Mr. Thomas at this number.''

''Oh, right,'' he said. ''I see what happened. I'm the person who called you, but they made a slight mistake on the name. I didn't say 'Thomas,' I said 'Tom S.' ''

''I guess I must know you from the rooms.''

''Actually,'' he said, ''I don't think you know me at all. In fact I'm not a hundred percent positive I got the right person. Let me ask you something. Did you ever speak at a meeting called Here and Now?''

''Here and Now.''

''It's a Brooklyn group, we meet Tuesdays and Fridays in the Lutheran church on Gerritsen Avenue.''

"I remember now. It was a three-speaker meeting, and a fellow named Quincy had a car so he drove. And we got lost and barely got there in time. That must be a good two years ago."

"More like three. I can be fairly precise about the date because I'd just made my ninety days. In fact I announced it at that meeting and got a round of applause."

I almost congratulated him.

"Let me just make sure I got the right person," he went on. "You were a New York City cop, you quit the police department, and you became a private detective."

"You've got a good memory."

"Well, nowadays I'll hear somebody's qualification and forget it ten minutes later, but the ones you listen to in the first few months make a deep impression. And the night you spoke I was hanging on every word. Let me ask you, are you still doing the same thing? Working as a private detective?"

"That's right."

"Good. That's what I was hoping. Look, Matt—excuse me, is it all right to call you Matt?"

"I guess so," I said. "And I'll call you Tom, since that's the name I've got for you so far."

"Jeez, that's right. I still didn't say my last name. I dunno, I'm not handling this so good, am I? Maybe that's the best place to start, with my name. The *S* stands for Sadecki."

It took a minute, but then the penny dropped. "Oh," I said.

"George Sadecki's my brother. I didn't want to leave the name before because, well, I just didn't. Not that I'm ashamed of my brother. Don't think that, because I'm not. He was always a hero to me. Certain ways he still is."

"I gather he's been having a rough time."

"For years. He hasn't been right since they brought him back from Vietnam. Oh, he had his problems before then, you can't go and blame everything on the war, but you can't deny it changed him. At first we kept waiting for his life to straighten out, for him to get a handle on it. But it's more'n twenty years, Chrissake, and a while back it became clear nothing was going to change.

"Early on he had different jobs but he never held on to one for very long. He couldn't get along with people. He didn't start fights or anything, he just couldn't get along with people.

"Then he became completely unemployable, because his manner got very strange and he would have these weird facial expressions, and also he stopped being clean about his person. I know your home group's on Ninth Avenue and you live in the neighborhood, so maybe you knew George."

"Just by sight."

"So you know what I'm talking about. He wouldn't bathe and he wouldn't change his clothes, and of course the beard and the hair. If you bought clothes for him you were just wasting your money because he would wear one pair of pants until they fell apart even if he had six other pairs hanging in his closet.

"It was like he had a certain way to live and nothing was going to make him change. He had a place to live, you know, or maybe you don't know. They hung that homeless tag on him and that's all you hear, but actually he had a basement room on Fifty-sixth Street. He found it himself and he paid the rent on it."

"By taking back aluminum cans?"

"He gets a couple of checks each month, the V.A. and SSI, and that covered his rent with a little left over. Right after he got the room, my sister and I made an arrangement with the landlord, that if George ever missed coming up with the rent we'd take care of it.

Never happened once. You see a guy, dirty bum on a park bench, you figure here's a person incapable of functioning. Yet he paid the rent on time each month. In the sense of doing the things that mattered to him, you would have to say he functioned."

"How is he holding up now?"

"All right, I guess. I had a very brief visit with him yesterday afternoon. They had him on Rikers Island and I drove all the way out there only to find that they'd moved him to Bellevue for psychiatric evaluation. He was in the prison ward on the nineteenth floor. I only had a few minutes with him. I hated to leave him, but I got to tell you I was glad to get out of there."

"How did he look to you?"

"Oh, I don't know. I suppose most people would say he looks good because they cleaned him up some, but all I could notice was the look in his eyes. George tends to stare, it's one of the things about him that puts people off, but now he's got this haunted look in his eyes that could break your heart."

"I assume he has an attorney."

"Oh, sure. I was gonna get a lawyer for him but they had already appointed someone and the guy seems all right. He's weighing a couple of options right now. He can plead my brother not guilty by reason of insanity or diminished capacity, or he can avoid a trial altogether by arranging for him to plead guilty to some sort of reduced charge and be sentenced to a long term in a treatment facility. It amounts to about the same thing either way. He winds up institutionalized, but it's not prison and there's the possibility he can get some help."

"How does George feel about it?"

"He's okay with it. He says he might as well plead, seeing as he figures he did it."

"Then he admits he killed Holtzmann."

"No, he *figures* he did it, figures he must have done

it. He doesn't remember it but he understands the evidence against him and he's not stupid, he knows how strong their case is. His take on it is he can't swear he did it but he can't swear he didn't, either, so they're probably right.''

"Was he in a blackout?''

"No, but his memory is never what you'd call reliable. He'll recollect events but be completely wrong about their sequence, or he'll misremember something, he'll have an incident or a conversation different from the way it actually happened.''

"I see.''

"You've been very patient with me, Matt, and I appreciate it. I know I'm taking all day to get to the point.''

"That's all right, Tom.''

"The thing is,'' he said, "everybody's satisfied, you know? The cops have the case cleared and the press off their backs. The D.A.'s looking at either a plea bargain or a trial he can't lose. George is ready to go along with whatever his lawyer decides, and the lawyer's ready to get the case off his desk with a minimum of aggravation, at the same time knowing he's doing the best thing for all concerned. My sister says once he's in a mental institution she won't have to lie awake worrying he's not getting enough to eat, or that he's in some sort of physical danger, dying of exposure or somebody hurting him. My wife says the same thing, and she also says that he's probably belonged in an institution for years, for his own protection and for the good of society. We're just lucky he didn't kill an innocent child, she says, and the real tragedy is that he wasn't put away earlier so that Glenn Holtzmann would be alive today.

"So everybody's telling everybody else how it's all working out for the best, and I'm sitting here feeling like the only fly in the ointment. I'm the pain in everybody's ass. You think my brother's crazy? I'm the crazy one.''

"Why's that, Tom?''

"Because I don't believe he did it,'' he said. "I know how ridiculous that sounds. I can't help it. I just do not believe he killed that man.''

5

"**I** appreciate this," he said. He spooned sugar into his coffee as he talked, stirred, added milk, stirred some more. "You know," he said, "I almost let it go. I came this close to not calling. I looked up private investigators in the Yellow Pages. Well, all I knew was your first name, and I didn't see any guys listed named Matt, and I figured maybe I'm supposed to keep my hands off this one. Let go and let God, right?"

"That's what the bumper stickers say."

"Then I thought, Tommy, take one shot and see what happens. Don't knock your brains out, don't go and hire another detective to look for this detective, but at least pick up the phone and see where it gets you. Don't push the river, but at least get your feet wet, and who knows? Maybe you catch a wave, maybe you can go with the flow."

The flow thus far had led him to the Flame, where we were sharing a booth in the smoking section. Years ago I used to meet prospective clients in bars. Now I meet them in coffee shops. I've gone with the flow myself, and look how far it's carried me.

"So I called Intergroup," he said, "and I asked for a contact person at Keep It Simple, because I knew that was your home group. Unless you switched home groups since then, or moved to another neighborhood or out of the city altogether. Or even picked up a drink, because who knows, right?''

"Right."

"Anyway, they gave me a guy to call, and I called it and I told a lie. I said I met you at a meeting and you gave me your number and I lost it, and that I never did get your last name. He didn't know your last name either, but he knew right off who I meant, so that let me know you were still sober and still in the area. He gave me another number to call, a fellow named Rich, and I don't know his last name either, but he knew *your* last name, and he had your number in his book. So I called, last night and again this morning, and you called back, and here I am." He drew a breath. "And now you can tell me I'm crazy and I'll go home."

"Are you crazy, Tom?"

"I don't know," he said. "You tell me."

He looked sane enough. He was about five-eight or -nine, the same height but a little thicker in the body than those welterweights I was currently missing on *Wide World.* He had a round face, its boyishness offset by frown lines on his forehead and creases at the corners of his mouth. His light brown hair was worn short and thinning on top. He had wire-rimmed eyeglasses, and I guess they should have been bifocals, because he took them off to study the menu before ordering his cup of coffee.

He wore a light blue sport shirt tucked into pleated chinos. His shoes were brown penny loafers with crepe soles. On the seat next to him he'd placed his jacket. It was teal trimmed in navy, with an L.L. Bean logo over the breast pocket. He wore a plain gold wedding band on the appropriate finger and a Timex digital watch with a stainless-steel band, and he had a pack of Camels in his shirt pocket and a lit one in the ashtray. He didn't look like a style-setter, but he certainly looked all of a piece, a Brooklyn neighborhood guy, a family man who worked hard and made a living at it. He didn't look crazy.

I said, "Why don't you tell me why you think George is innocent?"

"I don't even know if I got a reason." He picked up his cigarette, flicked ashes from it, put it back down again. "He's five years older'n me," he said. "Did I mention that? There was him, then my sister, then me. Growing up, of course I looked up to him. I was fourteen when he went into the service, and by then I knew there was something different about George, the way he had of staring off into the distance and sometimes not responding to questions. I knew this, but still I looked up to him." He frowned. "What am I trying to say? That I know him and he could never kill another human being? Anybody could. I came this close myself."

"What happened?"

"This is maybe two years before I got sober, okay? I'm in a bar. Nothing unusual in that, right? So there's an argument, guy pushes me, I push back, he shoves, I shove, he swings, I swing. He goes down, not because I give him such a good shot. He more or less trips over his own feet. Wham, hits his head on something, the bar rail, base of a barstool, I don't know what, and he's in a coma for three days and they don't know if he's gonna live, and if he dies I'm on the hook for manslaughter. What am I gonna say, I didn't mean for it to happen? That's what manslaughter is, when you don't mean it." He shook his head at the memory. "Long story short, he comes out of it on the third day and refuses to press charges. Wouldn't hear of it. Next thing you know I run into him in a bar. I buy him a drink, he buys back, and now we're the best of friends." He picked up his cigarette, looked at it, stubbed it out. "He wound up getting killed about a year after that."

"Another bar fight?"

"A holdup. He was assistant manager of a check-cashing place on Ralph Avenue and there was three of them shot, him and a security guard and a customer. He was the only one died. Well, shit happens, and maybe his number was up, but if his number'd been up a year earlier I'd be a guy'd done time in prison, a guy you'd describe as having a history of violent behavior, and all because a guy gave me a push and I pushed him back."

"You were lucky."

"I been lucky all my life," he said. "My poor fucking brother's had no luck at all. He's a man who walks away from confrontations, but all the same he could find himself in a fight, given the right set of circumstances. Life he led, violence is always waiting for you around the next bend in the road." He straightened up in his seat. "But what happened last week," he said, "it doesn't make sense. It doesn't fit George."

"How do you mean?"

"Okay," he said. "Here's how the police reconstruct it. Holtzmann's on the corner making a call from a pay phone. George approaches him, asks him for money. Holtzmann ignores him, tells him no, maybe tells him to go fuck himself. George pulls out a gun and starts blasting."

"What's wrong with that?"

"You saw George around the neighborhood. Did you ever see him ask anybody for money?"

"Not that I can recall."

"Believe me, you didn't. George didn't panhandle. He didn't like to ask anybody for anything. If he was really broke and he wanted to scrape a few bucks together and he couldn't do it hustling bottles and cans, maybe he'd go up to cars at a stoplight and wipe windshields. But even then he wouldn't press hard for the money. He certainly wouldn't disturb some guy in a business suit talking on the phone. George walked right by guys like that.''

"Maybe George asked the time of day and didn't like the answer he got.''

"I'm telling you, George wouldn't even have spoken to the guy.''

"Maybe he had a flashback, thought he was in a fire-fight.''

"Triggered by what? The sight of a man making a phone call?''

"I see what you're saying,'' I said, "but it's all theoretical, isn't it? But when you look at the evidence—''

"Okay,'' he said, leaning forward. "Good, let's talk about the evidence. As far as I'm concerned, that's where their whole case breaks down.''

"Really? I thought it was pretty persuasive.''

"Oh, it looks solid at first glance,'' he said. "I'll grant you that. Witnesses placing him on the scene, but what's so remarkable about that? He lives just around the corner from there, he must walk past that pay phone every day of his life. They're supposed to have another witness says he was talking about guns and shooting, but who are these witnesses? Other street people? They'll tell the cops anything they want to hear.''

"What about the physical evidence?''

"I guess you're talking about the cartridge casings.''

"Four of them,'' I said, "matching the four nine-millimeter slugs they took out of the victim. They would have been ejected automatically from the murder weapon when the shots were fired, but they weren't at the crime scene when the cops got there. Instead they turned up in the pocket of your brother's army jacket when the police picked him up.''

"It's strong evidence," he admitted.

"A lot of people would call it conclusive."

"But to me it just proves what we already know, that he was there at the approximate time the shooting took place. Maybe he was just steps away, standing in a doorway. Holtzmann wouldna seen him and neither would the killer. Holtzmann's on the phone, the killer shows up, maybe on foot, maybe he hops out of a car, who knows? Bang bang bang bang, Holtzmann's dead and the killer's out of there, takes off running or jumps back in his car, whatever. Then George comes forward. Maybe he watched the whole thing, maybe he was nodding and the shots woke him up, but now there's a man down and the light from the streetlamp is glinting off four pieces of metal on the sidewalk." He broke off, lowered his eyes. "I'm getting carried away here. I better stop before you figure I'm crazier than my brother."

"Keep talking."

"Yeah? Okay, so he steps forward to get a good look at the victim. That's something he might do. And he sees the casings, and he was in the military, he knows what they are. You remember what he said to the police? 'You have to police the area,' he told them. 'You have to pick up your own brass.' "

"Doesn't that suggest that he was responsible for their presence? That they'd come out of his own gun?"

"It suggests to me that he was confused. There was a dead man on the ground and cartridge casings alongside it and his only reference for that was Vietnam. He remembered right off what they told him about picking up shell casings on patrol and that told him what to do in the present situation."

"Isn't it simpler to assume he was trying to conceal evidence of his own involvement?"

"But what the hell did he conceal? He dropped the goddamn things in his jacket pocket, he walked around with them for a full day until they picked him up. If he wanted to get rid of them, he had plenty of chances. They say he walked over to the river to get rid of the gun, that he flung it off a pier into the water. He threw away the gun but kept the casings? He could have tossed them anywhere, a trash can, a Dumpster, a sewer grate, but instead he carried them in his pocket all day? Where's the sense in that?''

''Maybe he forgot they were there.''

''Four brass casings? They'da rattled around in there. No, it's senseless, Matt. Senseless.''

''I don't think anyone's tried to argue that your brother was behaving rationally.''

''Even so, Matt. Even so. Look, speaking of the gun. The murder weapon was a nine-millimeter pistol, right? The bullets they dug out of Holtzmann were nine-millimeter, and so were the casings in George's pocket.''

''So?''

''So George had a forty-five.''

''How do you know?''

''I saw it.''

''When?''

''Maybe a year ago. Maybe a little less than that. I came looking for him, I had some stuff for him, and I drove around until I found him. He was in one of his usual spots, near the entrance to Roosevelt Hospital.'' He drank some coffee. ''We walked back to his room so he could stow what I'd brought, clothes mostly, and a couple of bags of cookies. He always liked those Nutter Butter cookies, with the peanut-butter filling. From the time we were kids, that was his favorite kind of cookie. I always brought him some whenever I went looking for him.'' He closed his eyes for a moment, opened them and said, ''We got to his room and he told me he had something to show me. The place was a mess, piles of crap everywhere, but he knew right where to look and he moved some junk out of the way and came up with a gun. He had it wrapped in this filthy hand towel, but he unwrapped it and showed it to me.''

"And you were able to identify it as a forty-five?"

He hesitated. "I don't know a lot about guns," he said. "I've got a revolver I keep at the store, a thirty-eight, it sits on a shelf under the cash register and I don't even touch it from one month to the next. We're on Kings Highway west of Ocean Avenue, household appliances, we'll sell you anything from a Waring blender to a washer-dryer, and there's not a whole lot of cash comes over the counter. It's all checks or plastic nowadays, but they'll hold up anything, they smoke a little crack and they can't think straight, and if the cash register's empty they'll shoot you to make a point. So the gun's there, but I pray to God I never have to use it.

"It's a revolver, I don't know if I mentioned that. The gun George showed me wasn't, it didn't have a cylinder like mine. It was L-shaped, rectangular.''

He sketched its outline on the tabletop. I told him it sounded like a pistol, but how did he know it was a forty-five?

"George said that's what it was. He called it a forty-five-caliber pistol. What was the other phrase he used? A military sidearm, that's it. He said it was a government-issue military sidearm.''

"Where did he get it?"

"I don't know. I asked him and he said something about carrying it in Vietnam, but I don't believe he brought it back with him. I think he may have had one like it over there. My guess is he found this one or bought it on the street. I don't know if it was loaded or if he even had any bullets for it. The cops turned up people from the neighborhood who said he used to carry a gun and he'd take it out and show it around. Maybe he did. Life he led, I can see him carrying a gun for protection, even using it to defend himself. But why would he have to defend himself from a man making a phone call? And anyway, you can't shoot nine-millimeter bullets out of a forty-five, can you?''

''What happened to the gun?''

''The one I saw? You got me. It wasn't on him when they picked him up. They didn't find it when they searched his room. They say George told them some story about throwing it off a pier into the Hudson. They sent divers down and came up empty, but who even knows if they had the right pier. You want to know what I think happened?''

''What?''

''George threw his gun in the river months ago. One reason or another he decides it's not safe to carry it and he ditches it, and then when they pick him up and ask him what happened to the gun, he says he tossed it. He can't say when because he doesn't have that kind of memory. Or here's another possibility—he gets worried after the murder, after he picks up the cartridge casings, and decides he better get rid of the gun, so he goes home and finds it and tosses it. Or here's another way it could have happened—''

He went on working out scenarios to fit the evidence while leaving his brother innocent of all charges. Finally he ran out of theories and looked at me and asked me what I thought.

I said, ''What do I think? I think the cops arrested the right man. I think your brother showed you a nine-millimeter pistol and said it was a forty-five because they look similar and that was the type of semiautomatic handgun he was familiar with. I think he probably found the gun in a garbage can while he was searching for redeemable cans and bottles. I think there were bullets in the clip when he found it. I think the previous owner used the gun in the commission of a felony and got rid of it afterward, which is generally how guns find their way into garbage cans and Dumpsters and the river.''

''Jesus,'' he said.

''I think your brother was nodding in a doorway when Glenn Holtzmann went to make his phone call. I think something roused him out of a dream or reverie. Something he saw or heard, on the street or in his dream, convinced him that Holtzmann was a threat. I think he reacted instinctively, drawing the gun and firing three times before he really knew where he was or what he was doing. I think he put the fourth and final bullet in the back of Holtzmann's neck because that's how you executed people in Southeast Asia.

''I think he picked up the casings because he was taught to, and also because they might tie him to the shooting. I think he got rid of the gun for that reason, and I think he would have thrown the casings in after it if he hadn't forgotten they were there, or that he was supposed to get rid of them. I think he has no memory of shooting Holtzmann because he was only partially aware of what he was doing at the time. He was in a dream or a flashback.''

He sat back, looking as though he'd just taken a stiff right to the solar plexus. ''Whew,'' he said. ''I thought . . . well, never mind what I thought.''

''Go ahead, Tom.''

''Well, see, I figured on having to spend a few thousand dollars on a lawyer for George, and it turned out they'd already appointed an attorney, and on account of him being an indigent person the attorney's fees are paid out of public funds. And the lawyer was as good as anybody I could hire, plus he'd already seen George and had some rapport with him.'' He shrugged. ''So I've got this money I thought I was going to spend, and I thought, you know, maybe I could hire somebody to do a little detective work, find out if maybe George is innocent. Soon as I thought 'detective' I thought of you. But if you're stone certain the man is guilty—''

"That's not what I said."

"No? That's what it sounded like."

I shook my head. "I said I think he's guilty. Or that he did it; words like 'guilty' seem ill-chosen when the person involved may have thought he was executing a sniper somewhere north of Saigon. But that's just what I think, and it's an opinion based on the existing evidence. I could hardly think anything else, given the data available to me. There may be more data that neither of us knows about, and if it was brought to my attention I might have to revise that opinion. So yes, I think he did it, but I also think it's possible I'm wrong."

"Say he didn't do it. Is there a way to prove it?"

"You'd have to prove it," I said, "because I don't think you could get him off by discrediting the prosecution's case. Even if you impugned some of the eyewitness testimony, the cartridge casings are solid physical evidence and the next best thing to a smoking gun. Since they've got enough to prove him guilty, your only defense is to provide actual proof of innocence, probably by establishing that somebody else did it. Because Holtzmann sure as hell didn't commit suicide, and if George didn't kill him somebody else did."

"So you'd have to find the real killer."

"Not quite. You wouldn't have to identify him or develop a case against him."

"You wouldn't?"

"Not really. Say a flying saucer descended from the skies and a Martian hopped out, put four bullets in Holtzmann, got back in his saucer, and took off for outer space. If you can substantiate that, if you can prove it happened, you don't have to produce the saucer or subpoena the Martian."

"I get it." He got out a cigarette, lit it with a Zippo.

Through a cloud of smoke he said, "Well, what do you think? You want to go looking for that Martian?"

"I don't know."

"You don't know?"

"I may be the wrong person for this," I said. "See, I was acquainted with Glenn Holtzmann."

"You knew him?"

"Not well," I said, "but better than I knew your brother. I was up to his apartment once. I've met his wife. I talked to him a few times on the street and I had coffee with him once a block from here." I frowned. "I wouldn't say we were friends. As a matter of fact, I can't say I liked him much. But I don't think I'd be comfortable trying to get his killer off the hook."

"Neither would I."

"How's that?"

"If George did it," he said, "I don't want him off the hook either. If he pulled the trigger then he's a danger to himself and others and he belongs in a locked ward somewhere. I only want him cleared if he didn't do it, and if that's the case where's your conflict? You'd only be helping George if he turns out to be innocent. And you just said it yourself, if he didn't do it then somebody else did. If George goes away for it, then the real killer's getting away with it."

"I see what you mean."

"The fact that you knew the victim," he said, "to my mind that makes you the perfect man for the job. You knew Holtzmann, you know George, you know the neighborhood. That gives you a head start, the way it looks to me. If anybody's got a shot at it, I'd say you do."

"I'm not sure that means much," I said. "I think the chance that your brother didn't do it is slim, and the likelihood of establishing it is slimmer still. I'm afraid you'd be throwing your money away."

"It's my money, Matt."

"That's a point, and I guess you're entitled to throw it away if you want to. The thing is, it's my time, and I don't much like to throw it away even if I'm getting paid for it."

"If there's a chance he's innocent—"

"That's another thing," I said. "You believe he's innocent, in part because that's what you'd prefer to believe. Well, let's suppose that he is, and that if you just sit back and do nothing he's going to go away for the rest of his life for a crime he didn't commit."

"That's the thought that drives me crazy."

"Well, is it the worst thing in the world, Tom? You said yourself that he wouldn't be in a conventional penitentiary, that he'd wind up in some sort of mental facility where his needs would be met and he'd get some sort of help. Even if he's innocent, even if he got there for the wrong reason, is that so bad? They'll feed him, they'll see that he bathes and takes care of himself, he'll get treatment—"

"Thorazine's what he'll get. They'll turn him into a fucking zombie."

"Maybe."

He took off his glasses, pinched the bridge of his nose. "You don't know my brother," he said. "You've seen him but you don't know him. He's not homeless, he's got a room, but he might as well be homeless for all the time he spends there. He can't take being cooped up. He's got a bed that he hardly ever sleeps in. He doesn't sleep like a normal person, lies down at night and gets up in the morning. He sleeps like an animal, half an hour or an hour at a time, on and off throughout the day and night. He'll stretch out on a bench or curl up in a doorway and nap like a cat.

"He likes the open air. Even in the winter he's out of his room all the time. It's only the coldest nights'll drive him inside. As bitter as it gets he'll just put on more clothes until he's got everything he owns stuffed under that army jacket of his. And he'll walk to keep warm. Hours on end he'll walk, mile after mile.

"Day in, day out, he wore that army jacket. I never saw him without it. Well, they took it away from him and they burned it. They took everything he was wearing and tossed it in the incinerator. What else were they gonna do? When I saw him they had him in all clean clothes. They'd bathed him and cleaned him up. They didn't shave him or cut his hair because they're not allowed to do that, not without his consent, but that's Bellevue and Rikers. When he's in a permanent facility the rules'll be different.

"They burned up his army jacket. Well, what else were they supposed to do with it, the state it was in? But it's hard to imagine George without it.

"You can say my brother's crazy, and I guess he is, but he's been this way all his life and they're not about to change him now. I'm not saying it'll kill him to be locked up because maybe it won't, maybe he'll just pull himself a little further away from reality and crawl deeper inside his own mind and create his own world in there."

He looked straight at me. With his glasses off he looked more vulnerable, but somehow tougher, too.

He said, "I don't want to glamorize the life he leads, make him sound like some kind of Noble Savage. It's a horrible life. He lives like an animal, he lives in fear and torment. If he doesn't wind up in a locked ward with a Thorazine straitjacket he'll fall in front of a subway train or die of exposure, unless he gets really lucky and some teenage sadists set him on fire. Jesus Christ, Matt, I wouldn't lead his life for the world, but it's his life, do you follow me? It's his fucking life so let him fucking live it."

6

"**S**o I said I'd look into it," I told Elaine. "He put a thousand dollars on the table and I picked it up. Don't ask me why."

"Compassion," she said. "A sense of social responsibility. The need to see justice done."

"What else could it be?"

"Maybe you wanted the money."

"I was taught to grab what came my way," I allowed, "but it's a hard way to turn a buck. You work overtime trying to give the client his money's worth and walk away feeling fraudulent because you haven't accomplished anything. The fact that there was nothing to accomplish ought to carry some weight, but somehow it doesn't."

"You think George did it?"

"I think so, yes. For all the reasons I gave Tom."

"But there's room for doubt."

"Not much room," I said. "Not much doubt."

We had dinner in the Village and hit a couple of jazz clubs on Bleecker Street, then caught a cab back to her place. In the morning she made a pot of strong coffee, toasted a couple of poppy-seed bagels, and cut a papaya in half. Sunlight streamed in through the living-room

window, but Elaine, reading the *Times* we'd picked up
on the way home, informed me it wouldn't last. Cloud
cover would settle in by midday, with a strong proba-
bility of showers in the late afternoon and evening.
"Clearing tomorrow," she said. "A lot of good that
does me. Tomorrow's Monday. The museum's closed."

She was taking another photography course, this one
called "The Urban Landscape Through the Camera's
Eye." There was a display uptown at the Museum of
the City of New York and she was supposed to see it
before her next class.

"I guess I'll get rained on," she said. "What about
you?"

"I think I'll go walk around my neighborhood."

"I figured you might. Hell's Kitchen or Clinton?"

"Maybe a little of each. I'll wear out some shoe
leather and start earning the thousand dollars Tom Sadecki gave me. And I want to get to a meeting, and then
tonight I've got my usual Sunday dinner date with Jim
Faber."

"Well, I might go to the gym," she said, "or I might
say the hell with it and go straight to the museum. Then
I'll come home and plant myself in front of the television set. How come a television binge doesn't seem
nearly as degenerate when the programs are British?"

"It's the way they talk."

"It must be. *American Gladiators* would feel like an
edifying experience if they got Alistair Cooke to intro-
duce it. Call me tonight, if you get the chance, or I'll
talk to you in the morning. And say hello to Jim for
me."

I said I would. I somehow failed to mention my two
o'clock date with an old girlfriend.

Ages ago, when phone calls cost a dime, you made
them from little glassed-in booths with doors that closed

against traffic noise and weather. Maybe it's still that
way in other parts of the country, but in New York the
phone booths gradually evolved out of existence, providing less and less shelter with each model change.
Now all you get is a phone mounted on a post, and one
of these days they'll get rid of the post.

The phone I was interested in was on the southwest
corner of Eleventh Avenue and West Fifty-fifth Street,
and I knew it was the one Glenn Holtzmann had been
using on the night he died because it was the only one
around. It was about ten-thirty by the time I walked
across town from Elaine's. I looked over at the phone
while I waited for the light to change, then crossed the
street and took the receiver off the hook. I listened to
the dial tone and put it back.

For all the years I'd lived at the Northwestern, I had
spent precious little time on Eleventh Avenue. This
stretch of it ran to auto showrooms and warehouses,
building-supply outlets and collision repair shops. They
were all closed now, as they would have been on the
night of the shooting.

I walked around some, trying to get the feel of the
crime scene. There was nothing to identify it as such,
no chalk outline to mark where the body had lain, no
yellow plastic Crime Scene tape.

No visible bloodstains.

I could picture him standing there, lifting the receiver,
digging in his pocket for a quarter, dropping the coin in
the slot. Then something makes him turn—a sound, perhaps, or movement glimpsed out of the corner of his
eye. He starts to turn, and even as he's turning a shot
rings out, and he's hit.

The bullet takes him on the right side below the rib
cage. It pierces the liver and severs the portal vein, the
large blood vessel that services that organ.

A mortal wound, in all likelihood, but he won't live

long enough to die of it. He reels toward the shooter, who fires twice more from point-blank range. One slug glances off a rib and plows through muscle tissue, doing little serious damage. The other finds the heart and causes virtually instantaneous death.

He's on the ground now, sprawled full length on the sidewalk with his feet at the base of the post on which the phone is mounted. There's a fourth and final shot, a *coup de grâce*, fired into the back of his neck. It's as loud as the others, but he doesn't hear it.

Hard to say how long he lay there, or how much blood spilled out of him. Dead bodies don't bleed much, as a rule, and the heart wound would have brought death quickly, but I couldn't guess how much blood might have gouted from the liver wound before the heart stopped its pumping. In any event he lay there, first bleeding and then not bleeding, until someone picked up the dangling receiver and phoned it in.

Tom Sadecki had given me the address of the building where his brother rented a room. It was on Fifty-sixth just off the avenue, a red-brick old-law tenement with an identical building on its right and a rubble-strewn vacant lot on its left. A flight of steps led down to the basement entrance. The door at the bottom of the stairs had a glass window set at eye level, but I couldn't see anything through it. The door was locked. It didn't look as though it would be terribly hard to force it, but I didn't try. I don't know that I would have wanted to go in even if it had been unlocked.

I went back to the corner of Fifty-fifth and Eleventh, got out my notebook and made a rough sketch of the scene. There was a Honda dealership on the corner where Holtzmann was killed, a Midas Muffler franchise directly across the street. I remembered Tom Sadecki's scenario and tried to figure out where George might have lurked in the shadows while somebody else did the shooting. I didn't see any doorways, but there was a spot alongside the entrance to the Honda showroom where a person might have stood or crouched without being too conspicuous. There was a trash can on the corner, not ten yards from the pay phone, and others on the opposite curb and ranging alongside the muffler shop.

The sun had been shining when I left Elaine's apartment. Clouds obscured it by the time I reached the site of the murder, and the sky kept getting darker by the minute. The temperature was dropping, too, and it occurred to me that the jacket I was wearing wasn't going to be warm enough. I headed back to my hotel to change, and pick up an umbrella while I was at it.

But when I got to Ninth Avenue there was a bus just pulling up and I ran and caught it. Maybe the rain would hold off, I told myself. Maybe the sun would come out and warm things up again.

Sure.

It was almost twelve-thirty when I walked into a room on Houston Street, filled a Styrofoam cup with coffee, and took a couple of cookies from a chipped china plate. I found a chair, and someone stood up and read the AA preamble and introduced the speaker.

The group was mostly gay, and a lot of the sharing was about AIDS and HIV. At one-thirty we held hands and had a moment of silence, followed by the Serenity Prayer. The young man on my right said, "Do you know how they close the meetings at the agnostics' group? They have a moment of silence, followed by *another* moment of silence."

I walked down through SoHo, stopping at a pizza stand for a Sicilian slice and a Coke. Lispenard Street is just below Canal and only two blocks long, and Jan's loft is on the fifth floor of a six-story building wedged between two larger and more modern buildings. I stepped into the vestibule and rang her bell, then went back onto the sidewalk and waited for her to open the window and throw down the key.

That's what she'd done the night I met her, and on quite a few subsequent occasions. Then for a while I'd had a key of my own. I'd used it a final time on the afternoon I came to pick up my things. I had filled two shopping bags with my clothes and left the key on the kitchen counter, right next to the Mr. Coffee machine.

I looked up. The window opened and the key sailed out, hit the pavement, bounced, clattered, lay still. I picked it up and let myself into the building.

7

"Come on in," she said. "It was sweet of you to come. You're looking well, Matthew."

"So are you," I said. "You've lost weight."

"Hah," she said. "Finally." She tilted her head and looked me in the eye. "What do you think? Is it an improvement?"

"You've always looked good to me, Jan."

Her face clouded and she turned from me, saying that she'd just made a fresh pot of coffee. Did I still drink it black? I said I did. No sugar, right? Right, no sugar.

I went to the front of the loft, where floor-to-ceiling windows looked out over Lispenard Street. Her bronze head of Medusa, the hair a writhing mass of snakes, stood on its plinth to the right of the low sofa. It was early work; I'd seen it and remarked on it the night we met. Don't look her in the eye, Jan had told me, for her gaze turns men to stone.

Her own gaze when she brought the coffee, out of those large unflinching gray eyes, was almost as intimidating. She *had* lost weight, and I wasn't sure it was an improvement. She looked older than the last time I'd seen her.

Her hair was part of it. It was completely gray now.

It had been liberally salted with gray when I first met her, and never seemed to get any grayer. Now there were no dark hairs visible, and that coupled with the weight loss added years to her appearance.

She asked if the coffee was all right.

"It's fine," I said. "Aren't you having any?"

"I haven't been drinking much coffee lately," she said. Then she said, "Oh, what the hell. Why not?" She disappeared into the kitchen and came back with a cup of her own. "It *is* good," she said. "I'd almost forgotten how much I like the stuff."

"What have you been doing, trying to switch to decaf?"

"I pretty much got away from coffee altogether," she said. "But let's not have one of those deadly AA conversations about all the things we don't do anymore. What's that story about the old guy in the Salvation Army band? 'Yes, brothers and sisters, I used to drink, I used to smoke, I used to gamble, I used to go with wild, wild women, and now all I do is beat this goddamn drum.' " She took another sip of coffee and set the cup down. "Bring me up to date, Matthew. What have you been doing?"

"Beating my goddamn drum. Doing a little day work for a big agency. Working when I get a client, coasting when I don't. Going to meetings. Hanging out. Keeping company with Elaine."

"That's going well, then? I'm glad. She seemed very nice. Matthew, I told you I wanted to ask a favor."

"Yes."

"So I'll just come right out and ask it. I was wondering if you could get me a gun."

"A gun."

"There's so much crime these days," she said levelly. "You can't pick up the paper without seeing something awful on every page. It used to be that people were safe in decent neighborhoods, but now it doesn't seem to matter where you are or what time of day it is. The incident last week, with the young publisher. Right in your neighborhood, wasn't it?''

"Just a couple of blocks away.''

"Terrible,'' she said.

"Why do you want a gun, Jan?''

"For protection, of course.''

"Of course.''

"I don't really know anything about them,'' she said thoughtfully. "Of course I would want a handgun, but there are different styles and sizes, aren't there? I wouldn't know what kind to pick.''

"You need a permit to own a gun in this city,'' I said.

"Aren't they difficult to get?''

"Very difficult. About the best way is to join a gun club and take a course, and in return for a fairly stiff fee they'll help you fill out an application and steer you through the whole process. The training's not a bad idea, actually, but the entire procedure takes a while and it's not cheap.''

"I see.''

"If you went that route you could probably get a permit entitling you to maintain a handgun on the premises, and to transport it in a locked case to and from a firing range. That's sufficient if you want protection from burglars, but you wouldn't be able to tuck the gun in your purse for protection on the street. For that you'd need a carry permit, and they're very slow to pass those out nowadays. If you had a store and routinely carried large sums of cash to the bank, then you might qualify. But you're a sculptor and live and work in the same location. I knew a goldsmith years ago who was able to get a carry permit because he frequently transported quantities of precious metals, but you couldn't claim that without paperwork to back it up.''

"Clay and bronze don't cut it, huh?"

"I'm afraid not."

"Actually," she said, "I wouldn't need to carry the gun. Anyway, I'm not all that concerned about the legality of it."

"Oh?"

"I don't want to go through a lot of red tape applying for a permit. For heaven's sake, is it my imagination or do half the people in this city have guns? They're installing metal detectors in the schools because so many students are bringing guns to class. Even the homeless are armed. That poor derelict was living out of garbage cans and *he* managed to have a gun."

"And you want one."

"Yes."

I picked up my coffee cup and found it empty. I couldn't remember finishing it. I put it back down again and said, "Just who is it you want to kill, Jan?"

"Oh, Matthew," she said. "You're looking at her."

"It started in the spring," she said. "I noticed I'd lost a few pounds without even making an effort. I thought, hey, great, I'm finally getting a handle on my weight.

"I didn't feel so hot. Low energy, a little nausea. I didn't attach much significance to it. I'd felt that way in December, but I always have a bad time around the holidays, I get depressed and I feel lousy. Doesn't everybody? I chalked it up to seasonal malaise and let it go at that, and when it came back a couple of months later I still didn't pay much attention to it.

"Then my stomach started bothering me. I had a pain right here, and one day I realized I'd been having it on and off for weeks. I didn't want to go to the doctor because if it was nothing I'd be wasting time and money and if it was an ulcer I didn't want to know about it. I figured if I ignored it maybe it would go away. So I did and it didn't. It got to the point where I had to go to sleep in a half-seated posture because sitting up relieved the pain. Well, denial can only get you so far, and finally I decided I was being ridiculous and I went to the doctor, and the good news was I didn't have an ulcer after all. Now you're supposed to ask me what the bad news was."

I didn't say anything.

"Cancer of the pancreas," she said. "Do you want some more good news and bad news? The good news is they can cure it if they catch it early enough. All they have to do is remove the pancreas and the duodenum and reattach the stomach to the small intestine. You have to shoot yourself up with insulin and digestive enzymes a couple of times a day for the rest of your life, and your diet is extremely restricted, but that's the good news. The bad news is they never catch it in time."

"Never?"

"Almost never. By the time noticeable symptoms appear, the cancer has invariably spread to other abdominal organs. You know, I beat myself up at first for ignoring the weight loss and the other symptoms, but the doctor made me let myself off the hook. He told me it had unquestionably metastasized before I felt the first twinge or lost the first ounce."

"And the prognosis?"

"It couldn't be much worse. Ninety percent of people with pancreatic cancer are dead within a year of initial diagnosis. The rest of us are dead within five years. Nobody gets out of this alive."

"Isn't there any kind of treatment they can try?"

"There is, but it doesn't keep you alive. They can do certain things to make you more comfortable. I had a surgical procedure last month to bypass a blocked bile duct. They connected—well, what's the difference what they did, but it relieved the pain and got rid of the jaundice. It also left me feeling the way you'd expect to feel if they cut you open and sewed you back up again, but I think it was worth it. The first thing I noticed after surgery was that I'd gone completely gray, but that probably would have happened anyway. And if it bothers me I can always dye it, right?''

"Right.''

"It won't fall out, because there's no point in trying radiation or chemotherapy. Aw, Jesus, it just seems so ... I was going to say unfair, but life's unfair, everybody knows that. What it seems is so fucking arbitrary. Do you know what I mean? God picks your name out of a hat and you're it.''

"What causes it, do they know?''

"Not really. Statistically alcohol and tobacco seem to be factors. Much higher incidence among drinkers and smokers. Seventh-Day Adventists and Mormons hardly ever get it, but they hardly ever get anything. It's a wonder they don't all live forever. What else? A high-fat diet may play a role. And they think there's a connection with coffee consumption, but it's hard to tell because eighty percent of the population drinks the stuff. Not Mormons, of course, or Seventh-Day Adventists, God bless 'em. All they do is beat their goddamn drums. Well, that's about all I do, isn't it? I drank for as long as I could, and I smoked like a chimney for years. And of course I've always been a heavy coffee drinker, and that's one vice that certainly didn't stop when I got sober. Quite the opposite, in fact.''

"Is that why you've been staying away from it lately?''

"Of course. What else do you do once the horse is stolen? You buy a new lock for the stable door.'' She heaved a sigh. "Although I swear I don't think coffee had a damn thing to do with it. And I think the real reason I stopped drinking it is because that kind of behavior is automatic for people in Twelve-Step programs. What do we do in times of stress? We give up something that gives us pleasure." She got to her feet. "I'm going to have another cup," she announced. "Can I bring you some?"

"Sit down. I'll get it."

"Don't be silly," she said. "I don't have to conserve my strength. I'm not an invalid. I'm just dying."

A little later she said, "I don't want to give you the impression that I'm sick of the world and can't wait to get out of it. Every day is very precious to me. I want to have as many of them as I possibly can."

"Then what do you want with a gun?"

"That's for when I run out of good days. I went over to the library and read up on the subject, and it seems that when the good days run out the bad days are pretty bad. You don't just turn your face to the wall and expire. It's apt to be pretty agonizing, and it can go on for a while."

"Aren't there things they can give you for the pain?"

"I don't want that. I missed whole chunks of my life because I was too full of Smirnoff's to know what was going on. I don't want to jump out of this world and into the next one with a head all muddled with morphine. I had Demerol after surgery and I couldn't stand the way it made me feel. I made them take me off it and give me Tylenol instead. 'But you've got breakthrough pain,' the resident said. 'Tylenol won't touch it.' 'Then I'll live with it,' I told him, and it wasn't so bad. Do you think I was being a martyr?"

"I don't know."

"Because I don't think so. Dammit, I've got too much invested in a sober life to settle for anything less than a sober death. I'd rather have the pain than something to cover it up. What the hell, this is the hand I was dealt.

I figure I'll stay in the game as long as I possibly can. Then I'll fold. It's my hand, I can fold when I want to.''

I looked out the window. It had grown darker still, as if the sun were setting. But it was hours too early for that.

"I don't consider it suicide," she said. "There's a part of me that's still Catholic enough to find suicide unacceptable. God gives you your life and it's a sin to take it. But I don't see this as a case of taking my life. I'd just be giving myself a gift." She smiled gently. "The gift of lead. Do you know the poem?"

"What poem?"

"Robinson Jeffers, 'Hurt Hawks.' He finds an injured hawk in the woods near his home and he goes on about how he admires hawks, how if the penalties were the same he'd sooner kill a man than a hawk. He brings food to this one and tries to help it, but the day comes when the only thing he can do for the bird is put it out of its misery. 'I gave him the lead gift in the twilight,' I think that's how the line goes. Meaning a bullet. He shot the hawk, and then it was able to take flight.''

I thought it over, and said, "Maybe it works better with hawks.''

"What do you mean?"

"Gun suicides are messy. And they don't always work. When I was fresh out of the academy I heard about a guy who put a gun to his temple and shot himself. Bullet glanced off the bone and plowed a furrow up the side of the skull, tunneled underneath the scalp and came out the other side. The poor bastard bled like a stuck pig, deafened himself permanently in one ear, and had a headache he couldn't even begin to describe.''

"And lived."

"Oh, sure. He never even lost consciousness. I've known of other cases where people managed to put a bullet in their brain but lived anyway, including a Housing Authority cop who's spent the past ten or twelve years in a profound vegetative state. But assuming you'd get it right the first time, is it really the kind of gift you want to give yourself? It's such a violent physical insult to the body. You wind up with the top of your skull gone and your brains all over the wall. I'm sorry, I don't mean to be graphic, but—''

''That's all right.''

''Aren't there gentler ways, Jan? Isn't there a book on the subject?''

''Indeed there is,'' she said. ''I've got a copy on my bedside table. I had to buy the damned thing, too. I went to the library and there were sixteen people on the waiting list. I couldn't believe it, I thought I was at Zabar's trying to buy half a pound of lox. You want to kill yourself in this town, you have to take a number and wait.''

''How do they get it back?''

''How does who get what back? You lost me.''

''The book,'' I said. ''If it does its job, who's around to return it to the library?''

''Oh, that's rich,'' she said. ''You'd have to make a provision. 'I, Janice Elizabeth Keane, being of sound mind—' ''

''That's your story and you stick with it.''

'' '—do hereby request that my just debts and funeral expenses be paid, and that my copy of *Final Exit* be returned forthwith to the Hudson Park branch of the New York Public Library—' ''

'' '—in the hope that others may get as much out of it as I have.' ''

''Oh, Christ, that's wonderful,'' she said. ''And then they call the next person on the list. 'Hello, Mr. Nussbaum? We have the book you requested. Please get your affairs in order.' ''

How we howled.

*   *   *

The problem with the book, she said, was that most of the recommended methods involved ingesting some sort of mood-altering substance. Typically you were advised to swallow a fistful of sleeping pills and wash them down with a glass of whiskey. Since one of her prime motives for suicide was the desire to die sober, such methods struck her as counterproductive.

And suppose it didn't work? Suppose she woke up twelve hours later with a hangover, and all she'd managed to do was lose her sobriety? *My name is Jan and I've got one day back and two weeks to live.* No, to hell with that.

"They also recommended carbon monoxide," she said. "You attach a hose to the tailpipe and run it through the window. Tough to do without a car, though. I suppose you could rent one, but what would I do, park it on the street? Just as I was fading out some crackhead would break in and steal the radio."

So a gun seemed like her best choice. She was going to be cremated anyway, so what did it matter what she looked like? The person who discovered her body might have a bad moment or two, but that was just too bad, and life was full of bad moments, wasn't it?

She had thought of traveling to some southern state where they'd sell a handgun to anybody who wanted one, but she wasn't sure just how the laws worked. Could you buy one if you were from out of state? Or did you have to show local ID? Maybe you could establish residence, the way people used to do to get a Nevada divorce. Anyway, how would you go about getting the gun back on the plane? She could always make the return trip on Amtrak, but she hated the idea of spending that many hours on a train. For that matter, she wasn't crazy about the idea of flying anywhere, either.

"And then I thought, for God's sake, the city's full of unregistered guns, and it shouldn't be that hard to get one. If schoolchildren can get them, if homeless derelicts walk around armed, how tricky can it be? And I asked myself if I had a friend who would know how to get his hands on a gun, and who maybe loved me enough to do it. And you, my dear, were the only person who came to mind.''

''I guess I'm flattered.''

''And thrilled in the bargain, huh?''

Was it raining outside? It looked as though it might be raining.

I said, ''You know, I hate all this. I hate that you're sick. I hate the idea of you dying.''

''I'm not crazy about it myself.''

I said, ''I'll get you the gun.''

''You will?''

''Why not?'' I said. ''What are friends for?''

8

Outside, there was a cold wind blowing. You could feel the storm coming. I walked to the IND station at Canal and Sixth. I must have just missed an A-train, because I had to wait fifteen minutes for the next one. The platform was empty when I got there, and almost as empty when the train finally showed up.

I got off at Columbus Circle, and when I hit the street it was pouring fiercely. The few people unfortunate enough to be out in it took shelter in doorways, or struggled with umbrellas, trying to keep the wind from twisting them out of shape. On the far side of Fifty-seventh Street I saw a man trying to cover his head with a newspaper, and another man scurrying along with his shoulders drawn in, as if to present the rain with the smallest possible target. I didn't bother to adopt any of these strategies. I just resigned myself to getting soaked and walked right on through it.

When I hit the lobby, Jacob looked across the desk at me and whistled softly. "Lord, you better get yourself upstairs and into a hot tub," he said. "Catch your death walkin' around like that."

"Nobody lives forever," I said.

He gave me a curious look, then went back to the

73

Times crossword. I went up to my room and got out of my wet clothes and under the shower. I stood there a long time, willing myself to feel nothing but the hot spray on my neck and shoulders. By the time I turned off the taps and stepped out of the tub, the little room looked like a Turkish bath.

The mirror over the sink was steamed up. I left it that way. I had a pretty good idea how old and tired I looked, and I didn't feel the need to see for myself.

I got dressed and tried to find something to watch on television. I settled for the news on CNN but it didn't matter what I was watching because I couldn't pay any attention to it.

After a while I turned it off. I'd had the overhead light on, and I turned that off, too, and sat looking out the window at the rain.

I met Jim Faber at the Hunan Lion on Ninth Avenue. I got there at six-thirty, having walked the several blocks with an umbrella for protection. It didn't blow inside out, either. The rain was still coming down hard, but the wind had eased up considerably.

Jim was already there, and as soon as I sat down the waiter came over with menus. There was already a pot of tea on the table, and two cups.

I opened the menu and nothing looked very appealing. "You may be eating for two tonight," I said. "I haven't got much of an appetite."

"What's the matter?"

"Oh, nothing." He gave me a look. He is my AA sponsor and my friend, and we've had a standing Sunday night dinner date for a few years now, so it's not surprising that he can tell when I'm being evasive. "Well, I had a call yesterday," I said. "From Jan."

"Oh?"

"She wanted me to come down to her place."

"Isn't that interesting."

"Not in the way you're thinking. She had something she wanted to tell me. I went down there this afternoon, and she told me."

"And?"

I said the words in a rush, not wanting to give them a chance to get stuck in my throat. "She's dying. She's been diagnosed with pancreatic cancer, she's got less than a year to live."

"Jesus Christ."

"I guess it hit me pretty hard."

"I guess it would," he said, and then the waiter turned up with pad and pencil at the ready. "Listen," Jim said, "why don't I just go ahead and order? Bring us one order of the cold noodles, an order of the spicy shrimp with broccoli, and General Tzo's famous chicken." He squinted at the menu. "Except he seems to be known as General Tsung at this particular establishment. Another menu, another spelling. I suppose it's all the same general. God knows it's always the same chicken."

"Is good dish," the waiter said.

"I'm sure it'll be fine. And we'll have brown rice with that, if you have it."

"On'y white rice."

"Then we'll have white rice." He handed back the menu and refilled our teacups. To me he said, "If you and I lived in China, would we be going out every Sunday night for General Schwarzkopf's chicken? Somehow I doubt it. Matt, that's horrible news, just awful. It's an absolute certainty? There's nothing at all they can try?"

"Evidently not. According to her the diagnosis is a death sentence. Worse than a death sentence, because you can't delay it by filing appeals. It's like frontier justice in the Old West. They pronounce sentence in the afternoon and hang you at sunrise."

"What a hell of a thing. How old is Jan, do you happen to know?"

"Forty-three, forty-four. Something like that."

"That's not very old."

A little older than Elaine, a little younger than I. I said, "I guess it's as old as she's going to get to be."

"What a hell of a thing."

"Afterward I went back to my room and sat by the window and watched it rain. I wanted a drink."

"Now there's a surprise."

"I never entertained the idea of having one. I knew it wasn't something I wanted to do. But the physical desire was as strong as I can remember it. Every cell in my body cried out for alcohol."

"Who wouldn't want a drink under the circumstances? Isn't that what it's for? Isn't that why they put the stuff in bottles? But wantin' ain't drinkin'. And it's a good thing, or there wouldn't be but one AA meeting a week in New York, and you could hold it in a phone booth."

If you could find a booth to hold it in, I thought. They didn't have them anymore. But why was I thinking about phone booths?

"Nothing easier than staying sober when you don't feel like drinking," he went on. "But what amazes me is the way we manage to stay sober even when we do feel like drinking. And that's what strengthens us, too. That's where the growth comes from."

Oh, right. I'd been thinking about phone booths earlier in the day, standing on the corner of Fifty-fifth and Eleventh and looking at the phone Holtzmann was using when he died. Where would Superman change his clothes, now that the city was out of phone booths?

"I don't think I've ever gone through a difficult time without getting something out of it," Jim was saying.

" 'I must go on. I can't go on. I'll go on.' I forget who said that."

"Samuel Beckett."

"Really? Well, it's the whole program in, what, ten words? 'I must stay sober, I can't stay sober, I'll stay sober.' "

"That's eleven words."

"Is it? 'I must stay sober, I can't stay sober, I'll stay sober.' All right, it's eleven words. I stand corrected. Ah, cold noodles with sesame sauce, and not a moment too soon. Here, help yourself to some of these. I can't eat the whole thing."

"They'll just sit on my plate."

"So? Everything's got to be someplace."

When the waiter had cleared away our dirty dishes, Jim said I'd done pretty well for a man with no appetite. It was the chopsticks, I explained. You wanted to look like you knew what you were doing.

I said, "I still feel empty. Eating didn't change that."

"Have you cried for her?"

"I never cry. You know the last time I wept? The first time I spoke up at a meeting and admitted I was an alcoholic."

"I remember."

"It's not that I make an effort to hold back the tears. I'd be perfectly willing to cry. But it's evidently the way I am. I'm not about to rip off my shirt and go beat a drum in the woods with Iron Mike and the boys."

"I think you mean Iron John."

"Do I?"

"I think so. Iron Mike's the fellow who coaches the Chicago Bears, and I don't figure he's much of a drummer."

"Strictly a bass player, huh?"

"That would be my guess."

I drank some tea. I said, "I hate the thought of losing her."

He didn't say anything.

I said, "When Jan and I broke up, when we finally called it quits and I got my stuff from her place and gave her back her key, I remember telling you how much it saddened me to see the relationship end. Do you remember what you said to me?"

"I hope it was profound."

"You told me that relationships don't end, they just take a different form."

"I said that?"

"Yes, and I found the words very comforting. For the next few days I was running them through my mind like a mantra. 'Relationships don't end, they just take a different form.' It helped me keep from feeling that I'd lost something, that something valuable had been taken from me."

"It's funny," he said, "because not only don't I remember the conversation, but I can't even recall ever having had the thought. But I'm glad it was a comfort."

"It was," I said, "but after a couple of days I thought about it, and I decided it was a cold comfort. Because this particular relationship had changed its form, all right. It had changed from two people who spent half their nights together and spoke at least once a day to two people who made a particular point of staying out of each other's way. The new form the relationship had taken was one of nonexistence."

"Maybe that's why I didn't remember the line. Maybe my unconscious mind had the good sense to spot it for the horseshit it was."

"But it's not horseshit," I said, "because when all is said and done you were absolutely right. Jan and I were cordial when we ran into each other, but how often did that happen? Once or twice a year? I can tell you the last two times I spoke to her over the phone. That lunatic Motley was running around killing any woman he could find who'd ever had anything to do with me, and I called my ex-wife to tell her to lay low, and I called Jan, too. Then I called her again afterward to tell her the coast was clear.

"But she's always been there whether I see her or not, whether I talk to her or not, whether I consciously think of her or not. Relationships change their form, yes, but there's something about them that doesn't change. I'll tell you, I hate to think of a world that doesn't have her in it. I'm going to lose something when she dies. My life's going to be a little smaller."

"And a little closer to the end."

"Maybe."

"All our mourning's for ourselves."

"You think so? Maybe. When I was a kid I couldn't understand why people had to die. You want to know something? I still can't."

"You were young when you lost your father, weren't you?"

"Very young. I thought the whole thing was a colossal mistake on God's part. Not my father's death in particular but the way the system worked. I still don't get it."

Neither did he, and we batted that one around for a while. Then he said, "Getting back to my words of wisdom about relationships enduring. Maybe death doesn't change things, either."

"You mean the spirit lives on? I'm not sure I buy that."

"I don't know that I do, either, although I keep an open mind on the subject. But that's not what I'm getting at. Do you honestly think Jan'll stop being a part of your life when her own life comes to an end?"

"Well, it'll be a little harder to get her on the phone."

"My mother died over six years ago," he said, "and I can't get her on the phone, but I don't have to. I can hear her voice. I don't mean that she's necessarily out there somewhere, in an afterworld or on another plane of existence. The voice I hear is the part of her that's become a part of me and lives on in my mind." He fell silent for a moment, and then he said, "My father's been gone over twenty years, and I've still got his voice in my head, too, the old bastard. Telling me I'm no damn good, telling me I'll never amount to anything."

"I sat at the window and watched it rain," I said, "and I thought of all the people I've lost over the years. That's what comes of living this long. It's a hell of a choice life gives you. Either you die young or you lose a lot of people. But they're not gone if I still think of them, right?"

"More cold comfort, huh?"

"Well, it's better than no comfort at all."

He signaled for the check. "There's a new Big Book meeting Sundays at Holy Name," he said. "If we leave now we should be right on time for it. Want to check it out?"

"I went to a meeting this morning."

"So?"

There are several different formats for AA meetings. There are speaker meetings and discussion meetings, and there are formats which combine the two elements. There are step meetings, which center each week upon one of the program's twelve steps, and tradition meetings, which do the same for AA's twelve traditions. Promise meetings focus on the benefits of recovery, which are presumably assured to everyone who follows the directions. (There are twelve promises, too. If Moses had been an alcoholic, I've heard it said, we'd be stuck with twelve commandments instead of ten.)

The Big Book is the oldest and most important piece of AA literature, written by the first members over fifty years ago. Its opening chapters explain the program's principles, and the rest of the book consists of members telling their personal stories, much as we tell them now when we speak at meetings, telling what our lives used to be like, what happened, and what it's like now.

When I was first getting sober Jim kept telling me to read the Big Book, and I kept finding things I didn't like about it. The prose style was leaden, the tone was deadly earnest, and the sophistication level was that of a Rotary Club breakfast in a small town in Iowa. He said I should read it anyway. The writing's old-fashioned, I said. So's Shakespeare, he said. So's the King James Bible. So what? When I complained of insomnia, he told me to read the Big Book at bedtime. I tried it, and reported that it worked. Of course it works, he said; some of those chapters would stop a charging rhino in its tracks.

At a Big Book meeting, members typically take turns reading a couple of paragraphs of the sacred text. When the week's designated chapter has been completed, the rest of the hour is given over to a discussion of what was read, with people relating what they heard to their own personal histories and current situations.

This particular group, Clinton Big Book, had been meeting for the past eight Sundays in a first-floor classroom at Holy Name School, on Forty-eighth between Ninth and Tenth. There were fourteen of us and the chapter was a long one, so most of us got to read more than once. I didn't pay much conscious attention to the reading, but that was all right. It wasn't exactly new information.

It was still raining when the meeting ended. I walked a few blocks with Jim, neither of us saying much. At his corner he clapped me on the shoulder and told me to stay in touch. "Remember," he said, "it's not your fault. I don't know how Jan got cancer, never mind why, but there's one thing I do know. You didn't give it to her."

I was only a few blocks from Grogan's, but rather than walk past it I cut over to Ninth Avenue. It was no night for me to be sitting at a table with a bottle of good whiskey, even if another man was doing the drinking. Nor did I feel much like talking. I'd had enough conversation for one night, for all I'd left unsaid.

I hadn't said a word about the gun. Jim never asked the reason for Jan's call, assuming she'd just felt the need to share significant news with an old friend. If he'd asked I'd probably have told him about the mission she'd assigned to me, and that I had accepted it. But he hadn't asked and I hadn't mentioned it.

I called Elaine from my hotel room, and I didn't mention it to her, either. I didn't say much about my visit to the murder site, or about the rest of the day. We weren't on the phone all that long, and what we mostly talked about was her day, and the show she'd seen uptown at the museum. "Early photos of New York, and it's really a wonderful show," she said. "I think you'd enjoy it. It's up through the middle of next month, so maybe you can get to it. I walked out of there thinking I'll buy a camera, I'll walk around the city every day and take pictures of everything."

"You could do that."

"Yeah, but why? Because I like to look at photographs? Remember what W. C. Fields said."

" 'Never give a sucker an even break.' "

"He said women are like elephants. 'I like to look at them but I wouldn't want to own one.' "

"What has that got to do with photographs?"

"Well, I like to look at them, but . . . *I* don't know. Forget it. Does everything I say have to make sense?"

"No, and it's a good thing."

"I love you, you old bear. You sound tired. Long day?"

"Long day, cold day, wet day."

"Get some sleep. I'll talk to you tomorrow."

But I couldn't sleep for the longest time. I turned the TV on and off, picked up books and magazines, read a page here and a page there and put them down again. I even tried the Big Book, that time-honored soporific, but it didn't work. There are times when it doesn't, times when nothing works, and all you can do is look out the window at the rain.

9

"**I** hate to say it," Joe Durkin said, "but I've got a bad feeling about this. I wish you would give the guy his money back."

"That's something I never thought I'd hear you say."

"I know," he said. "It's not like me. When a man gets a chance to make an honest dollar, who am I to stand in his way?"

"So what's the problem?"

He leaned back in his chair, balancing it on its back legs. He said, "What's the problem? My friend, you're the problem."

We were in the detective squad room on the second floor of the Midtown North station house on Fifty-fourth Street. I'd walked over after breakfast, going a little bit out of my way in order to have another look at the Eleventh Avenue murder site. It was a lot livelier on a Monday morning, with most of the shops and showrooms open for business and more vehicular traffic on the avenue, but it didn't offer any fresh insights into the last moments of Glenn Holtzmann.

From there I'd gone to Midtown North, where I'd found Joe at his desk. I'd told him how Tom Sadecki

84

had given me a retainer, and now he was telling me to give it back.

"If you were almost anybody else," he said, "you'd do what almost anybody else would do, which is put in a dozen hours or so and then tell your client what he probably already knows, which is that his nut job of a brother did it. That way your client knows he did all he could, and you earn yourself a decent piece of change without busting your hump to do it.

"But you're a contrary bastard, and on top of that you're as stubborn as a fucking mule. Instead of just taking your guy and shining him on, which is all he really wanted in the first place, whether he knows it or not, you'll have to make sure you give him his money's worth. And you'll find a way to convince yourself there's a possibility the brother didn't do it, and you'll put in the hours, and you'll break everybody's balls, mine included. By the time you're done you'll have so much time invested that you'll be lucky to clear minimum wage for your troubles, and you'll have come to the reluctant conclusion that Lonesome George is every bit as guilty as everybody knows he is, but you'll have done everything in your power to fuck up an open-and-shut case. Why are you staring at me like that?"

"I was just wishing I had a tape of that speech. I could play it for prospective clients."

He laughed. "You think I went overboard there? Well, it's a Monday morning. You have to make allowances. Seriously, Matt, just go through the motions on this one, will you? It's a high-profile case. We solved it fast with some good police work, but the media's in love with the story. You don't want to give 'em an excuse to open it up again."

"What would they find?"

"Nothing. The case is solid. It was a good bust."

"Were you on the case, Joe?"

"The whole precinct was on it, along with half of Manhattan Homicide. I didn't have much to do with closing it. Once they picked him up it was closed. He had the brass in his pocket, for Chrissake. The casings. What more do you need?"

"How did you know to pick him up?"

"Information received."

"Received from whom?"

He shook his head. "Uh-uh. Can't tell you that."

"From a snitch?"

"No, from a priest who decided it was time to violate the seal of the confessional. Yes, of course from a snitch. As far as the identity of the snitch is concerned, don't ask."

"What did the snitch have to say?"

"I can't tell you that."

"I don't know why not," I said. "Was he on the scene? Did he see something, hear something? Or did somebody just pass on a rumor that led you to George?"

"We have an eyewitness," he said. "How's that?"

"An eyewitness to the actual shooting?"

He frowned. "I always tell you more than I planned," he said. "Why do you figure that is?"

"You know it's the best way to get rid of me. What did your eyewitness see?"

"I already said too much, Matt. There's a witness and there's hard physical evidence and there's the next best thing to a confession. Sadecki says he figures he probably did it. The case is so solid even the perp's convinced."

It had me convinced, too, but I had a fee to earn. "Suppose what the witness saw was the aftermath," I said. "George bending over the body, picking up the shells."

"After somebody else shot him."

"It's possible."

"Oh, sure, Matt. Somebody fired from the grassy knoll. You ask me, the CIA was in on it."

"Holtzmann could have been mugged," I said. "It's not exactly unheard-of in that neighborhood. He could have been shot resisting a robbery attempt."

"No evidence of it. He had a wallet on his hip with over three hundred dollars in it."

"The mugger panicked after the shooting."

"Funny way to panic. First he fires a very deliberate fourth shot into the back of the neck, then he panics."

"Who else was on the scene? Who else did the witness get a look at?"

"He saw George. That was enough."

"What was Holtzmann doing there? Did anybody bother to check that out?"

"He went for a walk. It's not like commercial aviation, you don't have to file a flight plan first. He was restless and he went for a walk."

"And he stopped to make a phone call? What was the matter with the phone in his apartment?"

"Maybe he was trying to call his apartment, tell his wife when he'd be home."

"How come he didn't reach her?"

"Maybe the line was busy. Maybe he had the number half-dialed when Boy George shot him. Who the hell knows, and what the hell difference does it make? God damn it, you're doing just what I knew you would do, you're trying to pick holes in a perfectly solid case."

"If it's really solid I won't be able to, will I?"

"No, but you'll make a real pain in the ass of yourself in the meantime."

I'm the one fly in the ointment, Tom Sadecki had said. I'm the pain in everybody's ass.

I said, "What do you know about Holtzmann, Joe?"

"I don't have to know anything about him. He's the victim."

"That's where a homicide investigation starts, isn't it? With the victim?"

"Not when you can cut to the chase. When you've already got the killer in custody, you don't have to turn the victim inside out. Why the thoughtful expression?"

"You know what's wrong with the case, Joe?"

"The only thing wrong with it is you're taking an interest. Aside from that it's perfect."

"What's wrong with it," I said, "is you solved it too fast. There are a lot of things you would have learned—about Holtzmann, about other people in the area—but you never had to pursue them because why bother? You already had the killer in custody."

"You think we've got the wrong man?"

"No," I said. "I think you've got the right man."

"You think the police work was slipshod? You think we missed something?"

"No, I think the police work was excellent. But I think there are some avenues you haven't needed to explore."

"And you figure you'll take a little walk down them."

"Well, I took the man's money," I said. "I have to do something."

The Donnell branch library is on Fifty-third off Fifth. I spent a couple of hours in the second-floor reading room going through all the local papers for the past ten days. Once I got past the hard news, most of which was already familiar to me, the bulk of the stories turned out to be non-stories, pieces about homelessness, about neighborhood gentrification, about crime in the streets. There were interviews with people who'd lived for years in the area's tenements and apartment houses, with others who'd recently moved into Holtzmann's high-rise, and with a few who lived on the street. Every columnist with an ax to grind found a way to hone it here. Some of it made interesting reading, but it didn't tell me much I hadn't already known.

There was one essay I particularly liked, a *Times* Op-Ed piece by an advertising copywriter who was identified as residing within two blocks of the Holtzmann apartment building. He had been unemployed since late May, and he explained how his economic circumstances altered his perspective.

"With every passing day," he wrote, "I identify a little less strongly with Glenn Holtzmann, a little more closely with George Sadecki. When the news first broke, I was shocked and horrified. That could have been me on the sidewalk, I told myself. A man just past entering the prime of life, a professional man with a bright future, living in Clinton, the most exciting area of the most stimulating city in the world.

"And as the hours and days slip by," he went on, "it is a subtly different mirror in which I see myself. That could be me on Rikers Island, I find myself thinking. A man on the verge of middle age, an unemployed idler in a dwindling job market, drifting through the days in Hell's Kitchen, the most unsettling area in the most desperate city on God's earth. I still ache for the man who was killed, but I ache too for the man who killed him. I could have found myself in either man's shoes, in Glenn Holtzmann's well-polished wing tips or in George Sadecki's thrift-shop sneakers."

I walked back to my hotel, pausing along the way for a hot dog and a papaya drink. I checked at the desk for messages but nobody had called. I picked up a container of coffee at the deli next door and carried it across the street to the little park adjacent to the Parc Vendôme. I found a place to sit and took the lid off my coffee, but it was too hot to drink. I set it down alongside me on the bench and got out my notebook.

I jotted things down, thinking on paper, beginning
with the assumption that George Sadecki was innocent.
Trying to prove it was a waste of time; what I had to
do was find someone else who could have done it.
Someone with a reason to kill Glenn Holtzmann, or
someone who might have done so with no more reason
than George had.

Glenn Holtzmann. From where I sat I could see the
top floors of his apartment building. If I turned around
I could see the table at the Morning Star where we'd
had our last conversation. Lisa had lost the baby, he'd
told me. I had felt for him that afternoon, but still had
remained disinclined to get close to him. I'd felt dis-
tanced from him, and was happy to keep him at a distance. I hadn't wanted to get to know him.

Now it looked as though I had to. A homicide investigation, I'd reminded Joe, properly starts with the victim. To find a killer you look for someone with a reason
to kill. To learn the reason you first learn who the victim
is.

If someone had a reason.

But maybe he had just been in the wrong place at the
wrong time. He could have been the victim of a failed
robbery attempt. Joe had made it sound unlikely, ridi-
culing the notion of a holdup man who would take the
time for a *coup de grâce,* then dash off without retriev-
ing the money. What he'd said made sense, but that's
more than most criminals do. They're disorganized.
They act impulsively, operate irrationally, and change
course abruptly. A relative handful are stable and well
organized, but the great majority do something stupid
every time they leave the house.

Not that a would-be mugger was the only sort of person who might have killed Holtzmann for no good reason. He could simply have spoken out of turn in a city
where altogether too many people walk about armed.

Any kind of argument—over the use of a public telephone, for example—had the potential to turn violent.

Or he could have been killed by mistake. That had happened a few years back at a restaurant in Murray Hill. Four men, three of them furriers and the fourth their accountant, had just taken a table and ordered a round of drinks. Two men came in the door and one took out an automatic weapon and sprayed the furriers' table, killing the four men and wounding a woman at the table next to theirs.

It was a very obvious mob hit, and for a week or two investigators probed for mob infiltration of the fur industry, or evidence linking any of the dead men with one of the five crime families. As it turned out, none of them had ever come any closer to organized crime than buying a candy bar from a vending machine. The intended target had been four other men, principals in a mobbed-up construction firm in Jersey City, who had been sitting on the other side of the restaurant when the hit occurred. The shooter, it turned out, was dyslexic, and had turned left when he should have turned right. (A DEADLY MISKATE was the *Post*'s headline.)

Well, these things happen. Everybody makes miskates.

So there were two ways to approach it. I could look to the victim or at the event itself. I was about ready to flip a coin when I saw a familiar face no more than twenty yards away. Hair like white Brillo, high cheekbones, a narrow nose, hornrimmed glasses, skin the color of my coffee. It was Barry, George Sadecki's friend, and he was sitting on an upturned milk crate, with a three-foot concrete cube serving him for a table. He had a chessboard set up on it and he was smoking a cigarette and studying the pieces on the board.

I walked over and greeted him by name and he looked

up at me, his mouth smiling easily even as his eyes labored to place me. "I know you," he said. "Your name'll come to me."

"It's Matt," I said.

"See? Came to me by special delivery. Sit down, Matt. You play chess?"

"I know how the pieces move."

"Then you know the game. That's all it is, you just move the pieces till somebody wins." He snatched up a pawn in each hand, held his hands behind his back, then presented me with both fists. I tapped one and he opened it to disclose a white pawn.

"See?" he said. "You're a winner already, you get to make the first move. Set 'em up and we'll play. No stakes, just to pass the time."

There was another plastic milk crate on the opposite side of the table from him. I perched on it and set up my men, studied them, then advanced the king's pawn two spaces. He answered in kind and we both made a few unsurprising opening moves. When I brought out my bishop to menace his knight he said, "Ah, the old Ruy Lopez."

"If you say so," I said. "Someone tried to teach me the names of the standard openings once, but it didn't stick. I'm afraid I've got no head for the game."

"I don't know," he said. "Way you keep badmouthing yourself, seems like you're trying to hustle me."

"Dream on," I said.

At first we both made our moves rapidly, but as the game developed I found it harder to come up with something and began spending more time studying the board. Ten or a dozen moves into the game we exchanged knights, and somehow I wound up a pawn down. A little further along he forced an exchange of his remaining knight for one of my rooks. With each move he was mobilizing his forces for an attack, and all I could do was await it. My position felt cramped, awkward, indefensible.

"I don't know," I said, trying to find a move that did me some good. "I suppose I could resign."

"You could," he agreed.

I extended a forefinger and toppled my king. He looked sad, lying there on his side.

Barry said, "We wasn't playin' for stakes, but that doesn't mean you couldn't duck across the street for a quart of Eight Hundred."

"I'm not drinking these days, Barry."

"Think I don't know that, man? But when did you hear me say anything about drinking? Drinking's one thing. Buying's another."

"That's a point."

"Basement of St. Paul's," he said. "That's where I know you from, am I right?"

"That's right."

"I don't hardly get there. Used to come around for the coffee, and just to sit with folks. Drinking's no problem for me."

"You're fortunate."

"Long as I stay with the beer I seem to be all right. Was a time it was tending to make me sick." He laid a hand on his right side, just beneath the rib cage. "Was hurting me some right about here."

"The liver," I said.

"I guess. What I think it was, I think it was the Night Train. That sweet wine's a killer. But the beer, she seems to agree with me." He grinned, showing a little gold at the corners of his smile. "For now, anyway. Beer'll pro'ly kill me herself someday, but a man has got to die of something. Live long enough, sooner or later you die of too much living. If it's not one thing it's another. Isn't that what they say?"

"That's what they say."

"And what do you say, then? You want to spring for a quart of OE and we'll play another game?"

I found a five and gave it to him. He touched his index finger to his eyebrow in a mock salute and headed for the Korean grocery across the street. I watched him move in a loose-limbed, effortless gait, his long arms swinging easily at his sides. He was wearing a navy pea jacket and faded jeans and high-top sneakers, and he had to be sixty years old at a minimum, and he loped across Ninth Avenue like a man who had it all together.

I caught myself thinking that maybe Barry had the right idea. Stick to beer and ale, go to an occasional meeting for the coffee and the company, work on your chess game, and hustle a buck now and then when you get thirsty.

Yeah, right. And get through life sitting on milk crates. And what kind of shape was I in, pray tell, if Barry was starting to look like a role model? I had to laugh at myself, recognizing the thought for what it was, just one more note in the siren's song of the booze. Its lure was endless, and infinitely resourceful, and whatever street you walked down it would be waiting around the next corner, ready to pop out and take you by surprise. You could make a million dollars and win two Nobel prizes and the Miss Congeniality award, and next thing you knew you'd walk past a Blarney Stone and find yourself wondering if the stew bums in the back booth knew something you didn't. Because they got to drink and you didn't, so how wrong could they be?

Barry came back with a quart of Olde English 800 in a paper bag. He twisted off the cap and drank without removing the bottle from the bag. He said I could have the black pieces this time or I could stay with white, whichever I'd rather. I said I figured that was enough chess for one day.

"Guess you don't have a real feel for the game," he said. "You'd think you would, though."

"Why?"

"Well, the figuring-out aspect of it. Must be a lot like police work, scoping out the moves, calculating you'll do this if I do that. You was a cop, right?"

"You have a good memory."

"Well, the both of us has been around the neighborhood enough years now. Be a surprise if we didn't reckanize each other. Guess I'd figure you for a cop anyway, on the basis of how you present and represent. This be about George?"

I nodded. "I saw you on television," I said.

"Man," he said, "is there anybody in this city didn't see me on television?" He sighed and shook his head, treated himself to another long pull on the Olde English bottle. "How many channels now? Sixty, seventy if you got cable? Must be everybody watches Channel Seven, because everybody seen Barry on television. Everybody but me. I swear I must be the only person in New York didn't see the damn program."

We talked some about George, and I sensed I was getting what everyone got who mentioned having seen the TV spot, a sort of reprise of The George Sadecki I Knew. I steered him to Holtzmann and asked him what he knew about the man who got shot.

"You live here," I said. "You keep your eyes open. You must have seen Glenn Holtzmann around the neighborhood."

"I don't think so," he said. "Don't recall him if I did. I seen his picture in the paper and didn't reckanize him. Terrible thing, wasn't it? Bright young man, whole life ahead of him."

"What are they saying about him on the street?"

"Like I just said. Saying what a fine young man he

was and what a bad thing happened. What else they gone say?''

"That would depend on what they knew.''

"Man, how would they know him? He didn't live here.''

"Of course he did," I said. "You can see his building from here.''

He made a show of following my finger as I pointed at the top floors of Holtzmann's apartment building. "Right," he said. "That's where he lived, up on the fortieth floor.''

The twenty-eighth, I thought.

"That's another country up there," he said. "Man commuted from the fortieth floor over there to some other fortieth floor where his office is at. Where you and me are is the street. Man like that, the street's just a place he's got to pass through twice a day, getting from one fortieth floor to another.''

"He was on the street a week ago Thursday.''

"To get some air, so they say.''

"Meaning?''

"Oh, I ain't signifying. Just seems to me there ought to be plenty of air up on the fortieth floor. Got nothing *but* air up there, wouldn't you say?''

"So what was he doing on the street?''

"Could be Fate. You believe in Fate?''

"I don't know.''

"Man's got to believe in something," Barry said. "What I believe, I believe I'll have another drink." He did, and all but smacked his lips. He said, "I'm hip that you don't drink, but are you sure you won't have a little taste?''

"Not today. What was there besides Fate and fresh air that could have brought Holtzmann to Eleventh Avenue?''

"Told you I didn't know the man.''

"I figured you might know the street."

" 'Leventh Avenue? I know where it's at."

"Did you ever go over to George's room?"

"Didn't even know he had one until just this past week. Knew there was some place he kep' his stuff but didn't know where. Far as Eleventh Avenue's concerned, nothing much to draw me there."

"You didn't have to take your car in for a brake job?"

He laughed richly. "No, the brakes is just fine. Maybe I take a run over there, let 'em rotate the tires." He had another pull of Olde English, and this time he drew the bottle halfway out of the bag and squinted at the label over the tops of his glasses.

"See," he said, "beer and malt liquor's just about the right speed for me. Wine an' whiskey's bad for me. Was a time they treated me decent, but those days is gone."

"So you said."

" 'Course I'll smoke a little herb once in a while if it happens to come my way, but I won't go looking for it. Man passes you a jay, offers you a taste, you want to be sociable, you follow me?"

"Sure."

"An' the last time they had me over to Roosevelt they cut me open an' gave me this Percodan after they sewed me up. One every four hours, and I swear they was nicer than the pain was bad. They gave me some to take with me when they discharged me, but they run out pretty soon, and they wouldn't refill the scrip. I went over to DeWitt Clinton Park and bought six pills off a skinny white boy with those mirror sunglasses, and they looked same as the ones they gave me at Roosevelt, same color, same markings on em, but they just didn't do me the same kind of good. Maybe there's such a thing as drug-company seconds, ones that don't measure up an' they sell 'em out the back door. What do you think?"

"I suppose it's possible."

"So I don't get over to Eleventh Avenue much," he said. "They ain't got nothing I need."

His Percodan story had put me in mind of Jan's decision to pass up painkillers rather than compromise her sobriety. My mind tracked that thought and I almost missed the implications of what Barry was saying.

Then my brain geared down and I said, "DeWitt Clinton Park. There's a little park a block or two below the corner where Holtzmann was shot. The west side of Eleventh. Is that the park you're talking about?"

"Uh-huh. Clinton Park. You ever go there, don't buy nothing off a white boy with mirror shades. Be wasting your money."

"That's a little out of my range," I said. "I didn't even know the name of the park. They sell a lot of drugs there?"

"Sell a lot of shit," Barry said. "Pill'd have to do more'n that for me before I'd call it a drug. There's always dealers there, if that's your question. This here's about the only park I know that don't have dealers in it, and that's on account of how small it is. No grass, no trees, just slabs for benches and tables. Call it a park, but it's just a wide part of the sidewalk. A genuine park, you sure to have drug dealers."

"They can't get much business over there."

"You selling what the people want, they come an' find you."

"I guess that's true."

"An' at night you get the girls. You know the girls I mean. They just hang around in case somebody in a car or a truck calls them over to ask directions."

"That's further downtown, isn't it? It used to be just north of the Lincoln Tunnel that the girls would work the traffic."

"Don't know about that," he said. "Girls I know

about is right here on Eleventh Avenue, strutting their stuff in the blond wigs and the hot pants. 'Cept they ain't girls, if you take my meaning.''

"You mean they're transsexuals."

"Transvestites, transsexuals. There's a difference, but I disremember which is which. Boys looking to be girls, and I must say there's some of 'em look mighty fine. Wouldn't you say?''

"Oh, I'm too old for that," I said.

He cackled happily. "You younger'n I am, and I ain't too old for it. The girls on Eleventh Avenue, though, they got an eye for the dollar. An' a lot of 'em sick nowadays, you go with 'em and you catch your death. No, when I get the old feeling, I'm better off with my schoolteacher.''

"Who's that?''

"Lady I know, lives up near Lincoln Center. Teaches the fourth grade up in Washington Heights. Likes that white wine, whatchacall Chardonnay. I believe that's how you say it. Always has beer in the icebox for me, though. And I can always have a hot bath there, and while I'm soaking in the tub she'll be down in the basement running my clothes through the washing machine. I can stay there on a cold night, an' she'll cook me breakfast in the morning, if she don't have too bad of a wine hangover.'' He uncapped the OE bottle and looked down into it. "She'll gen'ly come up with five or ten dollars, too, but I don't like to take money from her.'' He looked at me. "But sometimes I do," he said.

DeWitt Clinton Park covers two city blocks, extending from Fifty-second Street to Fifty-fourth Street and from Eleventh Avenue to Twelfth Avenue. A baseball field ringed by a twelve-foot cyclone fence takes up more than half the space, and most of what remains is given over to a playground for children, also fenced. The baseball field was deserted when I got there, but the playground was in use, with kids playing on the swings and slides and monkey bars, and clambering with abandon on the great outcropping of rock that had been allowed to remain for that purpose.

At the southeast corner of the park stood a World War I memorial, a larger-than-life statue of a Doughboy green with verdigris, a rifle on his shoulder. These six lines were engraved upon the small plinth on which he stood:

FROM ''FLANDERS FIELDS''
IF YE BREAK FAITH
WITH THOSE WHO DIED
WE SHALL NOT SLEEP

THOUGH POPPIES GROW
ON FLANDERS FIELDS

I remembered the poem from high school English. The author was one of the War Poets, but I couldn't recall which one, Rupert Brooke or Wilfred Owen or someone else. The plinth offered no clues; as far as it was concerned, the lines might have been the work of the Unknown Soldier.

To the Doughboy's right, two men many years younger than I stood close together, deep in conversation. One was black and wore a Chicago Bulls warm-up jacket, the other an Hispanic in acid-washed denim. Perhaps they were debating the authorship of the poem, but somehow I didn't think so. The poppies that interested them didn't grow on Flanders fields.

On my earlier visits to Eleventh Avenue I hadn't noticed any drug dealers, but then I'd barely taken notice of the park, deserted at that hour. Now, in the late afternoon, it was still a long way from being a drug supermarket like Bryant Park or Washington Square. There were young men scattered about, singly or in pairs, sitting on benches or leaning against the fence, perhaps eight of them in all. Two more sat behind home plate in the otherwise empty grandstand. Most of them eyed me, warily or in entrepreneurial anticipation, as I made my rounds. A few whispered enticements: "Smoke, good smoke."

At the park's western edge I looked across Twelfth Avenue and viewed the traffic, already beginning to thicken with commuters heading for the bridge and the northern suburbs. Beyond the stream of cars stood the Hudson piers. I tried to picture George Sadecki in his ratty army coat, dodging traffic so that he could heave his gun off one of those piers. But of course he'd have

run that particular fool's errand in the middle of the
night. There would have been less traffic to dodge.

I turned to watch a couple of fellows my age giving
each other a workout on the handball court. They had
piled their jackets and sweatpants at courtside and were
down to shorts and shoes and terrycloth sweatbands, and
they powered the ball as if determined to drive it through
the wall, playing with the singleminded devotion of the
middle-aged male. A few years ago Jan Keane and I had
come upon a similar display, a pickup basketball game
in the Village, and she had made a show of sniffing the
air. "Testosterone," she announced. "I can smell the
testosterone."

Bring me a gun, she'd said. I pictured her holding it
in her hands, sniffing the oiled steel. I imagined the shot,
heard her disembodied voice over its reverberation.
Cordite, she'd be saying. I can smell the cordite.

I left the park at its northwest corner, and the first pay
phone I came to was right there at Twelfth Avenue and
Fifty-fourth Street. I listened to the dial tone but held on
to my quarter because someone had removed the label
that gave the phone's number. You could call out from
the unit but no one could call you back.

There was a phone with its number intact at Fifty-
fourth and Eleventh, but it wouldn't take a quarter from
me. I tried four different coins and it found something
unacceptable about each of them, spewing them all back
to me. I retrieved them in turn and walked a block north,
and the phone I wound up calling from was the one
Glenn Holtzmann used for the last call he ever made. It
had its number posted, it provided a dial tone, and it
took my quarter. As long as nobody shot me I was in
good shape.

I dialed a number, and when a tone sounded I punched
in the number of the phone I was calling from. Then I

hung up and held the mute receiver to my ear while surreptitiously holding down the hook with my other hand, so that it would appear to passersby that I was actually using the phone, not simply waiting for it to ring.

I didn't have long to wait. I picked up and a voice said, "Who wants TJ?"

"The police of three continents," I said. "Among others."

"Hey, my man! Where's it at, Matt? You got something for TJ?"

"I might," I said. "Are you free this afternoon?"

"No, but I be reasonable. What you got?"

"I'm a block from DeWitt Clinton Park," I said. "I don't know if you know it."

"'Course I know it. That's the park and not the school? Say I meet you by the statue of the captain."

"You mean the soldier."

"I know he's a soldier. I don't know his name, so I call him Captain Flanders."

"I think you've got the rank wrong," I said. "He's dressed like an enlisted man."

"Oh yeah? He white, so I figure he be an officer. Meet you there in twenty minutes?"

"I'm not sure that's a good idea."

"Then why'd you call, Paul? What you said—"

"I don't think we should meet in the park, that's all." I looked around for a place to meet but didn't see anything suitable on the avenue. "Tenth Avenue and Fifty-seventh," I said. "There's a coffee shop on the corner. Armstrong's is on one corner and there's a high-rise apartment building diagonally across from it, and on one of the other corners there's a coffee shop, a Greek place."

"That's three corners," he said. "What's on the fourth one?"

"I don't know offhand. What difference does it make?"

"Don't make none to me, man, but you already told me about two other places that don't make no difference either. You want to meet me at a coffee shop, all you got to tell me about is the coffee shop. I guess I find it all right. No need to give me landmarks."

"Twenty minutes?"

"Twenty minutes."

I took my time getting there, doing a little window shopping along Fifty-seventh Street. It took me fifteen minutes to get to the coffee shop, and TJ was already there, sitting in one of the front booths and working his way through a pair of cheeseburgers and a plate of well-done french fries. TJ is a black street kid, visually indistinguishable from all the others who hang out on West Forty-second Street between Bryant Park and the Port Authority Bus Terminal. A while back a case had led me to that blighted stretch of pavement, and that's where I met TJ.

By now we were old friends and business associates, but I still knew remarkably little about him. TJ was the only name I knew for him, and I had no idea what the letters stood for, or if indeed they stood for anything at all. I didn't know how old he was—sixteen, if I had to guess—or anything about his family. From his accent and speech pattern I'd have to guess he was Harlem born and bred, but he turned accents on and off, and I had heard him sound convincingly Brooks Brothers more than once.

He spent most of his waking hours in and around Times Square, practicing the survival skills you need to get over on the Deuce. I don't know where he slept. He insisted he wasn't homeless, that he had a place to live, but he was very secretive about the subject.

At first I'd had no way to reach him, and when he called me I was unable to return his calls. Then he took the money I paid him for a good night's work and bought himself a beeper, claiming it was an investment. He was very proud of the beeper and always managed to pay the monthly charge to keep it on-line. He thought I should have one, too, and couldn't understand why I didn't.

Whatever else he did for money, he seemed willing to drop it in a second if I called him with an offer of a day's work. When I failed to call he would call me, insisting I must have something for him, proclaiming that he was energetic and resourceful. God knows I didn't throw a whole lot of money his way, and I'm sure he got a better financial return on his time scamming on the Deuce, running errands for the players and shilling for the monte men. But he persisted in regarding the detective business as his chosen career, and looked forward to the day when the two of us would be partners. Meanwhile he seemed perfectly content to play Tonto.

While he ate I told him about Glenn Holtzmann and George Sadecki. He'd heard about the incident—it would have been hard for anyone in the tri-state area to miss it—but it had had less impact on the Deuce than in less volatile neighborhoods. I could understand this. *A dude shot a dude* is how the street kids would sum it up, and what after all was so remarkable about that? It happened all the time.

Now, though, he had a reason to pay attention to the fate of these particular dudes, and he listened closely while I laid it out for him. When I was done I motioned for the waiter and ordered more coffee for myself and a chocolate egg cream for TJ.

When his egg cream came he took a sip and nodded like a gourmet indicating that the Pommard was accept-able. Not outstanding, mind you, but perfectly accept-able. He said, "They's people in the park an' on the street. Be buyin' this an' sellin' that."

"Not so much in the daytime," I said, "but especially at night."

"An' it was nighttime when it went down, an' you think maybe somebody seen something. An' they take one look at you an' right away they make you for the Man, so you don't be gettin' no place with 'em."

"I didn't even try."

"Nobody be thinkin' I the Man."

"My thought exactly."

"They see me an' you together, they be puttin' two an' two. So that's why we here 'stead of meetin' in the park."

"Good thinking."

"Well, it don't take no rocket scientist." He lowered his head, worked on the egg cream. He came up for air and said, "I'd fit in better'n you would. No question. Might even bunk into some dude I already know. Might not, though. Clinton Park be off of my usual turf."

"Just by a few blocks, and you must have made the trip before. You remembered Captain Flanders."

"Oh, Cappy an' I be old friends, but this here's my city, Kitty. I be plannin' to know it all, time I'm through. That don't mean I know the dudes on the pavement everywhere I go. Most of your players, they don't move around too much. Somebody new comes on the scene, he be looked over pretty good. Maybe he competition, maybe he runnin' a game of his own. Maybe he the Man, or maybe he workin' for the Man. More he ask questions, more he start lookin' like trouble."

"If there's a risk involved," I said, "let's forget it."

"Be a risk in crossin' the street," he said. "Risk in *not* crossin' the street, too. Can't spend your life standin' on the corner. What you do, you look both ways an' then you cross."

"Meaning?"

"Just that it might could take a few days. Can't be walkin' up to people an' askin' questions right off. Got to take your time, build up to it."

"Take all the time you want," I said. "The only thing is that there's not much money in the case. Tom Sadecki didn't give me a great deal of it in advance, and I doubt there'll be more coming. As a matter of fact, I have a feeling I'll wind up giving all or part of his money back to him."

"Hate to hear you talk like that. Givin' money back."

"It goes against the grain," I said, "but sometimes I don't seem to have any choice."

"That case," he said, pushing the check across the table at me, "I guess I best let you pay for lunch. Might as well get the money out of you while you still got some."

After he'd headed off toward the park, I stood on the sidewalk in front of the coffee shop and looked at Glenn Holtzmann's building. I told myself I should have picked another coffee shop for my meeting with TJ. It's not as if my choices had been limited. There are almost as many coffee shops in Manhattan as there are Greeks in Astoria, all with essentially the same menu and about the same ambience, or lack thereof. Why did I have to pick one that would put me on this particular street corner, face-to-face with the task I least wanted to perform?

A homicide investigation begins with the victim. From where I stood I could count up twenty-eight stories and look at the victim's windows, behind which I might well find the victim's wife. Lisa Holtzmann was beyond question the first person I should be talking to, the one person most likely to have information I needed to know.

And she was the last person I wanted to talk to. I

hadn't called when she lost her unborn child. I hadn't
called when her husband was killed. I hadn't spoken to
her once since the evening the four of us spent together
in April, and I had rebuffed her husband's overtures of
friendship, and I felt uncomfortable about all of that, if
not precisely guilty. My discomfort grew geometrically
at the thought of disturbing her now, intruding upon her
grief with the kind of impolite questions it would be my
duty to ask.

I looked up, counted windows. I knew their apartment—*her* apartment—was on twenty-eight, but that
left me uncertain as to how many windows to count,
because I hadn't noticed whether or not the building had
a thirteenth floor. Most New York high-rises omit the
number, but a few builders over the years had refused
to cater to the superstition. (Harmon Ruttenstein, who'd
plunged from his terrace a week ago, had been particularly outspoken on the subject, and more than one article
had quoted his assertion that life was too short for tris-
kaidekaphobia, which sent people all over town running
to their dictionaries. Since he'd lived in one of his own
buildings, one of the obituary writers pointed out, his
sixty-second floor had actually been on the sixty-second
floor, not on the sixty-first as would have been the case
in most comparable buildings.)

Either way, I'd told Elaine, it's just the last half-inch
or so that you have to worry about.

For all I knew, the Holtzmanns had lived in a Harmon
Ruttenstein building, but for all I knew they hadn't, so
I couldn't really be sure which windows were theirs. I
was of course able to narrow it down to two possibilities,
and in any case I couldn't tell whether the apartments
in question were lit because the lowering sun was re-
flected in all the windows on the building's western face.

I thought, Jesus, spend a quarter, will you?

There were two pay phones on the corner but one was

out of order and the other wasn't built to accept coins, just NYNEX calling cards. They offered me a card with every monthly phone bill but I had thus far resisted, seeing it as just one more thing to carry, but if the coin phones keep disappearing I suppose I'll have to get one. Then, as with everything else, I'll wonder how I'd ever got along without it.

I crossed the street and made the call from Armstrong's. In my early sobriety I'd made a great point of avoiding the place, having virtually lived there for so many years. In my absence Jimmy had lost his lease and moved the joint from the east side of Ninth just south of Fifty-eighth to its present location. I stayed out of the new place, too, and I also found myself avoiding the establishment that had replaced it, a perfectly innocent Chinese restaurant. (Once, when Jim Faber suggested it for our Sunday dinner, I told him I didn't think it was a good idea. "I used to drink in that place before it existed," I explained. He didn't question either the language of that sentence or the logic of my argument. Only another alcoholic would have understood either.)

Then one night another friend, also a sober alcoholic, suggested Armstrong's for a late supper, and since then I'd gone there when I had a reason. I had a reason now, but an inner voice challenged it. Weren't there any other phones in the neighborhood? What was the matter with the one in the coffee shop? And why was I looking for an excuse to hang out in a ginmill?

A mind may be a terrible thing to waste, but it's an even worse thing to have to listen to. I told mine Thanks for sharing and went ahead and made my phone calls, first to 411 and then to the number I copied down. Lisa Holtzmann's phone rang four times, and then I got to hear her husband's recorded voice advising me that no one was home and inviting me to leave my message at the beep. "Now be sure to wait for the beep," he said.

I waited for the beep, all right, and then I hung up.

It wasn't the first time I'd listened to a ghost. Years ago an English call girl named Portia Carr got herself killed by a client—her client, not mine—and one night I got drunk enough to call her number, and got sober in a hurry when she answered. But of course it was her machine, and as soon as I figured that out I was able to go back to being drunk again.

Machines were scarcer then. Now everybody's got one—everybody but me—and we're used to voices that outlive their owners. Not long ago I called a friend and Humphrey Bogart answered his phone. I called him again a week later and got Tallulah Bankhead. There was a tape you could buy, a triumph of modern technology which allowed long-dead celebrities to answer your phone. "Here's looking at you, shweetheart. My pal Jerry Palmieri can't come to the phone right now, but if you leave your number he'll get back to you when we round up the usual suspects."

Glenn Holtzmann's voice was less of a shock than Portia Carr's and no more of a surprise than Tallulah's. But I was a little off-balance to begin with, making a call I was loath to make from a joint I didn't want to be in, and I'd jump at any excuse to short-circuit the process and get out of there. Under the circumstances, I'd have hung up on John Wayne.

Back at my hotel, I took another stab at it, but by the time I'd heard him again I'd talked myself out of leaving a message. Speaking to her was one thing, leaving word for her to call me was another. Once again I listened to the beep, and once again I left it unanswered.

I called Elaine and told her I couldn't remember if we had anything planned for the evening. She said we didn't. "But I'd love to see you," she said. "Only I don't really feel like leaving the house."

"Neither do I."

"That's going to make it tough for us to get together," she said. "Unless we spend the whole night on the phone, and that could really burn up the old message units."

We got that sorted out. "I don't mind leaving my house," I said. "I just don't want to leave yours."

"Well, you never have to," she said. "*Mí casa es su casa.* Come over anytime, I'll cook or we'll order in, and we'll spend a quiet evening at home."

"At *su casa.*"

"Yeah, *chez moi.* I've got some reading and paperwork to do, but it won't take me forever. You know what? Pick up a movie on the way over."

"Anything special?"

"No, surprise me. Nothing with monsters, that's all I ask."

"We get enough of those in real life."

"You said it. What time should I expect you?"

"I could catch an early meeting and get over there around eight. How does that sound?"

"As a matter of fact," she said, "it sounds terrific."

We spent a quiet evening at home. We had curry, delivered by an Indian restaurant that had just recently opened on First Avenue. According to Elaine, there was a key advantage to eating Indian food at home.

"In every Indian restaurant I have ever been to," she said, "there is one waiter whose last bath was in the Ganges, and when he comes near your table you could die."

I tried Lisa Holtzmann after dinner and rang off without a word when her machine answered. Elaine spent twenty minutes on paperwork and then popped a cassette in the VCR. I'd picked up *The Man Who Shot Liberty Valance*, with Lee Marvin playing the titular villain and John Wayne and Jimmy Stewart playing themselves.

Elaine said, "When I was a kid my parents would watch old movies on the late show. 'My God, look how young Franchot Tone is!' Or Janet Gaynor, or George Arliss, or whoever they were watching. It used to drive me crazy. And now I'm doing it. Throughout the whole movie all I could think of was how young Lee Marvin was."

"I know."

"But I didn't come out and say it until the picture

had ended. I think I showed commendable restraint.''

The phone rang and she answered it. "Oh, hi," she said. "How's it going? It's been a while, hasn't it?"

I tried not to hang on the words, even as the usual faint wave of jealousy rolled over me. Elaine still got calls now and then from former clients, and felt it was simpler to spend ten seconds announcing her retirement than go to the trouble of changing her number. I understood, but all the same I'd have preferred them to call when I was somewhere else.

"Just a minute," she said. "He's right here."

I took the phone and TJ said, "Man, I been to your hotel room. That room is small with just you in it. You shouldn't be bringin' a nice lady there."

"That was no nice lady," I said. "That was Elaine."

"Think I don't know that? Oh, now I get it. You ain't at your hotel."

"I knew you'd figure it out."

"You at her house. You got the whatchacall on. Call Forwarding."

"Good thinking."

"If you had a beeper," he said, "you wouldn't need stuff like that, confuse people when somebody else answers your phone. Why I called, I been hangin' out with the Captain."

"Captain Flanders."

"That's my man. Hey, the park changes some when the sun goes down, the park and the street both. Got a whole bunch of folks buyin' and sellin'."

"You've got that in the daytime," I said, "but then they're mostly buying and selling Hondas."

"Different shit now," he said. "Lotta crack. You see the empty vials on the ground. Just about anything you want, there be somebody here sell it to you. Lot of girls, too, an' some of 'em lookin' real fine. 'Cept they ain't girls. You know what they call 'em?"

"Transsexuals."

" 'Chicks with dicks' is what you hear people say. Say the other word again." I did, and he repeated it after me. "Transsexuals. I know there's people call 'em sex changes, but that's after they has the operation. Up until then they chicks with dicks. You happen to know if they born that way?"

"I'm fairly sure they're born with dicks."

"Gimme a break, Jake. You know what I mean."

The transsexuals I'd known all said they'd been that way as far back as they could remember. "I guess they're born that way," I said.

"How do they get the titties? It don't hardly come natural. What do they get, hormone shots? Implants?"

"Both, I think."

"An' then they hustlin', savin' up for the big operation. What they all want, get the operation so you can't tell 'em from a real woman, 'cept they standin' six-two and got big hands an' feet, which might give somebody a clue."

"Not all of them want the surgery."

"You mean they want to have it both ways? Why's that?"

"I don't know."

A pause, and then he said, "Just tryin' to feature myself walkin' down the street with titties bouncin' under my shirt. Weird."

"I guess."

"Get a headache thinkin' about it. You recollect what I told you first time I met you? When you was walkin' on the Deuce an' I couldn't get you to say what you was lookin' for?"

"I remember."

"I told you everybody got a jones. You can take that to the bank, Frank. Truest thing I ever said."

I said, "I wonder if Glenn Holtzmann had a jones."

"Nothin' to wonder. If he had a pulse he had a jones. Maybe we get lucky, find out what it was."

Elaine had caught enough key words to be interested, and I filled her in on the rest. "TJ's wonderful," she said. "One minute he's utterly hip slick and cool, and then his innocence peeks through. At that age the whole notion of transsexuals has to be disturbing."

"But not unfamiliar, not where he hangs out."

"I guess. I just hope he doesn't turn up with tits one of these days. I don't think I'm ready for that."

"I don't think TJ is, either."

"Good. You figure Glenn Holtzmann had a jones?"

"TJ says everybody does. That reminds me." I looked at my watch and decided it wasn't too late to call Holtzmann's widow, especially since she wasn't likely to be home. Nor was she. This time, though, I didn't listen dutifully to her late husband's voice. As soon as the machine picked up, I broke the connection.

I said, "Something took him to Eleventh Avenue. He could have been stretching his legs, but why stretch them in that direction? It could have been coincidence, or he could have been looking for something that Eleventh Avenue had to offer."

"He didn't strike me as the crackhead type."

"No, but he wouldn't be the first yuppie who ever did lines of coke."

"Do people like him buy it on the street?"

"Not usually, no. Maybe he had a sex jones, maybe he was looking for love in all the wrong places."

"With a wife like that at home?"

" 'A neater, sweeter maiden in a cleaner, greener land.' But what's that got to do with it?"

"Not much," she said. "Most men have wives at home, and they can't all be bowwows. Maybe he just got the urge for something different."

"Maybe he was partial to tall girls with big hands and feet."

"And dicks. He was taking a big chance, picking up a street-walker."

"No kidding."

"No, besides the usual. Remember the view from their apartment? If she'd been at the window she could have seen him on the corner. She might even have witnessed the shooting."

"Assuming the angles were right and the view wasn't obstructed. I doubt you could make much out at that distance, anyway."

"I guess not. You think she'll keep the apartment?"

"I have no idea."

"Would you like to live there? Not that particular apartment, necessarily, but something like it?"

"Way up in the sky, you mean?"

"Way up in the sky with a drop-dead view. If and when we get around to moving in together—but maybe you don't feel like talking about it now."

"No, I don't mind."

"Well, I love this apartment, but I was thinking we might be better off someplace new. This place has an awful lot of history."

"All the times we've made love here."

"That's not what I was thinking of."

"I know."

"I'm not in the game anymore, and I'm still living in the same apartment. I'm not sure that's such a good idea. Even if we didn't move in together, I'm not sure it's a good idea."

"Would you sell this place?"

"I could. The way the market is now, I'd probably be better off renting it out. The company that manages my other real estate holdings could take care of it."

"Ms. Rich Bitch."

"Well, I'm not going to apologize for it. I didn't steal it and nobody left it to me. I made it the old-fashioned way."

"I know you did."

"I fucked for it. So? It's honest work. It may not be legal but it's honest. I worked hard and saved my money and invested it wisely. Are those things to be ashamed of?"

"Of course not."

"I sound defensive, don't I?"

"A little," I said, "but so what? Nobody's perfect. Where would you want to live?"

"I've been trying to figure that out. I like this neighborhood, but if the apartment's got a history so does the neighborhood. What about you? You might want to keep your hotel room as an office."

"Some office."

"It's a place to meet clients."

"I used to meet them in bars," I said, "and now I meet them in coffee shops."

"Would you want to give it up?"

"I don't know."

"It's so cheap," she said. "Rent-controlled and all. It might be worth keeping just so that you'd have some private space when you wanted it. Living together might be less threatening if you knew you had a place of your own nearby."

"What would it be, an escape hatch?"

"Maybe."

"You'd have one, too, if you rented this place instead of selling it."

"No," she said. "Once I'm out of here, that's it. Fifty-first Street won't see me again. Even if things don't work out, even if we find out we can't, uh, live together, I'm never coming back here. As a matter of fact—"

"Yes?"

"Well, even if we're not ready to live together, maybe I ought to think about getting out of here. It seems silly to go to the trouble of finding some interim place if we're going to be looking for an apartment together, but I think it's time I got the hell out."

"Why the urgency?"

"I don't know."

"Oh?"

After a moment she said, "I got a phone call today. One of my old regulars."

"He didn't know you'd retired?"

"He knew."

"Oh?"

"He's called a few times over the past year. To make sure this retirement hadn't turned out to be a passing fancy."

"I see."

"It's understandable. Somebody sells her ass for twenty years, then takes it off the market, you don't assume it's permanent."

"I suppose."

"A few times he called just to chat. So he said. Well, we knew each other for years, and it was a friendly relationship, so you don't like to tell a guy like that to shit in his hat. But I don't need chatty conversations with former johns, either, so I always managed to cut it short. No hard feelings, gotta go, 'bye."

"Good."

"Today he asked if he could come over. No, I said, you can't. Just to talk, he said, because he's going through something difficult and he needs to talk to somebody who really knows him. Which is bullshit, because I don't. Really know him, I mean. So I said no, you can't come over, I'm very sorry but that's the way it is. I'll pay you, he says. I'll give you two hundred dollars, just let me come over and talk."

"What did you do?"

"I told him no. I told him I wasn't in the therapy business, either, and I told him not to call me anymore. He didn't just want to talk. You probably figured that much out on your own."

"Yes."

"He figured once he got in the door he could get in the bedroom. He figured once I took money I'd do something to earn it. But it wasn't really about sex, it was about power. He liked the idea of getting me to do something I didn't want to do."

"Who is he?"

"What's the difference?"

"I could have a talk with him."

"No, Matt. Absolutely not."

"All right."

"If I hear further from him, but I don't think I will, not more than once every couple of months and I can live with that. No, I don't need to be protected. Not from this particular jerk."

"If you're sure."

"I'm sure."

"But I think you should change your number."

"When I move. New apartment, new phone number."

"Both at once."

"Right."

I thought about it. I said, "Maybe we should start looking for a new place."

"Or at least think about it. You'd prefer the neighborhood where you are now, wouldn't you?"

"Well, I'm used to it," I said, "the same way you're used to Turtle Bay. I've got certain restaurants and coffee shops I go to, and of course I've got my regular meetings. Mick's joint is a short walk from me. So are Lincoln Center and Carnegie Hall and most of the city's theaters, not that we go all that often, but it's nice to know they're there.

"But it's not the only part of town I like, or even my favorite in a lot of ways. I like the West Village, I like Chelsea, I like Gramercy Park."

"Or farther downtown. SoHo, Tribeca."

But those places had a history of their own. "Or a little farther up on the West Side," I went on. "Say the West Seventies. I'd be an easy walk or a short bus ride from where I am now, so I could keep the hotel room as an office and still go to the same AA meetings. Now that I think about it, though, the possibilities are vast. We could live almost anywhere."

"Not out of Manhattan, though."

"No, definitely not."

"Unless we move to Albuquerque."

Shortly before Christmas I'd had a windfall; I took a case on a contingency basis and it paid off. When her school's semester break came around after the first of the year we'd flown out to New Mexico and spent two weeks driving around the northern part of the state, much of it among the Indian pueblos. We'd both responded to the adobe architecture in Albuquerque and Santa Fe.

"We could have a whole house there," I said, "with swirls and minarets and curved walls. And it wouldn't matter where it was, because we'd have to drive everywhere anyway, and whatever neighborhood we picked would be safer and more comfortable than anywhere in New York."

"Would you like to do that?"

"No."

"Thank God," she said, "because neither would I. The whole country's full of places that are much nicer than New York and I wouldn't want to live in any of them. And you're the same way, aren't you?"

"I'm afraid so."

"It's good we found each other. And if we start to yearn for the sight of adobe, we can always fly out to Albuquerque for a visit, can't we?"

"Anytime we want," I said. "It's not going anywhere."

It must have been around midnight when we went to bed. An hour later I gave up on sleep and tiptoed out to the living room. There was a rack full of magazines and a bookcase full of books, and of course there was always the TV, but I was too restless to sit still. I got dressed and stood at the living-room window, looking at the red neon Pepsi-Cola sign across the river. New buildings had eclipsed much of her view since Elaine moved in, but you could still see the Pepsi ad. Would I miss it if we moved? Would she?

Downstairs the doorman nodded wordlessly, then returned his gaze to the middle distance. He was a young fellow, a recent immigrant from somewhere in the Arab world, and he always had a Walkman headset plugged into his ears. I'd assumed he was hooked on Top 40 radio until I found out one night that he listened relentlessly to self-improvement tapes that exhorted him to take charge of his life, boost his money-generating capacity, and lose weight and keep it off.

I walked down First Avenue, past the UN building, clear to Forty-second Street. There I turned right, walked a block, and headed back uptown on Second Avenue. I passed a few saloons, and while they did not call to me I cannot say I was entirely unaware of their appeal. I could have looked for Mick at Grogan's, but if I found him it meant a late night, and even if we cut it short I'd be clear over on the West Side and not much inclined to come all the way back to East Fifty-first.

Living together would solve that problem. And bring what others in its place?

There's an all-night coffee shop at the corner of Second and Forty-ninth. I took a seat at the counter and ordered a prune Danish and a glass of milk. Someone had left an early edition of the *Times* behind, and I started to read it but couldn't keep my mind on what I was reading. Maybe I needed some self-improvement tapes. *Develop the Hidden Powers of Your Mind! Take Charge of Your Life!*

I didn't need to develop any hidden powers. I had enough brain cells left to figure out what was going on.

Jan Keane had come back into my life, even as she was nearing the end of her own. She and I had almost lived together, had indeed been groping in that direction, and then the relationship had instead broken down, and we had lost each other.

And now Elaine and I were in a similar situation, and at a similar stage. I had space in her closet, a drawer in her dresser, and a side of her bed on which I slept several nights a week. Because this stage was transitional, because it was undefined and perhaps indefinable, everything had to be considered and assessed. Should I automatically put on Call Forwarding when I was going to be spending the night on East Fifty-first? Should I apologize fervently when I forgot to disconnect it afterward? Should we have a second line installed?

Or should we move? Should I keep my hotel room? Should we choose my neighborhood, or her neighborhood, or some piece of neutral ground?

Should we discuss it? Should we avoid discussing it?

Ordinarily all of this was tolerable enough, and sometimes even amusing. But Jan was dying, and that somehow cast a yellow shadow over everything.

I was afraid, of course. I was afraid that what had happened to one relationship would happen to another, and that one of these days I would come for my clothes, and leave my keys behind on the kitchen counter. I was afraid the shabby little hotel room I held on to like grim death would be my home for the rest of my life, that I'd be perched on the edge of my narrow bed in my underwear when Grim Death himself came calling. That they'd have to haul me out of there in a body bag.

Afraid things would fall apart, because they always do. Afraid it would all end badly, because it always does. And afraid, perhaps more than anything, that when all was said and done it would all turn out to have been my fault. Because, somewhere down inside, somewhere deep in the blood and bone, I believe it always is.

I drank my milk and went home, and this time the doorman greeted me by name and gave me a big smile. (*Remember Names and Faces! Let Your Smile Brighten the World!*) When I slipped into the bedroom Elaine stirred but did not awaken. I got into bed and lay alongside her in the darkness, feeling her warmth.

Sleep took me by surprise, and the next thing I knew I was dreaming that I was following a man and trying to catch a glimpse of his face. I tailed him over precarious catwalks and down endless staircases, and at last he turned, and he had a mirror for a face. When I sought a reflection in it, all that was shown to me was pure white light, blinding in its intensity. I wrenched myself awake, reached out to touch Elaine's arm, and fell back asleep almost instantly.

When I awoke again it was nine o'clock and I was alone in the apartment. There was hot coffee in the kitchen. I had a cup, showered, dressed, and was pouring a second cup when she got back from the health club, announcing that it was a beautiful day outside. "Blue skies," she said. "Canadian air. We give them acid rain, they give us fresh air and Leonard Cohen. What a deal."

I called Lisa Holtzmann and hung up as usual when the machine answered. Elaine said, "Gimme. What's her number?" She dialed it and winced when Holtzmann's message played. Then she said, "Lisa, this is Elaine Mardell, we had a class together last semester at Hunter. I should have called ages ago, and I'm terribly sorry for what you've had to go through. I'm sure you're busy, but could you call me as soon as you get a chance? It's sort of important, and—oh, hi, Lisa. Yes, well, I thought you might be monitoring the machine because Matt called you half a dozen times and got the machine each time. He felt funny about leaving a message. Uh-huh. Sure."

She asked some questions, said some traditionally sympathetic things. Then she said, "Well, why don't I put Matt on? He's right here. All right, and you and I'll get together one of these days. Will you call me? Don't forget. All right, hold on. Here's Matt."

I took the phone and said, "Matthew Scudder, Mrs. Holtzmann. I'm very sorry to disturb you. If this is a bad time to talk—"

"No, it's fine," she said. "As a matter of fact—"

"Yes?"

"Actually, I was planning to call you, but I was putting it off. So I'm glad you called."

"I wonder if I could see you."

"When?"

"As soon as you've got the time available. Today, if that's possible."

"I have to meet someone for lunch," she said. "And then I have appointments all afternoon."

"How does tomorrow look?"

"I'm supposed to see someone from the insurance company at two tomorrow afternoon, but I don't know how long that will take. Uh, do you have any free time this evening? Or don't you like to make appointments after business hours?''

"My work sets its own hours," I said. "Tonight would be fine, if you're sure it's convenient for you."

"It's perfectly convenient. Nine o'clock? Or is that too late?''

"It's fine. I'll come to your place at nine, unless I hear otherwise. I'll give you my number in case you have to cancel." I did, and added that she could call the hotel desk if she misplaced the number. "I'm at the Northwestern," I said.

"Just down the street. Glenn told me a couple of times how he ran into you in the neighborhood. If *you* have to cancel, call and leave a message. I haven't been picking up the phone until I know who it is. The kind of calls I've been getting—"

"I can imagine."

"Can you? I couldn't. Well. I'll expect you at nine, Mr. Scudder. And thank you."

I hung up and Elaine said, "I hope I wasn't interfering. I just had this image of that poor girl sitting next to the phone, scared to pick it up because it might be another jerk calling from one of the supermarket tabloids. And I figured it wouldn't be awkward for me to leave a message, and then when I spoke to her I could tell her to get in touch with you."

"That was good thinking."

"But maybe I should have asked you first."

"You did fine. I'm going to be seeing her tonight."

"Nine o'clock, you said."

"Uh-huh. She said she'd been planning to call me."

"She didn't tell me that. What about, I wonder?"

"I don't know," I said. "That's one of the things I'll have to find out."

I went back to my hotel and turned off Call Forwarding. There must be a way to do that from a distance, but I've never been able to manage it. I never would have had Call Forwarding in the first place, but it had been a gift from a couple of computer hackers who'd invaded the phone-company computer system on my behalf. While they were in there, they'd arranged for me to get Call Forwarding without having to pay the monthly service charge. They also gave me free long-distance service by routing my long-distance calls through Sprint without telling Sprint's billing system about it. (When I raised ethical objections, they asked me if defrauding the phone company was really going to trouble my conscience. So far I'm forced to admit that it hasn't.)

I caught a noon meeting at the Y on West Sixty-third. The speaker was celebrating his ninety days, which is the minimum amount of sober time you have to have before you can lead a meeting. He was pleased as un-spiked punch to be sober, and his qualification was giddily buoyant. During the break the woman sitting beside me said, "I was like that. Then when I fell off my pink cloud it shook the earth."

"And now?"

"Now I'm happy, joyous, and free," she said. "What else?"

Afterward I bought coffee and a sandwich at a deli and picnicked on a bench in Central Park, breathing some of that Canadian air Elaine had spoken so highly of. I could think of things to do but they could wait, and probably ought to; most of them centered on Glenn Holtzmann, and it made sense to put them on Hold until I'd learned what his wife had to tell me.

I spent a couple of hours in the park. I walked up to the zoo and watched the bears. At the expanse called Strawberry Fields, I thought of John Lennon and figured out how old he would be, if a bullet hadn't assured that he'd stay forty forever. If you could see the world from God's perspective, I'd heard someone say once, you would realize that every life lasts precisely as long as it ought to, and that everything happens as it should. But I can't see the world, or anything else, from God's perspective. When I try, all I get for my troubles is a stiff neck.

Of course there are those who'd say I've had that all my life.

There were messages at the desk from Jan and TJ. I called him first and beeped him. When five minutes passed without a call back, I rang Jan's number. I got her machine and said I was returning her call, and that she could call me anytime.

I turned on CNN and was paying precious little attention to it when the phone rang and it was TJ, apologetic for taking so long to answer his beeper. "Couldn't find a phone," he said, " 'cept there be somebody on it. Whole stretch of Eighth Avenue, the phones is gone, Dawn."

"They're all out of order?"

"Out of order? They out of state, Nate. What dudes'll

do, 'stead of breakin' 'em open, they'll wrap a chain around 'em an' attach it to their car bumper, pull off an' rip the whole box off the wall. You figure they go through all that just for the quarters, or can they get something for the phones?''

"I don't know who would buy them," I said. "Unless they can work out a way to sell them back to the phone company."

"Slow way to get rich, Mitch. Hey, what I called to tell you. Could be I findin' somethin' out. What I heard on the street, somebody saw what happened."

"You found a witness?"

"I didn't find nobody yet. I don't even know her name. All's I know is the name of somebody who knows her. But I think I be gettin' somewhere."

"The witness is a woman?"

"More like what we was talkin' about last night. A chick with a dick, 'cept you told me a different word. Transsexual?"

"That's right."

"I keep hangin' around you, I gone be educated. This here chick with a dick, I think I most likely be able to find her. Might take a while, is all."

"Just be careful."

"You mean like safe sex?"

"Jesus," I said. "I mean don't do anything that'll get you shot."

"Hey, no prob', Bob. That's why it might take time, 'cause I bein' careful. An' these transwhatchacalls ain't too swift. 'Tween the drugs and the hormones, they inclined to be on the vague side. Tell you, though. I don't think George did it."

"What makes you say that?"

"Ain't he our client? And don't we be the good guys?"

"I guess you're right, Dwight."

"You learnin'," he said. "You comin' along fine."

Elaine called, to tell me about her day and ask about mine. We agreed that it had been a beautiful day, and that the autumn was the best time of the year. "There was something I wanted to ask you," she said, "but of course I can't think of it now. I hate it when that happens."

"I know."

"And it happens more and more. Somebody told me about an herb you can take that's supposed to help your memory, but do you think for one minute I can remember what the hell it is?"

"If you could—"

"—I wouldn't need it. I know, I thought of that. Well, it'll come to me. You're seeing Lisa tonight, aren't you? Call me afterward if you feel like it."

"If I think of it. And if it's not too late."

"Or even if it is," she said. "You know what? I love you."

"And I love you."

Jan called again while I was taking some shirts to the laundry around the corner. I was gone less than ten minutes and walked right past the desk without checking for messages, but the clerk spotted me entering the elevator and rang my room with the message. I called her right back, and once again I got her goddamn machine.

"We seem to be playing tag," I said. "I'm going out in a few minutes, and I've got a business appointment this evening. I'll keep trying you."

It was exactly nine o'clock when I gave my name to the lobby attendant and told him Mrs. Holtzmann was expecting me. His expression turned wary when he heard her name. I sensed that she'd had her share of visitors since her husband's death, the bulk of them unexpected and unwelcome.

He used the intercom and cupped the mouthpiece in his hands, pitching his voice too low for me to hear him. Her reply allowed him to relax. He wasn't going to be called upon to throw me out or summon the police, and his gratitude was visible. "You go right on up," he said.

She was standing in the doorway of her apartment when I got off the elevator, looking prettier than I remembered her, and older, too, as if recent events had sculpted character into her face. She still looked young, but now it wasn't so difficult to credit her with the thirty-two years the news articles had mentioned. (She was thirty-two and he was thirty-eight, I found myself thinking. And George Sadecki was forty-four. And John Lennon was still forty.)

"I'm glad you could come," she said. "I don't remember what to call you. Is it Matt or Matthew?"

"Whichever you prefer."

"I called you Mr. Scudder on the phone this morning. I couldn't remember what I called you the night we all had dinner. Elaine calls you Matt. So I guess I will. Won't you come in? Won't you come in, *Matt*?"

I followed her into the living room, where two couches stood at a right angle to one another. She seated herself on one and gestured toward the other. I sat down. Both couches were placed to take full advantage of the western view, and I looked out through the window at the last vestiges of the sunset, a pink and purple stain at the edge of the darkening sky.

"Those high-rises across the way are in Weehawken," she said. "If you think this is something, imagine the view they've got. They can see the whole Manhattan skyline from there. But then when they go downstairs and out the door, they're in New Jersey."

"Poor devils."

"Maybe they're not so bad off, living there. From the day I came to New York I assumed Manhattan was the only place to be. I grew up in White Bear Lake. That's in Minnesota, and I know it sounds as though you'd have nothing but moose and Eskimos for neighbors, but it's actually more or less a suburb of the Twin Cities. Well, I got off the Northwest flight with an MFA from the University of Minnesota and I don't know what else. A sketch pad, I suppose, and the phone number of a friend of a friend. I spent the night at the Chelsea Hotel, and the next day I had a share in an apartment on Tenth Street east of Tompkins Square Park. If there's a better definition of culture shock, I don't know what it is."

"But you adjusted."

"Oh, yes. I didn't stay long in Alphabet City because it just didn't feel safe to me. Nothing ever happened to me, but I kept hearing about people on the block who'd been mugged or raped or stabbed, and as soon as I could I moved to Madison Street. That's on the Lower East Side."

"I know where it is. It's not exactly Sutton Place either."

"No, it's a slum. Anywhere else in America it would all be torn down, but it wasn't as drug-infested as East Tenth Street and I felt safer there. My first place was a share, but then I got an apartment of my own, three little rabbit-warren rooms in a tenement where the hallways smelled of mice and urine and marijuana smoke. And nothing ever happened, nobody ever bothered me on the street or in the building, nobody ever forced the door or came in off the fire escape. Not once. And then I met a man who swept me off my feet and took me away from all that and moved me into this incredible place, everything's new, nothing smells, there's an attendant in the lobby twenty-four hours a day.

"And here I am," she said, her voice rising. "Here I am, sitting on a new sofa with my feet on a new oriental rug, everything's new, and I'm looking out my window and I can see for miles. And I'm here in this safe place, this clean safe place, and I've got a dead baby and a dead husband, and how did that happen? Would you mind explaining that to me? How did it happen?"

I didn't say anything. I don't suppose she expected an answer. I watched her face while she worked to get control of herself. It was a perfect oval, the features regular and even. She was dressed neatly, wearing a dove-gray cardigan over a matching crew-neck sweater and a pleated navy skirt. Her shoes were black and plain, with one-inch heels. The overall effect was of a grown-up parochial-school girl, but what had been prettiness six months ago now verged on beauty.

"I'm sorry," she said. "I thought I had myself under control."

"You do."

"Can I get you something to drink? We've got scotch and vodka, and I don't know what else. Oh, and there's beer in the refrigerator. And I've got to stop saying 'we.' What can I get you, Matt?"

"Nothing just now, thanks."

"Coffee? There's some made, and I think that's what I'm going to have. I'm afraid it's not decaf, if that matters."

"Actually, I prefer regular."

"So do I, but Glenn could only drink decaf at night. We went to a restaurant a few months ago and the waiter actually asked if we wanted decaf or non-decaf. Can you imagine?"

"I don't think I've heard that one before."

"I hope I never hear it again. How do you take your coffee? Your non-decaf coffee?"

I told her and she went into the kitchen to get it. When

she came back I was at the window looking down at Hell's Kitchen or Clinton, as you prefer. I could see DeWitt Clinton Park and wondered if TJ was down there.

She said, "You can't quite see it from here. The corner of that building's in the way." She was at my shoulder, pointing. "I went over there the day after it happened, or maybe it was the day after that. I don't remember. Just to see for myself. I don't know what I expected. It's just a street corner."

"I know."

"Have you been?"

"Yes."

"I put your coffee on the table. Tell me if it's all right." I sat down and tasted it. It was good, and I told her so. "Good coffee's a weakness of mine," she said, "and decaf never tastes right to me. I don't know why." She sat down and drank some of her own coffee. "This is going to be hard to get used to," she said. "Being a widow. I was just getting used to the idea of being a wife."

"How long were you married?"

"It was a year in May, so that's what, seventeen months? Not quite a year and a half."

"When did you move in here?"

"The day we got back from the honeymoon. When we met Glenn had a studio apartment in Yorkville and of course I was still on Madison Street. After the wedding we flew to Bermuda for a week, and when we came back there was a limousine waiting for us at the airport. We came right here and I thought the driver got the address wrong, I thought we were going to live at Glenn's place until we found something larger. The next thing I knew Glenn was carrying me over the threshold. He said if I didn't like it we could move. If I didn't like it!"

"Quite a surprise."

"He was full of surprises."

"Oh?"

She started to say something, then caught herself. "I should be businesslike," she said. "But I don't know exactly what I'm supposed to do. I've never hired a detective before."

"I already have a client, Lisa."

"Oh? Did he hire you?"

"Did who hire me?"

"Glenn."

"No," I said. "Why would he have hired me?"

"I don't know."

I plunged in. "A man named Thomas Sadecki hired me," I said. "His brother was arrested for Glenn's murder."

"And he hired you—"

"To explore the possibility that his brother didn't do it. You should understand that I'm not trying to get Sadecki off if he's guilty. But there's a slim chance that he's innocent, in which case your husband's real killer is walking around free."

"Yes, of course." She thought about it. "You're trying to find someone in Glenn's life with a reason to kill him."

"That's one possibility. The other is that he was shot down by a stranger, but that the killer was someone other than George Sadecki. Eleventh Avenue is different at night than it is by day. They stop selling cars and brake jobs and switch over to drugs and sex. That kind of activity puts a lot of wrong people on the street, and it could have been one of them who ran into Glenn."

"Or it could have been someone he knew."

"Yes, that's possible, too. I met Glenn for the first time in April, and of course I did see him a couple of times after that around the neighborhood. But I didn't really know him.''

"Neither did I.''

"Oh?''

"I told you he swept me off my feet. That was no exaggeration. We met at his office, I think that came up in conversation the night we all got together—''

"Yes, I remember.''

"He made a real play for me, courted me as I'd never been courted before. He gave me a real rush. I talked with him every day. If we didn't go out, he would call me on the phone. I'd had boyfriends before, I'd had men who were interested in me, but nothing like this.

"And at the same time he didn't pressure me sexually. We went together for a month before we went to bed, and during that time we probably saw each other an average of three or four times a week. Well, AIDS and all, people don't automatically go to bed on the third or fourth date anymore, but do they wait a month?''

"I don't know.''

"I'd have worried about it, but I had the sense that he was in charge and he knew what he was doing. I always had that feeling. And one night we had dinner in his neighborhood and he took me back to his apartment. 'You'll stay over,' he said. And I thought, okay, great. And we went to bed. And two days later he proposed marriage. 'We'll get married,' he said. Okay, great.''

"Very romantic.''

"God, yes. How could I help being in love with him? And even if I weren't, to tell you the truth I think I would have married him anyway. He was bright, he was rich, he was handsome, and he was crazy about me. If I married him I could have babies, and I could quit struggling to make a living and concentrate on the kind of art I really wanted to do. No more Madison Street, no more chasing around town on the subway, showing my book to art directors who were more interested in my figure than my work, except for the ones who weren't interested in women at all. If I'd met someone like Glenn a few years earlier he would have scared the daylights out of me, the way he took charge of everything, but I'd had enough years of coping with things on my own. This is a tough town.''

"That's the truth.''

"I was ready to let somebody else take the helm. And it never felt as though he was pushing me around. With the honeymoon, he chose the destination and made all the arrangements. But he picked a place he knew I would like. And with this apartment, he knew I liked the neighborhood and he knew I loved the idea of being way up high and looking out over the city.

"It was all ready, too. He had it all furnished. Anything I didn't like could go right back to the store, he said. He hadn't wanted to bring me home to an empty apartment, but he wanted to make sure it was to my liking, so I should feel free to change anything I wasn't crazy about. There was one rug I didn't care for, and we took it right back to Einstein Moomjy and got that one instead, and there was really nothing the matter with the original rug but I felt as though I ought to make some little change, as though he expected me to. Do you know what I mean?''

"Sure.''

"He was a wonderful husband,'' she said. ''Thoughtful, considerate. When I lost the baby he was really there for me. It was a hard time for me and I didn't really have anyone but Glenn. I never made close friends in New York. I was friendly with a few people in Alphabet City and I lost touch with them when I moved to Madison Street, and the same thing happened with my Madison Street friends when I got married and moved here.

It's the way I am. I'm friendly and I get along with people, but I don't really connect with them, not in any lasting way.

"That meant I spent a lot of time alone, because Glenn had to work late some nights, and he sometimes had business appointments evenings and weekends. I took classes—that's how I met Elaine—and of course I had my drawing and painting. And I would take myself to the movies, or on a Wednesday afternoon I might go to a matinee. And there are always concerts. With Carnegie Hall and Lincoln Center so close, it's not hard to find something to do. And I never minded spending time by myself. Can I get you more coffee?"

"Not right now."

"Since the murder," she said, "I find I keep turning on the television set. I never watched when I was home by myself. Now I seem to watch it all the time. But I suppose I'll get over that."

"Right now it's company," I said.

"I think that's exactly what it is. I started watching it for the news. I had this need to see every newscast because there might be something having to do with Glenn's death, some new development in the case. Then once they'd arrested that man—I'm sorry, I have a block, I can never remember his name."

"George Sadecki."

"Of course. Once they arrested him, I didn't care about the news, but I still wanted to hear voices in the house. That's what the television is, human voices. I think I'm going to stop turning it on. If I need voices I can always talk to myself, can't I?"

"I don't see why not."

She closed her eyes for a moment. When she opened them and resumed speaking her voice sounded tired, strained. "I've come to realize that I didn't know my husband at all," she said. "Isn't that curious? I thought

I knew him, or at least I didn't give any thought to the fact that I didn't know him. And then he was killed, and now I can see that I never knew him at all.''

"What makes you say that?"

"Sometime last month," she said, "he in a very off-hand way brought up the possibility of his death. If anything ever happened to him, he said, I wouldn't have to worry about losing the apartment. Because there was mortgage insurance. If he should happen to die, the mortgage would automatically be paid off in full.''

"And you haven't been able to find the policy?"

"There is no policy."

"People sometimes lie about having insurance coverage," I told her. "It seems innocent enough to them because they don't expect to die. He probably just wanted to set your mind to rest. And are you absolutely certain there's no policy? It might be worthwhile to check with the lender.''

"There's no policy," she said. "There's no lender."

"What do you mean?"

"I mean there's no mortgage," she said. "I own the apartment free and clear. There was never a mortgage. Glenn bought it outright for cash.''

"Maybe that's what he was saying, that there was no lien against the property.''

"No, he was very specific. He explained exactly what the policy was and how it worked. It was reducing term insurance, with the amount of coverage decreasing each year as the mortgage was amortized. It was all very clear, and it was all a complete fabrication. He did have insurance coverage, as a matter of fact, a group policy at work and a whole-life policy he took out on his own, both with me as sole beneficiary. But he didn't have any reducing term insurance, and there was never any mortgage.''

"I gather he handled the family finances."

"Of course. If I had been paying the bills each month—"

"You would have noticed there was no mortgage payment to make."

"He took care of everything," she said. She started to say something else, then stopped and got to her feet. She went over to the window. It was fully dark now, and you could see stars. You can't always see them over New York, even on clear nights, because of the pollution. But they sparkled now, thanks to the clean Canadian air.

She said, "I don't know if I should tell you."

"Tell me what?"

"I wonder if I can trust you." She turned around and fastened those big blue eyes on me. They looked trusting enough. There was precious little calculation in their gaze. "I wish I could hire you," she said. "But you've already got a client."

"Do you think your interests are opposed to his?"

"I don't know what my interests are."

I waited for more. When she didn't say anything I asked her how her husband had been able to buy the apartment for cash.

"I don't know," she said. "He had money he'd inherited on the death of his parents, that's how he'd been able to afford the down payment. He said."

"Maybe there was enough family money so that he didn't need a mortgage."

"Maybe."

"And maybe he was secretive about it because he didn't want to let you know that you were married to a wealthy man. Some rich people are like that, afraid they'll be loved for their money alone. And if there was a great discrepancy between your net worth and his—"

"Mine was about a dollar ninety-eight."

"Well, that might explain it."

"Then where's the money?" she demanded. "If he was rich, shouldn't there be bank accounts, CDs, stocks and bonds? I can't find any of that. There are the insurance policies, I told you about them, and there's a few thousand dollars in a checking account, and that's it."

"There may be other resources you aren't aware of yet. He could have had a safe-deposit box you don't know about, or brokerage accounts, or any number of things. If no money turns up in the next few months I'll grant it's a strange situation, but it'll take that long to tell what's out there."

"Some money did turn up," she said.

"Oh?"

She took a deep breath, let it out, and made her decision. She went into another room and came back a moment later with a metal strongbox about the size of a shoe box.

"I found this in the closet," she said, "just a couple of days ago. I was thinking that I ought to go through his things and give his clothes to the Goodwill. And I found this on the top shelf. I didn't know the combination and I was going to try to break it open with a hammer and screwdriver, and then I realized it was just a three-number dial so there could only be a thousand combinations, and if I started with three zeroes and ran the numbers in turn up to nine ninety-nine, well, how long could it take? And what else did I have to do? Then when I hit the number I started to cry, because it was five-one-one, and that's our anniversary, May eleventh, five-eleven. I looked at the dial and I started to cry, and I was still crying as I lifted the lid."

"What did you find?"

For answer she worked the dial and opened the box and showed it to me half-filled with banded stacks of bills. The ones I could see were all hundreds.

"I was expecting stock certificates and personal papers," she said. "But after all that buildup you must have known what I was going to show you."

"Not necessarily."

"What else could it have been?"

Dozens of things, I thought. A secret diary. A drug stash, for sale or for personal use. Pornography. A gun. Audio tapes. Company secrets. Love letters, old or new. Heirloom jewelry. Anything.

"I figured it was probably money," I said.

"I counted it," she said. "There's close to three hundred thousand dollars here."

"And nothing to indicate where it came from."

"No."

"I don't suppose it's what's left of his inheritance."

"I don't know if there was any inheritance. For all I know his parents are still alive. Matt, I'm frightened."

"Has anybody tried to throw a scare into you?"

"What do you mean?"

"Any strange phone calls?"

"Just reporters, and not many of those this past week. Who else would call?"

"Somebody who wants his money back."

"You think Glenn stole this?"

"I don't know how he got it," I said, "or where it came from, or how long he's had it. I'm not sure it's a good idea for you to keep it around the house."

"That occurred to me, but I'm not sure where I can put it, either."

"Don't you have a safe-deposit box?"

"No, because I never had anything valuable enough to keep in one."

"You do now."

"But is it a good idea? If there's an IRS investigation—"

"You're right. Wherever this came from, it's a pretty sure bet he didn't pay taxes on it. If they run an audit they'll get a court order to open any boxes in either of your names.''

"Do you have a box? If you were to hold it for me—''

I shook my head. A few minutes ago she was unsure whether or not to trust me with the information. Now she wanted to hand me the money. "I don't think that's such a good idea," I said. "Do you have a lawyer?''

"Not really. There was a guy on East Broadway I used once when I had a hassle with my old landlord, but I don't really know anything about him.''

"Well, there's somebody I can recommend. He's across the Brooklyn Bridge, but I think he's worth the trip. I can give you his number, or if you want I could call him for you.''

"Would you?''

"First thing tomorrow. He'll give you good advice, and he can probably keep the money in his safe. It'll be more secure there than in your closet, and I think attorney-client privilege would apply. I'll have to ask him about that.''

"And until then—''

"Until then it can stay in the closet. It's been safe there so far, and I'm not going to tell anyone it's there.''

"I'll be glad when it's out of here," she said. "I've been nervous ever since I found it.''

"I'd be nervous myself," I said. "It's a lot of money. But I don't think you should give it to the Goodwill.''

"**D**o you know," Mick said, "my mother always swore I had the second sight, and sometimes I believe the good woman was right. I was just now thinking I ought to give you a call. And here you are."

"I just dropped in to use the phone," I said.

"Did you now. When I was just a bit of a boy, there was a woman a flight up from us sent me every day to Featherstone's on the corner to fetch her a bucket of beer. They'd sell it to you like that then, by the pail. A little galvanized-iron pail it was, about so big. They filled it up for her for a dollar, and she paid me a quarter to run the errand."

"And that's how you got your start."

"Saving those twenty-five cent pieces," he said, "and investing them wisely. And look where I am today. No, sad to say, I spent the money on candy. A terrible sweet tooth I had in those days." He shook his head at the memory. "The point of the story—"

"You mean there is one?"

"—is that the woman wouldn't have you thinking she ever drank the beer. 'Mickey, there's a good lad, and would ye ever run down to Featherstone's for me, as I need to be washin' me hair.' I asked my mother how come Mrs. Riley used beer to wash her hair. 'It's her belly she's after washin',' says herself, 'for if Biddie Riley washed her hair for every bucket of beer she bought, she'd wash herself baldheaded.' "

"That's the point?"

"The point is she only wanted the beer for a hair rinse, and you're only here to use the fucking telephone. Have ye no phone in your room?"

"You found me out," I said. "I actually dropped in for a wash and set."

He clapped me on the shoulder. "If you've a call to make," he said, "use the phone in my office. You don't want the whole world listening."

There were three men at the bar and one behind it. Andy Buckley and a man I recognized but didn't know by name were playing darts in back, and two or three tables were occupied. So the whole world wouldn't have heard if I'd used the pay phone on the wall, but I was grateful all the same for the privacy of his office.

It is a good-sized room, with an oak desk and chair and a green metal filing cabinet. There was a huge old Mosler safe, no doubt at least as sturdy as the one in Drew Kaplan's law office, but unprotected by lawyer-client privilege. Hand-colored steel engravings in plain black frames formed two groups on the wall. Those over the desk were of the west of Ireland, where his mother's people had come from. The ones over the old leather couch showed scenes in the south of France, once home to his father.

The phone on the desk had a rotary dial, but that was all right because I wasn't calling TJ's beeper. I called Jan, and for a change I actually reached her instead of her machine. She said hello, her voice thick with sleep.

"I'm sorry," I said. "I didn't realize it would be too late to call you."

"It's not. I was reading and I dozed off with the book

on my lap. I'm glad you called. I've been thinking about the conversation we had the other day.''

"Oh?"

"And it occurred to me that I might have overstepped the bounds of our friendship."

"How?"

"By putting you in an awkward position. By asking something I had no right to ask."

"I would have said something."

"Would you? I don't know. Maybe, maybe not. You might have felt under an obligation. At any rate, I wanted to call and give you another chance."

"To do what?"

"To tell me to go fly a kite."

"Don't be silly," I said. "Unless you've been having second thoughts."

"About wanting the—"

"The item."

"The item. Ah. That's what we're calling it?"

"On the phone, yes."

"I see. No, no second thoughts. I still want the item."

"Well," I said, "it turns out to be a little harder to get hold of than I'd thought, but I'm working on it."

"I didn't want to rush you. I just wanted to give you a graceful way out, if you wanted to take it. After all, that's what this is about, isn't it?"

"What?"

"A graceful way out."

I asked her how she was feeling.

"Not bad," she said. "And wasn't it a beautiful day? That's why I kept being out when you called. I couldn't bear to stay inside. I love October, but I guess everybody does."

"Everybody with any sense."

"And how are you, Matthew?"

"Fine. Very busy, suddenly, but that's how it is with

me. Long stretches with nothing to do, and then a batch of things all at once.''

''That's how you like it.''

''I guess so, but it does get hectic. But I will take care of that little matter for you. I've been working on it.''

''Well, now,'' Mick said. ''What shall I look for on my next phone bill? Have you called China?''

''Just Tribeca.''

''There's those would call it another country, but the phone rates don't reflect their view. You've time for a little chat, haven't you? Burke's just started a fresh pot of coffee.''

''No coffee right now. I've been drinking it all day.''

''A Coca-Cola, then.''

''Maybe some club soda.''

''By God, you're a cheap date,'' he said. ''Sit down, I'll fetch something for both of us.''

He brought his private bottle of twelve-year-old Jameson and the Waterford tumbler he liked to drink from, and for me he provided a stemmed glass and a bottle of Perrier. I hadn't even known he stocked the stuff. I couldn't believe many of his customers called for it, or even knew how to pronounce it.

''We'll make it an early night,'' I said. ''I'm not in shape for a marathon.''

''Are you all right, man? Are you feeling fit?''

''I'm fine, but I'm working a case that's starting to heat up. I want to be able to get an early start tomorrow.''

''Is that all it is? Because you look troubled.''

I thought about it. ''Well,'' I said, ''I guess I am.''

''Ah.''

''A woman I know,'' I said, ''is very ill.''

''Very ill, you say.''

''Pancreatic cancer. It's incurable, and it looks as

though she doesn't have very much time.''

Carefully he said, ''Do I know her, man?''

I had to think. ''I don't believe you do,'' I said. ''She and I had stopped seeing each other by the time you and I got acquainted. I've stayed on friendly terms with her, but I'm sure I never brought her here.''

''Thanks be to God,'' he said, visibly relieved. ''You gave me a turn for a moment there.''

''How? Oh, you thought I was talking about—''

''About herself,'' he said, unwilling even to say Elaine's name in such a context. ''Which God forbid. She's well, then?''

''She's fine. She sends her best.''

''And you'll give her mine. But that's hard news about the other one. Not much time, you said.'' He filled his glass, held it to the light. It had a fine color to it. He said, ''You don't know what to wish someone in such circumstances. Sometimes it's better if it's over sooner.''

''That's how she wants it.''

''Oh?''

''And that's probably part of why I look troubled. She's decided she wants to shoot herself, and she's picked me to get her the gun.''

I don't know what I expected, but certainly not the shock that showed on his face. He asked if I'd accepted the mission, and I said that I had.

''You were not raised in the church,'' he said. ''For all that I drag ye along to mass, you weren't brought up Catholic.''

''So?''

''So I could never do what you've undertaken to do. Aid and abet a suicide? I'm a terrible Catholic, but I couldn't do it. They take a hard line on suicide, you know.''

''They're pretty strict on homicide, too, aren't they?

I seem to remember a whole commandment on the subject.''

'' 'Thou shalt not kill.' ''

"But maybe they don't take it seriously. Or maybe it went by the board with the Latin mass and eating meat on Friday."

"They take it seriously," he said. "And I have killed men. You know that."

"Yes."

"I've taken life," he said, "and I'll likely die with my sins unconfessed, and as likely burn for them. But taking your own life is a very grave matter."

"Why? I've never understood that. You're not harming anybody but yourself."

"The thought is that you're hurting God."

"How?"

"You're saying you know better than Himself how long you should live. You're saying, 'Thanks very much for this gift of life, but why don't You take it and shove it up Your ass.' You're committing the one sin that cannot be undone, and cannot be confessed because you're not around to confess it. Oh, I'm no theologian, I can't explain it worth a damn."

"I think I understand."

"Do you? You'd likely have to be born to it for it to make sense to you. I take it your friend's not Catholic."

"Not anymore."

"She was raised in the church? There's few of us ever get over it, you know. It doesn't bother her, what she plans to do?"

"It bothers her."

"But she's resolved to do it anyway?"

"It's likely to get very bad in the later stages," I said. "She doesn't want to go through all that."

"Nor would anyone, but are there not things they can give her for the pain?"

"She doesn't want to take them."

"Why not, for God's sake? And, you know, she could always take a little too much. It's easy to grow confused under the circumstances, and before you know it you've gone and taken the whole bottle."

"And isn't that suicide? The worst sin of all, you just finished explaining."

"Ah, but you wouldn't be in full possession of your faculties at the time. It doesn't count against you if you're not in your right mind. Besides," he said, "don't you think the Lord would overlook it if you gave Him half a chance?"

"Do you think so, Mick?"

"I do," he said, "but I told you I'm no theologian. Theology aside, aren't pills easier to get hold of than a gun? And isn't it a gentler death they offer you?"

"It is if you do it right," I said, "but not everybody does. Sometimes people come out of it choking on their own vomit. But that's not the real reason she'd prefer a gun."

I explained Jan's commitment to sobriety, and how in her eyes that ruled out drugs either to kill the pain or to ease the passage. His green eyes were first incredulous and then thoughtful as he took it all in.

He freshened his drink while he thought about it. At length he said, "Your lot takes this business very seriously."

"Not all of us would make the choices Jan has made," I said. "Most of us would take something for the pain, and I don't know how many of us would see a gun as providing a more sober way out than a handful of Seconal. But yes, you could say that we take sobriety pretty seriously."

"As seriously as our lot takes suicide." He drank, regarded me over the brim of the glass. "Let me ask you this. What would you do in her position?"

"I don't know," I said. "I'm not in her shoes, and that makes it impossible for me to say what I'd do if I were. I think I'd take painkillers, but on the other hand I'd want a clear head at the end. As for killing myself, well, I don't think that's a choice I would make. But who can say? I'm not in her shoes."

"Nor am I, thanks be to God. And I'm just as glad not to be in yours, either."

"What would you do, Mick?"

"Ah, Jesus, that's a good question. If I loved her, how could I refuse her? Yet how could I do her such a horrible service? I'm sorry for her trouble, but I'm grateful it's not me she asked."

"And if it were I that asked you?"

"God, what a question," he said. "It's not, is it? You that's asking."

"No," I said. "Of course not."

We talked of other things, but not for too much longer. I made it a fairly early night.

On the way home I thought about Lisa Holtzmann and the money she had shown me. I wondered where it had come from and what was going to become of it.

Did Kaplan even have a safe in his office? It seemed to me he must, that any lawyer would require one. I hoped his was roomy, and as secure as Mick's huge old Mosler.

I'd seen that Mosler open on more than one occasion. I knew some of the items it typically contained. Money, of course, both U.S. and foreign. Records of his outstanding loans—money he had out working on the street, yielding usurious interest and collected, if need be, by violence or the threat of violence. Occasional articles of value—watches, jewelry, presumably stolen.

And guns, of course. He always had a few guns in the safe. Now and then I'd needed a gun, and he'd provided one without question, and refused to take any money for it. Sitting in his office, talking on the phone with the old-fashioned rotary dial, I'd looked over at the safe and figured I'd get the gun from Mick.

He'd have furnished it with no questions asked. But now I'd have to get it somewhere else.

Because now he would know what I wanted it for. He might provide it, but my asking for it would be an abuse of our friendship. And that is something I take seriously. Like sobriety, or suicide.

Waddell & Yount had offices on the eighth floor of a twelve-story building at Nineteenth and Broadway. Two stores shared the ground floor, one selling cameras and darkroom supplies, the other a stationer. The building directory included a supplier of advertising specialty items and an environmentalist magazine. The floor immediately below Waddell & Yount was occupied by a men's discount clothier, offering closeouts and bankrupt stock at bargain prices.

The building was an old one, and the Waddell & Yount offices had not been recently refurbished. The carpet was maroon and threadbare, and the furniture ran to scarred sixty-inch wooden desks with matching swivel chairs and glassed-in stacking mahogany bookshelves. The overhead lighting consisted of bare bulbs in green metal shades. The period look was convincing, with technology providing the only anachronism; there were computers and digital phones on the old desks, and here and there a FAX and a copier. But at least one Luddite still clung to an old-fashioned typewriter. I could hear it clacking away as I followed Eleanor Yount through a maze of cubicles to her office.

She was a handsome woman in her early sixties, stout

now, with iron-gray hair and alert blue eyes. She wore a cameo brooch on the lapel of her navy suit, a gold band set with diamonds on her left ring finger. When I'd called at ten that morning to ask for an appointment she had told me to come in an hour. I'd taken my time walking there, stopping for a cup of coffee along the way, and now it was eleven and she was seating herself at her desk and pointing to a chair for me.

She said, "Here's a funny thing. After we spoke I began to wonder about the propriety of this meeting. I wanted advice, and the first thought I had was that I ought to consult Glenn." She smiled gently. "But of course that's not possible, is it? I called my personal attorney and explained the situation to him. He pointed out that, since I had nothing either to conceal or reveal, I needn't worry about being indiscreet." She picked up a pencil from the desk top. "So there's my good and bad news, Mr. Scudder. It's all right for me to talk with you, but I'm afraid I have next to nothing to say."

"How long did Glenn Holtzmann work for you?"

"A little over three years. I hired him shortly after my husband's death. Howard died in April, and I believe Glenn started here the first week in June. I interviewed him right before ABA. That's the annual booksellers' convention, it's always Memorial Day weekend." She turned the pencil in her hand. "My husband was his own in-house attorney. He was a graduate of Columbia Law School and a member of the bar, so of course he trusted himself to read contracts."

"And after Mr. Yount died—"

"Mr. Waddell," she said. "At home we were Mr. and Mrs. Waddell, while here we were Mr. Waddell and Ms. Yount. Of course that was Miss Yount for many years, before Ms. became a part of the language. To Howard's great dismay, I might add, and not for reasons of male chauvinism. He just couldn't brook the notion of an abbreviation that wasn't an abbreviation *of* anything." Her eyes aimed themselves somewhere past my left shoulder, gazing down the years. "Eisenhower was president when we moved into these offices," she said. "And we had only half our present space, we shared the suite with a man named Morrie Kelton who was a booking agent for dance bands and strippers and the most hopeless sort of latter-day vaudevillians. The strangest people in New York were apt to walk in that door. Did you ever see *Broadway Danny Rose?* We saw it and thought right away of Morrie. I wonder what happened to him. I suppose he's gone. He'd have to be close to ninety by now."

The typewriter clattered in the distance. "Morrie Kelton," she said. "He was a crude, hard-bitten little man, but he had a sweetness about him. Do you wear reading glasses, Mr. Scudder?"

"I beg your pardon?"

"You're of an age to need them. Do you wear glasses to read?"

"No," I said. "I could probably use them, but I can get by without them. As long as the light's not too dim."

"Then I don't suppose you're a customer of ours. If you don't need reading glasses, you probably don't buy large-print editions."

"Not yet."

"You're a patient man," she said. "Letting me traipse down Memory Lane and putting up with my impertinent questions. I asked because I was thinking of the firm's early days. When I met Howard Waddell he was drawing contracts and selling subsidiary rights at Newbold Brothers. They were a small trade house, acquired a few years ago by Macmillan, but still thriving when Howard went out on his own. And do you know what propelled him?"

"What?"

"Presbyopia. He was squinting at fine print, holding the paper at arm's length, avoiding paperbacks because the print was too small. A week after he got his first pair of reading glasses he started looking for office space. Within a month he'd signed a lease here and given notice at Newbold. I was an assistant in the production department there, on the phone every day arguing with printers while I dreamed about becoming the next Maxwell Perkins and fanning some young spark into the next literary bonfire. 'Ellie,' he said, 'the world is filling up with old farts with weak eyes and there's nothing out there for them to read. Once you get past thirty-odd editions of the Bible, the only large-type books are *The Power of Positive Thinking* and *The Book of Mormon*. If this isn't an opportunity I don't know what one is. Why don't you come work for me? You'll never get to meet a real writer or wear out a blue pencil, and I don't figure we'll ever get rich, but I bet we have fun.' "

"And you went to work for him."

"Without a second thought. What did I have to lose? And we did have fun, and somewhere along the way we got rich. Not at first, God knows. We both worked twelve-hour days. Howard gave up his apartment and slept on a couch here, claiming that saved him rent and bus fare and an hour's commuting time every day. He brought in a hot plate and a tiny refrigerator and we ate at our desks. For years our only market was libraries and we were selling to very few of them. But we stayed with it, and our business grew.

"And we fell in love, of course. And it was genuinely romantic, because each of us quietly assumed what we felt was unrequited, and so we were in love for a long time before we let on. Then we made up for lost time, except that I don't think there is any such thing, do you?"

I thought of the drinking years, the burned-out days, the blacked-out nights. I remembered Freddie Fender's song, "Wasted Days and Wasted Nights." But were they?

"No," I said. "I don't think any time is wasted."

"But how we rushed to make up for it! For a week he spent every night at my apartment. I lived in two little rooms on East End Avenue. Five flights up, and no elevator, and Howard was in his mid-forties by then, and in no condition to appreciate climbing five flights of stairs. He didn't enjoy taking two buses to work in the morning, either. After a week he said, 'Ellie, this is ridiculous. I've just spoken with a real estate agent. There's a perfectly suitable apartment available on Gramercy Park. Two bedrooms, sunken living room, key to the park. We can walk to work. Look at it, will you? I'll trust your judgment. If it looks all right to you, tell him we'll take it.' And, almost as if it went without saying, he added, 'We'll get married. In fact we can do that right away, whether you like the apartment or not.'"

"Just like that."

"Just like that. We changed my name to Mrs. Howard Waddell, and we changed the firm's name to Waddell & Yount, and we had thirty years. We never moved the offices, we just took Morrie Kelton's space and added on another adjoining suite when it became available. This area is fashionable now, all sorts of publishers are moving in. And we're still here, and I'm still on Gramercy Park. The apartment's too big for me, all by myself, but then the office is too small, so I suppose it averages out. I *am* sorry, Mr. Scudder. You should have steered me back on track."

"I was interested."

"Then I'll withdraw my apology. Glenn Holtzmann, Glenn Holtzmann. He sent over his résumé at the suggestion of a friend of his at the firm we used on the rare occasions when we required outside counsel. Sullivan, Bienstock, Rowan and Hayes, they had offices in the Empire State Building, but I don't think they exist anymore as a firm. It's not important, I don't even know the name of Glenn's friend there, and I believe he must have been somebody very junior.

"Glenn was unemployed at the time. He grew up in western Pennsylvania, in a town called Roaring Spring. I believe the closest town of any size is Altoona. He attended Penn State University. And no, I didn't have all of this committed to memory. I checked the files after I spoke to you on the phone."

"I was beginning to wonder."

"After college he worked for several years in Altoona. An uncle of his had an insurance agency and Glenn worked for him. Then his mother died—his father was already dead—and he took the insurance money and the proceeds from the sale of the house and moved to New York, where he attended New York Law School. When your eye hits that on a résumé, you tend to read it as 'New York University Law School,' but there's a rather considerable difference. Still, he did well there, and he passed the bar exam on his first try, and moved up to White Plains and went to work for a small firm there. He said the New York firms weren't hiring, which I take it to mean they weren't hiring boys with Penn State and New York Law on their résumés."

But he hadn't liked living and working in Westchester County, and before too long he hooked on with a publishing house in the city, working in their legal department. He'd been let go as part of the wholesale sacking of the department that occurred when the house was gobbled up by a Dutch conglomerate in a hostile takeover. Then Howard Waddell had died, and Glenn had sent over his résumé, and there had been no need to interview anyone else.

"At first," she said, "there wasn't much for him to do. The vast majority of our transactions are with American trade publishers with whom we've done business for years. Our contracts are straightforward and clear-cut. As pure reprinters, we don't have to secure permissions or concern ourselves about possible libel. We don't commission original works, so we don't have to sue to recover advances when authors fail to deliver manuscripts. You see, Glenn was being hired to handle what had amounted to only a small portion of Howard's work.

"This didn't mean we could have done without him. How can I best explain?" She frowned, hunting for an analogy. "My secretary has a typewriter," she said. "Now of course she also has a computer, which she uses for almost everything. But every now and then there's a form that has to be filled out, and you can't do that on a computer. It uses its own paper, you see, so when you want to type a few lines on an already existing piece of paper, you need a typewriter. Frequently days go by without that typewriter's being used, but that doesn't mean we could get along without it."

"I think I heard it earlier."

"No, I know what you heard. My secretary's typewriter is a demure little electronic model that's very nearly as silent as her computer. What you heard was an old Underwood that sounds like the city room in *The Front Page*. Our foreign-rights person insists on using it and nothing else for all correspondence. It's a hideous old machine, too, with its keys out of alignment and the *o* and *e* filled in with ink. She produces these disgraceful letters full of corrections and strikeovers and FAXes them all over the world. And this is a twenty-eight-year-old woman, mind you, presumably a part of the computer generation." She sighed. "I don't mean to imply there was anything old-fashioned about Glenn, because there wasn't. But like the typewriter he was indispensable when we needed him, but that was only now and then.''

"What did he do with the rest of his time?''

"He spent a good share of it reading at his desk. His area was history and world affairs, and we took on several books on the basis of his recommendations. And he pitched in in other areas as well.'' Her eyes narrowed. "When Glenn started here,'' she said, "I thought he might become a good deal more than our in-house counsel. As a matter of fact, I saw him as a possible successor.''

"Really.''

"Remember, my husband had started out with a legal background. And I thought Glenn might use his position as a platform from which to reach out into all aspects of the business. I'm by no means ready to retire, but in a few years I might be, especially if I had the right sort of person standing in the wings. I never came out and said this to Glenn, but it ought to have been implicit. His was a job with a future.''

"But he didn't exploit it.''

"No. One of my husband's final projects was our large-print book club. The club start-up called for a lot of legal work, and it got most of Glenn's attention at the beginning. The master plan called for us to develop additional clubs for readers with specialized interests— mysteries, science fiction, cookbooks. It was an area of the business with real growth potential, and all Glenn had to do was make it his baby, moving out of the legal area and expanding the whole operation. But he didn't do it, and six or eight months after he started here, I realized that he was evidently content to remain a small frog in our little pond. At first I thought he was just biding his time here, that he'd jump to another firm when he got the chance, probably a corporate law firm. Then time passed and I saw I was wrong, that he was quite happy where he was. I decided he wasn't terribly ambitious.''

"Were you disappointed?"

"I suppose I must have been. I'd envisioned him as another Howard Waddell, and he was a far cry from that. And I had thought my own retirement might come about sooner rather than later. As things stand I expect to hang on to the reins for five more years, and I think I know who'll take them from me when the time comes.''

"Your foreign-rights person," I said.

"That's exactly right! And by then her typing won't stand in her way, because she'll have a secretary of her own. Now tell me how you knew that.''

"Just a lucky guess."

"Nonsense. You weren't guessing. You spoke with absolute assurance. How on earth did you know?''

"Something in your voice when you were talking about her. And a look in your eye."

"Nothing more concrete than that?"

"No."

"Remarkable. *She* doesn't know what I have planned for her, and neither does anyone else. You must be very good at what you do, Mr. Scudder. Is that your whole job, talking to people and listening to what they say? And watching their faces while they say it?''

"That's most of it," I said. "It's the part I like the best." We talked a little about my work, and then I asked about Glenn Holtzmann's salary.

"He got annual raises," she said, "but he was still earning considerably less than the large corporate law firms pay to associates fresh out of law school. Of course they get seventy or eighty hours a week out of their people, and I've told you how little we demanded of Glenn. He earned enough to live decently. He was single

when he started here, and then when he did marry he
was clever enough to pick someone with money. Have
I said something wrong?''

"Did he tell you his wife was rich?"

"Perhaps not in so many words, but that was certainly
the impression I got.''

"She was an artist," I said, "supporting herself as a
free-lance illustrator. She lived in a run-down tenement
on the Lower East Side.''

"That's extraordinary.''

"He met her here," I went on. "She came to show
samples of her work to your art director, and he spotted
her, and I gather it was quite romantic, though in a very
different way from your own courtship.''

"If courtship is even the right word for it," she said.
"But please go on. This is fascinating.''

"He swept her off her feet. He proposed a month after
they met.''

"I had the impression they kept company longer than
that.''

"You never met his wife?"

"No. I know she was from Denver, and the wedding
took place there. No one from the office attended. I gathered that it was a family affair.''

"She's from a suburb of Minneapolis," I said, "but
I get the impression she cut her ties with her family
when she moved to New York. They were married at
City Hall and honeymooned in Bermuda.''

"I don't suppose her father built ski resorts in Vail
and Aspen.''

"I can't recall that she told me anything about her
father, but no, I don't think he did anything of the sort.
When they got back from the honeymoon Glenn surprised her with a new apartment. He made the down
payment with money left over from his parents' estate.''

"My impression was that he'd had barely enough to get him through law school."

"Maybe he saved his lunch money."

"The apartment—"

"A small two-bedroom condo with a spectacular view. I'd say a minimum of a quarter of a million dollars."

"It's a new building, isn't it? The builders arrange financing with as little as ten percent down. He would only have needed twenty-five thousand dollars. But wouldn't he have had trouble with the payments?"

The payments, I explained, had been a cinch; he'd bought the property outright for cash.

She stared at me. "Where did he get the money?"

"I don't know."

"Of course the first thing I have to think is that he might have embezzled it. A quarter of a million dollars? I'm tempted to say it's impossible, but everybody always says that. I've heard of two embezzlements in publishing in the past year or so. One of them ran into six figures. Both were very quickly hushed up, and both involved cocaine, which seems to foster that sort of behavior. It creates a compelling economic motive and undermines character and judgment at the same time. Did Glenn use cocaine?"

"Did you suspect him of it?"

"Certainly not. I don't even think he drank very much."

I asked about cash. Was there ever much around?

"We keep substantial funds on deposit," she said. "They would be listed as cash assets on a balance sheet. But I don't suppose that's what you mean."

"I was talking about currency," I said. "Green money."

" 'Green money.' Well, Mr. Scudder, my secretary keeps a petty-cash box in the top right-hand drawer of her desk. She dips into it when we have to tip a delivery boy. I suppose there's fifty dollars in there on a good day, but it would take an extremely resourceful person to steal a quarter of a million dollars out of it.''

"I think Holtzmann got his money in cash. If he found some way to steal from you it would have involved unwarranted payments to dummy accounts, and I don't see any sign of any of that.''

"That relieves my concern but not my curiosity. Where do you suppose he got the money?''

"I don't know.''

"Maybe he just had it all along. Maybe *his* parents were wealthy, maybe they left him a really substantial amount of money, and he didn't want anyone to know. He used some of the money to get through law school and he just kept the rest.''

"In cash? There would be bank accounts, certificates of deposit. Unless it was already in cash when he inherited it.''

"How could that be?''

"Maybe it was fruit-jar money, untaxed cash his parents squirreled away that came to him upon their death. When is he supposed to have come to New York? Ten years ago?''

"At least that long. I could have Enid look it up.''

"It's not important. Ten years. The bills I saw looked recent enough, but I didn't check the series dates or the signatures, so—''

"The bills you saw?''

I hadn't meant to let that out. "There was some cash in the apartment,'' I said.

"A substantial amount?''

"I'd call it that.''

We both fell silent. At length she asked me who my client was. I told her. She wanted to know if this meant that George Sadecki was innocent. Not necessarily, I said. It might only mean that he was guilty of killing a man with a secret. I might know more when I unearthed Glenn Holtzmann's secret, but at this point all I'd managed to establish was that he had one.

"He worked late frequently," I said. "At least that's what he told his wife. But if his work load was as light as you've said—"

"I don't know that he ever stayed at his desk past five o'clock."

"I wonder where he went."

"I've no idea."

"He had some evening appointments as well. Business appointments, but I gather the business wasn't Waddell & Yount's."

She shook her head. "This is all so incomprehensible to me," she said. "I don't think I'm particularly naive. But if there was ever an unlikely candidate for the title role in *A Double Life*, it was Glenn."

"I met him once."

"You hadn't mentioned that."

"Well, it didn't amount to much. My girlfriend and I saw them socially, him and his wife. That was in the spring. Then I ran into him a couple of times in the neighborhood. I live just a block from him. He wanted to talk to me about writing a book."

"Are you a writer?"

"No, and I wasn't at all interested, but the implication was that he'd be interested in publishing a book about my experiences. From what he'd already said about your firm I had the impression that you were strictly a reprint publisher."

"Yes, that's correct."

"And I also had the impression that Glenn had no more interest in my writing a book than I did. He wanted something from me, and he didn't want to let me know what it was. I was uneasy around him. He always seemed sneaky to me.''

"Evidently your instincts were better than mine.''

"Or maybe he didn't have a hidden agenda here,'' I suggested. "Maybe he saved his dark side for when he was away from the office.''

She was the boss, she told me. If Glenn had had a dark side, or even a light side, he'd have been less likely to expose it to the woman who signed his paycheck. She took me around the office and introduced me to three of his fellow employees, including the young woman in charge of foreign rights, and a brief conversation with each of them added nothing substantial to my store of knowledge. Lately his work had centered largely upon a proposed large-print book club, and the legal ramifications of requiring members to purchase a minimum number of books annually. I wound up learning a little more about the subject than I cared to know. I didn't figure it had much to do with money in a strongbox, or gunshots, and blood on the sidewalk.

Back in Eleanor Yount's office, she wanted to know my guesses on some of the case's unanswerable questions. I told her it was too early in the game for guesses. There wasn't enough to go on.

"I was afraid you'd say that,'' she said. "I'd like to know how this turns out, and I have the feeling I won't get to read about it in the newspapers.''

"You might.''

"Even so, they won't have the whole story, will they?''

"They usually don't.''

"Will you come back and tell me? And of course I intend to have my accountant make very certain that W&Y didn't pay for Glenn's apartment. I'll let you

know if there are any irregularities. If you could let me
have a card—''

I gave her one of my cards. She said, ''A name, a
number, and nothing else. A minimalist business card.
You're an interesting man, Mr. Scudder. I *don't* publish
originals, but I'm friendly with just about everyone in
this town who does, so if there should happen to be a
book you've been wanting to write—''

''There really isn't.''

''That's remarkable,'' she said. ''I didn't think there
was a policeman or private detective anywhere in New
York who wasn't trying to get a book published. Nobody's out looking for criminals these days. They're all
looking for an agent.''

15

I had called Drew Kaplan earlier but he'd been in court. I called again from Waddell & Yount. His secretary said she'd spoken to him and he could see me in his office at three o'clock. And yes, she said, Mr. Kaplan had a safe in his office. Her tone left me feeling faintly foolish for having asked.

I called Lisa Holtzmann and listened again to Glenn's voice. If I had to hear a voice from the grave, I would have preferred something a little more informative. All he did was tell me to leave a message. I waited him out and identified myself, and she picked up right away. I told her she had a three o'clock appointment with Drew Kaplan at his Court Street office.

"Will you be able to come with me, Matt?"

"I was planning on it," I said. "I figured you might want company."

"I'd be nervous making the trip by myself."

I told her I'd be at her place at two, that that would leave us plenty of time. I had another call to make, to TJ's beeper, but I didn't want to loiter in the Waddell & Yount office waiting for a callback, nor did I think "Who wants TJ?" would go over well with the girl on the switchboard. I went out and called from the street, punched in my number at the tone, and waited for his call.

After five minutes without a callback and a couple of dirty looks from passersby looking for a phone, I spent a quarter and called my hotel. The only slips in my box were a pair of calls from TJ. No message, just his beeper number. I fed the phone another quarter and called Elaine and got her machine. ''It's Matt,'' I said. ''Are you there?'' When there was no response I said, ''I'd like to see you tonight but things are starting to heat up. We could have dinner if I get done in time, or else I can come over late. I'll call as soon as I have a better picture of my schedule.'' It seemed as though there ought to be something to add to that, but I couldn't think what, and then the tape ran out and saved me the trouble.

I depressed the hook and held on to the receiver, hoping for TJ's call. Of course he could have called while I was talking to my hotel or Elaine's machine, in which case he'd have gotten a busy signal. I was thinking this through when a man in a dark suit and a porkpie hat asked me if I was going to make my call or what. ''Because if what you want's a private office,'' he said, ''there's buildings up and down Broadway got plenty of vacancies, more'n they know what to do with. Talk to 'em, they'll fix you up with a desk, a chair, phone company'll put in your own private phone.''

''Sorry.''

''Hey, no problem,'' he said, and dropped his own quarter in the slot.

A block away I spent another quarter and called AA's Intergroup office. I asked the volunteer who answered if there was a lunchtime meeting nearby. She sent me to a community center just off Union Square and I got there as they were reading the preamble. I sat down and stayed put for an hour, but I was barely aware of what they were saying. My mind was too busy with Glenn Holtzmann to have room for much else. Still, it was as good a place to think as any, and the coffee wasn't bad, and the buck I put in the basket was as much as anyone expected from me. And if I'd declined to throw that in no one would have cared. Nobody suggested I go rent myself an office, nor did anyone advise the old fellow sleeping two rows in front of me to look for a hotel room.

I got to Fifty-seventh and Tenth a few minutes early. There was a different doorman on duty, but when I gave him her name he was every bit as suspicious as the one the night before. I gave him my name as well and told him I was expected, and once he'd confirmed this we were old friends.

Up on Twenty-eight, she opened the door just as I knocked and closed it as soon as I'd cleared the threshold. She took hold of my arm just above the elbow and told me she was glad I was there. "You're five minutes early," she said, "and in the past ten minutes I must have looked at my watch twenty times."

"You're anxious."

"I've been anxious ever since you left last night. The money made me nervous from the moment I discovered it, but it wasn't entirely real until I showed it to you and we talked about it. I should have made you take it with you."

"Why would you want to do that?"

"Because it kept me up most of the night. It just scared me, that's all. At one point I decided it wasn't safe in the closet, that was the first place they would look."

"The first place who would look?"

"I have no idea. I hopped out of bed and got the box down from the shelf and stowed it under the bed. Then I decided *that* was the first place they'd look. I decided the money was dangerous and all I wanted was to be rid of it. I had the idea of opening the box and throwing all the money out the window.''

''That's some idea.''

''You know what stopped me? I was afraid to open the window. I was afraid I wouldn't be able to keep from jumping. In fact I got so I was scared to stand close to the window even with it shut and locked. Heights don't usually scare me, but it wasn't the height, it was my own mind I was afraid of. Look at me.''

''You look all right.''

''Do I?''

She looked fine to me. She was wearing tan flannel slacks, a moss-green turtleneck, a brass-buttoned navy blazer. She had lipstick on, and a little makeup. And she was wearing perfume, a woodsy scent.

There was coffee made and I agreed we had time for a cup. After she'd poured it she went into the bedroom and came back with the strongbox. I took it from her and felt its weight, then set the dial to 511 and lifted the lid.

She said, ''You remembered the combination.''

''I remember stuff.'' I took out a stack of bills and flipped through them, giving them a close look. She asked, her voice rising, if there was anything wrong with the money. I told her the bills looked good to me. They weren't counterfeit. They hadn't been stuffed in fruit jars and buried out behind a stone barn somewhere in Pennsylvania, either. Some of them were older—hundreds circulate at a more sedate pace than smaller denominations, and take longer to wear out—but most bore dates within the past decade. They were not part of Holtzmann's legendary patrimony. I told her I was glad she hadn't thrown them out the window.

''I was going to undo the wrappers,'' she said, ''so

as not to hurt anybody. Imagine being killed by falling money."

"You wouldn't want that on your conscience."

"No. But I thought how pretty it would look, all those bills floating through the air, tossed here and there by the breeze. And think of how many people I would have made happy."

"Even so," I said.

We went downstairs and hailed three cabs to find one willing to make the trip. Cabbies these days apply for a hack license as soon as they clear Immigration, and the first five words of English they learn are, "I don't go to Brooklyn." The first two showed off their command of the language and drove away smiling. The third, a Nigerian who'd grown up speaking English, had nothing to prove and was willing to go wherever we wanted. He didn't know how to get there, but he took direction well.

Of course the subway would have been faster and easier, and about fifteen dollars cheaper, but who in his right mind would take three hundred thousand in cash for a ride on the subway? You might as well toss it out the window.

Drew Kaplan sat at his desk and listened attentively while I filled him in on who Lisa was and why we were there. I told him just about everything, but didn't say anything about the contents of the metal strongbox I'd placed on his desk. When I'd run through it he went back over a couple of points, but he didn't say a word about the box, either. Then he tipped his chair back and gazed up at the ceiling.

"Needs a paint job," I offered.

"So? You could use a haircut, but am I insensitive enough to bring that up?"

"Evidently."

"Evidently. Mrs. Holtzmann, first let me offer my

sympathies. Of course I read the press coverage of the case. I'm sorry for your loss."

"Thank you."

"On the basis of what I've just been told, I think you definitely need someone to look after your interests. I gather you'd like to put that"—he indicated the strongbox—"in a safe place. You haven't told me what's in it and I don't see any reason why you should, but perhaps Matt here would like to take, say, three wild guesses as to what it might conceivably contain."

"Three guesses?" I said.

"Sure. Shot-in-the-dark time."

"Okay," I said. "Well, there might be several tusks of poached ivory in the box, smuggled in from Tanzania."

"There's a possibility."

"Or Judge Crater might be in there."

"Could be," Drew said, enjoying himself. "He's been missing a long time."

"What's that, two guesses?"

"Uh-huh. One to go."

"Well, I suppose there could be a substantial amount of cash in the box."

"And if by some wild coincidence there really was cash in there, would you like to take another wild guess where it came from?"

"Uh-uh. Not a clue."

"As much of a mystery as the apartment equity, and everything else about this mysterious man. All right." He laid a hand on top of the strongbox. "I'm going to take this for safekeeping," he announced, "with the understanding that I have no idea what it contains, and that not only my custodianship of the box but its very existence are confidential matters. I'll give you a receipt for the box, Mrs. Holtzmann, or should that be Ms.?"

"On the receipt? I don't care."

"On the receipt it will just say Lisa Holtzmann. I wanted to know how you preferred to be called."

"Lisa," she said. "Call me Lisa."

"Fine, and I'm Drew. As I said, I'll give you a receipt, but if this box disappears in a burglary you'll have to understand that there's no question of reimbursement or insurance coverage. I'd reimburse you for the strongbox, but not for what's in it."

She looked at me. I nodded, and she told Drew she understood.

"Set your mind at rest," he said. "I don't steal from clients, I just overcharge them. It's a lot more lucrative in the long run and you spend less time in prison. Lisa, if this box here were all we had to worry about I'd take it and charge you a few dollars for storage. Or I might suggest you go around the corner and lease a safe-deposit box in your maiden name, or in some name you always thought you might like to use." He sat up straight, clasped his hands. "But there's more at stake here. You've got your apartment, which those nice folks at Internal Revenue might take an interest in if your husband happened to buy it with unlaundered funds. You've also got insurance proceeds, which they shouldn't be able to attach, but might depending on the nature and ownership of the policies, and on just how Laughing Boy filed or didn't file his tax return." He frowned. "I'm sorry, I don't mean to make slighting references to your late husband. There's no disrespect intended, it's just he's left you in a tricky spot and that tends to inspire me to heights of sarcasm."

"But underneath it all," I said, "Drew's a prince."

He ignored me. "There's also a good possibility of hidden assets," he went on, "which might only come to you if you're aware of them. What I'd like from you, Lisa, is a check for five thousand dollars as a retainer.

That should cover the actions I undertake on your behalf.''

Again she looked at me. This time I said, "That's no good, Drew. She hasn't got it.''

"Oh?''

"Not in the bank. She'll get the insurance money eventually, but for the time being all she's got is a household account with enough dough in it to cover her day-to-day expenses.''

"I see.''

I shot a look at the strongbox. His eyes went to it and back to me.

"I'd like to get paid by check,'' he said. "If I went down the hall for a minute and didn't put that in the safe until I got back, and if she wrote out the check, maybe when she got back home she'd happen to discover five thousand dollars in the refrigerator, just enough to deposit in the bank so the check wouldn't bounce. What do you think?''

"I think that would leave a paper trail that wouldn't do her a whole lot of good. One look from anybody and the first thing they pick up is the cash deposit.''

"Yeah, you're right,'' he said. "Shit. Give me a minute.'' He sat back and closed his eyes. After a full minute he opened them and said, "Okay, here's how we'll do it. You brought your checkbook with you, I hope? I'd like you to write out a check payable to Drew Kaplan, Attorney-at-Law, in the amount of two hundred dollars.''

I said, "See? They're all alike. They start out high, but you can generally Jew them down.''

"I didn't hear that,'' he said. "Did you put the whole phrase, my name and Attorney-at-Law? Good.'' He picked up the phone and pushed the intercom button and said, "Karen, draw a check on the office account payable to Matthew Scudder, with the notation that it's for investigative services on behalf of Lisa Holtzmann.'' He spelled her name for Karen, then covered the mouthpiece and said, ''Investigative? Investigatory? Which is right?''

''Who cares?''

He shrugged. Into the phone he said, ''One hundred dollars, and hold on to it. He'll pick it up when he's ready to leave.''

''I like that,'' I said. ''Are we partners? Do we split everything fifty-fifty?''

He ignored me again. He said, ''Now here's what I'm going to do. I'm going down the hall for a minute, and when I get back I wouldn't be a bit surprised if Lisa has ten thousand dollars in her purse that she completely forgot about. And no, there hasn't been a sudden price increase. I'll be back in a moment.''

When he had left the room I opened the box and removed two stacks, each of fifty bills. She put them in her purse and I closed the box and spun the dial. We waited in silence until Drew returned with my check. ''A hundred dollars,'' he said. ''Now you can buy that Cadillac.''

''You'll never guess what Lisa found in her purse.''

''Tanzanian ivory would be my guess, but I'm willing to be proved wrong.''

A glance from Lisa, another nod from me. She drew out both stacks of bills and placed them on his desk.

He sighed and said, ''You try to do it by the book, you try not to take cash, but how can you operate that way and serve the best interests of the client? This is how lawyers get in trouble.'' He thought about that and said, ''Well, it's one way. There are others.'' He picked up one packet of bills, weighed it in his hand, tossed it to me. He took the other, riffled the edges, sighed again, and put it in his inside breast pocket. To Lisa he said, ''Do you understand what just took place?''

"I think so."

"If there's anything you don't understand Matt will be able to explain it. You have a lawyer now and you have a detective, and because I wrote out the check retaining our friend here, anything you tell him or he finds out on his own is privileged information. He can't be compelled to divulge it. Not that he would anyway, but this way his ass is covered, if you'll pardon the plain speech." He hefted the strongbox. "You forget how heavy ivory is," he said. "Especially the poached kind. Lisa, I'll be in touch. Call me if anything happens and refer all matters to me. Don't answer any questions from anybody about anything. Don't allow anyone access to your apartment without a warrant, and call me if anybody shows up with one. Matthew, always a pleasure."

There was a cab at the hack stand down the block and the driver was untroubled by our destination of Tenth Avenue and Fifty-seventh Street. "That's Manhattan," I said, and he assured me it was not a problem. Lisa wondered why I had specified the borough; did Brooklyn have a Tenth Avenue and a Fifty-seventh Street? Indeed it did, I said, and they intersected near where Sunset Park and Bay Ridge abutted one another. She said she didn't know Brooklyn at all, that she'd been to Williamsburg where some artists she knew had lofts, but we weren't anywhere near there now, were we? No, I said, we weren't.

What conversation there was stayed at that level until we had reached our destination and gone on up to her apartment. "I'm going to have a drink," she announced. "I got out of the habit while I was pregnant, but there's no reason not to, is there? I think I'll have a scotch. What about you?"

"A little of that coffee, if there's any left."

"You don't drink?"

"I used to."

She took this in, started to say something, and changed her mind. She went into the kitchen and came back with coffee for me and what looked like a very weak scotch and soda for herself. We each picked a couch to sit on and went over what had taken place at the law office on Court Street. Drew hadn't wanted to take cash, I explained, because that was a good way for a lawyer to get in trouble. Several defense attorneys had run into problems when they accepted cash fees from drug dealers. The government had tried to impound the fees on the grounds that they were the proceeds of illegal traffic in narcotics, and had sometimes been able to pull this off even when the original case against the defendant wound up being dismissed.

"Was Glenn trafficking in drugs?"

"Who knows?" I said. "At this point no one can say what the hell he was doing, but the money is pretty likely to be dirty one way or another. At the very least it's untaxed income. And it's about to become untaxed income all over again, because Drew can't very easily enter it in his books and deposit it in his bank account without leaving it an open question as to where it came from. He has to keep it off the books."

"I thought people preferred income off the books."

"Not always. In this case the money he'll save in taxes is offset by the fact that he's going to be breaking the law. More to the point, two people will know he's broken the law."

"And the two people are—"

"You and I. He doesn't think we're likely to turn him in or he wouldn't have taken the cash, but he bought himself a little insurance by making sure I took five thousand dollars myself in his presence. Now my hands aren't any cleaner than his. Incidentally, I'll give that money back to you if you want."

"Why?"

"It's a lot of money."

"I was going to throw the whole kit and caboodle out the window a few hours ago, remember?"

"You wouldn't have done that."

"No, but I wanted to. I didn't know that money existed until a few days ago. Ever since I found it I've been afraid someone would take it away or kill me for it. Now there's a chance I may be able to keep some of it, and even if I don't I can at least stop worrying about it. If one of those packets of bills goes to you and the other to a lawyer in Brooklyn, what do I care?"

She punctuated the question with a long sip from her drink. It triggered a flash of sense memory—the faintly medicinal taste of scotch, cooled by the ice cubes, diluted by the soda, the tongue tingling from the soda's bubbles, from the whiskey's alcohol. Jesus, I could damn near hear the background music, Brubeck or Chico Hamilton, say. Or Chet Baker, playing a trumpet solo, then putting the horn down and singing in that voice as thin as her drink, as cool, as enduring in memory

"I have to make a couple of calls."

"All right," she said. "Do you want to use the phone in the bedroom? You'd have more privacy."

"This is fine," I said.

I called Elaine. "It's been a long day," I said, "and it's not over yet."

"Do you want to skip it?"

"No, I don't. I've got a few things to take care of, and then I want to go home and shower and lie down for half an hour. Suppose I came over around eight? We can eat at that little place around the corner."

"Which little place? Which corner?"

"Your choice."

"Deal," she said. "Eight o'clock?"

"Eight o'clock."

I broke the connection and dialed TJ and punched in Lisa's number at the tone. "A friend with a beeper," I explained. "He'll probably be calling back any minute. When it rings, one of us ought to answer before the machine picks up."

"Why don't you answer it, Matt? I don't want to talk to anybody. If it's not for you just tell them they've got the wrong number."

"Wouldn't they just call back?"

"Fuck 'em," she said, and giggled. "I haven't had a drink in a *while*," she said. "I think I'm feeling this one. Were you talking to Elaine just now?"

"That's right."

"I like Elaine."

"So do I."

"I'm warm," she announced, and got to her feet. "That's the trouble with facing west. It gets so hot in the afternoon. This summer I had to close the blinds every afternoon to keep the place from heating up faster than the air-conditioning could cope with it. And then I had to remember to open them in time for the sunset." She took off her blazer, hung it over the back of a chair. "Are you going to be able to stay for the sunset, Matt?"

"I don't think so."

"We've got a VCR. I could plug it right into the window and try taping it for you. Oh, fuck, I did it again."

"Did what?"

"Said 'we' instead of 'I.' *I've* got a VCR. But you can't tape sunsets, can you? You have to catch them live and in person. Except they have this video of an aquarium, have you seen it?"

"I think I heard something about it."

"Glenn actually rented it once, if you can believe it. To see what it was like. It was uncanny, you'd swear you had real fish swimming in your television set, that the TV was an aquarium. You know what they could have?''

''What?''

''Like a huge TV screen,'' she said, ''that you'd hang on a wall that doesn't have windows, or right over the window if you're in the back with a view of the air shaft. And they could sell you sunset videos, and it would be like looking out your own window if you had one, except better, because you could play it any time of day you wanted. You could have a spectacular sunset at like two in the morning. Don't you think that's a brilliant idea?''

''Brilliant.''

''*I* think so. Matt, you know what I wish?''

''What?''

The phone rang. ''I wish you'd answer that,'' she said.

It was TJ, complaining that he'd been trying to reach me all day. ''I found her,'' he said, ''an' then I lost her.''

''The witness?''

''She seen it go down,'' he said. ''What's hard is gettin' the story out of her. She a shy child.''

''What's her name?''

''We on the phone, Joan. Don't want to be sayin' names. Name she gave me's most likely a street name anyway. It a girl's name, so you know it ain't the name she was born with.''

''She's a transsexual?''

'' 'TS' is her word for it. Always thought those letters stood for somethin' else. I told her, hey, you TS, I'm TJ, maybe we be kin of some kind. Kissin' cousins, she say.''

''Is she a working girl?''

''She workin' at bein' a girl. I hung around with her long as I could, all the time tryin' to reach you. One time you beeped me I couldn't get to a phone. Time I did, I called the number an' got a busy signal. Finally got through, got some weird dude barely spoke English. Told him, man, what business you got answerin' the phone when it ain't for you? He still be figurin' that out.''

"You say she's a witness. What did she see?"

"Saw the two men we talkin' about."

"Glenn and George?"

"Okay to say on the phone? Yeah, those two."

"Did she see the shooting?"

"Says she didn't. Saw just before an' just after. Saw the one lyin' there an' the other goin' through his pockets.''

"Or bending over him and picking up shell casings."

"What I was thinkin'. You pro'ly got questions to ask her.''

"A whole bunch," I said. "Where is she?"

"Out an' about. Had a doctor appointment at four, wouldn't let me tag along with her. 'Now TJ, I trust you have better ways to occupy your time.' I tried followin' her.''

"You did?"

"Ain't that what detectives do? Only you best give me some lessons. I didn't do too good at it."

"It's not easy."

"I followed her into the subway an' the train pulled out before I could catch it. I hopped the turnstile but I still didn't have no shot at it, plus I had a fool wanted to report me for fare-beating. Man, I said, you get outta my face with this citizen's arrest shit, or I gonna make a cardiac arrest.'' He sighed. "But I lost her."

"Can you find her again?"

"Hope so. I gave her my number, told her to beep me after she done at the doctor's. If she don't, I be lookin' for her over by the Captain.''

"Is that where she works?"

"She work up an' down the avenue. Or she work down on West Street in the Village. She don't have to work as hard as some of 'em do, 'cause she ain't got a pimp or a cocaine jones."

"What kind of jones has she got?"

"Guess you'd say it was a doctor jones," he said. "Puttin' money by for this procedure an' that procedure. You wouldn't believe the shit they'll do to you if you crazy enough to want it."

"In the movies," I said, "the girl was always saving money for an operation, but it was so that her kid brother could walk again."

"Just go to show," he said. "Times has changed."

I would be at the same number for another fifteen or twenty minutes, I told TJ. After that I'd be at my hotel for a little while, and then at Elaine's. But I'd put Call Forwarding on when I left my hotel, so he could just call the usual number. Any time, I said. It didn't matter if it was late.

Lisa was silhouetted against the window, the contours of her body more apparent than when the blue blazer had cloaked them. My eyes were drawn to her breasts and buttocks. She said, "I heard you say you'd be here another twenty minutes."

"If it's all right."

"Of course it's all right. Was that an informant you were talking to? Has there been a break in the case? What's so funny?"

"Nothing. I was just talking to a kid who does some work for me. He's not an informant, although there are a couple of informants I probably ought to be talking to." My friend Danny Boy Bell, for instance. "He found an eyewitness to the shooting, or at least to its aftermath. Is that a break in the case? Probably not. I'll have to find out just what she saw, or thinks she saw, and make some estimate of her reliability.''

"It's a woman, then?''

"Not exactly. Whatever I get from the eyewitness, it'll probably be less of a revelation than what I learned this morning at Waddell & Yount.''

"You mentioned you were there. You didn't say what you found out.''

And that took the allotted twenty minutes, and five or ten more in the bargain. I recounted most of what I'd got from Eleanor Yount and checked it against what Lisa Holtzmann knew about her husband. I asked a lot of questions and filled a few pages in my notebook, and along the way she went back to the kitchen and freshened her drink. It seemed to me that its contents were a little darker this time around, but that may have been a trick of the lighting. We were starting to get that sunset.

Eventually I got up from the couch and told her it was time I was on my way. "I know,'' she said. "You're meeting Elaine at eight o'clock, and having dinner at the little place around the corner.''

"You were paying attention.''

"I offered you the privacy of the bedroom,'' she said. She let the line hang in the air for a moment, then said, "First you'll go back to your hotel to shower.'' She extended a hand, touched my cheek, ran her fingers upward against the grain. "You'll probably want to shave, too.''

"Probably.''

"I'm going to pull a chair over to the window and watch the sun go down. I wish I didn't have to do it alone.'' I didn't say anything, and she took my arm and walked me to the door. Her hip bumped against mine, and I could smell the scotch on her breath and the woodsy scent of her perfume.

In the doorway she said, "Call me if you find out anything I should know about."

"I will."

"Or just to talk," she said. "I get lonely."

16

Before I left my hotel, I slipped the deck of fifty hundred-dollar bills into the top drawer of my dresser. *That's the first place they'll look,* a little voice told me. That was fine, I decided. Let them find it right away instead of tearing up the whole place. I closed the drawer and went out to catch a cab to Elaine's.

Dinner wasn't a great success. The restaurant she picked was indeed a little place around the corner, a French bistro that called itself Chien Bizarre, its logo featuring a severely clipped and presumably deranged poodle. Elaine, a vegetarian, couldn't find anything on the menu that hadn't flown or swum or crept sometime in recent memory. This has happened before, and she is generally cheerful about it and orders a vegetable plate. On this occasion she wasn't cheerful about it, nor did her spirits brighten when I reminded her who had picked the restaurant. The waiter helped out by being deliberately obtuse when she explained what she wanted, and the kitchen overcooked the vegetables and then overcharged for them.

The service was slow, too, and neither of us was in a mood that fostered conversation. There were a lot of long silences. Sometimes that's fine. There's an AA group I go to occasionally structured along Quaker lines, with members speaking up when moved to do so. The silence is apt to stretch between speakers, and nobody gets nervous about it. The silence is considered a part of the meeting. Elaine and I have shared silences that enhance the conversation in much the same fashion.

Not this time. These were edgy silences, uncomfortable and disquieting. I tried not to look at my watch, but there were times when I couldn't help myself, and when she caught me at it the silence only deepened.

On the way home she said, "The one thing I'm glad of is that they're in the neighborhood. I'd hate for us to have spent cab fare on that meal."

"If they weren't in the neighborhood," I said, "we wouldn't have gone."

"That was supposed to be a joke," she said.

"Oh. Sorry."

The doorman that evening was an old Irishman who'd been with the building since V-J Day. "Evening, Miss Mardell," he said cheerily, his eyes not registering my presence.

"Evening, Tim," she said. "Lovely out, isn't it?"

"Ah, beautiful," he said.

In the elevator I said, "You know, the son of a bitch makes me feel invisible. Why doesn't he acknowledge my presence? Does he think you're trying to keep me a secret?"

"He's an old man," she said. "It's just the way he is."

"Everybody in the world's either too young to know better or too old to change," I said. "Have you noticed that?"

"As a matter of fact," she said, "I have."

There was a message on her machine. It was TJ, leaving a number for me to call. I told Elaine I should probably call him right away. Go ahead, she said.

I dialed the number and it was answered on the second ring. Someone with a throaty voice said, "How may I help you, dear?"

I asked for TJ. He came on the line and said, "Here's the deal, Lucille. Now's a good time to come on down and see us."

I glanced at Elaine. She was sitting in the black-and-white wing chair, making faces at the clothes in the Lands' End catalog. I covered the mouthpiece and said, "It's TJ."

"Isn't that who you called?"

"He's managed to track down a witness. I probably ought to run over there and question her before she lights out again."

"So? You're going, right?"

"Well, we had plans."

"I guess we'd better change them, wouldn't you say?"

"Let me have the address," I said to TJ.

"Four eighty-eight West Eighteenth, 'tween Ninth and Tenth. No name on the buzzer, but you ring number forty-two. It's up on the top floor."

"I'll be there in a few minutes."

"We be waitin', Dayton. Oh, 'fore I forget." His voice dropped. "What I told her, I said there be a couple dollars in it for her. Was that cool?"

"No problem."

"Because I know we on a tight budget."

"It's a little looser than it was," I said. "We got another client."

I hung up and got my topcoat from the front closet. Elaine asked me about my new client.

"Lisa Holtzmann," I said.

"Oh?"

"Glenn was sneakier than we thought. He bought that apartment of theirs for cash."

"Where did he get the cash?"

"That's one of the things she wants me to find out," I said.

"So you've got two clients now."

"Right."

"And a witness. Things are really looking up."

"I guess. I don't know how long I'll be."

"Where do you have to go?"

"Chelsea. I shouldn't be gone much more than an hour."

"And then you're planning to come back here?"

"That was the idea, yes."

"Oh," she said.

"Is something wrong?"

She was still holding the Lands' End catalog. She threw it down and said, "We got off on the wrong foot tonight. I don't know why. It's probably my fault. But at this point it's impossible to get back on track. You'll rush through the examination of this witness because you'll feel you have to get home to me, and you'll resent me for it—"

"No I won't."

"—and I'll be pissed at you for staying out late, or for coming home with an attitude. And you're really into your work right now, and there are probably other things you'd like to be doing tonight, after you get done with the witness. Am I right?"

"I probably ought to talk to Danny Boy," I admitted.

"Among others. But all of that can wait."

"Why should it? Because we're having so much fun together? Call me in the morning. How's that?"

I told her it was fine.

*   *   *

The address TJ had given me turned out to be a red-brick tenement three doors from the corner of Tenth Avenue. When I'd climbed four flights of stairs TJ called down, "One more, my man. You can do it, Prewitt."

The two of them were waiting in the doorway of a rear apartment on the top floor. TJ was beaming with a sort of self-conscious pride. He said, "Julia, like for you to meet Matthew Scudder, man I work for, man I told you about. Matt, this here is Julia."

"Matthew," she said, extending her hand. "It's so lovely of you to come. Won't you step inside?"

She led me into a room that had been done to a turn. The wide-board pine floors, sanded and painted and polyurethaned, were a rich scarlet. The walls were a pale lemon yellow, and so thickly hung with art that little of their color showed through. The artwork had been professionally matted and framed, and ranged from drawings and engravings a few inches square to a signed Keith Haring poster, and, over the daybed, a poster for the film *Paris Is Burning*. The lighting was indirect, supplied by a variety of floor and table lamps, including two with black panther bases and several with leaded-glass shades. Beaded curtains screened a Pullman kitchen and the doorway to the bathroom. Many of the beads were faceted glass, and sparkled like diamonds.

"It's much," she said, "but it's home. Won't you have a seat, Matthew? I think you'll find that chair comfortable. And I think I'm going to have a glass of sherry. May I bring you one?"

"No, thank you."

"He don't drink," TJ said. "Told you that."

"I know you did," Julia said, "but it's only polite to offer. I also have Coke, Matthew. That's Coca-Cola, of course."

"That would be fine."

"Over ice? With a twist of lemon peel?"

She fixed it for me, and sherry for herself. TJ already had a Coke, but without the lemon twist. She seated herself on the daybed, folded her legs under her, and patted the place beside her. When TJ didn't respond she gave him a look and patted the daybed again. He sat down.

She was quite an exotic creature, with tawny skin that glowed as if lit from within. She had small ears, a long narrow nose, a full red-lipped mouth. Her eyes and high cheekbones lent a faintly Eurasian cast to her features. Her cheeks were downy, providing no sign that she'd ever had to shave. Her hair, cut à la Sassoon, was a streaky blond, quite becoming if genetically improbable. She was slender, and stood about five-eight, with most of her height in her legs. The harem pajamas she wore showed off her figure, full in the bust, slim at the waist, very trim in the rear. She wore lipstick and nail polish and dangly earrings and beaded slippers, and she looked entirely elegant.

I said the first thing that came into my mind. "You'd fool anyone," I said.

"Thank you."

"Your name is Julia?"

"It was Julio," she said, giving it the Spanish pronunciation. "I used to be a male Hispanic. Now I'm a female of undetermined origin."

"How long have you been living as a woman?"

"Five years, in the sense you mean. All my life, in another sense."

"Have you had the surgery?"

"*The* surgery? I've had several surgeries. I'll have more. But I haven't had *the* surgery."

"I see."

"I've had facial surgery and breast enhancement." She cupped her breasts. "Silicone completed what hormone treatments began. I've had a couple of moles removed. My next surgery, when I've raised the money and got up the courage, will be right here.'' She touched a finger to her throat. ''They shave the Adam's apple. It's a dead giveaway, but they can reduce it dramatically. It's scary, though, to think of them cutting there. But I think it's worth it, and you won't even be able to see the scar.'' She sipped the amber sherry. ''And it's not as nervous-making as *the* surgery.''

''I can imagine.''

She laughed. ''Well, I guess you *can*,'' she said. ''And there's something so irreversible about it. You can't go and tell the doctor you changed your mind, please sew them back on. Look at TJ, it makes him squirm when I even talk about it.''

''Don't bother me none,'' he said.

''Oh, is that right? Matthew, don't you agree that TJ would make a lovely girl?''

''Stop that.''

''I thought it didn't bother you? See, TJ's a good height, not ridiculously tall like some TS's. A little broad in the shoulders, but we can work with that.'' She turned to him and put a hand on his chest. ''You'll love it, TJ,'' she said. ''We can be girls together. We can play with each other's titties, we can rub pussies.''

''Why you gotta talk like that?''

''I'm sorry,'' she said. ''You're right. It's not lady-like.''

''Just stop that shit.''

I said, ''Julia, I understand you were on the street the night Glenn Holtzmann was shot.''

''Getting down to business, are we?''

''I think we'd better.''

She sighed. ''Men,'' she said. ''Always rushing through foreplay. What's the *hurry*? Why not take time to smell the, uh, flowers?'' When I hesitated she laughed throatily and leaned over to pat me companionably on the knee. "Forgive me," she said. "Sometimes I work a little too hard at being outrageous. Yes, I was there."

"What exactly did you see?"

"I saw Glenn."

"Did you know him?"

"No. Oh, because I called him by name just now? Well, the man's dead, so why be formal? But no, I never met him."

"Had you seen him before that night?"

"On the street, you mean? I don't think so. Have you spent much time yourself on Eleventh Avenue? Because I don't think I've seen you there."

"I **live** nearby," I said, "but I haven't been there much, no."

"Nobody has. There's not much pedestrian traffic, not of the sauntering sort. Except for those of us with something to sell. Prospective buyers rarely show up on foot. They're apt to be in cars. Or vans, but you're taking your life in your hands getting into a van. I paid entirely too much for these tits to let some psychopath cut them off. That actually happened to a girl on the East Side last year. You probably read about it."

"Yes."

"He was walking," she said. "Glenn. An attractive man, nicely dressed. At first I took him for a john, but he wasn't looking at the girls. Even the shy types, the ones scared to come up to you or say anything, they'll look. They may be sneaking peeks rather than staring, but at least they're looking at you."

"And he wasn't."

"No. Which suggested that he wasn't interested in *moi,* which in turn diminished my interest in him. I had a living to earn and I put my mind to that and didn't pay him any more attention. Then I happened to look over there, and he was on the phone."

"I don't suppose you noticed the time."

"Please," she said. "I know it was night because it was dark out."

"Got it."

"Then I got a date," she said. "A gentleman I've dated before, although I wouldn't call him a regular. Drives a Volvo station wagon with Jersey plates. One of your secret swingers. We went around the corner and parked." She put her index finger in her mouth and sucked on it, her eyes on me all the while. "It didn't take long," she said.

I glanced at TJ. His face was as expressionless as he could make it.

"Then," she said, "I was back in my usual spot. Let's see now. I was on the opposite side of the avenue from him, and closer to the corner of Fifty-fourth Street. He was at the corner of Fifty-fifth, in front of the Honda showroom. Did I see him then? I don't think so. I don't believe I had any reason to look over there."

"And?"

"And right about then a car pulled up and a man rolled down the window and we entered into a discussion. Before long we broke off negotiations, but while they were still ongoing someone fired a gun."

"Across the street."

"That's what it sounded like, but I couldn't tell for sure. I couldn't be positive it was gunfire, although that's what I took it to be."

"How many shots?"

"Three, but I know that from the news. I wasn't counting at the time. In fact I wasn't paying attention, I was busy with negotiations that were fast breaking down. This admirer of mine wanted to fuck me without benefit of condom. 'I'm not worried,' he said. 'I can tell you're clean and healthy.' Right, and determined to stay that way, thank you very much. So I had more on my mind than gunshots. Then we agreed to disagree, and I stepped back and he drove off, and just then there was a fourth shot.''

''How long between the third and fourth shot?''

''I don't know. What went through my mind when I heard the fourth shot was something along the lines of, oh, right, there were shots before. They had registered, but I wasn't thinking about them.''

''What did you do?''

''Looked toward the sound of the shot. But the car was still in front of me when the shot rang out, and then there was other traffic on the avenue that blocked my view of the corner. By the time I could see over there, all I saw was Glenn lying on the sidewalk. Except I didn't know it was him.''

''Because you hadn't heard his name yet.''

''No, I didn't even know it was the gentleman I'd seen earlier, because he was lying facedown and could have been anybody. For all I knew, the man I'd seen before had gone home while I was trying to talk business with Mr. Machismo. Later on, of course, I saw his picture in the paper, and then I knew I'd seen him. But at the time the only person I recognized was George.''

''George Sadecki, but you wouldn't have known him either, would you? Until you saw him in the paper, or on TV.''

She shook her head. ''I used to see George all the time,'' she said. ''I was afraid of him at first, the way he would stare at you, but everybody said, oh, that's George, he's harmless. So I would say hello to him when I saw him. 'Hi, George!' But he never answered.''

''And you saw him the night of the shooting?''

''Bending over the body.''

''Was that the first time you'd seen him that night?''

''No idea. You have to remember that George was part of the scenery. There was no reason to remember seeing him, or to distinguish one sighting from another.

I could have seen him earlier, or I might not have seen him for the past week. Did I see him and Glenn together? No, not until after the shooting.''

"And he was bending over the body? What did you think he was doing?''

"I couldn't tell. Possibly checking to see if the man was alive or dead. Possibly going for his wallet.''

"Did you assume he had shot Holtzmann?''

"No, because I saw right away it was George, and I was used to thinking of him as harmless.''

"You didn't know that he carried a gun.''

"No one ever mentioned it, and he certainly never showed it to me.''

"You didn't see a gun in his hand when he was leaning over the body.''

"No, but I was at a distance. I was wearing my contacts but even so I don't think I could have seen if he was holding something. But my impression is he had both his hands free.''

I went back and forth over it with her without getting a whole lot more than that. She was clearer about what she had seen than I had feared she might be, but she'd missed the shooting itself. If her testimony made the hypothesis of George's innocence a little more plausible, that was about all it did. It certainly didn't offer a clue as to the killer's identity.

I asked about other possible witnesses.

"I don't know,'' she said. "That street doesn't really come into its own until midnight, and the real action is between two and four-thirty in the morning. A lot of the johns like to do their drinking first. The bars close at four, and a half hour after that everybody goes home, or to an after-hours.''

"You were out there early.''

"I like it early. The early mongoose gets the cobra, as our dusky sisters from the subcontinent like to say.

Fewer johns, but less competition. Not that I have anything to fear from competition.'' She shot me a sidelong
glance. ''More to the point, I'd rather have my dates
before they get all liquored up. Married men. You're not
married, are you? You're not wearing a ring.''

''I'm not, no.''

''But TJ says you've got somebody.''

''Yes.''

She sighed. ''All the good men are taken. What was
I saying? Oh, yes, about getting an early start. I like to
go out early and have my dates and close the store as
soon as I can afford to. That gives me the rest of the
night to be me. But first I have to take care of business.
Speaking of which—''

''Yes?''

''Well, I hate to bring it up, but TJ did say I'd be
reimbursed for my time.'' I found a pair of fifties in my
wallet. She made a show of tucking them into the neck-
line of the harem pajamas. ''Thank you,'' she said. ''It
seems tacky to take money for sitting around and having
a conversation, but you wouldn't believe what those
doctors charge, and Blue Cross won't pick up any of it.
If I had Blue Cross in the first place, which I don't.''
She touched her Adam's apple. ''Pretty soon,'' she said,
''I'll have this little flaw corrected, and you'll have the
satisfaction of having contributed. But I'm sure your
work is full of satisfactions.''

''Not so full as you might think.''

''Oh, you're too modest,'' she said. ''I think I'll be
able to have the apple peeled by Christmas. As for
this''—she patted herself between the legs—''I'm just
not sure. You know, every man I go with wants to know
when I'm going to have it done. Like then I'll be a real
woman, and ever so much more desirable.''

''And?''

''And nine out of ten of them can't keep their hands

off it. If it's so loathsome, if it's something they want to have nothing to do with, why do they want to be touching it while I'm doing them? And they don't just want to touch. They want to elicit a response. They want it in their mouth, however inexpert their performance. They want it everywhere you could imagine.'' She looked at her wineglass and set it down when she saw it was empty. "These are straight men," she said. "Most of them are wearing wedding rings. They wouldn't even accept oral sex from another male, let alone perform it. But they see me as a woman and that liberates them. It sets them free to enjoy themselves with my cock." She shrugged. "If it's such a prize," she said, "maybe I ought to keep it."

We established that there was no question of her testifying, in or out of court. "I couldn't," she said, "because I was home alone that night, watching *A Star Is Born* and gorging on microwave popcorn. I'm serious. There are pimps out there who'd just love to have a reason to do a number on a girl who works independent. Just talk to a cop, tell him how sweet he looks in his uniform, and somebody might decide to teach you a lesson. No way I sit down with anybody official.''

I finished my Coke and said it was time I got going.

"Well, now that you know how to get here," she said, "I hope you'll come back. Are you running off too, TJ? He's sweet, isn't he, Matthew? It's so much fun to tease this child. I just wish he was a little lighter-skinned so I could see him blush. I can tell when he's blushing but I'd like to be able to see it.''

She went up to TJ and put her arms around him. She was an inch or two taller. She pressed up against him and whispered something in his ear, then released him and danced, laughing, to the door.

I followed him down the five flights, neither of us

saying a word. Outside I said I wanted to get some coffee. We walked to Tenth Avenue but I didn't see anything open outside of a couple of ginmills. We walked back to Ninth and found a Cuban-Chinese joint with one lone customer at the counter. We took a table and I ordered *café con leche*. TJ said he'd have a glass of milk.

"That there was Julia," he said.

"I'd have thought you were old friends," I said, "the way she was acting."

"Yeah, well, she the type makes friends in a hurry, Murray. She pretty weird, huh?"

"I liked her."

"Yeah?"

"Uh-huh."

"Pretty good witness, anyway."

"Very good," I said. "She didn't see everything, but she was very clear on the part she saw. You did good work finding her."

"Yeah, well, just part of the service, Jervis."

"Something the matter, TJ?"

"No, everything cool."

We fell silent. The waiter, walking as though his feet were killing him, brought TJ's milk and my coffee.

I said, "There is one other thing you might be able to help me with."

"Say what?"

"I need a gun."

His eyes widened, but only for an instant. "What kind?"

"Revolver'd be best."

"Caliber?"

"Thirty-eight or thereabouts."

"Box of shells with it?"

"Just so it's loaded."

He thought about it. "Cost a few dollars," he said.

"How much do you figure?"

"Dunno. Never bought no gun before." He drank some milk, wiped his mouth with the back of his hand, used a paper napkin to wipe his hand. "I know two, three dudes got shit to sell. Won't be no problem. Say a hundred, somethin' like that?"

I counted out bills, palmed them to him. He dropped his hand into his lap so it wasn't visible from the street and fanned the bills, then looked quizzically across at me. "Three hundred," I said. "A hundred's for the work you've done so far, just to keep us current. The rest is for the gun. It may cost more than you think. Whatever it costs, you can keep the difference."

"That's cool."

"Something's bothering you," I said. "If you don't feel you're getting paid enough, let me know about it."

"Shit," he said. "That ain't it."

"All right."

"You want to know what it is? It's that Julia, man."

"Oh."

"I mean, what is she? She a man or a woman?"

"Well, we keep saying 'she.' We wouldn't do that if we didn't think of her as female."

"She ain't like no dude I ever met."

"No."

"Don't look like none, either. See her on the street, you never 'spect she anything but a woman."

"You wouldn't."

"Even up close you wouldn't. Lot of 'em, you can tell right away, but she'd fool you."

"I agree."

"Say a dude goes with her, what do that make him?"

"Probably make him happy."

"Be serious, man. Would it make him gay?"

"I don't know."

"If you was gay," he said, "then you be wantin'

men, right? So why'd you be lookin' to get down with someone looks like a woman?''

"You wouldn't."

"But if you wanted a woman," he went on, "why would you pick one's got a dick on her?"

"Beats me."

"And why'd she say that shit about how I'd make a good girl?" He held his hands in front of his chest as if cupping breasts and frowned down at them. "Crazy damn thing to say to me," he said.

"She just gets a kick out of being outrageous."

"Yeah, well, she good at it. You ever been with somebody like her?"

"No."

"Would you?"

"I don't know."

"You with Elaine now, but if you wasn't—"

"I don't know."

"You know what she said to me, whisperin' in my ear like she did?"

"She said to come back once you got rid of me."

"You heard her, huh?"

"Just a guess."

"Pretty good guess, Bess. Place is nice, way she got it all fixed up. Never seen no red floor before, 'less it was linoleum."

"No."

"All them pictures. Take you days to look at 'em all."

"Are you going back?"

"Thinkin' on it. Bitch's got me all mixed up. I don't know what I want to do, you know what I mean?"

"I know what you mean."

"If I go I gone feel weird, and if I don't go I gone feel weird. You know?" He shook his head, clucked his tongue, sighed heavily. "Maybe I scared," he said. "Scared of what I apt to find there."

"And if you don't look?"

He grinned suddenly. "Scared what I might miss."

I found Danny Boy at Poogan's, a regular spot of his on West Seventy-second Street. He was at his usual table, with an iced bottle of vodka alongside. He had his right leg folded so that the foot was propped up on his left knee, and he was studying his shoe. It was a half-boot, actually, beige in color, with a slight heel.

"I don't know about this," he said. "You recognize the leather?"

"Ostrich, isn't it?"

"It is," he said, "and that's what bothers me. Ever see an ostrich?"

"Years ago at the zoo."

"I've only seen them on Channel Thirteen. *Nature.* *National Geographic* specials. Spectacular creatures. Can't fly, but they can run like hell. Imagine killing something like that just so you can skin it and make boots."

"I understand they're doing remarkable things these days with Naugahyde."

"It's not the killing that bothers me," he said. "It's the waste. All they use is the outside, for God's sake. It'd be different if they ate the meat, but it can't be very tasty or they'd have it on the menu all over town."

"Ostrich piccata," I suggested.

"I was thinking of Ostrich Wellington. But you follow me, don't you? I have this vision of the flayed corpses of ostriches rotting by the thousands, like buffalo on the Great Plains."

"Victims of rapacious ostrich skinners," I said.

"Led by the legendary Ostrich Bill Cody. Don't you agree with me that it's wasteful?"

"I suppose so. They're good-looking boots."

"Thank you. Long-wearing, they tell me. Makes a great leather, ostrich. And maybe it's a good thing we kill them for their hides. Otherwise I suppose we'd be up to here in ostriches. They'd be worse than rats. God knows they're bigger."

"Probably run faster, too."

"They'd ruin Jones Beach," he said. "Be no place to put your towel. Every few yards you've got another fucking ostrich with his head in the sand."

Maybe he'd seen Jones Beach on Channel Thirteen. It was a sure bet he'd never been there. Danny Boy Bell, short in stature and elegant in dress, is the albino son of black parents, and he is no more apt than Dracula to venture out in daylight. At night you can find him at Poogan's or Mother Goose, drinking Stoly or Finlandia and brokering information. In the daytime you can't find him at all.

I asked him what he'd heard about Glenn Holtzmann. Nothing, he said. All he knew was what he read in the papers, a story of an innocent victim, an armed derelict, and crime-ridden streets. I let out that it might not have happened that way, and that the deceased had handled a lot of cash for someone who got paid by check.

"Ah," Danny Boy said. "Lived life off the books, did he? I never heard a word."

"Maybe you could ask around."

"Maybe I could. And how's *your* life, Matthew? How

is the beautiful Elaine, and when are you going to make
an honest woman of her?''

"Gee, I was going to ask you that, Danny Boy," I
said. "You're the man with all the answers."

I took a couple of cabs and dropped in on a couple
of other people who kept their ears open as assiduously
as Danny Boy. They didn't dress as well or run as en-
gaging a line of small talk, but sometimes they heard
things and that made them worth a visit.

By the time I was finished it was past midnight and I
was at the counter at Tiffany's, not the jeweler on Fifth
Avenue but the all-night coffee shop on Sheridan
Square. There's a midnight meeting a short walk from
there on Houston Street, in premises occupied for years
by the Village's most notorious after-hours club. I
thought about dropping in, but I'd already missed half
the meeting. They had a two A.M. meeting, too, but I
didn't want to stay up that late.

Too late to call Elaine.

Much too late to call Tom Sadecki, although it was
time I let him hear from me. What had originally looked
a lot like tilting at windmills was turning out to be a
halfway rational mission. The more I thought about it,
the more persuaded I was that George Sadecki was innocent of Glenn Holtzmann's murder.

With a little luck I'd be able to prove it. If I turned
over Holtzmann's life I'd find someone with a motive,
and that's half the battle, as often as not. Once you know
who did it all you need to do is prove it, and I didn't
need enough proof to get a conviction in a court of law.
I just had to persuade people in a position to get the
charges dropped. Then George could go back to his
life's work of being a danger to himself and a nuisance
to others.

I ordered another cup of coffee. A man and woman

got up from a front booth and went to the cashier's desk. The man gave me a nod. I waved back. I recognized him from the Perry Street meeting a few blocks away. I went there sometimes when I was in the neighborhood.

Maybe we ought to move down here, I thought. I'd certainly spent enough time in the Village, working a long hitch out of the Sixth Precinct. That's where I'd been when Elaine and I first met, all those years ago.

The neighborhood had gone through changes since then, but all in all it had changed less than the rest of the city. Much of it was an official historic district, its buildings protected as landmarks. There were fewer high-rises, and the crooked streets with their three-story Federal houses were on a more human scale than her present neighborhood, or mine. I'd have plenty of meetings to choose from, Elaine could walk to classes at NYU or the New School, and the SoHo art galleries were ten minutes away.

Was that what I wanted to do?

I knew what I wanted to do.

"It's Matt," I told her machine. "It's late but I, uh, felt like talking if you were awake. I'll call you in the morning."

She picked up. "Hello," she said.

"It's late."

"It's not that late."

"I hope I didn't wake you."

"No, and it wouldn't matter if you did. I was hoping you'd call."

"Oh?"

"Yes."

"I was thinking," I said.

"Oh?"

"I was wondering if you felt like company. But I guess it's too late."

"No," she said. "It's not that late."

*   *   *

My cab took Eighth Avenue uptown, turned left at Fifty-seventh, caught a red light at Ninth just past the entrance to my hotel. In my mind I heard myself tell the driver that this was fine, that I'd get off here. But the words remained unspoken and the light changed and we went another block west. He made an illegal but not uncommon U-turn and dropped me at my destination.

The lobby attendant, so suspicious the night before, smiled in recognition this time. He called upstairs anyway, then smiled again and motioned to the elevator. On Twenty-eight, her door opened to my knock. She closed the door after me and put the chain on, then turned to give me a long look from those deep blue eyes.

She was wearing a robe, dark green with yellow piping. Under it was a nightgown of some sort, something pinky and filmy. Her feet were bare.

I could smell her perfume, or thought I could. Hard to tell. I'd been smelling it all the way up in the cab.

She said something and I said something, but I don't remember our lines. Then I said something about its being a restless night, and she said she thought maybe the moon was full and went over to the window to look for it.

I followed her there and stood behind her. I didn't notice the moon. I wasn't looking for the moon. Not literally, anyway.

I put my hands on her shoulders. She sighed and leaned back against me. I felt the warmth of her body through the robe. She turned in my arms and looked up at me, her mouth slack, her eyes enormous. I gazed into them, scared of what I might find.

And kissed her, scared of what I might miss.

Afterward I lay there, feeling the sweat cooling on my skin, listening to the beating of my own heart. I felt gloriously, joyously alive, and at once filled to overflowing with sorrow and regret.

I said, "I'd better be going."

"Why?"

"It's late."

"You said that when you called," she said, "and you said that when you got here."

"It's getting truer by the minute. And I've got a lot to do tomorrow."

"You could stay here."

"I don't think so."

"Why not? I'd let you sleep."

"Would you?"

"A little, anyway." She was lying on her back, her hands folded on her flat stomach, her eyes pointed at the ceiling. There was a faint sheen of perspiration on her upper lip. The silence stretched, and she broke it to say, "I like Elaine very much."

"Oh?"

"I do."

I was propped up on an elbow, looking down at her. "So do I," I said.

"I know that, and—"

"I love Elaine," I said. "Elaine and I belong to each other. None of this has anything to do with me and Elaine. It doesn't affect us."

"Then what are you doing here, Matt?"

"I don't know."

"You called me, didn't you? That was you on the phone, wasn't it?"

"Yes."

"So what's this all about? Is it all just part of the service? 'Excuse me, honey, I hate to eat and run, but I've got to go fuck the client.'"

"Cut it out."

" 'She's a widow, and you know how they get. The poor thing's probably dying for it.' "

"And where would I get an idea like that?"

She looked at me.

"You didn't want me to leave this afternoon," I said. "You wanted help watching the sunset."

"I was lonely."

"And that's all?"

"No. No, I was attracted to you. And I knew you were attracted to me, at least I was pretty sure you were. And I wanted this to happen."

"And it did."

"And it did. And now you wish I would turn into a pumpkin. Or a pizza, or a puff of smoke. Because you love Elaine."

I didn't say anything.

"Believe me," she said. "I don't want to complicate your life. I don't want to wear your ring or bear your children. I don't even want flowers. I'd like you to go on being the detective I hired you to be, and I'd like for you to be my friend."

"That's easy."

"Is it?"

"Uh-huh. Except that there's a potential for conflict between the two roles."

"What do you mean?"

"A detective can't help taking note when you tell a lie. A friend is supposed to overlook it."

"When did I tell you a lie?"

"Well, it was a pretty fair-skinned lie. When I called, you said you'd been awake. But you had already retired for the night."

"What makes you say that?"

"You can't fool the Great Detective," I said. "When I showed up you were wearing a robe and a nightgown."

"So I must have been sleeping when you called."

"Right."

"In the nightgown, and when I got up I put on the robe."

"Right again."

"When you called," she said, "I was sitting in the living room watching *The Fabulous Baker Boys* on HBO. I was wearing what you saw me in this afternoon."

"Tan slacks and a green turtleneck."

"Exactly. When I finished talking to you I turned off the TV and took off all my clothes. I dabbed on a little more perfume, freshened my makeup, and put on the nightie and the robe."

"Oh."

"Which probably makes me a slut, but who cares? I don't." She took my hand in both of hers. "Come back to bed, Great Detective. We'll search for clues."

It was well after four when I left. The bars were closed, and I was just as glad.

I walked home across Fifty-seventh Street, feeling too many things all at once even to take note of what they were. Rather than sort out the signals, I just wanted to turn off the set.

I went straight to my room without even stopping at the desk, got out of my clothes and under the shower. Sometimes there's no hot water at that hour but this time there was plenty and I must have used most of it.

I dried myself off and went straight to bed. I had a long list of things to think about but I was too tired to start. I closed my eyes and put my head on the pillow and I was gone.

I did manage to set my clock first, and it jarred me loose from a dream at half past nine. By the time I had the alarm shut off, the dream was completely gone. All I could recall was that there had been a lot of people in the room with me, and that I didn't have any clothes on.

I took another shower and shaved and got dressed. On my way out I stopped at the desk for the messages I hadn't picked up earlier, and there weren't any. I thought that was odd, and I had one foot out the door before I realized I had never turned off Call Forwarding after I'd left Elaine's. I had gone straight down to Chelsea, and never returned to the hotel until just before dawn.

I went upstairs and did what you had to do. I thought about calling Elaine to check for messages, but if there'd been anything crucial she would have called the hotel desk directly. She'd done just that in the past, when I'd been similarly forgetful.

Besides, she was probably toning her muscles at the gym. And if not, well, I didn't feel quite ready to talk to her yet.

I had plenty to do. I grabbed a quick breakfast around the corner, took the subway downtown to Chambers Street, and made the rounds of various city and state offices. I learned a few things about Glenn Holtzmann, the most interesting having to do with the ownership of the apartment where I had just committed what certainly felt like adultery. The original owner was a corporation called MultiCircle Productions, which had purchased the unit three years ago from the builder. MultiCircle had evidently lost it to foreclosure, because Glenn Holtzmann had acquired it a year and a half ago from an outfit called US Asset Reduction Corp. They deeded it to him on the thirteenth of April, a month before he and Lisa were married.

That was before he'd proposed to her, and in order to close on that date he'd have had to enter negotiations before he even met the girl, which seemed odd. Maybe he fell for her because he already had a place for them to live. And maybe he bought it because the deal was too good to turn down, but what *was* the deal? I couldn't find out what he'd paid for it. That was supposed to be a matter of record, but I couldn't find the record.

Around four I used a phone and caught Joe Durkin at his desk. I said, "You know, it's the damnedest thing. I'm right around the corner from One Police Plaza and I don't know a soul well enough to ask a favor."

"So you called me."

"I did. One quick question, won't take a minute."

"Of my valuable time."

"Of your valuable time. Did Glenn Holtzmann have a record?"

"Jesus Christ on stilts. What the hell are you jerking yourself off with now?"

"Did he?"

"Of course not."

"You know that for a fact? Your own personal knowledge?"

"Come on, Matt. You don't think somebody would have checked? Case generated more heat than anything since the Lindbergh kidnapping. You know how many people we had on it?"

"Each of them assuming somebody else did the obvious thing."

"Come on."

"Humor me," I said. "What does it hurt to check?"

"What good could it do? Especially at this stage. I swear I can't figure out why you're still screwing around with this piece of shit. What's the point?"

"Take you twenty seconds. You just punch it up on your computer. It'll tell you straight out and then we'll both know."

"All it ever tells me straight out is Invalid Request, or else it tells me Access Not Authorized. You're lucky you got out before these fuckers came in. The worst thing about it is the way kids fresh out of cop school pick it all up in about a minute and a half. Makes me feel like a fucking dinosaur. . . . Shit . . . Okay, here we go. No record. What a surprise.''

"You're sure?''

"Yeah, I'm sure, at least as far as felony and misdemeanor arrests are concerned. Maybe he ran a red light once. Maybe he was a scofflaw, had a lot of unpaid parking tickets. I wouldn't fucking know, and don't tell me to get my computer to talk to the computer at the Parking Violations Bureau, because I don't want to.''

"He didn't have a car.''

"He could have rented one. You can get a traffic ticket in a rented car.''

"Actually,'' I said, "I don't really care about traffic tickets.''

"I don't care about any of this. Seriously, what's the matter with you? Why are you still pursuing this?''

"Joe, I've been on it less than a week.''

"So? Look, I gotta go. Call me some day when you're done playing with yourself, you can take me out and buy me a hamburger.''

I bought myself a cup of coffee and wondered what had him in such a fierce mood. If I was starting with the victim, a perfectly traditional approach, why wouldn't I want to make certain that the victim didn't have an arrest record? It was more than odds-on that somebody would have checked, but why wouldn't I double-check? And where did he get off being astonished, even contemptuous, of the fact that I was still on the case?

It had been Saturday afternoon when I sat across a table from Tom Sadecki and took a thousand dollars from him. It was Thursday now. I had been on it four days. I didn't get it.

That reminded me, though, that I'd been planning on calling my client. I checked my notebook and tried him at the store. A woman answered, and called him to the phone without asking my name.

I said, "Tom, it's Matt Scudder. It occurred to me that I ought to be giving you a progress report."

"What do you mean?"

"Just that I was reluctant to take the case initially, but now it's beginning to look as though there's a very real possibility your brother is innocent. I don't have anything to take to the D.A., but I feel a hundred percent more hopeful than I did Saturday."

"You do, huh."

"Definitely," I said, "and I figured you would want to know about it."

There was a lengthy pause. Then he said, "First thing I thought, I thought this is your idea of a joke. But how could you possibly think it was funny? Next thing, and it's interesting how a person's mind works, next thing I thought is Jesus, the son of a bitch isn't sober, he's been sneaking drinks all along, and it's made him nuts and that explains it. The thought just flashed through my mind, it was that sudden."

"I don't know what you're talking about, Tom."

"You don't," he said. "You really don't. It was on the late news last night and it was in all the papers this morning, but I guess you didn't look at the news or read the paper."

I felt sick. "Tell me," I said.

"George," he said. "My brother George. They transferred him, Bellevue back to Rikers. Last night somebody stuck a knife in him, the poor bastard. He's dead. My brother George is dead."

18

"Tom," I said, "I'm sorry. I'm terribly sorry."

"Yeah, I know you are. First I heard, I got a call from my sister last night, she seen it on Channel Four. We weren't officially notified for another half hour. You imagine that?"

"What happened?"

"Aw, Jesus. Another guy, an inmate there. Also in Bellevue, where he and George had an argument. Then this guy's returned to the psychiatric wing or block or whatever they call it at Rikers, and a day or two later so is George. And the guy goes for him and stabs him."

"That's awful."

"Get this. Guy's in a wheelchair."

"The man who—"

"Yeah, the guy who stabs him. Paralyzed from the waist down, can't wiggle his fucking toes but he can stab George. Not the first time, either. He's in there for stabbing his mother. Difference is she lived."

"How'd he get the knife?"

"It was a scalpel. He stole it in Bellevue."

"He stole it in Bellevue and smuggled it back to Rikers Island?"

"Yeah, taped to the bottom of the wheelchair. And

he had tape wrapped around the base of the blade so it wouldn't be brittle. I mean, some of these people are crazy as a shithouse rat, but that don't make 'em stupid.''

"No."

"My sister said the oddest thing. 'Now I don't have to worry about him.' That he's getting enough to eat, that he's in trouble, that he's got someplace to sleep. Same as she said it was a relief having him locked up, now it's even more of a relief to have him dead. The thing is, I know what she means. He's safe now. Nobody can hurt him, and he can't hurt himself. And do you want to know something?''

"What, Tom?"

"He's gone less than a day, and already it's changed how I remember him. My grandmother on my mother's side got Alzheimer's. By the time she finally died she was this pathetic creature. You know how they get.''

"Yes."

"We all told each other that the cruelest thing about it was the way it changed how we saw her. This was a strong woman, came over from the old country, raised five children, spoke four languages, cooked and cleaned like she had a black belt in housework, and all you saw was this woman drooling and wetting the bed and making noises that didn't even sound human.

"But then she died, and it had a magical effect, Matt, because overnight I remembered what she used to be like, and that was all I remembered. When I picture my grandmother now she's always in the kitchen wearing an apron and stirring something on the stove. I have to work at it to picture her in bed at the nursing home.

"And already it's starting to be the same way with George. These memories have been flooding in, things I haven't thought about in years. Before he went in the service, before he started to lose it. Back when we were boys together.''

After a moment he added, ''It's sad, though.''

''Yes.''

''What you were saying, that he might be innocent. What an irony, huh?''

''It seems like a real possibility.''

''My first reaction is to be angry about it. Like if they hadn't locked him up this wouldn't happen. But that's bullshit, isn't it? I mean, look how he died, stabbed to death by a guy in a wheelchair. That happens to you, you got to say it was meant to be. Fate, karma, God's will, whatever you want to call it, it was just plain in the cards.''

''I see what you mean.''

''You want to hear something'll make you sick? I got calls from two different lawyers telling me how I gotta bring suit against the city of New York. I've got a legitimate action for wrongful death, on account of there's my brother in their custody and he gets killed through no fault of his own. You see me suing the city over this? What do I do, claim loss of services? And how do they figure what his life was worth, add up the cans and bottles he might have redeemed over the remainder of his anticipated lifespan?''

''Everybody sues nowadays.''

''Tell me about it. I had a customer last year—well, the hell with that. Put it this way, average American gets hit by lightning, 'stead of giving thanks he lived through it, he runs to his lawyer and sues God. I don't want to live that way.''

''I don't blame you.''

''Anyway,'' he said, ''I want to thank you for taking a shot at it. If I owe you anything on top of what I already gave you, just let me know and I'll send you a check.''

"No question of that. And if I find out anything further—"

"Why would you? My brother's dead. Case closed, right?"

"I'm sure that would be the official view."

"Be my view, too, Matt. Far as trying to clear his name, what's the point? Wherever he is now, it can't make a bit of difference to him. He's at peace now, God bless him."

I called Joe right away. Before he could say anything I said, "Don't start. I just now found out that Sadecki got killed last night."

"You must have been the last man in the city to get the news."

"I slept late and didn't buy a paper. I read the headlines on the run but the story didn't make the front pages. Everybody's giving top billing to the senator and his bimbo. I wondered why you were so steamed before."

"And I wondered why you were beating a dead horse. Or giving it mouth-to-mouth resuscitation."

"There's a charming image."

"Yeah, well, I'm a charming guy."

"I don't know anything more than what I just got from my client. I gather another prisoner did it."

"Another nut case, in there for attempting to do his own mother. Confined to a wheelchair—I hope you got that part."

"I did."

"That's the best part," he said. "I was editing the *Post,* God forbid, I'd bump the senator's secret nookie and spread the wheelchair across page one. He's a skinny kid, too, looks like a bank teller, but I guess he's a resourceful son of a bitch. Wheelchair, shit, he'd be a menace in a full-body cast."

"No question he did it?"

"None whatsoever. He did it in front of guards, for Chrissake. Makes 'em look stupid, something like that goes down in front of their noses, but what are you gonna do? Fucker was quick as a cobra."

"Why did he do it, do they happen to know?"

"Why does anybody do anything? He and George evidently got into it a little at Bellevue. Maybe George said something about Gunther's mother, something really nasty like she wasn't worth killing."

"That's his name? Gunther?"

"Gunther Bauer, from a good German family in Ridgewood. Here you got two guys, one kills the other, and they're both of European extraction. How often does that happen? It's like seeing two white kids facing each other in the ring."

"You see that."

"Yeah, on cable, and the fight's taking place in the veterans' hall in Bismarck, North Dakota. Does that cover it, Matt? Because I'm kind of busy here."

"I've got one more question," I said, "but I'm afraid you'll get mad at me if I ask it."

"I probably will, but why don't you ask it anyway."

"Is there any chance at all that somebody could have set this guy up to take George out?"

"Like the CIA? Controlling him through the fillings in his teeth? Next I suppose they'll hit Gunther. You been watching a lot of Oliver Stone movies lately?"

"From what you've said, Gunther Bauer makes an unlikely Jack Ruby."

"I'd say so, yeah."

"But so did Jack Ruby. I'm just trying to rule it out, that's all."

"What are you looking to do, squeeze a few more dollars out of the brother? Get him to feed more quarters into the meter?"

"I've got another client."

"No shit. You wouldn't want to say who?"

"I can't."

"Interesting," he said. "I still think there's less to this than meets the eye, but I'll make a phone call. What the hell."

I walked for a long time. Over an hour, certainly. I wasn't really aware of the time, and hadn't been ever since I started the paper chase. There was something exhilarating about it, whether or not it yielded anything of substance.

And I couldn't tell what I had. There were pages of fresh notes in my notebook, data I'd run down and thoughts and fancies I'd wanted to commit to paper, but did they amount to anything?

And did it matter at all whether they did or not? George Sadecki was dead, and his brother was right, there was nothing more to be done. Clearing the poor bastard's name made as much sense as the efforts of those crackpots who spend their lives trying to restore the reputation of Richard the Third.

Of course I had another client. I had five thousand dollars of her money in the top drawer of my dresser— if indeed it was her money, and if indeed it was still where I'd left it. I was in no mood to take anything for granted.

I covered a few blocks just making certain in my mind that it had been Drew Kaplan's idea for her to hire me, not something I'd brought about through manipulation. Not because I wanted the money, but in order to wind up in her bed.

Something else to think about, how I'd wound up in her bed. His bed, their bed, her bed. Our bed, for a couple of hours there.

Jesus, I hadn't called her. I wasn't supposed to send

her flowers, that was very clear, but I had to call her, didn't I? If I hadn't gone to bed with her I would probably have called her by now, but did our dalliance last night change anything?

Probably. It very likely changed everything.

I hadn't called Elaine, either. *You'll call me in the morning,* she'd said, but I hadn't. It seemed to me that, while the evening had been strained and uncomfortable, we'd resolved it well enough and had parted on good terms, with no unfinished business.

We had some now.

I decided I'd call them both as soon as I got the chance, but not from the street, not with traffic noise for background music. Right now I didn't want to talk to anybody, anyway. I just wanted to walk. It was the best exercise, walking. That's what all the authorities were saying lately. Just get out there, forget your troubles, and walk.

Right.

It must have been around six when I walked into an Italian-style coffeehouse on Tenth Street east of Second Avenue. The place called itself Caffè Literati, and along with the usual bentwood chairs and marble-topped tables and Quattrocento reproductions they had a couple of floor-to-ceiling bookcases, with real books in them. A sign advised that the books were there for customers' reading pleasure, but all were available for purchase as well at the marked prices.

There was only one other customer in the place, a fellow in his thirties who already had one of those horse-player faces you see in the OTB parlor. He had a folded newspaper on the table in front of him and he was working something out on a pocket calculator.

The room smelled of cigarettes and fresh-ground coffee, and the faint but unmistakable trace of one of those little De Nobili cigars hung in the still air.

Classical music played. It sounded familiar but I couldn't guess what it was. I asked the waitress who brought my double espresso. She looked as though she'd be likely to know, dressed all in black, with her long blond hair in a braid and her no-nonsense glasses.

"I think it's Bach," she said.

"Really?"

"I think."

I sipped my coffee and tried to figure out what the hell I was doing. I dug out my notebook and paged through it, making what I could of it.

What was the US Asset Reduction Corporation? Liquidators of foreclosed properties, most likely, and there were plenty of those lately, given the state of the economy. Why would Glenn Holtzmann, a single fellow comfortably ensconced in a studio apartment in Yorkville, make a private deal with a liquidator? It had very likely been a bargain, but how did he happen to be in the market? And where did he get the money to pay for it? And why wasn't there any record of the transaction?

Assume he had cash. Maybe US Asset Reduction had a profitable sideline as a money laundry. You paid them with a suitcase full of green money and then you sold the apartment, or mortgaged it for the maximum and walked away with legitimate reportable money. Maybe you mortgaged it with them, and they could foreclose again, run the same game over and over.

Would that work?

Even if it would, why weren't the numbers a matter of public record? Wouldn't anybody trying to make dirty money look clean want to be on the record?

Of course they would have given him documentation, paper that would say whatever he wanted it to say, paper that would look just fine at an IRS audit. But how did they do that and at the same time manage to keep it out of the city records?

And where did he get the money, the son of a bitch? I still didn't have a clue where he got the money.

"Boccherini."

I looked up, puzzled.

"Not Bach," she said. "Boccherini. I like walked away and listened to it for the first time, and I'm like, That doesn't *sound* like Bach. So I checked, and it's Boccherini."

"It's pretty," I said.

"I guess."

I tried to think about Holtzmann some more but I had lost the thread. No go. I sipped my coffee and listened to Boccherini. There was a pay phone on the wall across from the rest room, and my eyes kept being drawn to it. Boccherini was still playing when I gave up and made my calls.

"Thank God," Elaine said. "I've been worried about you. Are you all right?"

"Of course I'm all right. Why were you worried?"

"Because last night was a mess. Because I thought you were going to call this morning. Because George Sadecki was killed."

I explained how I'd only found that out a couple of hours ago. "The detective," I said, "is always the last to know."

"I was afraid of how you might take it."

"Afraid it would drive me to drink?"

"Mostly just concerned that you'd feel bad."

"I felt pretty stupid," I admitted, and told her about the conversations I'd had with Joe Durkin and Tom Sadecki. She agreed that the whole thing was pretty embarrassing.

"But if you think about it," she said, "all it really

shows is how dedicated you are to your work. If you'd been sitting around in your underwear watching TV, or if you just took time to eat a decent breakfast and read the paper—''

''I might have known what everybody else in town knew. That's pretty good spin control you've got there, but I still don't think this is something I'm going to trot out years from now to impress prospective clients.''

''No.''

''Anyway, I'm not walking around racked with guilt. I didn't contribute to George's death. I just took a long time to find out about it.''

''It's sad, isn't it?''

''It's sad but it's not tragic, except in the sense that his whole life was tragic. I'm sorry for Tom, but he'll get over it. And this simplifies his life, and he's enough of a realist to know it. He loved his brother, but George must have been a hard guy to love. It'll be easier to love his memory.''

I told her what Tom had told me, about his recollection of George having been changed by the fact of his death, with brighter early memories supplanting the later ones. We talked about that some.

She said, ''You know, you caught me on my way out the door. There's a lecture at Town Hall. In fact you could meet me there, I'm sure there are still tickets available, except you'd be bored to tears. Do you want to meet afterward? But not at Chien Bizarre.''

''You'll be coming from Town Hall, and I want to get to a meeting. Paris Green? Say a quarter after ten?''

''Perfect.''

''I've had a busy day,'' I told Lisa. ''George Sadecki was stabbed to death by another prisoner, but I suppose you knew that.''

''It was on CNN this morning.''

That figured. I told her a little of what I'd found and hadn't found in various government records. She said she'd heard from Drew, but as far as I could tell his call had been designed just to keep the client happy.

Maybe you could say the same for my call.

"I'm going to be busy tonight," I said. "I'll talk with you tomorrow."

While I was on the phone, one of the library books caught my eye. It was an anthology of twentieth-century British and American poetry, and I'd recognized the volume because Jan Keane owned a copy. I thought I might be able to find the Robinson Jeffers poem about the wounded hawk, but it wasn't in there. There were half a dozen others by Jeffers included. I read one called "Shine, Perishing Republic" that suggested he had a low opinion of human beings, Americans in particular.

I read the opening of "The Waste Land," with its observations about April's cruelty. October, I thought, could be fairly savage in its own right. I read a few other things, and then I read a poem of the First World War, "I Have a Rendezvous With Death," by Alan Seeger. I had read it before, but that was no reason not to read it again.

It reminded me of the poem at the base of the statue in DeWitt Clinton Park. I didn't know the author, but there was a title index and I found it that way. The author was John McCrae, and the lines on the monument were from the third and final stanza. Here's the complete poem:

> In Flanders fields, the poppies blow
> Between the crosses, row on row
> That mark our place; and in the sky

The larks, still bravely singing, fly
Scarce heard amid the guns below.

We are the Dead. Short days ago
We lived, felt dawn, saw sunset glow,
Loved and were loved; and now we lie
                    In Flanders fields.

Take up our quarrel with the foe!
To you, from failing hands, we throw
The torch. Be yours to hold it high!
If ye break faith with us who die
We shall not sleep, though poppies grow
                    In Flanders fields.

I was all set to copy it down when I thought to look inside the front cover. For five dollars I could own it. I paid for it and my coffee and went home.

It was close to ten-thirty when I got to Paris Green. Elaine was at the bar drinking a Perrier. I apologized for being late and she said she'd made good use of the time, that she'd spent it flirting with Gary. Gary, Paris Green's bartender, had announced at the beginning of the summer that he was through hiding from the world; he had accordingly shaved the great oriole's nest of a beard he'd worn as long as I'd known him.

Now he was growing it back. "Time to hide," he explained. "Lot to be said for hiding."

We went to our table and ordered, the large garden salad for her, fish for me. She assured me I would have hated every minute of the lecture. "*I* hated it," she said, "and I was interested in the subject."

I had the book with me, and back at her place I found the poem again and read it to her.

"That's why I was late," I said.

"You were busy grabbing the torch?"

"I walked a few blocks out of my way," I said. "To Clinton Park, where the last three lines are carved at the base of a war memorial. Except they got it wrong."

"What do you mean?"

"They misquoted it." I got out my notebook. "Here's how they've got it on the monument. 'If ye break faith / With those who died / We shall not sleep / Though poppies grow / On Flanders fields.' "

"Isn't that what you just read me?"

"Not quite. Somebody changed 'us' to 'those' and 'die' to 'died.' And 'in' to 'on.' They used eighteen words from the poem and got three of them wrong. And they left off the author's name."

"Maybe he insisted on it, like a disenchanted screenwriter taking his name off a movie."

"I don't think he was in a position to insist on anything. I think he finished the war beneath the poppies."

"But his words live on. *That's* what I keep forgetting to ask you. Something you said a few days ago about Lisa Holtzmann."

"What about her?"

"Something about a cleaner, greener maiden, but that can't be right."

" 'I've a neater, sweeter maiden in a cleaner, greener land.' "

"That's it, and it's been driving me crazy. I know the line, but where do I know it from?"

"It's Kipling," I said. " 'The Road to Mandalay.' "

"Oh, of course. And that explains why I know it. You sing it in the shower."

"What do you say we keep that to ourselves?"

"I had no idea who wrote it. I thought it must be the title song from a Bob Hope–Bing Crosby movie. Wasn't there a movie called that, or am I nuts?"

"Or (C) Both of the above."

"Nice. Kipling, huh? What do you think, are you in the mood for a little Kipling?"

"Sure," I said. "Let's kipple."

Afterward she said, "Wow. I'd have to say we haven't lost our touch. You know something, you old bear? I love you."

"I love you."

"You didn't talk with TJ, did you? I hope Julia's not teaching him how to dress for success."

"He'll be all right."

"How did you know the inscription was off?"

"It just wasn't the way I remembered it."

"That's some memory."

"Not really. I just read it a couple of days ago. If I had a great memory I'd have known then and there that they'd got it wrong. After all, I read it in high school."

The next day was Friday, and I spent it downtown having another crack at government records before they locked them all away for the weekend. I didn't learn much.

I quit in time to beat the rush hour and rode uptown on the subway. There was a message to call Eleanor Yount. It was almost five o'clock but I managed to catch her at her desk.

She was delighted to report that there had been no embezzlement. "My accountant was quite startled when I suggested the possibility," she said, "and very much relieved when he was able to rule it out. I hate to think that Glenn might have been a thief, but it does make the thought less unsettling to know he didn't steal anything from me."

I hadn't really figured him as an embezzler. Nor had I pictured an enraged Eleanor Yount keeping a rendezvous in Hell's Kitchen and pumping four bullets into her in-house counsel.

She asked me if I'd learned anything.

Not much, I said. I knew a few things I hadn't known before, but I couldn't make them add up to anything.

"I wonder when it started," she said.

I asked her what she meant.

"I always wonder," she said. "Don't you? Whether someone's a born criminal, or is it the scar of some childhood experience, or is there some pivotal incident later on. Glenn seemed such a supremely ordinary young man. But he seems to have told so many lies, and lived a life so different from what it appeared. I suppose it will turn out that he was beaten by his father or molested by his uncle. And then one day a cartoon light bulb formed over his head and he said, 'Aha! I'll commit embezzlement!' Or traffic in drugs, or blackmail some-one. It would be convenient if one knew what exactly it was that he did."

There was a message from TJ as well. I beeped him and he called me back, but the things we had to talk about weren't suited to an open line, so we didn't say much. I gathered that he didn't have the gun yet but he was working on it.

He didn't volunteer anything about Julia, and I didn't ask.

At St. Paul's that night the speaker was from Co-op City in the Bronx. He worked construction, mostly as a window installer, and he told a good basic drinking story. My attention drifted some, but he brought me back when he said, very solemnly, "And every single night I would lock myself in my furnished room and drink myself to Bolivia."

Jim Faber was there, and during the break he said, "Did you happen to catch that one? I thought you had to drop LSD if you wanted to take a trip, but this fellow got all the way to La Paz on Clan MacGregor. They could use that in their ads."

"I guess he thinks that's the expression, drinking yourself to Bolivia. I mean, it wasn't a slip of the tongue."

"No, he meant to say it. Well, many's the time I tried

drinking myself to Bolivia. And nine times out of ten I wound up in Cleveland.''

When the meeting ended we established that we were on for Sunday dinner. I asked him if he felt like a cup of coffee but he had to get home. I thought about calling Lisa, maybe dropping in on her. Instead I hooked up with a few others from the meeting and went over to the Flame. When I got out of there I still felt like calling Lisa, but I didn't. I went home and called Elaine to confirm our Saturday night date.

Afterward I watched CNN for a little while, then turned off the set and looked through the book of poems until I found one that gave me something to think about. Sometime after midnight I turned out the light and went to bed.

It was like not drinking, I thought, like staying away from a drink a day at a time. If I could stay away from bourbon that way, I ought to be able to resist Lisa Holtzmann.

Saturday afternoon I got a call from TJ. He said, ''You know the bagel shop in the bus station?''

''Like the back of my hand.''

''You ask me, they better at doughnuts than bagels. You want to meet me there?''

''What time?''

''You say. Won't take me five minutes.''

I said it would take me a little longer than that, and it was closer to half an hour before I was seated next to him at the counter of Lite Bite Bagels on the ground floor of the Port Authority Bus Terminal. He had a doughnut and a Coke. I ordered a cup of coffee.

''They got good doughnuts,'' he said. ''Sure you don't want one?''

''Not right now.''

''The bagels is mushy. You eatin' a bagel, you 'spect

it to fight back some. Doughnuts, you don't mind if they's mushy. Weird, huh?''

"The world's a mysterious place."

"And that's the truth, Ruth. Almost called you last night, woulda been real late. Dude had a Uzi he lookin' to sell.''

"That's not what I was looking for."

"Yeah, I know. It was pretty slick, though. Had an extra clip, had this case to carry it in, all fitted an' all. Cheap, too, 'cause all he wanted was to get high.''

I pictured Jan trying to kill herself firing at full automatic. "I don't think so," I said.

"Oh, must be he sold it by now. Else he used it to hold somebody up. Anyway, I got what you want.''

"Where?"

He patted the blue canvas Kangaroo pouch he was wearing around his waist. "Right in here," he said softly. "Thirty-eight revolver, three bullets for it. Holds five, but he didn't have but three. Maybe he went an' shot two people. Three bullets be enough?''

I nodded. One was enough.

"Know the men's room around to the right? I'll catch you there in a minute or two.''

He slipped off his stool and left the bagel shop. I finished my coffee and paid for both of us. I found him in the men's room, leaning over a sink, checking his hair in the mirror. I moved to the sink beside him and washed my hands while the fellow at the urinal finished up and left. When he was out the door TJ unclasped the pouch from around his waist and handed it to me. "Check it out," he said.

I went into one of the stalls. The gun was a Dienstag five-shot revolver with checkered grips and a two-inch barrel. It smelled as though it hadn't been cleaned since it was last fired. The front sight had been filed down. The cylinder was empty. The pouch held three bullets, each individually wrapped in tissue paper. I unwrapped one and made sure it fit the cylinder, then took it out and wrapped it back in the tissue paper. I put the three bullets in my pocket and tucked the gun under my belt in the small of my back. My jacket concealed it well enough, as long as it didn't slip.

I left the stall and handed the blue pouch to TJ. He started to ask what was wrong, then felt the weight of the pouch and realized that it was empty. He said, "Man, don't you want the Kangaroo? To carry it."

"I thought it was yours."

"It came with the goods. Here."

I returned to the stall and put the gun and the bullets into the pouch and adjusted the strap so that it would fit around my waist. The gun felt a lot more secure there than wedged under my belt. Outside, TJ explained that the pouches had become the holster of choice on both sides of the law.

"I believe it was cops started it," he said. "You know how they got to carry a gun when they off duty? Only they don't want no gun weighin' down their pocket or spoilin' the lines of their suit. Then a lot of the players, they was usin' these shoulder bags, but that's a little too much like a purse, you know? 'Sides, anything you carry like that, there be times you put it down an' forget to pick it back up again. The Kangaroos, they sell 'em everywhere, you don't even know you wearin' one. Leave the zipper open, you ready to quick-draw. An' they cheap. Ten, twelve dollars. 'Course you can buy one in leather an' spend more. I seen a dope dealer has one in eelskin. That be a fish or a snake?"

"A fish."

"Didn't know you could make leather out of no fish. Charge a lot for it, too. I guess you could get a Kangaroo made out of alligator if you was fool enough to want it."

"I guess."

I asked about Julia. "She a strange one," he said. "How old you think she is?"

"How old?"

"Take a guess, Les. How old you think?"

"I don't know. Nineteen or twenty."

"Twenty-two."

I shrugged. "Well, I was close."

"She seem younger," he said. "An' she seem older. One minute she this little girl an' you want to keep her safe. Next minute she your teacher, gone keep you after school. She know a whole lot of things, you know?"

"I'll bet she does."

"Not just what you thinkin'. She knows all kind of shit. She made those pajamas she was wearin'. You believe that? Designed 'em herself, too. Lotta ways she could make money. She don't have to be gettin' in cars on Eleventh Avenue. 'Course, right now she need the money."

"What about you?"

His eyes turned wary. "What about me?"

"I just wondered how we stand as far as money is concerned. Did you make out all right on the gun?"

"Yeah, we cool. Got a good deal on the gun. Only real expenses I had was all the dope I had to buy."

"What dope?"

"Well, hangin' out by the Captain an' all. You want to start askin' a bunch of questions, people got to know you all right. Best way is buy some drugs. They makin' money off you, they got a reason to like you."

"Did you have to spend very much? Because it's only right for me to reimburse you."

"No need, Reed. I made out fine."

"What do you mean?"

"Mean I took what I bought and sold it right here on the Deuce. Lost money on one deal but made some on another one. All said an' done, I come out a few dollars ahead.''

"You sold drugs."

"Well, shit, man, what else was I gonna do? I don't *use* none of that shit. I wasn't gonna throw the shit away. That's bread, Ed. I ain't in the business, not any more'n I'm in the gun business. Only business I want to be in is the detectin' business, but if I has to buy the shit I might as well get my money back. There be anything wrong with that?''

"I guess not," I said. "Not when you explain it like that.''

In my room I took the gun apart and cleaned it. I didn't have the right tools, but Q-tips and Three-in-One oil were better than nothing. When I was done I put the gun in the drawer with the five thousand dollars. I'd been meaning to put the cash in my safe-deposit box, but I had missed my chance. I'd have to wait until Monday.

I turned the TV on and off, then picked up the phone and called Jan. "I think I'm going to be able to get that item we discussed," I told her. "Before I follow through, I just wanted to make sure you were still in the market." She assured me that she was. "Well, I should have something by the end of next week," I said.

I hung up and checked the dresser drawer, as if the gun might have magically dematerialized while I was on the phone. No such luck.

That night I reprised most of my conversation with TJ for Elaine, of course leaving out the part about the gun. I told her how he'd bought and sold dope on my behalf, and how he seemed to be getting involved with a pre-op transsexual.

"Entranced by a transsexual," she said. "Or transfixed. Just how fascinated is he, do you know? What do we do if he shows up with tits?''

"That's a stretch. He's just experimenting.''

"That's all they were doing at the Manhattan Project, and look what happened to Hiroshima. What's the story? Are they an item?''

"I think she probably took him to bed and showed him a good time. I think the novelty of it impressed him and shook him up a little. That doesn't mean he'll be running down to the nearest clinic for electrolysis and hormone shots. Or that the two of them are going to be picking out drapes together.''

"I guess. Have you ever tried that?''

"Picking out drapes?''

"You know. Have you?''

"Not that I know of.''

"Not that you know of? How could you do it and not know it?''

"Well, strange things happen when you drink yourself to Bolivia. I did lots of things I don't remember, so how can I say for certain who I did them with? And if the girl was post-op, and if the surgeon did good work, how could you tell?''

"But you never did it that you know of. Would you?''

"I've already got a girlfriend.''

"Well, this is hypothetical. I wasn't propositioning you on behalf of Julia. How did you feel about her? Did you want to do her?''

"It never entered my mind.''

"Because you've got a cleaner greener maiden in a neater sweeter land, except I just got it backward, didn't I? A neater sweeter maiden. Will I ever get to meet Ms. Julia? Or do I have to take a walk on Eleventh Avenue?''

"No need,'' I said. "I'm sure they'll invite us to the wedding.''

*   *   *

I spent Saturday night at Elaine's. Sunday morning I
went back to my hotel right after breakfast and turned
off Call Forwarding. I checked the drawer, confirmed
the continuing existence of the gun and the money, and
called Jan.

I said, "Will you be home for the next hour or so?
I'd like to stop by."

"I'll be here," she said.

Half an hour later I was standing on the sidewalk on
Lispenard Street, waiting for her to toss down the key.
I was wearing the blue Kangaroo pouch. The zipper was
closed. I wasn't looking to make any quick draws.

When I got off the elevator she noticed the pouch
right away. "Very snazzy," she said. "And very sen-
sible. I never saw you as the backpack type, but that's
handy, isn't it?"

"It lets me keep my hands free."

"And blue's the right color for you."

"They come in eelskin, too."

"I don't think so, not for you. But come on in. Coffee? I just made a fresh pot."

I guess she looked the same. I don't know what
change I expected. It had only been a week. At first
glance her hair seemed grayer, but that was because it
had darkened some in my memory. She brought the coffee and we tried to find things to talk about. I remembered the speaker at the Friday meeting and told her how
he'd drunk himself to Bolivia, and we got through a cup
of coffee apiece by trotting out malapropisms and curious turns of phrase we'd heard in various AA rooms
over the years.

During a lull I said, "I brought you the gun."

"You did?"

I tapped the pouch.

"For heaven's sake," she said. "It never occurred to

me to wonder what you were carrying in that thing. From what you said yesterday I figured it would be the better part of a week before you managed to get it."

"I already had it when I called."

"Oh?"

"I guess I was hoping you'd tell me you didn't want it."

"I see."

"So I was stalling. At least I think that's what I was doing. I don't always know what I'm doing."

"Welcome to the club."

"What do you know about guns, Jan?"

"You pull the trigger and a bullet comes out. What do I know about them? Next to nothing. Is there a lot I have to know?"

I spent the next half hour teaching her some basic rules about handguns. There was an underlying absurdity in providing firearm-safety instruction to a potential suicide, but she didn't seem to think it was silly. "If I'm going to kill myself," she said, "I don't want to do it by accident." I taught her how to work the cylinder, how to load and unload the gun. I made sure it was unloaded, showed her how to make sure it was unloaded, and told her how to place the gun when the time came. The technique I suggested was the policeman's old favorite, the time-honored ritual known as eating one's gun. The barrel in the mouth, tilted upward, firing up through the soft palate and into the brain.

"That should do it," I told her. "The bullets are thirty-eight caliber, hollow-pointed so that they tend to expand upon impact." I must have winced because she asked me what was the matter. "I've seen people who did this," I said. "It's not pretty. It distorts the face."

"So does cancer."

"A smaller bullet doesn't make as much of a mess, but the chance of missing a vital spot—"

"No, this is better," she said. "What do I care what I look like?"

"I care."

"Oh, baby," she said. "I'm sorry. But it tastes terrible, doesn't it? Sticking a gun in your mouth. Have you ever done it?"

"Not in years."

"Were you—?"

"Considering it? I don't know. I remember one night, sitting up late in the house in Syosset. Anita was sleeping. I was still married, obviously, and still a cop."

"And drinking."

"That goes without saying, doesn't it? Anita was asleep, the boys were asleep. I was in the front room and I stuck the gun in my mouth to see what it was like."

"Were you depressed?"

"Not particularly. I was drunk, but I wouldn't say I was positively shitfaced. I probably would have blown the circuits on a Breathalyzer, but hell, I drove like that all the time."

"And never had an accident."

"Oh, I had a couple, but nothing serious, and I never got in trouble for it. A cop pretty much has to kill somebody to get cited for drunk driving. It never happened to me, and I did my share of it. Looking back, I'd have to say leaving the force and moving to the city probably saved my life. Because I stopped carrying a gun and I stopped driving a car, and either one would have killed me sooner or later."

"Tell me about the night you put the gun in your mouth."

"I don't know what more there is to tell. I remember the taste, metal and gun oil. I thought, *So this is what it feels like.* And I thought that all I had to do was do it, and I thought that I didn't want to."

"And you took the gun out of your mouth."

"And I took the gun out of my mouth, and didn't do it again. I thought about it some, living alone in New York, bottoming out on the booze. Of course I didn't have a gun anymore, but the city gives you plenty of ways to kill yourself. The easiest way was to do nothing and just go on drinking."

She picked up the gun, turned it over in her hands. "It's heavy," she said. "I didn't realize it would be that heavy."

"People are always surprised about that."

"I don't know why I didn't expect it. It's metal, of course it's heavy." She put it on the table. "I had a pretty good week," she said. "I'm not in any great rush to use this, believe me."

"I'm glad to hear that."

"But it's a relief to have it in the house. I know it's here for when I need it, and I find that very reassuring. Can you understand that?"

"I think so."

"You know," she said, "when people find out you've got cancer, you're really in for it. I haven't run around telling people, but I can't go to meetings and not talk about what's going on in my life. So a lot of people know about it. And as soon as they know that your doctor's given up on you, that what you've got is hopelessly incurable, then they come at you with the advice."

"What kind of advice?"

"Everything from macrobiotic diets and wheatgrass juice to the power of prayer and crystal healing. Quack clinics in Mexico. Getting your blood replaced in Switzerland."

"Oh, Jesus."

"I forgot him, but his name gets mentioned a lot, too. Everybody knows somebody who was given fifteen days to live and now they're out chopping wood and running marathons because of some stupid thing they tried that worked. And I'm not even saying they're full of crap. I believe these things work sometimes. I know miracles happen, too.''

"There's a thing you hear around the program—"

" 'Don't kill yourself five minutes before the miracle.' I know. I don't intend to. I believe in miracles, but I also believe I had my quota of miracles when I got sober. I don't expect another one.''

"You never know.''

"Sometimes you know. But here's what I was getting at. Here are all these people trying to help, each of them bringing me something and it's all useless. And you brought me the one thing I can use.'' She picked up the gun again. "Funny, huh? Don't you think it's funny?''

The sun had been shining that morning, but the sky was clouded over by the time I left Jan's loft. A week ago I'd had to go home in the rain. At least it wasn't raining yet.

Back at my hotel, I had five hours to get through before my dinner date with Jim. I thought of a way to get through them, and looked over at the telephone.

Like not drinking, I thought. You do it in manageable increments, a day at a time, an hour at a time, even a minute at a time when you have to. You don't pick up the phone, you don't call her, and you don't go over there.

Piece of cake.

Around two I reached for the phone. I didn't have to look up the number. While her husband's taped message ran its course, I thought instead of other words from the grave, those of John McCrae. *If ye break faith with us who die . . .*

I said, "It's Matt, Lisa. Are you there?'' She was. "I'd like to come by for a few minutes,'' I said. "There are a couple of things I'd like to go over with you."

"Oh, good," she said.

I went straight from her apartment to the restaurant. I showered first, so I don't suppose I could actually have been carrying her scent upon my skin. On my clothes, perhaps. Or on my mind.

Definitely on my mind, and several times I was on the point of saying something to Jim. I could have. One of the roles a sponsor plays is that of a nonjudgmental confessor. *I strangled my grandmother this morning,* you might say. *She probably had it coming,* he would reply, *and anyway the important thing is you didn't drink.*

I didn't mention it to Mick, either, although I might have if we'd made what he calls a proper night of it. I walked Jim home after the Big Book meeting at St. Clare's, then dropped by Grogan's, and one of the first things he told me was that we wouldn't be able to see the sun up together.

"Unless you want to drive up to the farm with me," he said, "for I'll be on my way in a couple of hours. I have to sit down with O'Mara."

"Is something the matter?"

"Not a thing," he said, "except that Rosenstein has it in his head that O'Mara might die."

Rosenstein is Mick's lawyer, O'Mara and his wife the co-managers of the country property he owns in Sullivan County. I asked if O'Mara was ill.

"He is not," Mick said. "Nor should he be, living the life he does, out in the open air every day, drinking the milk of my cow and eating the eggs of my hens. He's lived sixty years, has O'Mara, and should be good for sixty more. I said as much to Rosenstein. Ah, says he, but suppose he died, then where are you?"

"You'd have to hire someone else," I said. "Oh, wait a minute. Who's the owner of record?"

His smile held no joy. "O'Mara himself," he said. "You know I own nothing."

"The clothes on your back."

"The clothes on my back," he agreed, "and nothing else. There's another man's name on the lease of Grogan's, and another that owns the building itself. The car's not mine either, not legally. And the farm belongs to O'Mara and his wife. A man can't own anything or the bastards'll be after taking it away from him."

"You've always operated that way," I said. "At least as long as I've known you. You've never had any assets."

"And a good job, too. They had their hands out last year when they were trying to make their RICO case, ready to attach any assets they could find. Their fucking case fell apart, thanks to God and Rosenstein, but in the meantime they might have grabbed my holdings and sold them off. If I'd had the misfortune to own anything."

"So what's the problem with O'Mara?"

"Ah," he said. "If O'Mara dies, and herself with him, although women live forever—"

Not always, I thought.

"—then what happens to my farm? The O'Maras have no children. He has a niece and nephew in California, and herself has a brother, a priest in Providence, Rhode Island. Who stands to inherit depends on which O'Mara outlives the other, but sooner or later my farm's to be left to the niece and nephew or to the priest. And, Rosenstein wants to know, how do I propose to tell O'Mara's heirs that the farm is my own, and they're quite welcome to slop the hogs and collect the eggs, but I'll have the use of it when I see fit?"

Rosenstein had suggested ways to safeguard the farm,

ranging from an undated and unregistered transfer of ownership to a codicil to O'Mara's will. But any arrangement could be dismissed as a legal fiction if the federal authorities ever took a good look at the situation.

"So I'll talk to O'Mara," he said, "though I don't know what I'll say to him. 'Take care of yourself, man. Stay out of drafts.' But I know the answer. You must go through life owning nothing."

"You're already doing that."

"I am not," he said. "That's what Rosenstein called it, a legal fiction. However you own something, on paper or in secret, it can be taken from you." He looked at the glass in his hand, drank the whiskey. "But if you don't fucking care," he said, "then it seems to me you're all right. For God's sake, if O'Mara's fucking nephew gets my farm then I'll buy it from him. Or buy another one, or get along without one. It's being attached to bloody things that drags you down, that more than losing them. Here I am ready to drive half the night for fear O'Mara might die, and him not sick a day in his life."

"The Indians say men can't own land, that it all belongs to the Great Spirit. Man only has the use of it."

"And what is it we say of beer? You can't own it, you can only rent it."

"True of coffee, too," I said, getting to my feet.

"True of all property," he said. "True of everything."

It rained all day Monday. It had held off until I got home the night before, but it was coming down hard when I woke up.

I never left the hotel. When I moved in there was a coffee shop off the lobby, but it went out of business years ago. There had been several tenants in there since then; the current one sold women's clothing.

I called the Morning Star and ordered a big breakfast. The kid who delivered it came to my door looking like a drowned rat. I ate my breakfast and got on the phone, and I stayed on it all day long. I made call after call, and when I wasn't talking to someone or biding my time on Hold or drumming my fingers waiting for a callback, I was staring out the window and trying to figure out who to call next.

I spent a lot of time trying to chase down MultiCircle Productions, the previous owner of the Holtzmann apartment. It took a lot of digging to establish that their corporate charter had been written in the Caymans, which meant there was a veil there I could forget about penetrating.

The building manager for the condominium didn't know much about MultiCircle. She had never met anyone connected with the company, or indeed anyone who had occupied the premises prior to the Holtzmanns. It was her impression that the Holtzmanns had been the first people actually to live there, but she might be wrong about that. Nor had she had anything to do with the sale of the apartment, or of any of the units. The building had had a sales agent who had used one of the unsold apartments as an on-premises office, but of course all the apartments had been sold long ago and the sales agent had moved on. She could probably find out the agent's name, and a number that might or might not be current. Would I want her to do that?

The number wasn't current, as it turned out, but getting the right number wasn't any harder than calling 411 and asking for it. The hard part came when I tried to find someone at the sales agency who knew anything about the building at Fifty-seventh and Tenth. No one who'd sold space there still worked at the agency.

"There ought to be someone who can help you," a cheerful young man told me. "Hold on a minute, okay?" I held, and he came back with a name and a number. I called the number and asked for Kerry Vogel, spent a few more minutes on Hold, and was given another number to call.

When I reached her, Kerry Vogel had every bit as cheerful a voice and manner as the fellow who'd steered me to her. I have a feeling it's part of the job description. She remembered the building vividly, as well she might; she'd lived in it for a year and a half.

"We're gypsies," she said. "All of us in this business. It's a crazy life and not everybody can stay in it. You get a building and you pick an apartment. That's one of the perks, free rent, and it means you're there all the time, you can easily make appointments to fit the prospect's schedule. Also you're encouraged to pick one of the nicest units and fix it up attractively, because it's good psychology, your prospect right away sees himself living there. You rent good furniture, hang some nice art on the walls, and have the cleaning service come in once a week. And you'd be surprised how many times you'll take the person all over the building and they wind up, like, I want *your* apartment. So you write up the sale and you move.''

She had occupied five different apartments in the Holtzmann building, three of them in the same vertical line as the Holtzmann apartment, each of them in turn sold out from under her. She had trouble recalling the name MultiCircle Productions, but she remembered the apartment. I don't know what there was to remember, since she hadn't lived in it and since it was substantially identical to the ones above and below it, but then I'm not in that business.

She remembered now. A man had come by himself to look at apartments. He looked foreign, but he could have been European or South American, she couldn't tell which. He was tall and slim and dark and he hardly said a word. She'd rushed the sales pitch and didn't show him everything because he made her nervous.

And you had to follow your instincts, because the job was a dangerous one. For a woman, anyway. Because men were hitting on you all the time, and that was okay, it got to be a nuisance but you learned to live with it. But sometimes it wasn't just hitting on you, it didn't stay verbal, it turned physical. Sometimes it was rape.

Because it was easy for them. You were alone, you were in your own apartment, there was even a bed there to help them get the idea. And the building was generally half-empty at the very least, so there was no one around to hear you scream. Not that they could hear you anyway because that was a big selling point of the better new buildings. They were completely soundproof, and wasn't that a great thing to tell a potential rapist?

She'd been lucky so far, but she knew women who hadn't. This guy had spooked her some, so quiet and watchful and all, but nothing happened, he never hit on her at all. And when he left she was sure she would never see him again.

Which was true, actually, because she didn't. From then on the only person she saw was his lawyer, who was Hispanic. He didn't have an accent but his name was Spanish, and no, she couldn't remember it. Garcia? Rodriguez? It was a common Spanish name, that was all she remembered. She didn't remember the buyer's name, either, and she had a hunch she had never heard it, or else she probably would have known whether he was South American or European, wouldn't she? From the name?

She was pretty sure all anybody ever told her was MultiCircle Productions, whatever that was. See, anybody could buy a condo. With a co-op you had to go before the tenants' board and satisfy them that you were a decent person and you wouldn't be giving loud parties or being an unwelcome presence in the building. They could turn you down for any reason at all, or for no reason. They could discriminate in ways that were illegal for either a landlord or a private seller. Why, there was one East Side co-op that turned down Richard Nixon, for heaven's sake!

Condos were different. If you had a pulse and your check was good, you could buy a condo, and the other tenants couldn't keep you out. And once you had it you could sublet it, which a lot of co-ops didn't allow. So the luxury condos were very popular with foreigners who wanted a safe investment in the United States. And buyers of that sort were in turn quite popular with people selling condos, because they didn't expect you to finance their purchase, nor did they want a clause in the sales contract making the sale contingent upon their getting a mortgage. They generally wrote out a check and paid the full sum in cash.

Which was what this buyer had done. She remembered the closing, because nobody showed up for it, not even MultiCircle's lawyer. He sent the check by messenger.

Come to think of it, had she ever even met the lawyer? They'd spoken on the phone several times, and she had this mental picture of him that looked like the lieutenant on *Miami Vice,* but had she ever seen him?

She didn't remember the selling price, but she could ballpark it. All the apartments on a line varied in price— the higher you went, the more you had to pay—and that floor on that line would be, let's see, three-twenty? Well, give or take ten or fifteen thousand dollars, but that was close, anyway.

Probably a third of that was the view, and wasn't it spectacular? You didn't mind sitting around by the hour waiting for prospects when you had that to look out at. She'd enjoyed living there, although she hadn't been crazy about the neighborhood to begin with. But she liked it better as she got to know it more.

"There's a place right across the street," she said, "that's really super. Jimmy Armstrong's? Looks like nothing much from the outside, but it's nice and the food's sensational. Serious chili, and the selection of beers on tap is outstanding. You ought to check it out."

I assured her I would.

I called Elaine. "I had a hunch you'd be home," I said.

"I was out earlier, though. I went to the gym. Of course there were no cabs to be had, but I put on that plastic *shmatte* and I carried an umbrella. And I still got soaked going and coming, but it didn't kill me. You're home, I take it?"

"And staying put."

"Good, because it doesn't look as though it's going to quit soon. If I lived on a lower floor I'd start building an ark."

I told her what I'd learned about MultiCircle. "Foreign money," I said, "and no easy way to tell where it came from. One principal or a whole slew of them, and no way to tell that, either. A condo's an attractive investment, a good hedge against inflation and a way to shift some money here to guard against political or economic instability at home."

"Wherever home is."

"Although that probably wouldn't have been a big consideration, not if they were already incorporated in the Caymans and could stow the money in a dollar account there. Still, it's a good investment and you can rent it out. There's usually a minimum rental period, it's not like a hotel, although some resort condos have the minimum down to three days. In New York it's generally a month, sometimes longer."

"And in the Holtzmanns' building?"

"A month, but it didn't matter to MultiCircle because they never had a tenant in there. Glenn and his wife"— interesting how I avoided saying her name—"were the first people to spend a night there."

"And they'd been married all of a week at the time? I bet they did a good job of christening it."

"MultiCircle paid cash," I said. "They sent over a check in full payment."

"So?"

"So how did they lose it? I was thinking foreclosure, but how can you foreclose on a nonexistent mortgage? Sometimes a corporation has its assets seized to satisfy creditors, but this was some kind of shell in the Caymans. What kind of creditors would they have?"

"Their lawyer could probably tell you."

"Could but wouldn't. Assuming I knew who he was, which I don't. She didn't remember his name. It's probably on a piece of paper somewhere, and I'll try to find it, but even if I managed to find the guy I wouldn't get anything out of him. MultiCircle. You know what that sounds like to me?"

"Like going around in circles?"

"Like wheels within wheels," I said.

"Does it even matter who they are, or why they lost the property? I mean, if you were investigating me, would you want to know who lived here before I did?"

"This is different," I said. "There's something strange about MultiCircle Productions, and there's something strange about US Asset Reduction Corp., and God knows there's something strange about Holtzmann. All that strangeness, you've got to assume a connection."

"I guess."

"I have a feeling it's right in front of me," I said. "But I just can't see it yet."

I called Joe Durkin. "I actually tried you an hour ago," he said. "Two, three times. Your line was busy."

"I've been on it all morning."

"Well, just to set your mind at rest, Gunther Bauer was not the hired agent for an international conspiracy. I was lucky, guy I talked to was polite as can be. I could tell he wanted to laugh in my face, but he managed to control himself. Gunther's beef with George was personal and deeply felt, according to him. He was nobody's guided missile. Unless God told him to do it, which is possible, but he wasn't taking orders from any intermediary."

"I didn't really have much faith in that theory anyway."

"No, but you thought it was worth checking, and

you're an overly stubborn son of a bitch but you're not stupid.''

"Thanks."

"The idea was somebody put him up to it to keep George from talking, right?"

"Well, George wasn't much of a talker. But to close out the case."

"It was already closed out, though I'll grant you this slams the door. But if you're thinking about somebody pulling strings inside Rikers—"

"Which has been known to happen."

"Oh, no question, but it's not something your average citizen can do. You can't take a course at the Learning Annex, 'How to Arrange a Homicide Behind Prison Walls.' Might be a popular course, but they haven't offered it yet."

"No."

"So you're thinking in terms of somebody with reach. You must've found something indicates Holtzmann's dirty."

"Yes."

"What did he do?"

"Bought an apartment from a foreigner that nobody was living in."

"Well, Jesus, that's just as suspicious as hell, isn't it?"

"Why would a foreigner buy an apartment and not live in it or rent it out? You got any idea?"

"I don't know, Matt. Why would a foreigner do anything? Why would a foreigner join the police force?"

"Huh?"

"You didn't read about that? There's a proposal to do away with the citizenship requirement on the NYPD."

"Seriously? Why would they want to do that?"

"To make the department more representative of the

population at large. Which is a worthwhile goal, don't
misunderstand me, but that's a hell of a way to do it.
You should hear the PBA delegate on the subject.''

''I can imagine.''

'' 'Go all the way,' he says. 'Why should they even
need green cards? Take illegal aliens, take wetbacks.
Hang a fucking sign on the Rio Grande, *You too can be
a police officer.*' He was in rare form.''

''Well, it's an unusual idea.''

''It's a terrible idea,'' he said, ''and it won't do what
they want it to, because what you'll wind up with is half
the male population of Woodside and Fordham Road,
donkeys fresh off the Aer Lingus flight. Remember
when they did away with the height requirement? That
was supposed to get more Hispanics on the force.''

''Did it work?''

''No,'' he said. ''Of course not. All it brought in was
a lot of short Italians.''

I called Holtzmann's previous landlord, owner of the
building in Yorkville where he'd been living when he
met Lisa. When I was downtown I'd found the address
in an old city directory and got the landlord's name and
address from city real estate records. That's not always
easy, a lot of landlords hide behind corporate shells as
hard to penetrate as MultiCircle, but not this fellow. He
owned the building, lived with his wife in one of its
sixteen units, and served as its superintendent himself.

And he remembered Glenn Holtzmann, who had evidently lived there ever since he moved back to the city
from White Plains. The landlord, a Mr. Dozoretz, had
only good things to say about Holtzmann, who had paid
his rent on time, made no unreasonable demands, and
caused no problems with other tenants. He'd been sorry
to lose him as a tenant, but not surprised; the fourth-
floor studio was a tight fit for one person, and far too

small for two. A great shock, though, what had happened to Mr. Holtzmann. A tragedy.

Sometime after noon I called down to the deli and asked them to send up some coffee and a couple of sandwiches. Fifteen minutes later I was so lost in thought that the knock on my door came as a surprise. I ate my lunch dutifully, without really tasting it, and got back on the phone.

I called New York Law School and spoke to several different people before I managed to confirm the dates of Holtzmann's attendance there. No one I talked with remembered him, but his records indicated an unremarkable student. They had the name of the White Plains firm where Holtzmann had gone to work after graduation, and his address there, the Grandview Apartments on Hutchison Boulevard, but that was as recent as their information got; he hadn't bothered to keep them up to date.

The Westchester Information operator had no listing for the law firm, Kane, Breslow, Jespesson & Reade, but under *Attorneys* she had a Michael Jespesson listed. I called his office but he was out to lunch. I thought, in this weather? Why couldn't he order in from a deli and eat at his desk?

I might have tried the Grandview Apartments but I couldn't imagine what I might ask whoever took my call. Even so, it was a struggle to keep from calling them. There is an acronym in the New York Police Department, or at least there used to be. They taught it to new recruits at the Academy, and you heard it a lot in all the detective squad rooms. GOYAKOD, they said. It stood for Get Off Your Ass and Knock On Doors.

You hear it said that that's how most cases are closed, and that's not even close to true. Most cases close themselves. The wife calls 911 and announces she shot her husband, the holdup man runs out of the convenience store and into the arms of an off-duty patrolman, the ex-boyfriend has a knife under his mattress with the girl's blood still on it. And of the cases that require solution, a majority are closed through information received. If a workman is as good as his tools, a detective is no better than his snitches.

Now and then, though, a case won't solve itself and no one will be obliging enough to drop a dime on the bad guy. (Or on the good guy; snitches lie, too, like everybody else.) Sometimes it takes actual police work to clear a file, and that's when GOYAKOD comes into play.

It's what I was doing now. I was employing a foul-weather version of GOYAKOD. I was sitting on my ass and using the phone, waging the same kind of war of attrition on the blank wall of Glenn Holtzmann's death. The only thing wrong with it is that sometimes it becomes pointless and mechanical. You're at a dead end, but rather than admit it and try to figure out where you took a wrong turn, you keep on knocking on doors, grateful that there is an endless supply of doors to knock on, grateful that you can keep busy and tell yourself you're doing something useful.

So I didn't call the Grandview. But I didn't throw their number away, either. I kept it handy, in case I ran out of doors.

When I reached Michael Jespesson, he was shocked to learn that Glenn Holtzmann was dead. He had been aware of the murder but had paid very little attention to it; it was, after all, a street crime committed on streets well removed from his own. And it had been several years since Holtzmann had been associated with his late firm. Somehow the victim's name hadn't registered.

"Of course I remember him," he said. "We were a

small firm. Just a handful of associates plus a couple of paralegals. Holtzmann was a pleasant fellow. He was a few years older than the standard law-school graduate, but only a few years. The first impression he made was that of a real self-starter, but he turned out to be less ambitious than I'd guessed. He did his work, but he wasn't going to set the world on fire.''

That echoed what Eleanor Yount had told me. She'd initially seen him as a likely successor, then realized he lacked the drive. But somehow he'd driven himself all the way to the twenty-eighth floor. Add up the cash and the apartment and he'd left an estate well in excess of half a million dollars. Imagine what he could have accomplished if he'd had a little ambition.

"Maybe he was just in the wrong place," Jespesson said. "I wasn't surprised when he left. I never thought he'd stay. He was single, he hadn't grown up in the area, so what was he doing in White Plains? Not that he was a born New Yorker. He was from somewhere in the Midwest, wasn't he?''

"Pennsylvania.''

"Well, that's not the Midwest. But he wasn't from Philadelphia. He was from somewhere out in the sticks, if I remember correctly.''

"I think Altoona.''

"Altoona. New York is full of people from Altoona. White Plains isn't. So I wasn't surprised when he left us, and if he hadn't left then he'd have done so a few months later.''

"Why?''

"The firm broke up. Sorry, I took it for granted that you knew that, but there's no reason why you should. Nothing to do with Holtzmann, anyway, and I don't think he could have read the handwriting on the wall. I don't think there *was* any handwriting on the wall. I certainly didn't see it.''

I asked if there was anyone else I should talk to.

"I think I knew him as well as anyone," he said. "But how do you come to be investigating? I thought you had a man in custody."

"Routine follow-up," I said.

"But you do have the man responsible? A homeless derelict, if I remember correctly." He snorted. "I was going to say he should have stayed in White Plains, but we have our share of street crime here, I'm sorry to say. My wife and I live in a gated community. If you wanted to visit us I would have to leave your name with the guard. Can you imagine? A gated community. Like a stockade, or a medieval walled city."

"I understand they have them all over the country."

"Gated communities? Oh yes, they're quite the rage. But not in Altoona, I shouldn't think." Another snort. "Maybe he should have stayed in Altoona."

Why didn't he?

Why had he come to New York? He'd gone to college not far from home, returned home after graduation, and very likely fallen into the job selling insurance at his uncle's agency. Then when he came into a few dollars he moved to New York and went to law school.

Why? Didn't Penn State have a law school? It would have been cheaper than moving to New York, and would have been a logical preface to taking the Pennsylvania bar exam and practicing law not far from home. He could even have gone on selling insurance in his free time; he wouldn't have been the first person to work his way through law school in that fashion.

But instead he'd had a clean break. Hadn't looked back, as far as I could tell. Hadn't taken his bride back home, hadn't introduced her to his family.

What had he left behind? And what had he taken with

him when he made the move? How much had his parents left him?

Or had they left him anything at all?

Start with the uncle. I called Eleanor Yount to see if the firm's records had him listed by name. She had an assistant pull Glenn's résumé and reported that he had not been specific in listing his job experience prior to law school. Like his after-school jobs and summer employment, his career in insurance had been merely summarized. *Sales and administrative work at uncle's insurance office, Altoona, PA,* he'd written, along with the dates.

I got through to the Information operator in Altoona and had her check the Yellow Pages listings for an insurance agent named Holtzmann. There were a lot of Holtzmanns in the region, she told me, most but not all of them spelling it with two *N*'s, but none of them seemed to be in the insurance business.

Of course your uncle doesn't necessarily have the same last name as you. And there was a fair chance the uncle had died, or retired to Florida, or sold the business and bought a Burger King franchise.

Still, how big was Altoona? And how many insurance agents could it have, and wouldn't they tend to know each other?

I asked the operator for the names and numbers of the two insurance agencies with the largest Yellow Pages ads. She seemed to think that was an amusing request, but she gave me what I wanted. I called them both, in each case managing to get through to someone who'd been there a while. I explained that I was trying to contact a man who had been in the insurance business in Altoona and who may have been named Holtzmann, but who in any event had employed his nephew, whose name was in fact Holtzmann, Glenn Holtzmann.

No luck.

I called Information again and got the names of half a dozen of the two-*N* Holtzmanns. I took them in order. The first two didn't answer. The third was a woman with a voice like Ethel Merman's who assured me that she knew all the Holtzmanns in town, that they were all related, and that there was no one in the family named Glenn. Nothing wrong with the name, but no Holtzmann had ever used it, and she would know if they had.

I said I thought he was from Roaring Spring.

Now that was a different story, she said. She didn't quite say it, but she gave me the impression that people in Roaring Spring had tails. She knew there was a Holtzmann family in Roaring Spring, although she hadn't heard tell of them in years and couldn't say if any of them were still around. One thing she did know was that the Holtzmanns in Roaring Spring were not in any way related to the Holtzmanns in Altoona.

"Unless you go clear back to the Rhineland," she said.

I called Information and asked for Holtzmanns in Roaring Spring, wondering why it hadn't occurred to me to do so earlier. No matter. There weren't any.

I called Lisa. Did she happen to know the name of the uncle at whose insurance agency Glenn had worked in Altoona?

She said, "What a question. Did he ever mention any of his relatives by name? If he did I don't remember. The thing is, neither of us talked much about our families."

"What about his mother's maiden name? Did he happen to mention that?"

"I'm sure he didn't," she said. "But wait a minute, I just came across it on his group insurance policy. Hold on a minute." I held, and she came back to report that it was Benziger. " 'Father's name—John Holtzmann, Mother's maiden name—Hilda Benziger' " she read. "Does that help?"

"I don't know," I said.

I called Altoona Information again looking for an insurance agent named Benziger. There was none listed, and I didn't bother chasing the Benziger name any further than that. The uncle in question could have been an uncle by marriage, husband of the sister of one of Glenn's parents. He could even have been an honorary uncle, the father of a second cousin. There were just too many ways he could have a name that was neither Holtzmann nor Benziger.

I hung up the phone and sat there trying to figure out what to do next. It seemed to me that I was knocking on plenty of doors, but I kept getting them slammed in my face.

Was I going to have to make a trip to Altoona? God knows I didn't want to. It seemed a long way to go to chase down information that wasn't very likely to lead anywhere. But I didn't know if I could manage it from a distance. Up close, I could chase his parents' names through old city and county records, find out who all his relatives were, and come up with a name for the uncle in question.

Assuming the people I encountered were cooperative. I knew how to ensure cooperation from record clerks in New York. You bribe them. In Altoona that might not be possible.

Was I going to have to find out?

I glared at the phone, and I'll be damned if it didn't pick that moment to ring. It was Lisa. She said, "After I hung up I started thinking. Why insurance? Because he never told me he was ever in the insurance business."

"He told Eleanor Yount."

"He told me he sold cars," she said. "He sold Cad-

illacs and Chevrolets. And something else. Oldsmo-
biles?''

"When did he do that?"

"After college," she said. "Before he moved to New
York, before he went to law school."

"Under Auto Dealerships," I said. "Do you see the
name Holtzmann anywhere? Holtzmann Motors, Holtzmann Cadillac?''

They were remarkably patient at Altoona Information.
While she checked I pictured Glenn Holtzmann stretched
out on the pavement in front of a Honda dealership and
across the street from a muffler shop. The city's largest
Cadillac dealer was only a block or so away.

There were no Holtzmanns in the Altoona listings. I
asked her to try Benziger. That rang a bell, she said, but
she couldn't say why, or find a Benziger Motors on the
page. I told her I was looking for a dealership that sold
Chevrolet, Cadillac, and possibly Oldsmobile.

After a brief search she reported that only one local
dealership listed itself as an agency for Cadillac. They
had the other lines I mentioned, and GMC trucks, and
Toyota as well. "Sign of the times," she said of the last.
"That would be Nittany Motors," she said, "out on
Five Mile Road."

I took the number and dialed the call. The woman
who answered didn't believe there was a Mr. Holtzmann
present, unless it was a new man in the service department whose name she didn't know as yet. Was that who
I wanted?

"Then I guess Mr. Holtzmann's not the owner," I
said.

The idea seemed to tickle her. "Well, I guess *not*,"
she said. "Mr. Joseph Lamarck is the owner and has
been as long as there's been a Nittany Motors."

"And how long has that been?"

"Why, quite a few years now."

"And before that? Was there a time when it was Benziger Motors?"

"Why, yes," she said. "That was before my time, I'm afraid. May I ask the nature of your interest?"

I told her I was calling from New York, that I was involved in the investigation of a homicide. The deceased seemed to have been a former employee of Benziger Motors, and might have been a relative of Mr. Benziger.

"I think you ought to talk with Mr. Lamarck," she said, then came back to tell me he was busy on another line. Would I hold? I said I would.

I was lost in space when a deep male voice said, "Joe Lamarck here. Afraid I didn't get your name, sir."

I supplied it.

"And someone's been killed? Used to work here and a relative of Al Benziger's? I guess that would have to be Glenn Holtzmann."

"Did you know him?"

"Oh, sure. Not well, and I can't say I've thought of him in years, but he was a nice enough young fellow. He was Al's sister's boy, if I'm not mistaken. She raised young Glenn by herself and died about the time he went up to State College. I believe Al helped them some over the years, and then took Glenn on after he graduated."

"How did he do?"

"Oh, he did all right. I don't think he had any real feeling for the automobile business, but sometimes that comes with time. He left, though. I couldn't say what it was he was tired of, Altoona or the automobile business. May have been Al. Damn good man, but he could be hard to work for. I had to quit him."

"You used to work for Benziger?"

"Oh, sure, but I quit, oh, musta been a couple months after Glenn started. Nothing to do with Glenn, though.

Al chewed me out one time too many and I went down the street and worked for Ferris Ford. Then when Al had his troubles I came back and bought the place, but that's a whole 'nother story.''

"When did that happen?"

"Lord, fifteen years ago," he said. "History."

"That was after Glenn left."

"You bet. Several months after that Al had his troubles, and it was some time after that before I took over."

"What kind of troubles?"

There was a pause. "Well, I don't like to say," he said. "All just history now, anyway. There's nobody around played any part in it. Al and Marie left town soon as they could, and I couldn't guess where he is now. If he's alive at all, and it'd be my guess that he's not. He was a broken man when he left Altoona."

"What broke him?"

"The damn federal government," he said with feeling. "I wasn't going to say, but I'm not hurting anybody and you could find out easy enough. Al was keeping two sets of books, been doing it for years. His wife Marie was his bookkeeper and I guess they worked it out between them. He had an accountant, of course, Perry Preiss, and *he* was in trouble there for a while, until it turned out that Al and Marie had kept him in the dark all along. Still, I understand it hurt his practice.''

"What happened to the Benzigers?"

"They settled. No choice, was there now? IRS had 'em cold. It was out-and-out tax evasion, too, with a fraudulent set of books and some secret bank accounts. You couldn't say you made a mistake, you didn't report this and that because it slipped your mind. IRS wanted to, they could have put the both of them in jail. Had 'em over a barrel, and didn't show a lot of mercy, my opinion. Took Al Benziger for everything he had. I wound up buying this place. Somebody else bought their house, and somebody else got their summer place down by the lake.''

"And Glenn was gone when this happened.''

"Oh, sure. Didn't come back to rally round, either. If he even heard about it. Where was he at the time, New York?''

"New York,'' I said. "In law school, paying his way with the money he came into when his mother died.''

He asked me to repeat that. When I'd done so he said, "No, that part's wrong. Glenn Holtzmann grew up in a trailer in Roaring Spring, and they didn't even own the trailer. I don't guess his mother ever had a dime aside from what her brother gave her.''

"Maybe there was some insurance money.''

"Surprise me if there was, but anything like that would have been long gone. Didn't I say Glenn's mother died about the time he started college?''

"I guess you did.''

He said, "Raises a question, doesn't it? Where'd he get the money?''

"I don't know. How did the IRS know to come after Al Benziger?''

"My Lord,'' he said.

"Who knew about the second set of books?''

"An hour ago I'da said nobody knew. Perry Preiss didn't, I know that for a fact. *I* didn't know about it. I'da said Al and Marie and nobody else.''

"And now?''

"Now I'd have to wonder if maybe Glenn knew,'' he said. "My Lord, my Lord.''

"**H**e was a snitch," I told Drew. "A career informant, working free-lance. He got his start in Altoona selling cars for his uncle Al."

"Uncle Al in Altoona."

"He managed to find out that his aunt and uncle were evading taxes in high style. Two sets of books, secret bank accounts. I gather the uncle was a hard man to work for, so Glenn went to work for himself."

"He ratted them out to the IRS?"

"You can make money that way," I said. "I always knew that, but I never knew what a popular cottage industry it was. They've got an 800 number just for snitches. I called it yesterday and spoke with a woman who told me how the program worked. I asked her a lot of questions, and I didn't get the feeling she was hearing any of them for the first time. She must sit there all day long, chatting with the greedy and the resentful."

"Plenty of those to go around."

"I would think so. Your compensation is a percentage of the take in back taxes and penalties, and the percentage varies with the quality of the material you supply. If you bring in a set of books and make their whole case for them, that's worth more than if you just point the finger and tell them where to look.''

"Only fair.''

"You can stay anonymous, too, and I'm sure Glenn did. His uncle may have figured out who jobbed him, but maybe not. He had to step lively to stay out of Leavenworth. Sold everything he owned and left town in disgrace. I don't know how much he settled for, but Glenn's piece of the action was enough to put him through law school.''

"Did he have to pay taxes on it?''

"You know,'' I said, "I asked her about that. She said they like to collect it in advance, like withholding tax.''

"They would,'' he said.

We were in the Docket, on Joralemon Street around the corner from Brooklyn's Borough Hall. It's a nice room, high-ceilinged, the decor running to oak and brass and red leather. As the name would suggest, the patrons are lawyers for the most part, although the place is also popular with cops. Lunch hour is the busy time. They sell a lot of overstuffed sandwiches, pour a lot of drinks.

"Gorgeous day,'' Drew said.

"Beautiful,'' I said. "Last time I ate here it was like this. It was in the spring and I had lunch with a cop from Brooklyn Homicide. John Kelly, I saw him at the bar just now when I came in. It was such a nice day that I walked out of here and kept on walking clear out to Bay Ridge. I don't think I'll do that today. You know something? If yesterday had been warm and sunny I'd still be wondering where Glenn Holtzmann's money came from.''

"The weather kept you home.''

"And so I spent the whole day on the phone, and that turned out to be the right way to do it. Once I caught on to how he got his start, it wasn't hard to figure out who to call next and what to look for. When he passed the bar exam he went to work at a law firm in White Plains. Shortly after he left them the firm fell apart. The partner I talked to suggested idly that maybe Holtzmann had seen the handwriting on the wall.''

''I bet he wrote it himself.''

''And didn't sign his name. I called Jespesson back, that's the lawyer's name, to ask what had happened to the firm. The question must have caught him off base, because he didn't even ask why I wanted to know. It seems one of the other partners represented a couple of drug traffickers.''

''And the lawyer got paid in drug money and didn't report it and they sank his boat for it. You don't know how much I hate stories like this, Matt.''

''That's not quite how it went. The firm didn't do any criminal work, they represented these clients in other matters. And they got paid by check, or if any cash changed hands nobody knew about it. But this one partner developed a taste for cocaine.''

''Oh, don't tell me.''

''He funded his habit by doing a little dealing on his own. Then his partner in one of his deals turned out to be the DEA. They gave him a chance to roll over on his dealer clients, but I guess he figured a federal prison was better than an unmarked grave. By the time it was over it developed that he'd been stealing from clients, too. Jespesson gave me the impression that dissolving the firm was a cinch, that there wasn't much left to dissolve.''

''I'm assuming Holtzmann put the DEA onto the partner.''

''I'm assuming the same thing,'' I said. ''I can't call them up and ask. But I think it's a safe assumption.''

''I gather the DEA pays informants.''

''I did call and ask them that. They weren't as forthcoming as the nice lady at the tax office, but yes, they pay a bounty on drug dealers and a percentage on whatever they confiscate. I learned more about how it works from a fellow I know who knows a lot about information and its value in the open market.'' Danny Boy, and I'd called him at home; the weather had kept him indoors last night, too. ''The zero-tolerance policy may not be winning the war on drugs,'' I said, ''but it's starting to make the battles cost-effective. The first thing you do when you make a drug bust is confiscate everything within arm's reach. Vehicles, boats. Drugs, of course, but also the cash if the people you arrested came to buy. If any meetings took place in their houses, or if they stored product there, then you attach that. With so much property up for grabs, you've suddenly got a big budget for compensating informants.''

''The apartment,'' Drew said.

''It's suddenly obvious, isn't it? Some Europeans or South Americans bought it for cash under the shield of a Cayman Islands corporation. There's a dozen other things that could be besides drug money, but it's certainly up there on the list. And governmental seizure would explain how MultiCircle Productions lost the apartment when there was no mortgage for anybody to foreclose on. And then there's the US Asset Reduction Corp. I couldn't find a trace of them because they probably don't exist outside of a file folder in some government agency or other. They must be some sort of corporate shell for the liquidation of seized assets.''

''I thought they liked to get a lot of publicity with their seizures. Show the taxpayers how they're really socking it to the dope peddlers.''

''Not always,'' I said. ''Sometimes they'd just as soon keep it quiet. So nobody in Congress starts noticing how much money's passing through their hands.''

''Maybe some of it sticks to the occasional palm.''

"Not absolutely out of the question, is it?"

"And Holtzmann? What did he do to get the apartment, and who'd he do it to?"

"I don't know," I said. "My first thought was that he helped make a case against somebody in MultiCircle. But that would leave him with his cock on the block. If any of the people he screwed knew him, and then he's living in their apartment—"

"How else would he get it? It had to be compensation for some sort of informing he did."

"Say he ratted out Joe Blow and had a six-figure fee coming. And somebody said, 'Look, you need a decent place to live, and here's a list of confiscated properties up for grabs, why don't you pick one and we'll deed it to you?' "

"Virtue rewarded."

"It always is."

He got the waiter's attention and pointed to our empty coffee cups. When they'd been filled he said, "So who was Joe Blow? Any ideas?"

"No."

"Look at his résumé. He went from selling cars in Altoona to practicing law in White Plains. Where did he turn up next, this latter-day Jonah?"

"In the legal department of a publisher. That ship sank when a foreign conglomerate took them over."

"How'd he manage that?"

"I don't think he had a thing to do with it. From there he went to Waddell & Yount, and he was working there when he died. A publisher's legal department is a funny career slot for a professional snitch."

"So?"

"Well, I have a theory," I admitted. "It fits the facts, and I think it meshes with my own sense of Glenn Holtzmann."

"I keep forgetting you knew the guy."

"I didn't, really. I met him a couple of times, that's all."

"Let's hear your theory."

"I think he fell into it," I said. "I think he found out what his uncle was pulling and he felt a mixture of righteous anger and personal resentment. He did a job on Uncle Al and got himself out of Altoona in the process. He didn't take the IRS money and buy himself a Mercedes, either. He pieced it out, put himself through law school. He said it was an inheritance that enabled him to get his law degree, and I wouldn't be surprised if he saw the money as a sort of patrimony. Maybe he managed to tell himself the money should have been his in the first place, that Al Benziger got the gold mine while Glenn's mother got the shaft.

"He went to work in White Plains. Not his first choice, he'd have preferred a firm in the city, but it was the best he could do. He made a good initial impression but he turned out to have less drive than he led people to expect. The same thing happened at Waddell & Yount, incidentally. Eleanor Yount saw him as a possible successor when she took him on, but it didn't take long before she realized he didn't have it in him.

"In White Plains, he found out one of the partners was into coke in a big way. And maybe he was a little disillusioned with his job, and with the way his career was shaping up. Maybe his expenses were starting to edge out in front of his income. And here's this hotshot, using his nose for a vacuum cleaner, missing meals and doing deals. Glenn remembers Uncle Al and how satisfying it was to give him what he deserved. Profitable, too."

"So he drops a dime on him."

"Funny how we still call it that, considering how long a phone call's cost a quarter. But that's what he does. Once again he's out of there when the shit hits the fan.

He gets a job with a publishing house, stays there as long as he can, then settles in with another publisher. He's not ambitious and he's no high liver. He's in a small studio apartment in the East Eighties.

"Somewhere along the way he sees another chance to make a buck. My first thought was that he met Lisa, decided they needed a place to live, and quick found someone to sell out. But the timing's wrong. I think he was minding his own business when an opportunity came along and he grabbed it."

" 'I seen my opportunities and I took 'em.' " When I looked blank Drew said, "George Washington Plunkett, Tammany hack of the last century. He wrote this strangely candid political memoir, honest and self-serving at the same time. That's what he said. He seen his opportunities and he took 'em. I wonder what opportunity our friend saw."

"I don't know," I said. "If I had to guess, I'd say it had nothing to do with his work. It probably involved somebody he knew in Yorkville."

"Because he moved."

"That was his pattern, wasn't it? Screw somebody and then get the hell out. He did a job on someone and had a nice fee coming. 'Well, Glenn, how would you like the money?' 'Maybe you could pay me in real estate. What's available these days?' 'Let's see, here's something nice in a two-bedroom condo. High floor, river view, owned by a Corsican gentleman who only drove it on Sundays. Here's the keys, why don't you take it around the block?' "

"Is that how it works? They show you what's available and let you pick?"

"I don't know how it works. But I think that's essentially how he got the condo. This was right around the time he met Lisa. When that got serious he told them to push the paperwork, and by the time they got back from

Bermuda the place was ready for them to move in.''

"And the money in the strongbox?''

"Another job, I suppose. Or the same one. My guess is that something shifted for him when he got married, if it hadn't already. He began to see this sideline of his as a profession, not just something he'd fallen into once or twice. He started looking for opportunities.''

"How do you know that?''

"From his schedule. At work he had all he could do to fill eight hours, but he told Lisa stories about a heavy work load that kept him at his desk nights and weekends. I think he was out prospecting. I think that's why he was interested in me.''

"He figured he could clip you for tax evasion, huh? What would they seize, your extra pair of shoes?''

"It was my occupation that fascinated him,'' I said. "He told me he wanted to publish my memoirs. Well, that was a lot of crap. His firm didn't publish originals. What he wanted was to find out how a detective operates. He wanted me to teach him the tricks of the trade. He may have envisioned the two of us as partners, digging up dirt on people and transmuting it into gold. I never found out what he had in mind because I didn't like him enough to offer him any encouragement.''

"So he nosed around on his own.''

"Evidently.''

"Who killed him?''

"I don't know.''

"No idea?''

"None,'' I said. "I assume he was prospecting, sticking his nose in where it didn't belong. Someone must have tipped to what he was doing.''

"And shot him.''

"It's a chance you take when you run around setting up dope dealers. You run less of a risk turning in relatives for cheating on their taxes. But sooner or later you're going to run out of relatives, and dabblers like the lawyer in White Plains. When the other players are pros, you can wind up getting killed.''

"An occupational hazard.''

"I would say so. On the other hand, it's still odds-on that it happened the way the police figured it from the start.''

"George Sadecki.''

"There's a good chance he did it, and what difference does it make if he didn't? Clearing his name's not worth a dime to anybody. My guess is he's innocent, but I couldn't begin to back that up, let alone tell you who's guilty. Glenn didn't leave notes, or one of those traditional sealed envelopes to be opened in the event of his death.''

"Some people have no consideration. You want some more coffee?''

I shook my head. "Somebody's probably getting away with murder,'' I said, "but that happens all the time.''

"And it couldn't have happened to a nicer guy.''

"I don't know how bad a guy he was. On the one hand he was a paid rat, but you could make a case that he was an unheralded yuppie hero, collecting a bounty on bad guys. However you look at it, I don't have this sense of his ghost crying out for revenge.''

"What about our mutual client? Can she sleep nights if her husband's killer goes unpunished?''

"I don't see why not. You're her attorney. What's in her best interests?''

He thought about it. "To let it lie,'' he said.

"That's what I would have said.''

"Put in another few days looking for hidden assets. But I don't think we're going to find any.''

"No, neither do I.''

"On the other hand, I don't think we're going to get

any static from the IRS, either. I see her coming out of this with the deed to an apartment and a box full of money. That doesn't sound so bad.''

"No."

"You want it to come out neat," he said. "Be nice to know who killed him and how and why. Be even nicer to see the killer go away for it. I have to tell you, though, the best interests of the client are served with the whole thing closed out on the spot. Make a case out of this, generate a little press, and you just know some schmuck from the tax office is going to turn up with a million questions, and who needs that?''

"Nobody."

"Never get a conviction anyway. Whoever did it, by now he's sure to be alibied from here to St. Louis. Probably got proof he was playing pinochle with the pope and the Lubavitcher rebbe when Holtzmann got hit.''

"Must have been some game.''

"Well, you know the pope," Drew said. "No card sense, but he loves to play.''

22

A few days later I put on a suit and tie and went to the window, trying to guess if the weather would hold. It was sunny now, cool and clear, and I hoped it would stay that way.

Something drew my eye down to the benches alongside the Parc Vendôme, and I saw a familiar silhouette hunched over one of the stone cubes. I went downstairs, and instead of turning left for the subway I crossed the street and approached the lean black man with the white hair. He had a copy of the *Times* folded open to the chess column, and he was working out the problem with his own board and chessmen.

"You look nice," he said. "I like your necktie."

I thanked him. I said, "Barry, they're having a service for George this afternoon. I'm going out to Brooklyn for it."

"That right?"

"His brother called and told me about it. Just family, but he said I'd be welcome."

"Be a nice day for it," he said. " 'less it rains."

"You'd be welcome, too."

"At the funeral?"

"I thought maybe we could go together."

274

He looked at me, a long, appraising look. "No," he said. "I guess not."

"If you're thinking you won't fit in," I said, "well, hell, you'll fit in as well as I will."

"Guess you're right," he said. "We're both the same color, and dressed about the same."

"Oh, for Christ's sake."

"Thing is," he said, "it don't matter, fitting in or not fitting in. I don't care to go. You come back, tell me how it was. How's that?"

I rode out on the D-train. They buried him out of a funeral parlor on Nostrand Avenue, and there were more people in attendance than I would have expected, close to fifty in all. Tom, his wife, his sister, their relatives. Neighbors, employees, AA friends. The crowd was mostly white and a majority of the men wore ties and jackets, but there were a few black faces, a few gentlemen in shirtsleeves. Barry would not have been greatly out of place.

The casket was closed, the service brief. The clergyman who officiated hadn't known George, and he spoke of death as a liberation from the bondage of physical and mental infirmity. The veils drop away, he said, and blind eyes can see again. The spirit soars.

Tom followed him and said a few words. In a sense, he said, we'd all lost George a long time ago. "But we went on loving him," he said. "We loved the sweetness of him. And there was always the hope that someday the clouds would blow away and we'd get him back. And now he's gone and that can never happen. But in another sense we do have him back with us. He's with us now and he'll never lose his way again." His voice broke, but he squeezed the last words out. "I love you, George," he said.

There were two hymns, "Onward, Christian Soldiers" and "Abide With Me." A heavyset woman with dark hair to her waist sang them both unaccompanied, her voice filling the room. During the first hymn I thought of George in his army jacket, his pocket full of shell casings. The old soldier, fading away. Listening to the second, I remembered a version on a Thelonious Monk album, just eight bars long, just the melody. Haunting. Jan Keane owned the record. I hadn't heard it in years.

After the service there was a procession of cars following the hearse to a cemetery in Queens, but I passed on that and caught a train back to Manhattan. I found Barry right where I'd left him. I sat down across from him and told him all about George's funeral. He heard me through and suggested we play a little chess.

"One game," I said.

It didn't take him long to beat me. When I tipped my king over he suggested a toast to George's memory might be fitting. I gave him five dollars and he came back with a quart of malt liquor and a cup of coffee. After several long swallows he capped the bottle and said, "See, I don't never go to funerals. Don't believe in 'em. What's the point?"

"It's a way to say goodbye."

"Don't believe in that either. People come and people go. Just the way of the world."

"I suppose so."

"Matter of what you get used to, is all it is. George came around and I got used to him. Got used to him being around. Now he's gone and I'm used to that. Get used to anything, if you give yourself half a chance."

Early the following week they finally released Glenn Holtzmann's remains. I think they might have done so earlier if his widow had asked. I made a few calls for Lisa and arranged to have the body picked up at the morgue and cremated. There was no service.

"It seems incomplete," Elaine said. "Shouldn't there be some sort of service? There must be people who would come."

"You could probably round up a contingent from his office," I said, "but I don't think he had any friends as such. The easiest thing for her is a quick private cremation and no service."

"Will she have to attend? Do you think you ought to go with her?"

"She seems to have it all under control," I said, "and I'd just as soon start letting go."

So I didn't keep Lisa Holtzmann company when she picked up her husband's ashes. A day or two later, though, I left an AA meeting at ten o'clock and felt a restlessness I couldn't walk off, or talk myself out of.

I picked up the phone. "This is Matt," I said. "Do you feel like company?"

The following morning I walked over to Midtown North. Joe Durkin wasn't around, but I didn't need him for the task at hand. I talked to several different cops, explaining that I was working for Holtzmann's widow and that the personal effects returned to her had been incomplete. "She never got his keys back," I said. "He definitely would have had his keys with him, and she never got them back."

Nobody knew anything. "Well, shit," one cop said. "Tell her to change the locks."

I went through the same thing at Manhattan Homicide, and at Central Booking. I spent most of the day bothering people who had more important things to do, but by late afternoon I walked out of a police station with a set of keys in my pocket. It wasn't hard to establish that the keys were Holtzmann's—one of them fit the door to his and Lisa's apartment. It was easy to pick out the key to his safe-deposit box, and an officer at my own bank had a chart which enabled us to determine the bank and branch where we would find that box.

Drew Kaplan obtained authorization to open the box, and he and Lisa did so, accompanied by the inescapable representative of the Internal Revenue Service. I suppose everyone was hoping for cash and Krugerrands, but there was nothing inside to quicken anybody's pulse. A birth certificate, a marriage license. Old snapshots of unidentified persons, school pictures of Glenn.

"The prick from the IRS couldn't stand it," Drew reported. "Why have a box if he didn't have anything to keep in it? And why not have the smallest size? There must have been something else in there, he said. Obviously we got into the box, scooped the cash, and then called Uncle Sam. I suggested he look at the bank's records and confirm that no one had obtained access to the box since the boxholder's death. Which he already knew, the irritating little bastard, but he figured one way or another the government was getting screwed."

"Which they must have been."

"I would say so," he said. "If I had to guess, I'd say the money she found in the closet used to live in the safe-deposit box. Their records put him there a week to the day before he got hit. I'd say he went in there and took out his money and put it in a tin box and stuck it in his closet. Now why would he do that?"

"In case he needed it in a hurry."

"That's one. For a cash transaction, or just because he wanted to be able to cut and run. The other thought comes to me is maybe he had a premonition."

"I like that the best," I said. "He realizes he's in danger and wants to make sure she gets the money. That would explain why there was nothing else in the box that could embarrass anybody. He was already imagining the IRS looking over his widow's shoulder."

"And we know he knows all about the IRS, ever since he sicced them on Uncle Al."

"And we know he had good feelings toward her," I said, "because he picked their wedding anniversary for the strongbox combination."

"I didn't know that."

"Five-eleven," I said. "May eleventh."

"Nice touch," he said. "And nice job finding the keys."

"Oh, they'd have turned up sooner or later."

"Don't bet on it," he said. "You ever want to hide where you'll never be found, check into a police department warehouse and stretch out on a shelf. They got Peter Stuyvesant's wooden leg there, and you can use Boss Tweed's wallet for a pillow."

That should have been the end of it.

I'd done what I'd been hired to do. I hadn't established who'd pulled the trigger, but that had not been my assignment. I'd signed on to protect the financial interests of Lisa Holtzmann, and it seemed as though I'd done that. The last act I performed on her behalf consisted of accompanying her once more to Drew's office, where we collected the strongbox. We cabbed back to Manhattan and went to a bank on Second Avenue where she still had an account in her maiden name. She rented a safe-deposit box there and stowed the cash in it. It could stay there forever if it had to, or until someone figured out a good way to launder it.

I had been generously paid for my time, but it wasn't the most I'd ever earned for the least amount of work, and I don't think I felt grossly overpaid.

Anyway, it averages out. A week or so after I helped Lisa stash her money, I did some work for a woman who lived in a housing project in Chelsea. The job came to me through someone I knew from AA; this woman was the friend of a sister, or the sister of a friend, something like that. The woman had thrown out her live-in boyfriend when she found out he was molesting her nine-year-old daughter. The boyfriend didn't want to stay thrown out. He'd come back twice and beaten her up. After the second time she got an order of protection, but that's only useful after the fact; he'd promptly violated it, and violated the daughter while he was at it. She reported this, and the police had a warrant for the guy's arrest, but no one knew where he was living and they weren't about to launch a major manhunt over what the cops were inclined to categorize as a domestic disturbance.

I moved into the woman's apartment, staking it out from within. The woman was pretty in a lush, overblown way. She drank enough wine to stay permanently unfocused, smoked Newport Lights one after another, played solitaire by the hour, and never turned off the television set in the five days I spent in her apartment.

I would sit in a chair all day, reading a book or watching the TV if she happened to have it tuned to something I could stand. I used the phone a lot to keep from going crazy. Around midnight Eddie Rankin would come over. He's an occasional employee of the Reliable agency, a big towhead with quick reflexes and an appetite for violence. I figured the boyfriend was most likely to come around at night, and Eddie would be good if it got physical. He and I would tell lies for an hour or two, until I got drowsy enough to nap on the couch. At five he would wake me and I'd pay him a hundred dollars and send him home.

I don't think I could have stood it for more than a week, but the boyfriend showed up on the fifth night. It was around two-thirty. The kid was asleep in her bedroom. The woman had passed out in her chair in front of the TV, as she did every night. The set was still on, and Eddie was watching it while I was dozing lightly. I heard a key in the lock, and I was sitting up and throwing my legs over the side of the couch when the door burst open and the boyfriend came in, wild-eyed and roaring.

I never had to move. Eddie was on him before he got two steps in the door. He hit him with a hard left just below the rib cage, and he must have found the liver because it took the poor son of a bitch completely out of the play. He fell as if he'd been gutshot, and caught Eddie's knee in his face on the way down.

We could have called the cops and she could have pressed charges, assuming she would wake up enough to follow through with it. But he would have made bail, people like that always make bail, and he probably would have come over and killed her. He might have done that this time if we hadn't been there; I frisked him while he was lying there moaning, and took a seven-inch folding knife off him.

The idea was to keep him from coming back. "Maybe he fell off the roof," Eddie said, dragging the clown over to the window as he talked. "He strikes me as the kind of guy, he walks on roofs a lot, he tends to fall off."

But of course we didn't throw him off the roof, or out the window. What we did do was a pretty good job of beating the crap out of him. Eddie did it, actually—kicking him in the groin, in the ribs, stepping down hard on his hands. I'd have had to have been in a rage to do any of that, and once the situation itself was under control, so were my emotions. Eddie, on the other hand, was never far from rage, and could turn it on at will, with no provocation whatsoever.

If pressed, I could probably guess what kind of childhood he had.

When he'd had enough we got the boyfriend on his

feet and out the door. In the stairwell I took hold of him by the front of his shirt and told him I never wanted to see him again. "If you ever come around here again," I said, "I'll break your arms and your legs, and I'll put your eyes out, and I'll cut your dick off and make you eat it."

We got out of there and rode in Eddie's car to a diner he liked. "I was gonna have knockwurst," he said, "until you said that shit about making him eat his dick. You want to tell me something? How come the fucker had a key?"

"I guess she didn't change the lock."

"Jesus Christ."

"Well, it costs. She's not rolling in dough, as you may have guessed from a look around the place."

"Hey, she had money to pay us," he said. "You gave me, what, hundred a night for five nights, plus the extra yard for tonight"—I'd given him a bonus for combat duty—"is what, six bills? And how much are you getting, if you don't mind me asking?"

I admitted I wasn't getting paid, and told him when he pressed that his wages had come out of my pocket. He asked if she was family. I said no, and he frowned and asked if I was sleeping with her.

I said, "Jesus, Eddie."

"Well, shit," he said. "I mean, what are you, the March of fucking Dimes?"

"Lawyers call it 'pro bono,'" I said. "Once in a while I do one for free. She's a friend of a friend and she's got no money and you can't let a shitbag like that walk all over somebody that way."

"He was a shitbag, all right."

"So it was easier to help her out than explain why I couldn't," I said. "That's all. I don't make a habit of it."

"Shit, I should hope not," he said. And later, when

we were on our way out, he said, "One more time, Matt. You sure you're not poking her?"

"Yeah, I'm sure," I said. "And what difference does it make?"

"Well, I was thinking I might try my luck," he said. "But not if I'd be stepping on your toes."

"My toes'll be in another part of town," I said. "But are you serious?"

"Why not?"

"Well . . ."

"Look," he said, "I know she's a pig. But she's built nice, and she's got those sleepy eyes. Hey, I'm not talking love affair. I'd like to do her once, that's all."

"Be my guest."

"Those eyes an' that mouth. She looks like you could get her to do anything, you know what I mean?"

I was silent for a moment. Then I said, "Just don't touch the kid."

"Hey," he said. "What am I, an animal? Don't answer that."

"I won't."

"I may be an animal," he said, "but there's a limit."

It wasn't long after that that I celebrated my anniversary. Another sober year, a day at a time.

An accepted article of AA folk wisdom holds that we tend to experience a lot of anxiety around the anniversary of our last drink, and I suppose it's generally true. I'd be hard put to say how I felt this time around, and it seemed to me that I had more things to blame it on than my anniversary.

We celebrated the occasion. I qualified at an open meeting at a senior center on Ninth Avenue, and Elaine attended and got to hear me tell my story, and not for the first time. Afterward we went out for dinner with Jim and Beverly Faber.

"You'll see," Jim said. "It sneaks up on you. One of these days you'll wake up and realize you've got Long-Term Sobriety."

"I'll probably have serenity, too," I said.

"I don't know about that. But you might actually have enough time so that you can say you've been sober 'a few twenty-four hours.'"

"Never happen."

Some of the old-timers talk like that. I know a few who never acknowledge their own anniversaries, let alone celebrate the occasion. Just another day, they say, and maybe they're right.

Elaine and I went back to her place after dinner. We sat up talking for a while, then went to bed and made love. I was just about asleep, just slipping over the edge, and then something woke me. I don't know what it was. Elaine was lying on her side, facing away from me, her breathing slow and regular. I lay there, not wanting to move for fear of waking her. I hoped I'd drift off, but eventually I had to give up and go in the other room.

I sat on the couch with the lights off and tried to get rid of the thought that was keeping me awake. What I couldn't stop thinking was that someday I would drink again. It seemed perfectly inevitable to me.

And maybe that's why the old-timers don't think in terms of years. Maybe it's dangerous to take long views, or think long thoughts.

Every three or four days I would stop in at Grogan's and spend some time with Ballou. I would get there late, near closing time, and we'd sit at a table and drink. Irish whiskey for him, coffee or Coke or club soda for me. The best time was when the customers were gone, and the bartender put up the chairs and swept the floor and went home. Then we'd sit there with all the lights off but one and tell stories and share silences.

He liked the story about my pro bono work in Chelsea.

"You have to hurt the man," he said. "If you're not inclined to kill him—and you didn't want to kill him, did you?"

"No."

"It's kill them or throw the fear of God into them, and with some of them killing's the easier. You can hurt your man and throw a good scare into him, and then he gets drunk or takes some fucking drug and there's no fear in him. Do you know what I mean?"

"He forgets."

"That's it exactly. He forgets that he's afraid of you. It slips his fucking mind. So you must hurt him badly enough that he simply cannot forget it, he'd sooner forget his own name."

The words echoed in the still air. In the silence that followed I wondered if it wasn't simpler to kill, simpler and more certain. Especially if you were a man who killed easily, a man to whom it was second nature. I looked at my friend Mick Ballou, of whom I was uncommonly fond, and thought of another man of whom I had not been fond at all. The silence stretched, and I kept my night thoughts to myself.

When the night ran long, more often than not he'd urge me to join him at mass. He liked to close out the night at the eight o'clock mass at St. Bernard's on Fourteenth Street. His father had attended that mass every morning, cloaked in his white butcher's apron, kneeling in the little side chapel, receiving communion before he went off to wield his cleaver a block away.

Mick had his father's old apron, and he always wore it when he went to mass. He still owned the old man's cleaver, too, but he left that home. His father had begun each day at the butchers' mass; Mick would get up from his knees and go off to bed—in one of several apartments around town with a name other than his own on the deed or lease, at the farm upstate, or on the old leather couch in his office at Grogan's. And, unlike his father, he didn't ordinarily take communion.

Once, though, we had both stepped up to the altar, had in turn taken the wafer. He'd had the cleaver with him earlier that night, and had cut fresh meat with it. We had both of us bloodied our aprons before standing together in a singular act of sacrilege or piety, as you prefer.

Had my old friend put fresh blood on that apron?

Come to mass with me, he'd urge me now, as the night turned to morning. Not tonight, I'd always say. Another time, perhaps, but not tonight.

Elaine stopped going to her class.

One night we were at dinner and I realized that she was supposed to be in a classroom. I started to say something and she stopped me. "Don't worry about it," she said. "I dropped the course."

"Why?"

"Except I didn't do anything as formal as drop it. I just stopped going. When you're not taking these things for credit there's no point in withdrawing formally. That would be like sending a certified letter to Channel Thirteen telling them you were about to turn off *Nova*. Why bother? You can just click the remote and watch *Roseanne* like the rest of America."

I asked her how come she didn't want to go anymore.

"I don't know," she said.

"Oh."

"Because it's bullshit," she said. "Because I'm such a cliché, another old broad with time on her hands and nothing to do with it. I'm like the lilies of the field, I don't toil and I don't spin, and what fucking good am I?"

"I thought you enjoyed the classes."

"They're not my life."

"No."

"They can't be my life. I don't have a life. That's the problem."

I didn't know what to say, what to suggest. And, while I was trying to think of something, her mood changed. It was as if she'd hit a button on her own personal remote and switched herself to another channel.

"Enough of that," she said. "No long faces, no soul-searching in public places. People like to see you smile. At least that's what they taught us in Call Girl School."

Every few days I would pick up the phone and call Lisa. Sometimes I called her in the afternoon, sometimes late at night. She was almost always home. I would ask if I could come over. She would always tell me to come.

After a while she changed the message on her machine, replacing Glenn's final phrases with some equally bland lines of her own. My first reaction, once I'd realized that I hadn't dialed a wrong number, was one of relief that I wouldn't have to listen to that voice from the spirit world anymore, wouldn't have to hear the man out before I got to speak with his wife.

But the next time I heard her message I could hear his voice along with it, intoning lines from "Flanders Fields."

> *If ye break faith with us who die*
> *We shall not sleep . . .*

I never saw her outside of the apartment, never called her to talk, never took her downstairs for a cup of coffee or a bite to eat. I would go over there, early or late. She might be wearing anything—jeans and a sweatshirt, a skirt and sweater, a nightgown. We would talk. She told me about growing up in White Bear Lake, and about the way her father had started coming to her bed when she was nine or ten. He did everything but put it inside her. That would be wrong, he told her.

I told her war stories, sketched word portraits of some of the characters I'd known over the years, the unusual specimens I'd encountered on either side of the law. That way I could hold up my end of the conversation without revealing very much of myself, which was fine with me.

And we would go to bed.

One afternoon, with a Patsy Cline record playing in the background, she asked me what I figured we were doing. Just being together, I suggested.

"No," she said. "You know what I mean. What's the point? Why are you here?"

"Everybody's got to be someplace."

"I'm serious."

"I know you are. I don't have any answers. I'm here because I want to be here, but I don't know why that is."

Patsy was singing about faded love.

"I hardly leave this apartment," Lisa said. "I sit at the window and look at New Jersey. I could be out making the rounds, showing my book to art directors, calling the people I know, trying to get some work. Tomorrow, I tell myself. Next week, next month. After the first of the year. What the hell, everybody knows there's no work now. The economy's a mess. Everybody knows that."

"It's true, isn't it?"

"I don't know. I haven't been looking for work, so how do I know it's not out there? But how can I work up any enthusiasm for the struggle when I've got all that money just sitting there?''

"If you're not under any pressure—"

"I could be doing my own work," she said. "But I don't do that either. I sit around. I look at TV. I watch the sun go down. I wait for you to call. I hope you won't call, but that's what I'm waiting for. For you to call.''

I waited in similar fashion, waited for my own action, to call or not to call. I won't call her today, I would decide. And sometimes I'd stick to my decision. And sometimes I wouldn't.

"Why do you come over here, Matt?"

"I don't know.''

"What am I, do you figure? Am I a drug? Am I a bottle of booze?''

"Maybe.''

"My father drank. I know I told you that.''

"Yes.''

"The other day when you kissed me I had the sense that there was something missing, and I realized what it was. It was the smell of whiskey on your breath. We don't need a psychiatrist to figure that one out, do we?''

I didn't say anything. *I remember our faded love*, sang Patsy Cline.

"So I guess that's what's in it for me," she said. "I get to have Daddy in bed with me, and I don't have to worry that Mommy'll hear us because she's all the way across town. And he wouldn't put it in. He thought it was a sin.''

"So do I.''

"You do?''

I nodded. "But I do it anyway," I said.

Later that same day she talked about her late husband. We never talked about Elaine, I had ruled out that topic of conversation, but I couldn't presume to tell her I didn't want to hear about him either.

"I wonder if he expected this," she said.

"This?"

"Us. I think he did."

"What makes you say that?"

"I don't know. He admired you, I know that much."

"He thought I could be useful."

"It was more than that. He put it in my mind to call you. You called me, I realize that, but I was going to call you. I remember he told me once that if a person was ever in a jam, you'd be a good person to call. He said it with a certain intensity, too, as if he wanted to make sure I would remember later. It's as if he was telling me to call you if anything ever happened to him."

"You could be reading more into his words than he put there."

"I don't think so," she said, burrowing into the crook of my arm. "I think that was exactly what he meant. In fact I'm surprised there wasn't a note in the strongbox, along with the money. 'Call Matt Scudder, he'll tell you exactly what to do.'" Her hand reached for me. "Well? Aren't you going to tell me exactly what to do?"

And when I left her apartment that day I walked a block to Eleventh Avenue and down to the corner where he died. I stood there while the lights changed several times, then walked on down to DeWitt Clinton Park to pay my respects to the Captain. I read McCrae's misquoted words:

> IF YE BREAK FAITH
> WITH THOSE WHO DIED
> WE SHALL NOT SLEEP. . .

Had I broken faith, with Glenn Holtzmann, with George Sadecki? Was there more I could do, and was my inaction keeping their spirits restless?

What action could I take? And how could I bring myself to take it, if I was afraid of where it might lead?

Two weeks before Christmas Elaine and I had dinner with Ray and Bitsy Galindez at a Caribbean restaurant in the East Village. Ray is a police artist; working with eyewitnesses, he produces drawings of unidentified perpetrators for Wanted posters and NYPD circulars. His is an uncommon craft, and Ray is uncommonly good at what he does. I have used him twice in cases of my own, and on both occasions he did an extraordinary job of dredging up faces from some broom closet in my mind and making them visible on paper.

After dinner we went back to Elaine's, where the sketches he'd made for me were framed and hanging on the wall. They made a curious group. Two of the drawings showed murderers, the third a boy who had been a victim of one of the men. The other man—his name was James Leo Motley—had come very close to killing Elaine.

Bitsy Galindez had never been to Elaine's apartment before and had never seen the sketches. She looked at them and shuddered, saying she couldn't understand how Elaine could bear to look at them every day. Elaine told her they were works of art, that they transcended their subject matter. Ray, a little embarrassed, said they were decent draftsmanship, good likenesses, that it was true he had a knack, but that it was a hell of a stretch to call it art.

"You don't even know how good you are," Elaine countered. "I wish I had a gallery. I'd give you a show."

"A gallery," he said. "Have to be a rogues' gallery, wouldn't it?"

"I'm serious, Ray. In fact I was thinking of having you do a portrait of Matt."

"Who'd he kill? Just a joke."

"You do portraits, don't you?"

"When somebody asks." He held up his hands. "This is no false modesty, Elaine, but there's a hundred guys out on the street with easels and drawing pads who can do your portrait as good as I can, and maybe better. You sit for me and I do your portrait, it's not gonna be anything special. Believe me."

"That's probably true," she said, "because what makes your work unique is the way you draw a person without seeing him. What I was thinking was that you could draw Matt by working with me, as if he were a suspect and I an eyewitness."

"But I've already seen him."

"I know."

"So that would get in the way. But I see what you're saying, I do. It's an interesting idea."

"My father," she said.

"Beg your pardon?"

"You could do my father," she said. "He's dead, he died years ago. I have some photographs of him, of course. He's in one of the framed photos to the right of the front door, but don't look at it."

"I won't."

"In fact I'm going to take it down so you don't happen to glance at it by accident later on your way out.

This is an exciting idea for me, Ray. Could you do that, do you think? Could the two of us sit down and you'd do a drawing of my father?''

"I guess so," he said. "I don't see why not."

To me she said, "That's what I want for Christmas. I hope you didn't buy my present yet because this is what I really want."

"It's yours," I said.

"My daddy," she said. "You know, it's hard to picture him in my mind. I wonder if I'll be able to do it."

"The memory will come back when you need it."

She looked at me. "It's starting already," she said, and her eyes filled with tears. "Excuse me," she said, and got to her feet.

After they left she said, "I'm not crazy, you know. He really has an uncanny ability."

"I know."

"It'll be emotional, working with him. You saw how I got just thinking about it. But it's something I really want to do. If I cry a little, so be it. Kleenex is cheap, right?"

"Right."

"If I could, I'd give him a show."

"Why don't you?" She looked at me. "You've said that before," I said, "and not just about Ray. Maybe you ought to open a gallery."

"What a wacky idea."

"Maybe it's not so wacky."

"I've thought of it," she admitted. "It would be another fucking hobby, though, wouldn't it? And more expensive than taking courses at Hunter."

"Chance made a good thing out of it."

Chance was a friend of ours, a black man who had collected African art for years and now sold it quite successfully out of a gallery on upper Madison Avenue.

"Chance is different," she said. "By the time Chance went into the business he knew more about his field than ninety percent of the people who were dealing in it. But what the hell do I know about anything?"

I pointed at a large abstract canvas hanging near the window. "Tell me again what you paid for that one," I said, "and what it's worth now."

"That was luck."

"Or a good eye."

She shook her head. "I don't know enough about art. And I don't know a thing about merchandising it. Let's be realistic, okay? All I ever sold was pussy."

It was funny how the mood flattened out. We'd had a good time with Ray and Bitsy, and the prospect of collaborating on a portrait of her father had excited her, but now the blues rolled in like cloud cover. I had been planning on staying over, but a little before midnight I told her I felt the need for a meeting. "I'll just go back to the hotel afterward," I said, and she didn't try to talk me out of it.

There are two regular midnight meetings in Manhattan, one on West Forty-sixth Street, one downtown on Houston. I picked the closer of the two and sat on a rickety chair for an hour drinking bad coffee. The fellow who led the meeting had started out sniffing airplane glue at seven and had left no mind-altering substance unexplored in the years since then. He'd hit his first detox at fifteen, had arrested in an emergency room at eighteen, and had twice almost died of endocarditis contracted via IV heroin use. He was now twenty-four, had been sober two years and change, had sustained some permanent cardiovascular damage, and had just recently been diagnosed as HIV-positive.

"But I'm sober," he said.

At one point I looked around the room and realized I

was the oldest man in the room by a considerable margin, except for a wispy white-haired fellow in the corner who was arguably the oldest man in America. A couple of times during the discussion I was on the point of raising my hand, but something stopped me. I was at least as close to leaving before the meeting was over, but I didn't do that either, dutifully remaining until the hour was up.

Afterward I walked over to Tenth Avenue, and up to Grogan's Open House.

Mick said, "Do you remember the first time we talked? I made you take off your shirt."

"You wanted to make sure I wasn't wearing a wire."

"I did," he said. "By God, I hope you're not wearing one tonight."

Burke had gone for the night. The floor was swept, and all the tables but ours were topped with chairs. One light still burned. Mick had just told me a story that would have put him in jail if he'd told it in court. It had happened long ago, but it involved acts for which there is no statute of limitations.

"No wires," I said. I looked down into my glass. It held club soda, but the way I was gazing into it you'd have thought it was filled with something stronger. I used to stare like that into glasses of whiskey, as if they contained coded answers. All they did was dissolve the questions, but there was a time when that was enough. "No wires. No strings, either."

"Are you all right, man?"

"I suppose so," I said. "I finished up three days of per diem for Reliable yesterday. Then I spent this afternoon comforting a widow."

"Oh?"

"Or she comforted me. Right now it seems cold comfort all around."

He waited.

"A former client," I said finally. "You remember the fellow who was shot on Eleventh Avenue."

"I do. I thought you were done with that."

"I don't seem to be done with his wife."

"Ah."

Someone tried the door. It was locked and gated, but the one light burning and ourselves at a table was enough to kindle hope in the breast of some poor drunk every now and then. Mick stood, walked halfway to the door, and motioned for the fellow to go away. He tried the knob one more time before he gave up and moved on.

Mick sat down again and filled his glass. "He came in here a time or two," he said. "Did I ever tell you that?"

"Holtzmann?"

"Himself. This past summer we got our share of them that don't belong here. Part of it's the neighborhood changing, and then there was that fucking newspaper article."

Newsday had run a column on Grogan's, an affectionately Runyonesque report on the raffish crowd, with special emphasis on the legends surrounding Mick himself. I said, "That drew people? You'd have thought it would have scared them away."

"You would," he said, "but humans are a strange race of men. Your man came in around that time, looking around the way they'll do. As if he might spy a corpse in the corner."

"He was an informer," I said.

"Oh?"

"He sold out an uncle to the IRS, then set up another lawyer for a drug bust."

"By God," he said.

"He did pretty well at it. But it may have been what got him killed."

"It wasn't the other lad? Your man in the army jacket?"

"Well, it might have been. There's no telling."

"No telling," he said reflectively. "And if it wasn't the bum? Who then?"

"Someone he was setting up."

"Was he a blackmailer, then?"

"No, not unless he decided to branch out."

He frowned. "Then who'd know to kill him? The uncle? The lawyer?"

"It doesn't seem very likely."

"Not a case in progress, I shouldn't think, or ye'd have seen federal agents buzzing round like blowflies in carrion. Someone he was setting up, you said. And hadn't yet gone to the DEA or the IRS or whatever collection of initials he was planning to run to."

"Right."

"So how would your man know to kill him? And why kill him? Why not warn him off? What do you think he'd do if someone had a word with him?"

"Run like a rabbit."

"I'd say the same. Ye wouldn't even have to raise your hand to the man. If it had been me, I'd never have raised my voice. I'd have lowered it, I'd have spoken very softly."

"And carried a big stick?"

"You wouldn't need the stick for that lad."

"Maybe it was someone from the past," I said. "Not the uncle or the lawyer but someone from another job he did, one I don't know about. Someone who had a score to settle with Holtzmann."

"And found him on Eleventh Avenue? Was he to be found there often? Is that where a man would go looking for him?"

"Someone could have followed him there."

"And shot him down when he reached for the telephone?" He picked up his glass. "Ah, Jesus, who am I to tell you your business?"

"Somebody's got to do it," I said.

We talked of other things and let the silence stretch out between our stories. He wasn't hitting the Jameson bottle very hard, just topping up his glass often enough to keep from losing that edge. It was maintenance drinking, and I remembered it well; I had done my own share of it, until life took me to a point where maintaining was no longer possible because the traitorous booze would get me drunk before it would let me get comfortable.

Something was playing hide-and-seek in my memory, something I'd heard or read in the past day or two. But I couldn't quite manage to grab on to it. . . .

The days are short that time of year, but eventually the sky outside turned light. Mick went behind the bar and started a pot of coffee brewing. He filled two mugs and sweetened his with whiskey, and I'd hate to guess how many times I had mixed the two. The perfect combination—caffeine to enliven the mind, alcohol to silence the soul.

We drank our coffee. He looked at his watch, checked the time against the clock over the back bar. "Time for mass," he announced. "Will you come?"

The priest was Irish born, almost young enough to be an altar boy. There were only a dozen or so in the congregation, most of them nuns, and no one but Mick robed in butcher's white. I think the two of us were the only ones who didn't take communion.

He'd parked the silver Cadillac in front of the funeral parlor next door to the church. We got in and he put the key in the ignition but didn't start the car right away. He said, "Are ye all right, man?"

"I think so."

"How is it with you and herself?"

He meant Elaine. "It's a little strained," I said.

"Does she know about the other one?"

"No."

"And do ye care for her? The other one, I mean."

"She's a decent woman," I said. "I wish her well."

He waited.

"No," I said. "I don't care for her. I don't know what the hell I'm doing in her life. I don't know what the hell she's doing in mine."

"Ah, Jesus," he said. "You don't drink."

As if that explained everything.

"So?"

"So a man has to do something, some fucking thing or other." He turned the key in the ignition, fed gas to the big engine. "It's nature," he said.

There was a message at the hotel desk. *Call Jan Keane.*

"Happy anniversary," she said. "I'm what, a month late?"

"A little less than that."

"Close enough. You know, I remembered the date, I had myself all set to call you, and then it slipped my mind entirely. Fell right through a hole in my brain."

"It happens."

"With increasing frequency, as a matter of fact. I'd be afraid it was the early stages of Alzheimer's, but you know what? That's really not something I'm going to have to worry about."

I said, "How are you, Jan?"

"Oh, Matthew, I'm not so bad. Not so hot but not so bad. I'm sorry I missed your anniversary. Was it a good one?"

"It was fine."

"I'm glad," she said. "Can I ask you a favor? And I promise it's a less exacting favor than the last one I asked you. Can you come see me?"

"Sure," I said. "When?"

"The sooner the better."

I'd been up all night but I wasn't tired. "Now?"

"Perfect."

"It's what, twenty to ten? I'll be there sometime around eleven."

"I'll be here," she said.

I was a few minutes early, showered and shaved and wearing clean clothes. I rang her bell and went out to wait for the key. She tossed it straight at me and I caught it on the fly. She applauded, and clapped her hands some more when I got off the elevator.

"It was a lucky catch," I said.

"That's the best kind. Okay, now say it. 'You look like hell, Jan.' "

"You don't look so bad."

"Oh, come on. My eyes still work and so does the mirror. Although I've been thinking of covering mine. Jews do that, don't they? When somebody dies?"

"I think the Orthodox do."

"Well, I'd say they're on the right track but their timing's off. It's when you're dying that the mirror ought to be covered. After you're dead what difference does it make?"

I wasn't going to say it, but she didn't look good. Her complexion was off, sallow, with a yellow cast to it. The skin on her face had drawn closer to the bone, and her nose and ears and brow seemed to have grown, even as her eyes had sunk back into her skull. Her impending death had been real enough before, but now it was undeniable. It stared you in the face.

"Hang on," she said. "I've got fresh coffee made." And, when we each had a cup, she said, "First things first. I want to thank you one more time for the gun. It has made all the difference."

"Oh?"

"All the difference. I wake up in the morning and I

ask myself, well, old girl, do you have to use that thing? Is it time? And I say to myself, no, not yet, it's not time yet. And then I'm free to enjoy the day.''

"I see.''

"So I thank you again. But that's not what I dragged you down here for. I could have managed that part over the phone. Matthew, I'm leaving you my Medusa.''

I looked at her.

"You have only yourself to blame,'' she said. "You admired her extravagantly the first night we met.''

"You warned me not to look her in the eye. Her gaze turns men to stone, you said.''

"I may have been warning you about myself. Either way, you didn't listen. Stubborn bastard, aren't you?''

"That's what everybody tells me.''

"Seriously,'' she said, "you've always been drawn to that piece, so either you genuinely like it—''

"Of course I do.''

"—or you're trapped in your own lies, because I want you to have it.''

"It's a great piece of work,'' I said, "and I am indeed very fond of it, and I hope I have to wait a long time for it.''

"Ha!'' She clapped her hands. "That's why you're here this morning. She's going home with you. No, don't argue. I don't want to go through all that crap of codicils in my will and everybody waiting until it goes through probate. I remember how much fun it was when my grandmother died and the family fought pitched battles over the table linens and the silverware. My own mother went to her grave convinced that her brother Pat slipped Grandma's good earrings in his pocket the morning of the wake. And nobody in the family *had* anything, so it's not as though they were fighting over the Hope diamond. No, I'm distributing all my specific bequests in advance. That's one of the good things about knowing you've got a date with the Reaper. You can get all that stuff out of the way, and make sure things wind up where you want.''

"Suppose you live."

She gave me an incredulous look, then let out a bark of laughter. "Hey, a deal's a deal," she said. "You still get to keep the statue. How's that?"

"Now you're talking."

She had had the piece crated, and the wooden box stood on the floor alongside the plinth. The plinth was mine, too, she said, but it would be easier if I came back another time for it. The crated bronze was compact but heavy, the plinth easy to lift but hard to maneuver. Could I even manage the statue unassisted? I got a grip on the crate, hoisted it up onto my shoulder. The weight was substantial but manageable. I carried it through the loft and set it down in front of the elevator to catch my breath.

"Better take a cab," she suggested.

"No kidding."

"Let me look at you. You want to know something? You look like hell."

"Thanks."

"I'm serious. I know *I* look awful but I've got an excuse. Are you all right?"

"I was up all night."

"Couldn't sleep?"

"Didn't try. I was on my way to bed when I got your message."

"You should have said something. This could have waited."

"I wasn't all that sleepy. Tired, but not sleepy."

"I know the feeling. Most of my waking hours are like that these days." She frowned. "It's more than that, though. Something's bothering you."

I sighed.

"Look, I don't mean to—"

"No," I said. "No, you're right. Is there more of that coffee?"

I must have talked for a long time. When I ran out of words we sat in silence for a minute or two. Then she carried our coffee cups to the kitchen and brought them back full again.

She said, "What do you figure it is? Not sex."

"No."

"I didn't think so. What, then? The old boys-will-be-boys syndrome?"

"Maybe."

"Maybe not."

"When I'm with her," I said, "everything else is off in some other world where I don't have to deal with it. The sex is nothing special. She's young and beautiful, and that was exciting at first, just as the newness of it was exciting. But the sex is better with Elaine. With the other one—"

"You can say her name."

"With Lisa, I can't always perform. And sometimes the act is perfunctory. I'm there, we're having an affair, so we'd better get down to it or her presence in my life becomes even more inexplicable."

" 'Let's get away from it all.' "

"Uh-huh."

"Who have you told?"

"Nobody," I said. "No, that's not entirely true. I've told you, of course—"

"A nobody if there ever was one."

"And a few hours ago I told the fellow I sat up all night drinking with. Well, he was the one drinking. I stuck to club soda."

"Thank God for small mercies."

"I've wanted to talk about it with Jim. It sticks in my

throat. See, he knows Elaine. It's bad enough keeping something from her, but if other people know about it and she doesn't—''

"Not good."

"No. And of course there's the fact that talking about it makes it real, and I don't want it to be real. I want it to be a place I go in dreams, if it has to be anything at all. Lately every time I leave her apartment I tell myself it's over, that I won't go back there again. And then a couple of days later I pick up the phone."

"I don't suppose you've talked about it at meetings."

"No. Same reasons."

"You could try going to a meeting where nobody knows you. Some remote section of the Bronx where they've been marrying their cousins for the past three hundred years."

"And the children are born with webbed feet."

"That's the idea. You could say anything there."

"I could."

"Right. But you won't. Have you been going to meetings?"

"Of course."

"As many as usual?"

"I may have lightened up a little, I don't know. I've, uh, felt a little detached. My mind wanders. I wonder what the hell I'm doing there."

"Doesn't sound good, kiddo."

"No."

"You know," she said, "I think you may have picked just the right person to talk to. Dying turns out to be a very instructive process. You learn a lot this way. The only problem is you don't have any time to act on your newfound knowledge. But isn't that always the way? When I was fifteen years old I said to myself, 'Oh to be twelve again, knowing what I know now.' What the hell did I know when I was fifteen?"

"What do you know now?"

"I know that time's much too scarce to waste. I know that only the important things are important. I know not to sweat the small stuff." She made a face. "All these brilliant insights, and they come out sounding like bumper stickers. The worst part is it seems to me that I knew these things at fifteen. Maybe I knew them when I was twelve. But I know them differently now."

"I think I understand."

"Jesus, I hope you do, Matthew." She put a hand on my arm. "I care about you, you know. I really do. I don't want you to fuck it up."

Something in the newspapers. Something in the past couple of days.

I thought about it in the cab heading uptown, the crated bronze on the seat beside me. In front of my hotel I paid the driver and got the thing onto my shoulder again. I found a spot on the floor of my room where I wouldn't be likely to trip over it. I'd have to uncrate it, but that could wait. I'd have to go back for the plinth, but that could wait, too.

I went to the library, and it didn't take me long to find the story I was looking for. It had run three days earlier. I couldn't be sure where I'd read it, because all the local papers had it, and none of them offered much in the way of detail.

A man named Roger Prysock had been shot to death early the previous evening on the corner of Park Avenue South and East Twenty-eighth Street. According to the police, witnesses at the scene stated that the victim had been making a telephone call when a car pulled up alongside. A gunman emerged from the car, shot Prysock several times in the chest, fired a final shot into the back of the head, and got back into the car, which drove off. With its tires screaming, according to the *Post*. The deceased was said to have been thirty-six years old, and had a lengthy criminal record, with convictions for aggravated assault and possession of stolen property.

"He was a pimp," Danny Boy said. "I think he must have gotten his job through affirmative action."

"What do you mean?"

"He was white."

"He's not the first white pimp."

"No, but they're pretty scarce at the street level, and Dodger Prysock was strictly street."

"Dodger?"

"His *nom de la rue*. Damn near inevitable, isn't it? Roger the Dodger, and he was originally from Los Angeles."

"I'd have thought Brooklyn."

"That's because you have a sense of history. Mr. Prysock was not what you'd call a dominant figure in his chosen field, but he made a living."

"Enough to keep him in purple hats and zoot suits?"

"Not his style at all. The Dodger left that sort of thing for the brothers. Dressed very J. Press himself."

"Who killed him?"

"No idea," Danny Boy said. "Last I heard he was out of town. Then the first news I got of him was the story in the paper. Who killed him? Beats me. You didn't do it, did you?"

"No."

"Well, neither did I," he said, "but that still leaves a whole lot of people."

It was the middle of the afternoon when I got to the top floor at 488 West Eighteenth, but it would have looked the same in the middle of the night. No daylight came through the windows. The glass panes in their lower halves had been replaced with mirrors, the upper panes painted the same lemon yellow as the walls.

"We can't have anyone seeing in here," Julia said. "Not even the sun. Not even the Lord God."

She gave me a cup of tea, put me in a chair, sat on the daybed with her feet tucked under her. No harem pajamas this time. She was wearing snug black slacks and a fuchsia blouse. The blouse was silk, unbuttoned at the throat, and there didn't look to be anything under it that God or the surgeons hadn't given her.

I had beeped TJ, and there had been several phone calls back and forth. And now I had been granted an audience with Her Majesty.

"Roger Prysock," I said.

"Wasn't there an Arthur Prysock?" she wondered. "A musician, I seem to recall."

"This one's Roger."

"A relative, perhaps."

"Anything's possible," I said. "Roger the Dodger, they call him."

"Called him. He's dead."

"Shot down on the street while he was using the phone. Three or four in the chest and an extra for insurance. In the back of the head. Does that sound familiar?"

"It might ring a muted bell. How's that tea?"

"It's fine. He was a tall man, dark hair and eyes. Good-looking. Dressed well, if not as flashily as other members of his profession."

"Profession," she said archly.

"He died on a street that's been a hookers' stroll for as long as I can remember. Now who else do we know who was tall and dark and an Ivy League dresser and died just like that, on the same kind of street?"

"Oh, dear," she said. "Do you suppose we could fast-forward through the establishing shots?"

"Who killed him, Julia?"

"Well," she said, "it certainly *sounds* as though it was the same person who killed our friend Glenn, and I already told you I didn't know who that was."

" 'Didn't.' "

"Have I made a mistake in my tenses, Matthew?"

I shook my head. "You didn't know who killed him," I said, "but I think you do now. Because I think Glenn Holtzmann was killed by mistake. The man who killed him was looking for Roger Prysock. Maybe he only knew the Dodger by description, or maybe they were close enough in appearance to fool him in that light."

"I was all the way across the street," she said. "He didn't look like Dodger Prysock to me."

"You already knew he wasn't. You'd seen him up close earlier."

"That's true," she said. She examined a fingernail, then gnawed at the cuticle. "I didn't connect the two killings," she said. "The first one, Glenn, I haven't even thought about it in weeks now. And I didn't hear any details of the second shooting. I didn't know about the bullet in the back of the head."

"Sort of a signature."

"Yes." She studied her nails some more and blew on them, as if the polish were still wet. "I didn't even know he was back in town."

"Prysock."

"Yes. I haven't seen him in months. I heard he'd gone back to Los Angeles. I think that's where he's from."

"So I've heard."

"The first I heard he was back," she said, "was when I heard he was dead."

"Who had a beef with him?"

Her eyes avoided mine. "I don't have a pimp," she said. "Or a manager, as some of them like to be called these days. And I barely knew Roger the Dodger, and I didn't think very much of him. His clothes were conservatively cut, but he could put on a suit from Tripler and look like a ten-dollar whore in a bridesmaid's gown. Trust me.''

''All right.''

''Anything I could tell you would be secondhand. And you didn't get it from me, because I will never repeat *any* of this. Are we very clear on that?''

''Crystal clear.''

''What I heard,'' she said, ''and I didn't hear it until well after the Dodger disappeared, was that he'd gone to California for health reasons. In other words, somebody wanted to kill him.''

''Who?''

''I don't know the man. All I have's his street name, and I never met him because he doesn't walk down the same mean streets as this girl.''

''What do they call him?''

''Zoot.''

''Zoot,'' I said.

''After the sartorial statement he likes to make, which is far removed from that of the late Mr. Prysock.''

''He wears a zoot suit.''

''A genuine zoot suit,'' she said, ''if you even know what that is. People tend to stick that label to anything really tasteless and flashy, anything that goes with a floppy magenta hat and a pink Cadillac with fur upholstery, but the zoot suit was a particular style of the forties.''

''With a drape shape and a reet pleat,'' I said.

''You astonish me, my darling. It's tacky of me to say this, but you didn't strike me as terribly fashion-conscious. And now you turn out to be a veritable historian of the masculine couture.''

''Not quite,'' I said. ''Tell me about Zoot. Is he black?''

''And you never *told* me you were psychic.''

"Dark skin tone," I said. "Long pointed chin, more noticeable in profile than full face. Little button nose."

"It sounds as though you know him."

"I never met him either," I said. "But I saw him once wearing a powder-blue zoot suit and wraparound mirrored sunglasses. And a hat." I closed my eyes and focused. "A straw hat, cocoa brown, very narrow brim. And a very loud hatband."

"When did this happen?"

"A year ago, or maybe it was more like a year and a half. I heard a name for him, but it wasn't Zoot."

"What was he doing?"

"Sitting at a table with a friend of mine. Then he went away and I took his seat."

"And learned his name."

"But not his street name."

"And now for the big-money question. What color was the hatband?"

I frowned, concentrating, then shook my head. "Sorry," I said.

"Believe me, so am I," she said, "but it's not a total loss. You still get to keep the microwave oven and the home-entertainment unit. And thanks for being our guest on *Try to Remember*."

"Nicholson James," I told Joe Durkin. "He started out in life with the name James Nicholson, and somewhere along the way the name got reversed on some official document. My guess is it was a bench warrant, because that's the kind of official document he probably saw the most of. Whatever it was, he liked the look of it. As soon as he could he got his name changed legally, which may be the last legal thing he ever did."

"And his last illegal act?"

"Hard to say. He aced a fellow named Roger Prysock over on Park Avenue South, but that was a few nights ago, so he could have committed half a dozen class-A felonies since then. On the other hand, maybe he's taken holy orders. You never know."

"I never do," he agreed. "I can't say I care a whole lot, either, as long as your friend Nick stays the hell out of my precinct. Is that what he calls himself for short? Nick? Or does he prefer Jim?"

"Some people call him Zoot."

"Nice," he said. "Classy. Of course if he does become a man of the cloth they'll have to make that Father Zoot. Or maybe Sister Zoot, if he runs off and joins the Poor Clares. Tell me something, will you? What do I care about some asshole with his name on backwards who killed some other asshole in another precinct entirely?"

"Man he shot was about six-one, one-seventy, dark hair, dark eyes, well dressed, and talking on a public telephone at the time of the shooting. Zoot put a few in his chest and one in the back of his head."

He sat up straight. "All right," he said. "You've got my attention."

"Two months ago, whenever it was, Nicholson James developed a hard-on for Roger Prysock. I don't know what the beef was about. Girls or money, probably. One night the Zooter's taking a ride on Eleventh Avenue. Maybe he's looking for Prysock, maybe he just gets lucky, but there's the man he wants, talking on a pay phone the way Prysock always does and dressed all Ivy League, the way Prysock likes to dress."

"Only it's not Prysock."

"It's Glenn Holtzmann," I said, "out for a walk, and very possibly trying to put some scam of his own in motion, only we'll never know because he never got it off the ground. Zoot hops out of his car, shoots him three times. Holtzmann lands facedown, so if Zoot hasn't already seen that he got the wrong man, he's not going to notice it now. Anyway, it's nighttime, and it's not too bright.''

"And neither is Nicholson James."

"So he shoots him one more time and goes home," I went on, "or wherever you go to celebrate a job well done. Meanwhile, George Sadecki shuffles out of the shadows and decides he's walking point in the Mekong Delta and he better pick up his brass. Good police work scoops him up with a pocket full of evidence and George can't even swear he didn't do it."

"And the intended vic?"

"Roger the Dodger? Like the original Dodgers, he's skipped to L.A. As a matter of fact, he was probably already out of town when Zoot shot Holtzmann, either that or he was on his way shortly thereafter. George goes to Rikers and off to Bellevue and back to Rikers and gets stabbed to death. The case was already closed, and now there's not even going to be a trial to stir the ashes.''

"What about the word on the street? How come nobody knows Holtzmann got in the way of somebody else's bullets?"

"How would they know? Not that many people even knew Zoot had a beef with Prysock, and the ones who did couldn't have attached much weight to it. Pimps flare up at each other all the time. If they don't act on it right away, generally it blows over. And the people on the street didn't know that Holtzmann and Prysock looked alike, or that George wasn't the shooter the way the papers said he was. Hell, Prysock himself didn't know it was all that serious. He thought it was safe to come back. Nicholson James heard he was in town, drove around until he found the right pay phone and the right man using it, and then he did what he'd done before."

We went over it a couple of times. He asked me what I expected him to do.

"Maybe you could call whoever caught the Prysock homicide," I suggested. "Tell him they might like to check out Nicholson James for it."

"Also known as Zoot." His fingers drummed the desk top. "How do I know all this?"

"One of your snitches gave it to you."

"I suppose a little bird told him."

"The proverbial little bird," I said.

"They probably already got it, you know. Odds are Zoot ran his mouth in a players' bar on Lenox Avenue and three guys were trampled in the rush for the phone."

"It's possible."

"But you don't think so."

"If the word was out," I said, "there's a friend of mine who would have heard it. And he hasn't."

"I probably know who you're talking about."

"You probably do."

"And he hasn't heard it? That's interesting. Still, you could drop the dime yourself. Pick up any phone, just so it's not on Park or Eleventh Avenue. What do you need me for?"

"They'll pay more attention if it comes from you."

" 'When Durkin talks, people listen.' Remember that ad, remember E.F. Hutton? What the hell ever happened to them?"

"I don't know."

"Maybe people stopped listening." He frowned. "Matt, what's the punch line, huh? How does the story wind up?"

"With luck and good police work," I said, "Nicholson James goes away for the murder of Roger Prysock."

"What about your sleeping dogs?"

"Huh?"

"Holtzmann and Sadecki. It's a mess if that can of worms gets opened up again. You know Zoot'd skate on the Holtzmann shooting. In fact opening it up makes it harder to tag him with Prysock. It gives the defense something else to play with.''

''And I don't suppose it does the department a lot of good.''

''I know a couple of guys got commendations for the work they did bagging Sadecki. What I just called him and Holtzmann, sleeping dogs. Maybe we could let 'em lie. I don't suppose Zoot's gonna bring up the subject. He can't be that stupid.''

''No.''

''How about you, Matt? Could you let it be?''

''It's up to the client,'' I said. ''Let's see if I can sell it to him.''

I made the call from my hotel room, got Tom Sadecki at his store. I ran it down quickly for him and he listened without interrupting. When I had it all laid out I said, ''Here's where you have to make a decision. As it stands, the shooter may or may not stand trial for the murder of Roger Prysock, and if he does he may or may not be convicted. That depends on how good a case they can make against him. My guess is he'll either plead or stand trial, because the case is still fresh and they've got eyewitnesses, but it's too early to say for sure what will happen.

''If we try to connect the killer to Holtzmann and go public with what we have, it might weaken the case against him for Prysock. The most it could accomplish is to clear your brother's name. You told me a while ago that didn't matter, but you've got the right to change your mind if you want.''

''Jesus,'' he said. ''I thought I was done with all this.''

''You're not the only one.''

''What do you think I should do?''

"I can't answer that," I said. "It's easier for me if you let it go, and God knows it's easier for the cops, but the only real consideration is what you want, you and your family."

"George didn't do it? You're sure of that?"

"Absolutely."

"It's funny," he said. "Early on it was very important for me to believe that, and then it became important to just let go of it, you know? And now it looks as though I was right in the first place, and I'm glad to know that, but the importance isn't there anymore. Like the whole business doesn't have anything to do with George, or with any of us."

"I think I know what you mean."

"We'd just be putting him through it all over again, wouldn't we? Clearing his name. He doesn't need his name cleared. Let the world forget him. We remember him. That's enough."

"Then we'll just let it lie," I said.

I called Lisa. I said hello and she said hello, and she waited for me to invite myself over.

Instead I told her how her husband had been shot to death by someone who'd mistaken him for a pimp. "The case won't be reopened," I said. "The only person who might have wanted it was George Sadecki's brother, and he's decided against it. God knows the cops would rather leave well enough alone, and so would we."

"So it doesn't change anything."

"It ties off the loose ends," I said. "And it's reassuring to know Glenn wasn't killed by someone he'd informed on, or somebody he was trying to set up. But in practical terms, no, it doesn't change anything."

"It's funny the way he had a premonition."

"If that's what he had. Maybe he was working on something he thought might get him killed, and maybe it would have if the pimp hadn't gotten him first.''

We talked some more. She asked me if I wanted to come over.

"Not tonight," I said. "I'm exhausted."

"Get some sleep."

"I will," I said. "I'll call you."

I hung up the phone. I walked over to the window and stood looking out of it for a few minutes. Then I picked up the phone and made another call.

"Hi," I said. "Okay if I come over?"

"Now?"

"Did I pick a bad time?"

"I don't know," she said.

I said, "I really want to see you. I'm exhausted, I haven't been to bed since the night before last."

"Is something the matter?"

"No, but I've been busy. But I suppose it can wait until tomorrow."

"No," she said. "It's all right."

"Are you sure?"

"It's all right," she said.

25

"**H**e was killed by accident," I told Elaine. "That's how it looked from the beginning, that's how the police saw it. A guy from the twenty-eighth floor in the wrong place at the wrong time, a guy in a suit taking a walk on the wild side.

"They thought he ran into George Sadecki, and no matter how hard I tried I could never completely rule that out. But there was something wrong about Glenn Holtzmann, and the more I learned about him the more likely it seemed that he'd furnished somebody with a much better reason to kill him than poor George ever had. And the killing certainly felt purposeful to me. That last shot into the back of the head didn't seem characteristic of a mugging gone wrong, or a panhandler turned nasty. It was an execution. It was the sort of thing you don't do unless you damn well want somebody dead."

"And that's what it was after all," she said.

"That's exactly what it was. Nicholson James had what he must have felt was a very good reason to take out Roger Prysock, and that's what he thought he was doing when he killed Glenn. Then, when George shuffled along to take the rap for him, he must have felt God was watching over him. And of course he never went and told anyone what he'd done, because shooting the wrong fellow by mistake isn't good bragging material in the bars. He'd killed a stranger and another stranger was in custody for it, so it was the easiest thing in the world to pretend it never happened.

"Then Prysock turned up, figuring it was safe to come home, and Nicholson James found out about it and hit the Replay button. Same M.O., pay phone, three in the chest and a *coup de grâce,* only this time he got the right guy."

"And nobody made the connection?"

"No reason they should," I said. "There have been close to five hundred homicides in the five boroughs between Holtzmann's murder and Prysock's. Most of those have come as the result of gunfire, and a lot of them have taken place on the street. The similarities are striking, but you only see them if the Holtzmann killing is in the forefront of your mind, and every cop involved had other things to think about. Remember, Prysock was killed on the other side of town. Nobody on that case had had any connection to the Holtzmann case. And don't forget, Holtzmann's death was history. The case was closed, the perpetrator had not only been arrested but he was actually dead and gone. If you found a husband and wife murdered with an ax, you might think of Lizzie Borden. But you wouldn't try to make a case against her."

"I see what you mean."

"There was really only one person around who should have heard the penny drop. That was me, because I never really bought the idea that George did it. And, no matter how many homicides there'd been in the past few months, I had only one of them on my mind. So if anyone was going to draw a connection between Holtzmann and Prysock, it was me."

"And you did."

"No," I said, "that's the point. I didn't. The report of the Prysock killing ran in all four local papers, so I read it at least once. I obviously read it, because I remembered it a couple of days later. It even rang a bell, but I managed not to hear it."

"Why?"

"Because I went conveniently deaf. Irish deaf, my aunt Peg used to say. That's when you don't hear what you don't want to hear."

"Why didn't you want to hear it?"

"I'll tell you how I overcame my Irish deafness, and that should give you an idea of what caused it. After I left here last night I went to the midnight meeting at Alanon House. Then I went over to see Mick."

I told her about the hours I'd spent at Grogan's, and recapped the part of our conversation that had to do with Glenn Holtzmann. And I told her how the two of us had watched the sky turn light, and how we'd gone to St. Bernard's for the butchers' mass.

"But Mick was the only man there in a white apron," I said. "It was pretty much just us and the nuns."

"You thought he'd killed Holtzmann," she said.

"I was afraid of it. It was one of the first thoughts that struck me when I finally reached somebody in Altoona who could tell me where the money for law school came from. Here was Holtzmann, a career rat, and here was my friend Mick, with his car and his home and his place of business all deeded to other people so the government couldn't seize them. And he talked about it all the time, how they'd confiscate your assets if they could prove you had any, how his lawyer wanted him to make sure he didn't lose the farm if his tenants died on him and willed it to somebody else.

"I ran into Glenn once at Grogan's. I was drinking a Coke at the bar and he thought it was a glass of Guinness, which shows how well he blended in at your basic

Hell's Kitchen saloon. But he knew who owned the place, and he was full of questions about Butcher Ballou until I told him it was bad form to ask them. But that didn't mean he wouldn't have asked other people, and he might have learned something, and might have tried to use what he'd learned.

"Now it didn't really make sense to figure Mick killed him. Glenn did what he did in the shadows, and the two people he screwed that we know about never even knew what hit them. He certainly wouldn't have exposed himself to a man known to all as a stone killer. And if Mick did somehow get wind of what he was up to, it would have been the easiest thing in the world to warn him off.

"Here's where I went wrong," I said. "Instead of thinking it through, I shut down. I grabbed hold of the idea that my work was complete because I'd done all I could for both my clients. Lisa Holtzmann's money was safe and there was nothing more I could do for George Sadecki. And I had no leads to the real killer, so I could stop looking for him.

"Meanwhile, it gnawed at me. I couldn't stay out of Grogan's. I was seeking out Mick's company every couple of days, and I would sit up with him and never talk about what was foremost on my mind. And, as far as that goes, it *wasn't* foremost on my mind, not consciously, because I wasn't letting myself think about it.

"Then Nicholson James shot Roger the Dodger. And I read the goddamn story, and it didn't even register."

"And then you went and talked with Mick."

"I went and talked with him," I said, "and somehow the subject of Glenn Holtzmann came up." No need to say how that had come about. "And what he said made it abundantly clear that I'd let my anxiety keep me from thinking straight. And, miraculously, I began to remember that I'd read something recently that rang a bell. I didn't know what it was, but I knew it was something."

"Funny how minds work."

"You said it."

"Suppose he'd done it," she said.

"Mick?"

She nodded. "Suppose he admitted it, or suppose you came across some evidence that was absolutely unequivocal. Then what?"

"You mean what would I have done about it?"

"Uh-huh."

I didn't have to think it through. "I wouldn't have done a thing," I said. "The case was closed and I was through with it."

"It wouldn't have bothered you that he was getting away with murder?"

"I'd hate to guess how many murders Mick has gotten away with," I said. "I was an eyewitness to one of them and he's told me about plenty of others. If I can swallow all that, why should one more killing stick in my throat?"

"Even if it's one that involves you?"

"How am I involved? Because I was vaguely acquainted with the victim? Because the case dropped into my lap after the fact? It's not as though he would have killed somebody close to me, or as if the act itself were particularly reprehensible. If he *had* killed Glenn, I'd have said he had good reason."

"So suspecting him didn't change how you felt toward him."

"Not really, no."

"And it didn't affect your relationship."

"Why should it?"

"But you went to mass with him this morning," she said. "And you haven't done that in a long time."

"You Jewish girls," I said. "You don't miss a trick."

"Well?"

Jared Henderson 2 of 2
"I guess you're right," I said. "I guess I wouldn't allow myself to participate in that little ritual of ours as long as I suspected him. And once the suspicion was lifted I guess I felt a need to mark the occasion."

"And then you remembered the news item."

"I remembered that there was an item, and that it was recent. I read through back issues until I found what I was looking for. Then I started digging. The minute Julia mentioned a pimp named Zoot, I thought of the one person I remembered seeing in a zoot suit. That was Nicholson James, and I'd seen him talking with Danny Boy when I was working that abduction case. Kenan Khoury's wife. You remember."

"Of course."

"I talked to Danny Boy afterward, and he didn't even know there was bad blood between the two pimps, so it was good luck that Julia happened to know. But this whole business hasn't exactly been overflowing with good luck, so I'll take it."

"I don't blame you," she said. "God, you look tired, honey. I'd offer you more coffee but that's probably the last thing you need."

"You're probably right."

"I'm tired myself," she said. "I didn't get much sleep last night. I've had a lot on my mind lately."

"I know."

"I got scared when you called. Saying you'd been up all night and that you needed to talk to me. I was afraid of what you were going to say."

"I just wanted to tell you what happened."

"I know."

"And I didn't want to go to sleep by myself."

"Well, you don't have to," she said.

When I got into bed the thought came to me that, tired as I was, I was going to have trouble drifting off. The next thing I knew, sunlight was streaming in the bedroom window and the smell of fresh coffee permeated the apartment.

I was having my second cup when the phone rang. Elaine answered it, and I looked over at her and watched her face change. "Just a moment," she said. "He's right here."

She covered the mouthpiece and said, "It's for you. It's Janice Keane."

"Oh?"

She handed me the phone and stalked out of the room. I'd have gone after her but I had the goddamn telephone in my hand. I said, "Hello?"

"Matthew, I'm sorry, I picked a bad time, didn't I?"

"It's all right."

"Do you want to call me back?"

"No," I said. "It's okay."

"If you're sure," she said. "Because it's nothing urgent, except insofar as everything has acquired a certain urgency. I had a moment of what I'd have to call enlightenment yesterday, not long after you left. I almost called you then but I wanted to sleep on it and see if it was still there in the morning."

"And is it?"

"Uh-huh. And I wanted to share it with you, because it involves you, sort of."

"Oh?"

"I'm not going to kill myself," she said. "I'm not going to use that gun you brought me."

"Really."

"Yes. Do you want to know what happened? After you left I looked in the mirror, and I couldn't believe how lousy I looked. And I thought, well, so what? I can live with it. And I suddenly realized that I could live with whatever came along, for as long as I had to. I might not be able to do anything about it, but I could live with it, I could endure it.

"And this was news," she said. "There are things I can't control, like the pain and my appearance, and the completely unacceptable fact that I'm not going to be able to get out of this one alive. The gun gave me a kind of control. If I didn't like the way things were going I could always pull the plug. But who says I have to be in control, and who ever controls anything in this life in the first place? Oh, hell, I can stand a little pain. You never get more than you can handle, isn't that what they say?"

"That's what they say."

"You know what I suddenly understood? I don't want to miss anything. That's the whole point of sobriety, you stop missing out on your own life. Well, I want to be here for all of it. Dying's an experience, and it turns out to be one I'm not willing to miss. I always used to say I wanted death to take me by surprise. A stroke or a coronary, and preferably in my sleep so I wouldn't have even a split second's awareness of what was happening. Well, it turns out that's not what I want after all. I'd rather have time to let things wind down. If I went out like a light, I'd never have the chance to make sure my things go to the people I want to have them. Incidentally, don't forget you have to come back for the plinth."

"I know."

"So I guess I want to thank you one more time for getting me the gun," she said, "because I had to have it in order to know I don't need it. I don't know if I'm making any sense—"

"You're doing fine."

"Am I? Sometimes I wonder. You know the thought I had before I went to bed last night? I realized that what scared me most about dying was the fear that I'd fuck it up, that I wouldn't know how to do it. And then I thought, shit, just look at all the morons and losers who've managed it. How hard can it be? I mean, if my mother could do it, anybody can.''

"You're nuts," I said. "But I suppose you already know that.''

When I went into the bedroom Elaine was sitting on the stool looking at herself in the mirror over the dressing table. She swung around to face me.

"That was Jan," I said.

"I know who it was.''

"I don't know how she happened to call me here. I meant to ask her. I didn't think she had this number.''

"You had Call Forwarding on.''

"Can't be. I didn't put it on last night.''

"You didn't have to," she said. "You never took it off from the night before.''

"Oh, Jesus," I said. "You're kidding.''

"No.''

I thought back. "You're right," I said. "I never did.''

"She called yesterday morning, too.''

"She called here? Because there was a message at the desk when I got in.''

"I know. I was the one who left the message at the desk. 'Call Jan Keane,' I said. She didn't leave a number, and I figured you probably knew it.''

"Yes, of course.''

"Of course," she said. She got up from the little stool and walked to the window. It looks east toward the river, but the view is better from the living room.

I said, "You remember Jan. You met her in SoHo.''

"Oh, I remember, all right. Your old girlfriend.''

"That's right.''

She turned toward me, her face contorted. "Fuck," she said.

"What's the matter?''

"I was afraid we were going to have this conversation last night," she said. "I thought that was why you wanted to come over, so we could talk about it. And I didn't want to talk about it, but we have to, don't we?"

"What do you mean?"

"Jan Keane," she said, snapping out the syllables. "You're seeing her, aren't you? You're having an affair with her, aren't you? You're still in love with her, aren't you?"

"Jesus."

"I wasn't going to bring this up," she said. "I swear I wasn't, but it happened. Well, what do we do now? Pretend I never said anything?"

"Jan's dying," I said.

She's dying, I said. She has pancreatic cancer. She has only a few months left, they gave her a year and most of it's gone.

She called me a couple of months ago, I said. Right around the time Glenn Holtzmann got shot. To tell me she was dying, and to ask me for a favor. She wanted a gun. So she could kill herself when she couldn't take it anymore.

And she called yesterday, I said, because she wanted to give me a piece of her work. She's starting to distribute some of her possessions to make sure they go where she wants them to go. And I went down to her loft yesterday morning and picked up an early bronze of hers, and she didn't look good, so I guess it won't be too much longer.

And she called today, I said, to tell me she's not going to put the gun in her mouth and spray her brains all over the wall. She decided she wants to let death come at its own pace, and she wanted to let me know her decision, and how she'd come to it.

And yes, I said, I have been seeing her, though not

in the sense you mean. And no, I said, I'm not having an affair with her. And no, I said, I'm not in love with her. I love her, I care for her, she's been a very good friend to me, I said, but I'm not in love with her.

I'm in love with you, I said. You're the only person I'm in love with. You're the only person I've ever been in love with. I'm in love with you.

"I feel really stupid," she said.

"Why?"

"Because I was fiercely jealous of a woman who's dying. I spent all yesterday sitting around hating her. I feel stupid and mean-spirited and petty and unworthy. And nuts. Especially nuts."

"You didn't know."

"No," she said, "and that's another thing. How could you carry that around all this time and not say a word? It's been what, two months now? Why didn't you tell me?"

"I don't know."

"Did you talk to anybody about it?"

"I told Jim a little of it, but I didn't mention that she'd asked me to get her a gun. And I talked to Mick about it."

"And picked up a gun from him, I suppose."

"He's opposed to suicide."

"But not to murder?"

"Someday I'll explain the distinction he draws. I didn't ask him for a gun because I didn't want to put him in an awkward position."

"So where did you get the gun?"

"TJ bought it for me from somebody on the street."

"My God," she said. "You've got him buying guns and selling dope and hanging out with transsexuals. You're a wonderful positive influence on the boy. Did you tell him why you wanted it?"

"He didn't ask."

"Neither did I," she said, "but you could have told me. Why didn't you?"

I thought about it. "I guess I was afraid," I said.

"That I wouldn't understand?"

"Not that. You understand more than I do. Maybe that you wouldn't approve."

"Of your giving her the gun? How is it my business to approve or disapprove? Anyway, you'd do what you wanted, wouldn't you?"

"Probably."

"For the record, I approve of her decision to keep the gun out of her mouth. But I also approve of your decision to give her the gun and let her make her own choice. What I don't much care for is being left in the dark while you go through all sorts of agony. What were you planning to do when she died, skip the funeral? Or tell me you were on your way to a boxing match in Sunnyside?"

"I would have said something."

"That's comforting."

"I suppose there was some denial involved," I said. "Telling you about it would make it real."

"I can understand that."

"And there was something else I was afraid of."

"What?"

"That you'll die," I said.

"I'm not sick or anything."

"I know."

"So—"

"I hate it that Jan's dying," I said, "and I'll have lost something when she's gone, but it's the kind of thing that happens, losing people, and it's the kind of thing life teaches you to live with. But if anything happened to you I don't know what I would do. And it keeps being on my mind, and the only reason I don't think about it is I won't let myself. And sometimes when we're in bed I'll touch your breast and I find myself wondering if something's growing in there, or I'll find the scars on your middle where that bastard stabbed you and I'll start to wonder if he did any damage that they don't know about. It's been a few years since I became aware of my own mortality, and that wasn't much fun, but you adjust to it. Now what's happening to Jan has made me aware of your mortality, and I don't like it."

"Silly old bear. I'm gonna live forever. Didn't you know that?"

"You never told me."

"I have no choice," she said. "I'm in Al-Anon. I can't allow myself to die so long as there's a human being on earth that needs me. Oh, God, hold me, will you? Sweetie, I thought I was losing you."

"Never."

"I figured, well, she's interesting, she's accomplished, she's a fucking artist and everything, she's got to be more stimulating and admirable than somebody who spent her whole adult life fucking for a living."

"That's what you figured, huh?"

"Uh-huh. I figured she was the cleaner, greener malden."

"Shows what you know. *You're* the cleaner, greener maiden."

"Yeah?"

"No question."

"Me, huh?"

"You."

"So I was wrong," she said. "I stand corrected. Listen, do you think we could go back to bed? Not to do anything. Just to, you know, be close."

"Is that wise? We might lose control."

"We might," she said.

*   *   *

That afternoon I was standing at the living-room window. She came over and stood beside me. "It's supposed to be colder tonight," she said. "It might snow."

"Be the first snow of the year, wouldn't it?"

"Uh-huh. We could go out and walk in it or stay here and watch it. Depending on how close we want to get to the experience."

"I was thinking of when I first used to come to this apartment. You had a better view before some of those buildings went up."

"I know."

"I think it's time to move."

"Oh?"

"There are a couple of apartments for sale in the Parc Vendôme," I said, "and I'm sure there are others available in buildings all along West Fifty-seventh. I know you've always liked the one on the next block with the Art Deco lobby."

"And the one with the plaque that says Bela Bartok used to live there."

"Tomorrow or the day after," I said, "I think you should start looking for a place for the two of us. And as soon as you find something you like I think we should take it."

"Don't you want to look with me?"

"I'd just get in the way," I said. "I know I'll be perfectly happy in any place you pick. Jesus, how long have I lived in a hotel room the size of a walk-in closet? I'd like to have at least one window that I can sit and look out of, and with something more interesting on the other side of it than an air shaft. And I think we probably will want a second bedroom. But outside of that I'm pretty easy to please."

"And you want to stay in your neighborhood?"

"Well, it's that or SoHo, if you want to be able to walk to the gallery."

"Which gallery?"

"Your gallery," I said. "The stretch of Fifty-seventh with all the galleries is a five-minute walk from my hotel, and I think some of those buildings have space for rent."

"They ought to, at the rate galleries are going out of business these days. When did I decide to open a gallery?"

"You haven't yet," I said, "but I think you're going to. Or am I wrong?"

She thought about it. "I think you're probably right," she said. "What a scary thought."

"Another reason you'd better pick the apartment," I said, "is you're the one who'll be paying for it, or most of it. I decided I'd be stupid to let that bother me."

"You're right. You would."

"So I'll try not to."

"I'll list this apartment with a broker," she said. "I can do that right away. And I'll see about raising cash on some other properties so we won't have to wait around for this place to sell. I'll call now and see if I can set up some appointments for tomorrow and the next day. You want to know something? All of a sudden I can't wait to move."

"Good."

"We talked and talked about it, and then we stopped talking, and now—"

"Now we're ready," I said. I drew a breath. "When you've found a place, and when we're settled into the apartment and the neighborhood, and you've got everything more or less the way you want it, I'd like for us to get married."

"Just like that?"

I nodded. "Just like that."

It was the middle of January when I finally got down to Lispenard Street to pick up the plinth. I was there with Elaine during the week between Christmas and New Year's, along with eight or ten other friends of Jan's who'd come to celebrate the holidays. We'd had every intention of taking the plinth home with us and then forgot and left without it.

This time I made a special trip. "You look good," she told me. "How's the apartment? Are you in it yet?"

"The closing's set for the first of the month."

"That's great. I don't know if I told you, but I'm crazy about your lady. I hope you got her something nice for Christmas."

"I had a police artist draw a picture of her father."

"Why? Is he wanted for something?"

"He passed away years ago."

"And you found somebody to copy a photograph?"

"He worked from memory," I said. "Her memory." I explained the process. She thought it was fascinating, but a strange Christmas present. "It was what she wanted," I said. "It was a powerful emotional experience for her, working with the artist like that, and it

334

came out looking good. And I, uh, gave her something else, too.''

"Oh?"

"A ring."

"No kidding. Well, she's terrific, Matthew. You did okay.''

"I know."

"And so did she. I'm happy for both of you.''

"Thank you," I said. "*You're* looking good.''

"Ha! I am, aren't I? I'm thinner than I'd like to be, which is something I swear I never thought I'd hear myself say. But it's true, isn't it? I'm looking better.''

"Definitely."

"Well, I'm feeling better. I'm trying a few things.''

"Oh?"

"I've changed my diet around," she said, "and I'm doing this raw juice therapy, and I'm on a couple of other quack regimens I'd be embarrassed to describe to you. See, I've made a profound inner decision that I want to live.''

"That's wonderful."

"Well, I don't know that it's going to change anything. People have been drinking carrot juice and taking high colonics for years now and I haven't seen that many undertakers declaring bankruptcy. But I feel better. That ought to be worth something right there, wouldn't you say?''

"I would certainly think so.''

"And who knows, huh? Miracles happen. The medical profession just calls them something else, that's all. Spontaneous remission, they call it. Or they say the initial diagnosis must have been inaccurate. But who the hell cares what they call it?'' She shrugged. "To tell you the truth," she said, "I don't honestly expect a whole hell of a lot. But you never know.''

*　　*　　*

"You never know," Elaine said. "Doctors don't know everything."

"No."

"All they know is drugs and surgery and radiation. There are a lot of alternatives to traditional medicine, and sometimes they work a lot better. It sounds as though she's doing some really good things for herself. What could it hurt?"

"I don't see how it could."

"No, and the attitudinal change might make all the difference. I'm not saying it's all in her mind, it's very obviously in her body, but your state of mind makes a difference, don't you think?"

"Absolutely."

"And miracles happen, just the way she said they do. God, look at all the miracles we both know walking around. Look at us, for that matter. We're a miracle, aren't we?"

"I'd say so."

"So why shouldn't Jan be one? I'll tell you something. I think she's going to make it."

"Jesus, that would be great," I said. "I hope you're right."

"I think I am," she said. "I've got a feeling."

She died in April.

The cruelest month, Eliot wrote. Breeding lilacs out of the dead land. Mixing memory and desire. Stirring dull roots with spring rain.

That's about as much of the poem as I've ever felt I really understood, but it's enough.

The cruelest month, and I guess it got pretty cruel for her toward the end, but she made it through all right. She never did take any painkillers, although a few of us tried to talk her into it. She didn't shoot herself, either. She wouldn't part with the gun, wanting to have the option always available to her, but she never chose to use it.

Nicholson James was arrested in due course and charged with the murder of Roger Prysock. I haven't followed the case too closely, but it sounds solid. The police turned up both eyewitnesses and physical evidence, and whether he stands trial or pleads to manslaughter, he's a good bet to wind up doing some serious time. Meanwhile he's chilling out on Rikers Island while his lawyer keeps getting postponements.

I'm in my hotel room now. From where I sit I can see the Parc Vendôme across the street, but I can't see our apartment. We're on the fourteenth floor in the rear of the building, with good views south and west. This room is nominally my office, although I can't think why I would want to meet a client here. I can't say I use the place to house my files; what records I keep would fit handily in a cigar box.

But I still seem to like having this private space, and Elaine doesn't seem to mind.

I can see another building besides ours from my window. I have to look all the way to the right, and then I can just get a glimpse of the high-rise where Glenn Holtzmann lived, and where his widow continues to live. Again, I can't see her window. It's on the building's west side, looking out over the Hudson, looking across to New Jersey.

Sometimes I sit here and look over there, and sometimes her phone number pops unbidden into my mind. Because I remember stuff, I guess.

This is Matt, I could say. Would you like company?

Tough, Suspenseful Novels by
Edgar Award-winning Author

LAWRENCE BLOCK

FEATURING MATTHEW SCUDDER

A DANCE AT THE SLAUGHTERHOUSE
71374-8/ $4.99 US/ $5.99 Can

A TICKET TO THE BONEYARD
70994-5/ $4.99 US/ $5.99 Can

OUT ON THE CUTTING EDGE
70993-7/ $4.95 US/ $5.95 Can

THE SINS OF THE FATHERS
76363-X/ $4.99 US/ $5.99 Can

TIME TO MURDER AND CREATE
76365-6/ $4.99 US/ $5.99 Can

A STAB IN THE DARK
71574-0/ $4.50 US/ $5.50 Can

IN THE MIDST OF DEATH
76362-1/ $4.99 US/ $5.99 Can

EIGHT MILLION WAYS TO DIE
71573-2/ $4.99 US/ $5.99 Can

A WALK AMONG THE TOMBSTONES
71375-6/ $4.99 US/ $5.99 Can

Buy these books at your local bookstore or use this coupon for ordering:

....

Mail to: Avon Books, Dept BP, Box 767, Rte 2, Dresden, TN 38225   C
Please send me the book(s) I have checked above.
❏ My check or money order— no cash or CODs please— for $_____ is enclosed
(please add $1.50 to cover postage and handling for each book ordered— Canadian residents
add 7% GST).
❏ Charge my VISA/MC Acct#_____Exp Date_____
Minimum credit card order is two books or $6.00 (please add postage and handling charge of
$1.50 per book — Canadian residents add 7% GST).   For faster service, call
1-800-762-0779. Residents of Tennessee, please call 1-800-633-1607. Prices and numbers
are subject to change without notice. Please allow six to eight weeks for delivery.

Name_____
Address_____
City_____State/Zip_____
Telephone No._____   BLK 0494

CAJUN CRIME
FEATURING DAVE ROBICHEAUX
BY EDGAR AWARD-WINNING AUTHOR

JAMES LEE BURKE

IN THE ELECTRIC MIST
WITH CONFEDERATE DEAD
72121-X/ $5.99 US/ $6.99 Can
"Awesome"
The Wall Street Journal

A STAINED WHITE RADIANCE
72047-7/ $5.50 US/ $6.50 Can
"No one captures Louisiana culture
as well as James Lee Burke. . . it is also possible
that no one writes better detective novels."
Washington Post Book World

BLACK CHERRY BLUES
71204-0/ $5.50 US/ $6.50 Can
"Remarkable. . .A terrific story. . .
Not to be missed!"
Los Angeles Times Book Review

A MORNING FOR FLAMINGOS
71360-8/ $5.50 US/ $6.50 Can
"Truly astonishing"
Washington Post Book World

Buy these books at your local bookstore or use this coupon for ordering:

Mail to: Avon Books, Dept BP, Box 767, Rte 2, Dresden, TN 38225   C
Please send me the book(s) I have checked above.
❑ My check or money order— no cash or CODs please— for $_____ is enclosed
(please add $1.50 to cover postage and handling for each book ordered— Canadian residents
add 7% GST).
❑ Charge my VISA/MC Acct#_____ Exp Date_____
Minimum credit card order is two books or $6.00 (please add postage and handling charge of
$1.50 per book — Canadian residents add 7% GST). For faster service, call
1-800-762-0779. Residents of Tennessee, please call 1-800-633-1607. Prices and numbers
are subject to change without notice. Please allow six to eight weeks for delivery.

Name_____
Address_____
City_____State/Zip_____
Telephone No._____   BUR 0694